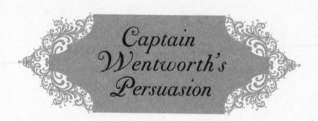

Captain
Wentworth's
Persuasion

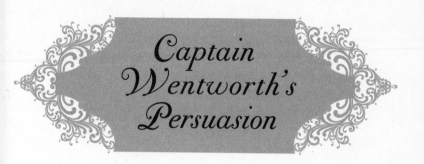

Captain Wentworth's Persuasion

JANE AUSTEN'S
Classic Retold
Through His Eyes

REGINA JEFFERS

Ulysses Press

Published in the United States by
ULYSSES PRESS
P.O. Box 3440
Berkeley, CA 94703
www.ulyssespress.com

ISBN: 978-1-56975-776-5
Library of Congress Catalog Number 2009940339

Acquisitions Editor: Kelly Reed
Managing Editor: Claire Chun
Editor: Kathy Kaiser
Editorial Associates: Lauren Harrison, Kelly Winton
Production: Judith Metzener
Cover design: what!design @ whatweb.com
Cover artwork: Joshua Reynolds "Captain Robert Orme";
    image thanks to the Art Renewal Center® www.artrenewal.org

Printed in the United States by Bang Printing

10 9 8 7 6 5 4 3 2 1

Distributed by Publishers Group West

*We remember fondly lost loves
and chances for happiness.*

"Time Does Not Bring Relief"
by Edna St. Vincent Millay

*Time does not bring relief; you all have lied
Who told me time would ease me of my pain!
I miss him in the weeping of the rain;
I want him at the shrinking of the tide;
The old snows melt from every mountain-side,
And last year's leaves are smoke in every lane;
But last year's bitter loving must remain
Heaped on my heart, and my old thoughts abide.
There are a hundred places where I fear
To go,—so with his memory they brim.
And entering with relief some quiet place
Where never fell his foot or shone his face
I say, "There is no memory of him here."
And so stand stricken, so remembering him.*

CHAPTER 1

By day or night, in weal or woe,
That heart, no longer free,
Must bear the love it cannot show
And silent ache for thee.
—Lord Byron, "On Parting"

"I have you, Captain!" the midshipman cried. "I need help over here!" the youth screamed over the turmoil on the deck, as he tried to support the weight of the slumped-over officer, who clung to his exhausted frame.

★ ★ ★

Captain Frederick Wentworth recognized the danger of pursuing the retreating French sloop, but he also recognized the need to keep the French from reaching reinforcements and from taking English secrets straight back to Bonaparte. He made the decision to take the French vessel despite the fact his wife traveled aboard *The Resolve* with him. He ordered his men to take the enemy craft. "If necessary, her crew cannot escape," he instructed them; the British had no reason to allow the French to live if they put up resistance. The countries, after all, were at war.

For two days, Wentworth's ship chased the French craft. In truth, he admired how the smaller French ship skimmed the water, trying to evade his own ship's best efforts to overtake the ketch. Frederick initiated his favorite maneuver in stopping his enemy— full broadsides, a lesson he learned from the tales of the infamous Blackbeard. *The Resolve* caught the French ship during the night. Dawn brought his enemy the knowledge it faced the full force of the British Navy, one of the finest to sail the seas.

Now, Anne gazed at her husband as he ordered her below deck, trying to protect her from the worst of the battle. Frederick Wentworth possessed a natural charisma; his men would follow him anywhere. A strong, formidable man, his intense eyes told the world he would tolerate nothing less than success. He made few errors in his choices, reasoning things out carefully before he made a decision. He lived for the adventure of the sea, but he was *her* Frederick, a practical man who had accomplished his dreams by organizing the chaos of his mind. She touched the weathered lines of his face with her fingertips before lightly brushing his lips with hers.

"You will be safe, my Love," he said as he cupped her chin in the palm of one large hand.

"Of course, I am safe," Anne insisted. "You are the captain of *The Resolve*; we are all safe under your command." She took his hand in hers, kissing the palm before releasing him. "Now, do what you must do, Frederick. I will be well." With that, she left him. She shivered when she saw him load his gun, knowing the strong possibility of hand-to-hand combat when the British boarded the sloop.

Wentworth glanced at her retreating form as she headed for the protection of the lower levels of the ship. He had loved her from the first time he saw her face; only her countenance brought him peace. In that moment long ago, he had set his sights on *his* Anne. It had taken nearly nine years for him to win her. Anne Elliot Wentworth epitomized the things to which Frederick Wentworth aspired: acceptance and love. Anne had overlooked his common origins; she had seen the man he was. He had sworn to prove to her aristocratic world she had not taken a step down with her choice of a husband. She symbolized why he fought this war against the French emperor.

He hoped to purchase an estate close to the shoreline for her. They would live there when he finally cashed in his commission from the service or at the end of the war. Anne, the daughter of a baronet, deserved the best he could give her. Frederick had lost her once, when youth demanded they make decisions not their own. Anne belonged to him now; he loved her beyond reason. Soon they could claim a place in society and start a family. He smiled briefly as the image played before him. Then he turned his attention to the other ship and prepared to strike at his enemy.

Wentworth felt the distant vibration as *The Resolve* ran out its guns. The ship readied itself for an assault. When he placed a spyglass to his eye, he saw the French scrambling to respond to the surprise. Older seamen shouted orders, but Frederick recognized the confusion and the dismay upon the younger sailors' faces. His men, on the other hand, stood their positions on the deck, awaiting the inevitable. His crew had kept a determined silent vigil throughout the night, using the darkness to overtake the French.

With a nod of his head, Wentworth ordered his men to attack. The gun ports were all pointed directly at the French warship, and shots rang out. He watched with satisfaction as the enemy's sails crashed to the deck. As the smoke cleared, he could readily see the gaping hole in the enemy's starboard tack. But the French powder magazines did not explode. "What the devil?" he muttered. The sloop's mizzenmast lay in multiple pieces on the deck. With the longboats in the water, Wentworth knew the French would fight, but he also knew he had managed another capture. Along with it would come the financial reward that would secure his future with Anne. Everything he had ever wanted was within his grasp.

Beside him, a sailor called to his partner, "We'll not be waiting!"

"They'll not surrender peacefully," a lieutenant cautioned his men.

"They're daft!" a man with a knife held tightly between his teeth hissed to the others gathering on the deck. A fierce curse sounded from the crow's nest above his head as Wentworth placed a rolled-up map in his assistant's hand.

He maneuvered *The Resolve* alongside the captured ship, readying to board her officially and claim her in the name of the Crown. Then—the unexpected, the unthinkable. A single shot rang out, and the heat seared through his side. Surprised, he touched the bloody opening in his jacket. *How?* he wondered as he slumped forward into the arms of the nearest midshipman. He was not close enough to the French ship for a French sailor to deliver such a blow. Instinctively, he raised his eyes to his attacker. The man, wearing a leather-fringed jacket and a floppy-brimmed hat, held a long rifle. Frederick recognized it as one American privateers used often to fight off personal attack. It had the distance the single-shot .60 musket that the British carried did not. "Give that to your good King George!" he heard the man's voice exclaim before British sailors surrounded him.

Frederick's pain came not from his French enemy but from an American assisting Bonaparte's Navy. He could hear the air gurgle in his throat as he sank to his knees. The pain and the fire radiated throughout his chest as he fell on his back, allowing his eyes to search the thin, smoky air for the blue sky with streaks of sunlight opening a new day. "Anne," he murmured as another midshipman cradled his captain's head for comfort.

"Help is on the way, Captain. Just stay with us," the man gasped through clenched teeth, fear coursing through his body.

Shipmates rushed forward. Lifting the gigantic frame of Frederick Wentworth onto a net stretcher, they quickly carried him to his quarters. As they settled him on the bed, Laraby, the sawbones assigned to the ship, rushed in, hustling various sailors from the room. "Get me plenty of rum!" the doctor demanded.

"Yes, Sir," one of the lieutenants snapped as he darted out the door.

Wentworth groaned deeply as another officer helped the doctor prop him up and remove his jacket. Then, as the officer kept Wentworth propped up, the physician cut the shirt away from the wound and began to clean away the seeping blood. "Easy, Captain," the doctor cautioned him. "Let me see what we have here."

The surgeon went through a mental checklist as he examined the captain's wound. "The bullet tore a zigzag path through part of your lower abdomen, Sir. There is quite a bit of damage. The good news is the bullet exited out your side. I need to sew you up, but I do not need to do any cutting."

Frederick finally got the words out, "Where is my wife?"

Another officer moved forward. "I will get her, Captain." The sight of all the blood had taken its toll on the man.

"I am giving you some laudanum." The doctor helped the first officer to ease Wentworth back onto the bed.

"Might I have some rum, too?" Wentworth's mouth went dry as his head touched the pillows.

The doctor half grinned. "That is why I ordered it." He supported Frederick's head while the captain took a large swig of the brew.

Anne rushed into the room and made her way to her husband's side. "Frederick," she said, whispering his name close to his ear as she brushed the hair from his eyes. "I am here, my Love." She interlaced her fingers with his.

With an effort, he squeezed her hand and opened his eyes to hers. "I need an angel watching over me," he whispered as she lowered her mouth to brush his lips lightly.

"Nothing can keep us apart—nothing ever again. I am here, Frederick. Let the doctor do his work. 'In sickness and in health,'" she murmured before kissing his temple.

Frederick made eye contact with the doctor and nodded his assent. Then his eyes rested again on Anne's face. He felt the laudanum begin to take its effect. His lids closed, but Anne's image remained with him.

★ ★ ★

Commander Frederick Wentworth made his way across Somerset. The sway of the public carriage along the uneven roadway reminded him of the rolling motion of the sea; at least, it did as long as he kept his eyes closed. When he had opened them an hour or so earlier, the grandmotherly woman sitting across the way had questioned him about the war and about his prospects. He assumed she had an eligible woman somewhere in her family, but Frederick had no intention of pursuing the subject. When he chose a wife, it would be a woman with whom he could share his hopes and dreams—one who would recognize his potential. So he had closed his eyes again, feigning sleep and imagining that he strode the decks of his own ship.

Passing through Uppercross, he finally allowed himself the pleasure of looking at the rolling countryside, which was peppered with herds of sheep and Brinny cattle grazing in the fields. His brother, Edward, resided as the curate at Monkford, and Frederick planned to spend part of his leave catching up with him. Quiet time was a pleasant prospect after the action he had seen of late. Of course, he had not been with his sister's husband, Benjamin Croft, and Nelson as they defeated Admiral Vileneuve at Trafalgar, but Frederick had seen his share of battles. Like Benjamin, he expected to use the war with the French emperor to make his fortune. Thoughts of his sister brought Frederick a pang of loneliness; Sophia and Benjamin shared a rare love. "Someday," he whispered to himself. "Someday, I will turn my head—"

The slowing of the horses interrupted his thoughts. "Upper-cross!" the driver shouted. "Changing horses!"

Frederick disembarked from the carriage and looked around. People hurried back and forth at the posting inn. Knowing he had not much further to go, he chose only to stretch his legs in the inn yard rather than spend his money on libation inside the crowded tavern.

"How much time?" he inquired of the groom as the man un-hitched the horses.

"More than a quarter hour—less than a half hour," the man responded. The driver leaned over the edge to take the mail pouch from the innkeeper.

Frederick looked at the village, which was a smattering of houses and shops. "I shall take a short walk," he told the driver as he started away toward the village.

The driver called to his retreating form, "We will not wait!"

Frederick did not even look back. He just raised his hand to let the man know he had heard the warning. Uppercross, a moderate-sized village, was designed in the old English style. He passed a gate, which led to a house, substantial and unmodernized, of superior appearance, especially when compared to those of the yeomen and laborers. With its high walls, great gates, and old trees, Frederick envisioned a veranda, French windows, and other prettiness, quite likely to catch the traveler's eye.

Strolling along the wooden walkways, he paused only to look in some of the shop windows. Seeing a fan he knew Sophia would love, he smiled. On impulse, he entered the shop; he would buy the fan for his sister. He could leave it with Edward to mail to her for her birthday. It would surprise the highly critical Sophia to know her seafarer brother had planned for her birthday long before the actual event.

Frederick chose the item and then, having paid for it, turned to leave; but he could not depart, for the shop's door swung open suddenly, and two ladies swept into the room. The first, a very handsome woman, dominated the space. A strong French perfume wafted over him as he allowed his eyes to assay her beauty. Her hair was nearly black, her eyes were brown, and her long nose had a distinctly aristocratic look. Belatedly, Frederick offered her a polite bow as she brushed past him, barely acknowledging his presence. "Miss Elliot!" he heard the shopkeeper say, his voice suddenly very alert.

Frederick had seen the type before. Usually, he preferred to avoid women of high Society, finding most of them too consumed with their own petty interests to be worth his time. Let them spend their days gossiping and shopping; he preferred a woman with an elegance of mind—a woman with a sweetness of character.

He stepped away from the domineering Miss Elliot and headed for the door; his carriage would be leaving soon. The second woman remained by the entry; he started to move around her, and then she raised her eyes to his. Frederick froze. Her delicate features and mild, dark eyes mesmerized him in an instant. For some reason, she did not look away, and neither did he. Instead, he stood before her, gazing down into her doe like eyes, watching them darken and sparkle and wondering if she could feel the fire burning in him. She flushed and raised her slim, slightly square jaw a bit; her ramrod-straight back made her appear taller than she was. In fact, she barely came to his shoulder. She said nothing, simply continued to look deeply into his eyes. Frederick found himself unexpectedly amused by the situation, and one eyebrow shot up.

"Come, Anne," the other woman demanded, and Frederick saw

a flash of embarrassment play across her face. She ducked her head, allowing her bonnet to shadow her features once again.

"Pardon me," he said, choking out the words; his throat was suddenly very dry. He desperately wanted to say more to her, but she had slipped away to her companion, who was thumbing through pages of fashion plates.

Frederick opened the door to depart, but he could not resist the urge to look at her one more time. His heart skipped a beat as she raised her head. She gave him a quick smile before turning her attention to bolts of material. Frederick paused; the faint smell of lavender surrounded him. He closed his eyes and inhaled deeply. Closing the shop's door and returning to the walkway, he murmured, "Beautiful." Smiling, he headed toward the inn yard.

Within the hour, Frederick found himself sitting in his brother's cottage. "You are a sight for sore eyes," Edward said as he handed his brother a cup of tea. "You have filled out since we last saw each other. The sea is good for your constitution."

Frederick chuckled. "It is, Edward; it is even better for my purse. I could leave the war with a governmental position, if I so wished, and a reasonable fortune."

Sitting down across the table from him, Edward nodded his agreement. "I know it is your wish, Frederick, to be acknowledged for your accomplishments. However, you must realize society is slow to change. Even a sizable fortune will not allow you to live within more than the fringes of fine society. An earl one step from debtor's prison will always be accepted quicker than a commoner with accrued wealth. Name is still more powerful than wealth."

"It should not be so." Frederick's words held a steely determination.

Edward added another sugar to his tea. "The aristocracy is not likely to change, my Brother, but if anyone can bend it to his will, it is you. Now, what would you like to do during your stay? I receive a few invitations on a regular basis. My position allows me some degree of respectability in country society, at least."

Frederick's thoughts went immediately to the dark eyes and the slender form of the woman called Anne. A fleeting smile turned up the corners of his lips. "Anything, Edward. I simply came to enjoy your company and to feel normal again. A taste for what I am fighting will go a long way when I must return to my ship."

"How is Harville?" Edward asked as he put his empty cup away.

Frederick chuckled. "He is in love once again. He swears this time he will marry the woman, but I have heard such protestations before. Like me, he returned home to visit his friends and family. His sister Fanny is coming of age soon, and Harville wants to assure himself that she will make no choices without his permission."

"I would hate to be in his shoes." Edward began to pick up Frederick's belongings to take them to his room. "With a mother and sisters and aunts for whom he is responsible, Harville will always be caring for some woman or another."

"Luckily, the man has a generous nature." Frederick rose to follow his brother. "If I ever needed someone on my side, Harville would be my first choice of all my shipmates."

★ ★ ★

The next evening found the Wentworth brothers at a neighborhood assembly. Edward Wentworth had earned the respect of the local gentry, and they welcomed his brother. Wearing his dress uniform, Frederick cut a fine figure, and more than one mother began to concoct ways to draw his address to her eligible daughter. He relished the attention; having been at sea for so long, Frederick craved the notice of English society, and now he imagined his place within the social structure of the country he called home.

He stood with Edward and several other men when he felt her enter the room. Even without turning around, Frederick knew that she was there. He knew it in his heart—he knew it in the shiver that ran down his spine. Turning slowly, he half expected to see "his Anne" standing in the doorway. Instead, he found a man of aristocratic rank posing in the entrance and waiting to be announced. Ostentatiously attired, a young woman—the same lady Frederick had noted in the village shop—stood by his side, her hand resting lightly on his proffered arm.

A voice rang out: "Sir Walter Elliot of Kellynch Hall. Miss Elizabeth Elliot. Lady Russell. Miss Anne Elliot." A path cleared as the members of the Elliot party walked the length of the assembly hall and took their places on the raised dais at the far end of the room. His body was correct; *she* was there. Miss Anne Elliot followed at the rear of her family, a tiny smile curving her lips. She fascinated him; as a woman of rank, Frederick knew she could easily marry a man of considerable wealth. But Miss Anne Elliot, unlike the rest of her family, did not possess vanity. What she had was a remarkable poise, a possession of the self.

"Steady, Frederick," Edward whispered in his ear. "Miss Elizabeth Elliot is not for you. She is to marry the heir apparent; at least, that is the accepted rumor."

Frederick's eyes never left Anne Elliot. "I am not looking at Miss Elliot."

Edward followed his brother's gaze. "Miss Anne?" he inquired. "She is the more *amiable* one."

"Let us get something to drink," Frederick added quickly, realizing his attention had become noticeable to those around him. Retrieving lemonades, the brothers moved off to speak privately. "Tell me what you know of the Elliots," Frederick commanded his brother.

"Sir Walter is a proud—no, *conceited*—aristocrat. Vanity is the beginning and end of Sir Walter Elliot's character: vanity of person and of situation. Reportedly, he was remarkably handsome as a youth; few women could think more of their appearance than he does of his own. He considers the blessing of beauty as inferior only to the blessing of a baronetcy."

"Where is Lady Elliot?" Frederick asked as he forced his eyes from Anne Elliot once more.

"She passed before I arrived in the area," Edward said. "Some six or seven years ago," he added. "I know little about her except what I have heard. She was a woman of very superior character from all reports—an excellent woman, sensible and amiable, whose judgment and conduct, if they might be pardoned the youthful infatuation which made her Lady Elliot, never required indulgence afterward." Frederick chuckled at his brother's attempt at sarcasm. "She humored, or softened, or concealed his failings, and promoted his real respectability for seventeen years; and though not the very happiest being in the world herself, she found enough in her duties, her friends, and her children, to attach her to life, and make it no matter of indifference to her when she was called on to quit them." Edward's eyes misted with the thought of how God often takes the best to heaven early. "Three girls, the two eldest sixteen and fourteen, was an awful legacy for a mother to bequeath; an awful charge rather, to confide to the authority and guidance of a conceited silly father."

Frederick could not resist asking the obvious question: "Why has Sir Walter never remarried?"

"Other than himself, Sir Walter is not likely to believe anyone worthy of his attention. Some thought he might choose Lady Russell; she was Lady Elliot's intimate friend, but they did not marry, whatever might have been anticipated on that head by their acquaintance. But he did bring her to live close by in the village of Kellynch, where she serves as a confidante for the daughters. It is said she holds great sway over their lives, especially over Miss Anne."

The music began again, and Frederick watched as Anne Elliot took the dance floor with a member of the local gentry. The man's slightly disheveled appearance and clumsy movements did little to win Anne's admiration. She looked politely at him and offered him a gentle smile, but Frederick could easily see that her eyes did not darken with pleasure, as they had with him. "Who is the gentleman?" He nodded toward the couple as Anne circled the man across from her.

"Charles Musgrove," Edward replied. "The Musgroves are the second most important family in the area. He is the eldest son and will inherit a substantial property. The Musgroves wish a match, but Lady Russell does not approve, from what I hear. She wishes more for Miss Anne. She favors her because, of the three girls, Anne Elliot most resembles her late mother."

"I believe it is time I return to the dance floor, Brother." Frederick started forward to choose a partner and to enter the quadrille already in progress.

Edward cautioned him, "If Lady Russell does not approve of Charles Musgrove, the brother of a curate will stand no chance."

"You will introduce me to Miss Anne later," Frederick instructed as the two men walked toward a cluster of eligible young ladies waiting to be escorted to the floor.

★ ★ ★

"Miss Anne," Edward said, bowing, "may I introduce my brother, Commander Frederick Wentworth?"

Frederick bowed. "Miss Anne."

"Commander." She curtsied and then brought her eyes to Frederick's face. She spoke to Edward but looked only at Frederick. "I believe, Mr. Wentworth, that your brother and I met briefly yesterday, although a formal introduction was not made at the time." Her soft voice weakened Frederick's knees, forcing him to shift his weight to maintain his stance.

"You honor me, Miss Anne, with your recognition." Frederick took her hand and lowered his head to kiss her gloved knuckles.

"What brings you to Somerset, Commander?" Anne withdrew her hand slowly, allowing Frederick the pleasure of holding it for a few seconds.

Frederick smiled at her. "Besides my brother's fine company, I seek the peace of the English countryside. I will be joining the crew of a new ship when I return to my duties. Hopefully, I will command my own ship before long."

"Then you have the prospect of advancement?" Interest flashed in her eyes, and Frederick realized she was not one to pretend.

"I do, Miss Anne." He nodded toward the dance floor. "If you have not already promised the next set, would you honor me with your company?"

Anne's face glowed as she smiled up at him. "It would be my pleasure, Commander."

They danced in silence for a few minutes, until Frederick

could bear it no longer. "Are we devoid of conversation so quickly, Miss Anne?"

"I would hope not." Her smile reached the corners of her eyes. "I was just contemplating the length of your name."

"It is a mouthful; is it not? Commander Frederick Wentworth. A man might expire before he could utter it in full." His laughter teased her ear as they passed each other in the dance form.

Anne's head turned to follow his progress through the twirls and turns that would bring them back together. "Imposing," she said, the word barely audible. "Both the man and the name."

Frederick felt his breath catch in his chest. Taking her hand as they proceeded down the line, he could not resist looking at her mouth. "Do you flatter me, Miss Anne?"

He watched as the flush of her cheeks reddened. "I—I apologize, Commander," she stammered.

"Please do not apologize, Miss Anne. To have the attention of such a beautiful woman would make any man puff up with pride."

"It is my sister Elizabeth who is the beauty of the family. I have a mirror, Commander. Please, no exaggeration." Those were her last words before they parted to circle other partners.

Frederick watched her as she wove her way around the other dancers. When the music brought them back together, he held her hand a little more tightly and lowered his voice so that only she could hear. "Miss Anne, I beg your forbearance with my words; I must speak the truth. I have traveled to the East Indies and many of the capitals of Europe; I have known the beauty of the world's greatest architecture and its most compelling musical scores, but I have yet to see such beauty—a face that instantly affected me as yours did. Please forgive me if I offend you; it is not my wish to do so."

Long seconds passed as Frederick waited for her response. Rarely did he act so impulsively, but he felt as though he had seen into the innermost being of Anne Elliot in the first moment he laid eyes on her. She would, he hoped, recognize the honesty of his words. He felt heat move through him. Even through her gloved hand, he imagined the sense of her bare one on his. "Miss Anne," he whispered again, his breath on the side of her face, "I should very much like to know your thoughts." He held his breath.

Anne lifted her chin, and Frederick fought the urge to move in closer. "I wondered, Commander, if we might sit together at supper?"

Frederick exhaled. The gentleman should ask the question, he reflected, but Anne Elliot clearly was no prisoner of societal convention. *Nor am I.* One corner of his mouth curled upward. "It would be my great pleasure, Miss Anne, but only on the condition that you agree to call me *Frederick.*"

There was a momentary hesitation before she responded. "Frederick." She smiled up at him as the dance ended. "Thank you, Commander," she said loudly for the benefit of those around her, but when she took his arm to go into supper, she said softly, "I look forward to your company, Frederick."

CHAPTER 2

And on that cheek, and o'er that brow,
So soft, so calm, yet eloquent,
That smiles that win, the tints that glow,
But tell of days in goodness spent,
A mind at peace with all below,
A heart whose love is innocent!
—Lord Byron, "She Walks in Beauty"

"To where are you off?" Edward inquired, giving Frederick a knowing grin, after having noted his brother's careful grooming that morning.

Frederick returned the smile. "I thought I might enjoy some of the countryside. A long walk perhaps."

"Would you care for some company?" his brother teased him.

A laugh escaped Frederick. "I do not think I care for *your* company this morning. I hope you are not offended, Edward."

"I am not offended. However, do not compromise Miss Anne's reputation. She deserves the best life has to offer."

"On that fact we do agree." Frederick stood to make his exit. Anne Elliot had not agreed to go walking with him that morning, but twice during supper she had told him specifically where she would be walking and what time she would be in the area.

Frederick grabbed a worn-looking blanket before he made his way out the door. At the bakery, he bought several fresh pastries and had them wrapped to take along with him. All night he had looked forward to seeing Anne Elliot again. His dreams had been filled with images of her. During supper the evening before, he had taken many opportunities to lean in close to her and to feel the heat simmering in her body. She was a flame; he was a moth.

She had taken a deep interest in his stories of the sea. To his surprise, sheltered, wealthy Anne Elliot knew about the important battles; she recognized the names of the larger ships and their skippers. Rarely did he meet a woman who did not wince and change the subject when confronted with the realities of war. Frederick held little back; he spoke freely of the maneuvers a ship made, of the mechanics of boarding an enemy ship, and of the tragedies of war. Never had he known a person not part of the Navy with whom he could share such memories. Most wanted only to know whether he was a war hero.

Now, in the early morning sun, he strode along the road leading out of town and toward the Kellynch estate. His heart felt light as he left the main road and cut across a field leading to a secluded lake. Then he spotted her, standing there under a river birch, leaning easily against its multiple trunks. Taking a deep breath, Frederick stepped forward. "Miss Anne?" he spoke to her profile as he approached.

She turned to see him standing there. Dropping a curtsy, she murmured, "Commander Wentworth."

Frederick stepped forward to take her hand and bowed over it. He raised his head and studied her expression to determine if he had overstepped his limits by meeting her there alone. "Do I disturb your solitude?"

Anne was silent for a moment as she seemed to weigh the propriety of the situation. Finally, she said, "I am glad, Frederick, that you attended to my words so closely last night."

"I assure you, Miss Anne, there was little about you to which I did not attend." Frederick risked everything by stepping forward to trace her jaw line with his thumb. "You are exquisite." For a moment, his breathing became shallow. Reluctantly, he forced his thoughts to the present situation. "May I walk with you?"

"Thank you, Frederick." She took his arm. "Why do you not leave your items here? We may return for them later."

"Excellent idea, Miss Anne." He wrapped everything in the blanket and secured it high in one of the branches of the river birch. Then they strolled along the hedgerows surrounding the adjoining field.

"My brother tells me that you lost your mother several years ago," he began. "We have that in common. For myself, I have only Edward and my sister Sophia. She is married to Benjamin Croft, another naval officer. I predict that my brother Croft will be an admiral someday soon."

Anne met his bold gaze. "I miss my mother desperately; Lady Russell tries to provide me with some sense of family, but it is not the same." She paused and flushed. "I—I cannot believe I am saying these things to you," she stammered. "I rattle on about personal matters, and we are barely more than strangers."

"We are, Miss Anne, clearly more than strangers. We were from the moment our eyes met in the milliner's shop." Frederick added, "I appreciate your not making me play the lengthy courtship games that others demand. My time in Somerset is short; I do not have the ability to call upon you daily for many months before I might hold your hand."

"Is this a courtship, Frederick?" The words hung in the air between them. They stopped walking and looked deeply in each other's eyes.

Frederick touched Anne's lips with his fingertips. "I stand enthralled," he whispered. "I wish to court you properly, Anne, or as properly as one might while on military leave. I intend to win your regard."

She looked about nervously. "I should have brought a maid with me."

Clearly, the young lady does not always *flout convention.* He smiled slightly. *Nor do I.* "I will be the perfect gentleman, Anne; you have nothing to fear from me." His tone, as he studied her, remained nonchalant.

"I do not fear you, Frederick," she said at last. To his eyes, Anne looked rather forlorn, even a bit lonely. Intuitively, he gathered her into his arms, needing to give her comfort; she relaxed, placing her head against his chest, resting her hand on the lapel of his jacket.

Frederick swallowed hard, forcing his desire for her away. When she became his, it would be through an honest proposal. His head made the decision, but his body fought him. He wanted Anne—wanted her completely—yet, he would not act on his desire; he would do the honorable thing. "I do not wish to release you, my Dear, but I fear that we need to walk once again." He lifted her chin with his fingertips and brushed Anne's lips lightly with his.

Anne blushed and moved away quickly. Frederick stepped up to take her hands in his. "Do not regret our intimacy, Anne. Ours will be a different relationship. We will offer each other honesty. I will write you love sonnets, and you will tell me how much more you prefer Lord Byron or Wordsworth." That brought a smile to her lips. "I will bring you wildflowers, and you will throw out the roses of other suitors; but most of all, I will give you of myself, as you will to me. Surely you must feel it, too?"

"I do feel it, Frederick." Her voice touched his heart with hope.

"Then let us return to the lake; I brought a blanket and a treat just for you, my Dear." She smiled. Frederick thought that he could become addicted to her smiles.

This time, she took his hand, and they walked silently back to the water. Frederick spread the blanket and then offered her the pastries. Anne's eyes sparkled, making her even more beautiful. She was everything for which he yearned. He would prove to her aristocratic father that he was worthy of the attentions of a baronet's daughter. "Tell me about yourself. What was your schooling like? And your friends?" He was intensely curious about this woman, already precious to him.

"After my mother passed, my father and Lady Russell felt it best that I return to school. I do not know how I would have survived in Bath without my friend Miss Hamilton. I returned unhappy to school, grieving for the loss of a mother I dearly loved, feeling the separation from home, and suffering as a girl of fourteen, of strong sensibility and not high spirits, must suffer at such a time. Miss Hamilton, three years older than I, but still suffering from the want of near relations and a settled home, remained another year at school. She was useful and good in a way, which considerably lessened my misery. I can never remember her with indifference."

"What happened to Miss Hamilton? I do not recall meeting her last night." Frederick broke off a piece of the pastry and fed it to her. Anne giggled like a schoolgirl, and then, unexpectedly, she boldly kissed his fingertips. Charmed, Frederick then brought his fingertips to his own lips.

"Miss Hamilton was not from this area. She left school, married not long afterward, was said to have married a man of fortune. That is all I know of her fate." Frederick's attention increased and Anne looked away, reluctant to meet the intensity growing in his eyes. "I—I am sorry," she stammered.

"Anne," he whispered. "Look at me." He reached out and gently caressed her cheek. She slowly brought her eyes up to his. "You will never have to be alone again. Do not feel remorse; I want to see only a smile on your pretty face." She closed her eyes, and he leaned in for a gentle kiss, his mouth lingering over hers. Then he pulled away. "I do not wish to say this, but I should return you to Kellynch Hall before you are missed."

Anne nodded. Frederick rose to his feet and helped Anne to hers. "May we meet again tomorrow?" His voice was raspy.

"Here, at the same time." She moved into his embrace, wrapping her arms around Frederick's waist.

He rested his chin on the top of her head. "Come, Anne," he said at last. "I must not ruin your reputation." With a deep sigh, he released her. "It will be a very long evening, my Love."

★ ★ ★

Thus began Frederick Wentworth's courtship of Anne Elliot. Unless it rained, they met daily; they walked the countryside, sharing conversations on nearly every subject possible. They had no idle drawing room chats. Instead, they spoke of the war, of crops, of family, of personal hopes and dreams, and of their growing affection for each other.

At least once weekly, they spent time together at a local soiree or enjoyed dinner out. When viewed by prying eyes, their behavior was usually entirely proper, even distant. Yet, Frederick found himself often reaching for her hand or resting his on Anne's back before catching himself. Likewise, Anne would lean into him when he came up behind her before realizing her error. The next day they would laugh about their actions and speculate on who might have seen them and what rumors they might face.

For well over a month, such was Frederick's life. "Do you plan to offer for Miss Anne before you return to the sea?" Edward asked suddenly one morning.

"I do." Frederick gazed levelly at his brother. "Do you object?"

"Heavens, no. I would be happy to see you finally content in your life. I simply wondered what you would do if she refused or if Sir Walter objected."

Frederick raised an eyebrow. "Do you believe Anne will refuse me?" he asked impatiently.

"From what I have noted of the woman, Miss Anne will not refuse you. She is obviously besotted with your charms. Yet, I do not believe that she will defy her father's or Lady Russell's wishes. If they refuse, Anne may turn down your proposal. You will need to be prepared for such a situation."

"Anne loves me," Frederick said with some assurance.

"I am sure she does." Edward replied. He said no more on the subject.

★ ★ ★

Frederick shored up his confidence. He planned to ask Sir Walter's permission on Saturday. He and Edward would attend an evening at Kellynch Hall on Friday. Knowing Anne had secured the invitation for them, he relished the idea of finally publicly acknowledging his feelings for her. He knew many people chose a mate as part of a business arrangement, but the match of Frederick Wentworth and Anne Elliot would be a true love match.

When the butler announced the Wentworth brothers' entrances into the drawing room, Frederick's eyes automatically found Anne. The Wentworths bowed to the room. An elderly parishioner of Edward's immediately engaged him in conversation. That left Frederick free to direct his attention to his love. Surreptitiously, Frederick and Anne circled the outer layers of the group, stopping to speak to honored guests and others included in the evening party. Frederick overheard that the heir presumptive, William Walter Elliot, Esq., great grandson of the second Sir Walter, was to be in attendance at the night's gathering. Miss Elizabeth Elliot, he noted, actually giggled nervously, almost like a schoolgirl; her eyes darted about the room in anticipation of Mr. Elliot's entrance.

The room was splendid. Antique treasures graced nearly every piece of furniture in the room; rich works of art lined the walls; ornate fabrics hung from the windows. Deep shades of green and gold intertwined in the carpeting, and throughout the room freshly polished gold pieces sparkled in the candlelight. The warmth of the room stood in contrast with the cool marble foyer. For a moment, Frederick realized the compromise Anne would be making in giving up such grandeur to be his wife.

Finally, Anne and Frederick were face-to-face. He bowed, and she returned a low curtsy. "Miss Anne," his voice held admiration, "you look fetching this evening."

"Thank you, Commander Wentworth." Her eyes sparkled with delight at seeing him in her home. "It pleases me that you were free to join us this evening."

Frederick's smile curved the corners of his eyes. "I understand we are to be blessed with the attendance of the elusive Mr. William Elliot."

Anne laughed lightly; previously, she had disclosed the frustration that her father and Elizabeth felt with the reception they received from William Elliot. Mr. Elliot was reportedly a very fine young man, currently engaged in the study of law. Elizabeth found him extremely agreeable, and every plan in his favor was confirmed. Elizabeth imagined becoming his wife and assuming her mother's former position as mistress of Kellynch Hall. The estate would thus remain in Sir Walter's family. Consequently, Sir Walter invited Mr. Elliot to Kellynch to foster a relationship with Elizabeth and to meet the local gentry. "Father is all aflutter, anxiously awaiting Mr. Elliot's approval of Kellynch. After all, it will be his someday. Father is not likely to remarry; even if he did, he would have to produce a male heir from any such union in order for him to remain in his home. The most for which he can hope is an alliance between Elizabeth and Mr. Elliot."

Frederick frowned. "The prospect of such a marriage does not appeal to me." He began to search her face, hoping to find a confirmation of what he thought to be Anne's feelings for him. "I have always wished to marry for love."

Anne flushed, but his soft words caressed her heart. She leaned toward him, and Frederick resisted the desire to stroke her face. "I am sure, Commander," she barely whispered, "that whomever you choose will love you in return."

Turning his back so the others could not see, his hand sought hers. For a few fleeting seconds, he clasped her fingertips in his. "Miss Anne," he began. He was so close to her that he could feel the warmth of her breath on his cheek. "With your consent, I would speak to your father tomorrow." Frederick waited. His heart seemed to be frozen in hopeful expectation.

He watched as Anne fought to make her words come. "Frederick," she murmured, "I would be pleased to entertain your entreaty."

Frederick's breath rushed out with her words. "Anne," was all he could get out. But what his mouth could not say, his facial expression did.

Before they parted in the drawing room, Frederick wanted to pull her into his arms and clasp her to him. Anne Elliot had welcomed his address. She returned his feelings for her with those of her own. His life seemed to grow more complete by the moment.

At supper, Frederick could scarcely keep his mind on the mundane conversations going on about him. All he could do was to fill his eyes with images of Anne. Although Sir Walter and Elizabeth Elliot barely hid their dismay at the absence of Mr. Elliot, Anne, obviously, felt none of their alarm. Frederick's heart leapt each time he heard her laugh. She sat between his brother, Edward, and Mr. Musgrove, giving both her attentions. With some effort, he caught her eye at last, and they exchanged a secret smile. Frederick closed his eyes and imagined his hands cupping her face, his fingers removing the pins from her hair to let it fall softly over her shoulders, and his thumbs tracing the outline of her bottom lip. When he opened them again, he found both Edward and Anne staring at him. Edward chuckled before turning to the lady seated on his right, but Anne held his gaze for a few seconds. Then she pursed her lips before touching them with her napkin. Frederick felt the heat rush to his body. Before she could look away, he winked at her and enjoyed seeing the color increase in her cheeks. Such romantic teasing was a new sensation for him, and he discovered he quite liked the results.

Sitting quietly, waiting for the next course, he began to imagine the life they would share. Frederick chastised himself for not economizing. He earned funds each time his ship did battle with a French one. Legally, as a British officer, he shared in the prizes of the French captures. He could win more; he *would* win more—for Anne. He currently held half of what he had earned in the victory at San Domingo. Looking at her, he knew that Anne deserved a fine home. He would give her all that she should have.

They would purchase an estate once he left the Navy. Soon, he would have his own ship, and Anne would sail with him, as his sister, Sophia, did with her husband. Fondly, he reflected on a conversation from the preceding morning. Her surprise when he had told her of the accommodations and food found on board ships had taken him aback. "Miss Anne," he had teased her, "surely you cannot be supposing that sailors live on board without anything to eat, or any cook to dress it if there were, or any servant to wait, or any knife and fork to use?" She had blushed profusely and Frederick lightly touched her lips with his. Happiness spread through his body with such musings; Anne would be his.

Later, Frederick lingered behind when the gentlemen left Sir Walter's study to rejoin the ladies in the drawing room. When only he and Sir Walter remained, he boldly approached his host. Frederick had not noted Sir Walter's growing anger as the evening progressed. The absence of Mr. Elliot—the man's obvious snub of Sir Walter's family—took its toll on Anne's father.

"Sir Walter, may I speak to you privately?" Frederick asked before the man could leave the room. The smell of port and half-smoked cheroots drifted Frederick's way.

Sir Walter offered his first cut. "I cannot imagine, Commander, that we have anything to discuss."

Frederick swallowed his irritation and tried another tactic. "I apologize, Sir. I would not intrude on your graciousness this evening. I simply request the honor to do so tomorrow morning."

"I will be to London tomorrow morning, Commander; your request is impossible." He started to make his way past Frederick.

Instinctively, Frederick reached to stop him physically but then thought better of it. "Sir Walter, I implore you," he begged the older man. "What I have to say is of great importance."

"Very well, Commander Wentworth." Sir Walter motioned to Frederick to follow him back into the study.

Sir Walter settled himself once more in his favorite wing chair, which faced the embers of a dying fire. Frederick began to pace, trying to right his thoughts. He had planned to approach Sir Walter on the morrow, but circumstances changed, and now he found himself frantically trying to find the right words to persuade Anne's father of the merits of his suit. The clearing of Sir Walter's throat jarred Frederick from his turmoil. He forced himself to take a stance beside the fireplace mantel. He swallowed hard and then spoke. "Sir Walter, since coming into Somersetshire, I have had the great honor of meeting your middle daughter, Miss Anne, on numerous occasions. During those times, I found my affections for Anne increasing. I am now of the persuasion to admit I think only of her and, with your consent, I wish to make Miss Anne my wife."

Sir Walter's eyebrow shot up. A smirk spread across his face. "You aspire to become a member of my family?" Sir Walter barely hid the sarcasm laced through his words.

Frederick stiffened, but he pushed away his anger, thinking only of Anne's need for her family. "I aspire to make Miss Anne a worthy husband." He controlled the contempt in his words. "The fact Anne is your child was never part of my decision."

Sir Walter laughed. "May I ask, Commander Wentworth, what you believe you could offer the daughter of a baronet?"

"I assume, Sir, you mean something besides my constancy and my ardent admiration?" he responded coolly.

"Commander Wentworth," Sir Walter's voice took on a reprimanding tone, "one cannot eat constancy; nor will your ardent admiration serve as protection for my daughter."

Feeling very much like a misbehaving schoolboy being called on the carpet by the headmaster, Frederick shot back, "I have a promising career in the British Navy; I expect to be given my own ship upon my return to my duties. As such, I foresee many opportunities to earn my fortune. I will eventually be able to provide for Miss Anne in the manner that she deserves."

Sir Walter snorted. "You will pardon me, Commander, if I address my concerns over parts of your declaration." Sir Walter motioned to Wentworth to sit in a chair across from him. He did not enjoy having the big man tower over him. "First, I am certain you will argue that the Navy has done much for us at home and that its members should have an equal claim with any other set of men."

Frederick disliked this turn of the conversation. "Defending our country has always been an honorable occupation for men such as I, as well as many second sons of the aristocracy," he retorted.

Sir Walter looked incredulous. "The profession has its utility, but I should be sorry to see any friend of mine belonging to it. Yes, it is in two points offensive to me; I have two strong grounds of objection to it. First, as being the means of bringing persons of obscure birth into undue distinction, and raising men of honors which their fathers and grandfathers never dreamt of; and secondly, as it cuts up a man's youth and vigor most horribly; a sailor grows old sooner than any other man; I have observed it all my life. A man is in greater danger in the Navy of being insulted by the rise of one whose father, his father might have disdained to speak to, and of becoming prematurely an object of disgust himself, than in any other line. When your brother came into the area, I inquired as to your family's connection to the earls of Strafford, as you have the same family name. I found that your family has no connections; you are not a man of property. One wonders how the names of many of our nobility become so common."

"Times are changing, Sir Walter," Frederick responded fervently, "and although you may object, our country chooses to reward its servants handsomely for hazardous work well done. I will exit the war and be able to offer Anne a place in society."

Sir Walter chuckled. "A place in society, you say, Commander? Where will Anne reside while you are off earning this handsome reward? Surely, you do not expect her to continue to live under my roof once she becomes your wife?"

"Anne will live with me aboard ship." Frederick knew that to Sir Walter this would probably sound ludicrous, but he and Anne had previously discussed his expectations for their living quarters. "A ship's captain is given adequate quarters for himself and his family."

Sir Walter leaned forward, resting his elbows on his knees. "You expect the daughter of a baronet, who is used to living in the luxury of a house such as is Kellynch Hall, to live in rooms no larger than some of my servants' quarters? You seem to believe that Anne is made of a firmer constitution than do I!"

"Miss Anne is aware of the conditions under which we will reside," Frederick protested firmly. "She expressed no qualms regarding the changes she will face as my wife." *Remember*, he told himself. *You are an officer of the Crown. Respond with honor.*

"My daughter agreed to such an alliance?" Sir Walter leaned back in his chair, attempting to discern what was not being said.

"She has, Sir." Frederick tried to keep his composure as he awaited Sir Walter's response.

After several infinitely long moments, Sir Walter played one more card with a sigh of resignation. "I do not expect that Anne will attract someone of better consequence. Her looks are too plain, and she is too compliant to earn a suitor worthy of her position." His words shot through Frederick. He felt a sudden desire to mar the perfection of Sir Walter's face with a well-placed thwack. "However," the older man continued, "I will not give my consent to such a union as you suggest, Commander." A hard thud struck Frederick's heart. Would Anne defy her father's wishes? "Yet, neither will I object to your marriage," the baronet went on. Frederick's thoughts rushed about chaotically. "If Anne chooses to marry you, I will let her go, but understand, I profess to do nothing for her. She will receive no dowry from me; the marriage you propose would be a very degrading alliance. I will wash my hands of her."

Stunned by this turn of events, Frederick forced himself to his feet. He bowed to Anne's father and started to take his leave. "I will inform Miss Anne of your decision, Sir." He paused and then said, "Sir Walter, I love Anne; I will make her my wife with or without your permission and with or without your money." With that, he strode from the room.

CHAPTER 3

As fair art thou, my bonnie lass,
So deep in luve am I,
And I will luve thee still, my dear,
Till a' the seas gang dry.
—Robert Burns, "O, My Luve's Like a Red, Red Rose"

He entered the music room only seconds before Sir Walter. The others gathered to hear Miss Elliot at the pianoforte took no notice, but Anne knew, when he stepped through the door, that Frederick Wentworth had been ill used by her father. She could see it in the tension in his shoulders and the set of his jaw. She watched him slip to the back of the group enjoying her sister's performance. As the song finished, she excused herself from Mrs. Musgrove's company and made her way to where he stood.

Frederick discreetly motioned to her to follow him. He slipped into the drawing room, and a few minutes later she did the same. Frederick eased the door partly closed to give them some privacy, while she took up a position in front of him. "Frederick, what is the matter? Did you speak to my father?"

Without thinking, he took her hand and brought her wrist to his lips. Keeping his eyes locked on hers, he found the peace he needed. "You are exquisite," he whispered.

She smiled. "I feared you had spoken to my father this evening. Lady Russell says he will travel to London tomorrow." Anne's voice caressed his being, and Frederick tried to shake off the disgust he still felt from the encounter with Sir Walter.

Taking a deep, calming breath, he confided, "I did speak to Sir Walter."

"And?" She touched his lips with her fingertips.

The words burst out of him, "And your father is an ass!" He turned away quickly.

"My father can be difficult," Anne admitted. She drew in a quick breath and lifted her chin. "Then he refused to consent to our marriage?"

Frederick did not turn to look at her. "Sir Walter did not refuse to allow the marriage to proceed."

"Then what makes you turn away? Do you no longer wish our union?"

Frederick turned quickly to find Anne sobbing silently a few feet away. He strode to her and took her into his arms, pulling her head to rest upon his chest. "I apologize, Anne. I thought only about how your father's words affected me; I did not consider how they would affect you, my Love." He stroked her back as he spoke. "Sir Walter will *allow* the marriage, although he says it would be a poor alliance on your part." Anne started to protest, but he clasped her tighter to him. "If you choose to marry me, your father will not honor you with a settlement; you will come to me with nothing."

Anne gasped and tried to pull away from him, but Frederick held her closer still. "I do not care for myself, Anne; I am used to what is adequate for my own survival. But I fear I cannot give you what you deserve. The only thing I can give you is my love and a promise that our way of life will not always be as it is now. I will make my fortune, and you will look back and be able to say you knew from the beginning that you would have your own estate." He loosened his hold on her, and then lifted her chin to look at her tear-stained face. "Anne, will you do me the honor of being my wife?"

She did not hesitate. "Oh yes, Frederick," she assured him. "Yes, I will marry you."

He lowered his head to kiss her lips gently. "Let us return to the music room," he said. "Meet me tomorrow. We will plan our life together."

"Yes," she whispered and then kissed him once again.

★ ★ ★

Frederick waited at the river birch. He slept little, but he never felt more alive. Anne had agreed to marry him; life was perfection. Finally, he spotted her coming across the field. She wore a light green muslin gown and a shawl over her ivory shoulders. Frederick found himself breathless just anticipating her presence. He went to meet her and spoke her name as she rushed into his arms. They stood entwined for a long time and then walked back to the blanket and the stream. "I am glad you are finally here," he whispered as he helped her settle on the coverlet.

She pulled her knees up, straightened her skirt, and encircled her knees with her arms. "With Father's departure, Kellynch took on a state of disarray for a few hours; I apologize if you waited for long."

"I would wait a lifetime for you." Frederick chuckled as she blushed. "Will you always blush when I tell you how much I desire you?" he teased.

"No." Her face flushed again.

He smiled at her denial. "How did I manage to win your heart, my Sweet? I ask myself that every day. Providence smiled on me when my eyes first rested upon your face."

"You saw me when others could not." Anne searched his weathered face, taking in the lines, each one so dear to her.

"Then may I assume you have not changed your mind about our marriage?"

She smiled. "I have not changed my mind. I love you, Frederick."

"And I love you, Anne." He cupped her face with the palms of his large hands. "I have barely a month left of my leave, but it will give us enough time to call the banns before we marry. We may start for Dover once we say our vows. I drafted a letter this morning to the Admiralty to inform them of our impending marriage, so accommodations will be made, and you may travel with me aboard ship. The question is, what will Sir Walter do once the banns are read for the first time?"

"I am only nineteen; without my father's permission, I may not marry. However, I was thinking about his doubts. I will speak to

Lady Russell and ask her to champion our cause with my father. She knows how to deal with him better than anyone else does. I am sure Father is just testing my determination; he will see more reason once he returns from his visit to his tailor in London. Lady Russell wants only my happiness."

"Will Lady Russell help us? Would she speak to our alliance? I truly do not care for myself; your father's money is of no significance to me."

"It is *my* inheritance, Frederick. It should not...he should not withhold it. If he does not object to our union, then I deserve the same consideration my father would give to Elizabeth or to Mary. That is what I will have Lady Russell argue."

"Then let us make our plans," he said softly. "We have much to decide."

★ ★ ★

Each day that they met added depth to their plans for the future. All his sanguine expectations, all his determination, and all his confidence would make him successful. He would prove it to her and to her family; he would distinguish himself and early gain another step in rank. Those were his guarantees to Anne.

The day after Sir Walter's return, Frederick waited for her, a rose in his hand. As usual, he met Anne by the lake. The moment he saw her coming across the field, he knew to expect trouble. Normally, Frederick went to meet her, but today something told him to wait—to wait for what was to come. A shiver of cold shot down his spine as she approached. Her eyes were red and swollen.

"Anne?" His voice was barely more than a whisper. His breath stirred a wisp of hair dislodged from her bonnet as he took her into his embrace.

She slid her arms around his waist, hearing his heart beat as she rested her head on his muscular chest. "I love you," she murmured. "Please remember that I love you." She buried her face in the folds of his jacket, trying to stop the tears.

"Will you tell me?" he said at last.

She shook her head. "I cannot."

"Lady Russell was unable to convince Sir Walter? Did your friend object to our union also? It is of no consequence. We will continue without their support."

"I cannot," she said again, but this time he knew that the words spelled doom.

"You cannot what, Anne?" he demanded.

Tears sprang to her eyes as she lifted her face to meet his gaze. "I cannot...I cannot marry you, Frederick." One lone tear trickled down her face.

"No!" He pulled her more tightly against him, silently vowing to never let her go. "I will not allow you to change your mind."

She craned her neck to look up at him. "Do you not see?" she pleaded.

"See what?" he asked, his voice cold, setting her forcibly from him. "I see a woman who breaks my heart with her words. I see a woman who promised to remain constant in her affections for me, but who turns away to the comfort of her four-poster bed as soon as she meets resistance. Is that not what I see, Miss Anne?" He took a step back from her.

His return to a formal address struck her forcibly, knocking the air from her. Anne fell to her knees. "Please, Frederick," she begged. "I love you; do you not see how much I love you? I have discussed it with Lady Russell, and she agrees. If I went with you, I would only hold you back."

He wanted to drop to his knees, too, and plead with her—to convince Anne that she did not know him if she thought he needed protection. Instead, he turned his back on the woman he loved. "Do not lie to me, Anne; do not invent reasons for not keeping your promise; you simply do not care for me enough to give up your fine society." The words sounded bitter; he could not disguise the fact that he felt betrayed. "Is there someone else?" he accused. "Has your father allowed you to accept Charles Musgrove? *He* can offer you the security I cannot!"

"Surely you know that is not true." She looked up into his eyes. Something she did not recognize flickered there.

His jaw tightened in annoyance. Taking a deep breath, he allowed his gaze to rest on her. "Anne, I will ask you once again to come with me—this day—this hour. We will travel to Gretna Green; we will marry, and I will love you with every ounce of my being."

He paused, waiting for her answer, but she hung her head and rocked herself for comfort. "I love you, Frederick," she sobbed. "Go with God." The words seemed to suffocate her, and she collapsed on the bank of the lake.

She could see the toes of his black Hessians as he stepped up beside her. "You do not know love," he said softly. He bent to lay the rose beside her head. Then he left her there, taking the devastation with him.

Leaving Anne behind nearly broke Frederick. Part of him wanted to take Anne into his arms and kiss her until she changed her mind. Part of him wanted to forcibly take her with him. He could hardly breathe. Reaching the summit of the last incline before the town road, he shouted curses at the open sky.

God gave him life when He had given him Anne, and now she had been ripped from him. Five weeks of happiness was not enough; he wanted more of Anne Elliot. A cry escaped his throat as he sank down in despair. How could she have turned on him so quickly? How could Anne have allowed her foolish, vain father and her misguided friend Lady Russell to persuade her to give him up? Belatedly, he saw how Anne's putting her trust in Lady Russell misfired. The woman did not approve of Charles Musgrove's plight. Why would she consider Frederick's a more honorable one? It was over! Anne was gone! Nothing—nothing could ever convince him to love anyone but her. Another cry of anguish filled the air before he began to recapture his composure, but anger and frustration still reigned.

Frederick sat for hours on the hillside, looking out over the land—but he saw none of it. His mind replayed the moments he had spent with Anne. Images of her, from her entrance into the village shop to the crumpled form he left lying on the bank of the lake, filled his brain. Her words—her gestures—the dream he held of their life together—everything he had ever wanted—he could not have asked for more. *Except—he wanted more—he wanted their time together to never end.*

As if in a trance, he made his way back to his brother's home. "I was beginning to worry!" Edward called from the kitchen. "How is Miss Anne today?"

"Miss Anne returned to Kellynch Hall." That was all he could say. Anne returned to her home. She would never be his bride—his wife; she did not love him enough. "I have correspondence to which I need to attend. Please excuse me, Edward," he said stiffly as he walked past his brother to the guest room.

"Certainly," Edward spoke with concern. "I will be here if you need anything."

Frederick did not answer; he could think of nothing but the image of Anne Elliot weeping beside the lake—a place that once held pleasant memories of a growing courtship. He lay down heavily on the bed in the small room and stared, unseeing, at the ceiling.

The room was in deep shadows when he heard his brother's voice and his light tap on the door. "Frederick, may I get you something to eat?"

"Nothing, Edward, thank you; I just need some time," he croaked. Frederick could not consider talking to anyone about Anne Elliot. The light in his life had disappeared.

"I will leave some fresh bread on the table."

Frederick did not answer; he was once more lost to his pain.

★ ★ ★

For three days he left the room only to attend to his bodily functions. He did not eat, and if he slept, Frederick could not remember doing so. All he knew was the desolation he felt every time he replayed her words in his head. His chest ached. Edward's appraisal of the aristocracy had been correct; even a successful naval officer would never be good enough for a daughter of the realm. He could die for England, but he could not marry into one of its honored families.

The emptiness inside ate at him. He would show them all.

Frederick Wentworth would become wealthy—he would win the praise of the King. He would make them all—Anne and her family—regret the day she turned from him. By that time, Anne would no longer mean anything to him. He would forget her as quickly as she forgot him.

And yet—and yet—Frederick knew she was his other half; he would always want her.

Finally, he appeared at the morning table. His brother noted the dark circles under Frederick's eyes and the sharp, angular cut of his cheekbones, but Edward chose not to comment on his obvious weight loss. "Good morning," he greeted as Frederick reached for a plate.

Frederick did not answer, but he did nod in his brother's direction. Filling his plate with fresh fruit and toast, he joined Edward at the oak table. They ate together in silence for several minutes. Noting the packed bag sitting near the doorway, Edward said carefully, "So you are to leave me today?"

"It is for the best." Frederick did not raise his head when he spoke. Instead, he seemed mesmerized by the action of spreading apple preserves on another piece of toast.

Edward hid his concern. "You have more than three weeks of leave remaining."

Frederick decidedly placed the knife beside his plate. "I will stay with Harville; he and I can return to our ship together. Forgive me, Edward, but I need the silence of a noisy household right now."

"Of course, Frederick—I understand." Edward leaned back in his chair and looked at his brother's demeanor. "I assume you would have the vicar delay the reading of the banns."

Frederick finally looked at his older brother. He forced steadiness into his words. "If you could attend to that duty for me, Edward, I would be most appreciative."

"I will see to it." Edward returned to his food. After an elongated silence, he ventured, "Will you take your leave of Miss Anne?"

"Miss Anne took her leave of me several days ago; I see no

reason to revisit what must be." Frederick's steely countenance told the story.

"I see." Edward sighed. "I will walk with you to the posting inn when you are ready to leave."

"Thank you, Edward, for your hospitality. You are more than a brother, and for that I am eternally grateful."

"Family is our greatest wealth." Edward knew Frederick suffered. "Men in our family wait to marry until we secure our futures. Then we marry for love." Edward shot a kindly look at his younger brother. "Possibly you need to question whether you were ready. Look at me; I am three years your senior, and I have yet to complete either of those tasks."

"Possibly," Frederick muttered. He laid his napkin on the table. "Sometimes I wonder whether the woman I thought Anne Elliot to be ever existed."

"You looked for perfection in Miss Anne," his brother reasoned. "But perfection is not to be achieved in this life. And consider, Frederick—you are willful. Can you really envision being able to tolerate Sir Walter's inane views of society? Those of the Elliots' world would never understand the overwhelming responsibilities you assume each day in your position."

"I know in my mind what you say is correct, Edward. However, it will take my heart some time to reconcile itself to those truths. My heart, unfortunately, knew only her."

Later that day, Frederick waited to board the carriage that would take him to Portsmouth and the Harvilles; Edward stood with him in silence. Frederick embraced his brother before stepping up into the carriage. "I should tell you," Edward shared with a smile, "I applied for positions in Herefordshire and Shropshire some months ago. When we next meet, it will not be here."

"I do not believe I would ever wish to return here." Frederick leaned out the coach window to shake his brother's hand. "I have seen all of Somerset I care to see. It will be my pleasure to visit you in your new home. It is time for you to complete the tasks; build your future, and marry for love. It would please me to see both you and Sophia well settled."

"I would wish the same for you."

Frederick looked at the surrounding buildings. "It looks to be a pleasant enough village."

"*Some* find it so," Edward remarked as the coach began to roll forward.

Frederick smiled and waved. "Then *they* may have it!" he shouted as the carriage pulled out of the inn yard and onto the main road.

★ ★ ★

"His fever is worse," the doctor cautioned as he placed another cooling cloth on Wentworth's forehead. "We have to find a way to break it soon. If not, he could die of his wounds."

"Tell me what else to do for him." Anne's voice betrayed her exhaustion. She had been by Frederick's side for more than six and thirty hours.

"You will make *yourself* a patient, Ma'am, if you do not get rest," he cautioned her.

"I will not leave him." She spoke with resolve. "What can I do for my husband?"

"Very well, Mrs. Wentworth," the man said. "We could try a bath of cold water. Submerging the captain would be risky, but I believe it would be worth trying."

"Then let us do it." Anne moved to take over the cold cloths for Frederick's care.

"I will have the men bring in the tub; we can haul in some of the seawater. It will be cooler than anything we have on board. I want to make sure his bandages do not become too wet. We cannot let the seawater get into the wounds." The doctor motioned for a midshipman as he opened the door to the captain's quarters. After relaying his orders, he returned to Frederick's bedside. "I shall have several men help me strip the captain and support him in the water as we lower his body into the coolness. You, Ma'am, should use the opportunity to freshen your own clothing and get something substantial to eat. It would embarrass the men to handle your husband as such with you in the room."

"I understand," Anne whispered. "I will tend him until you are ready." She smoothed the hair away from Frederick's forehead.

The doctor moved away as several sailors brought in the low tub. Men hauling buckets of icy seawater to fill the vessel followed them. Several glanced furtively at their commanding officer outstretched on his bed, unresponsive even to his wife's tender ministrations.

"Will he make it?" one of the men whispered to the doctor.

"We are doing everything we can to assure that he does." The physician motioned for another man to dump his bucket of seawater into the waiting tub.

When the cooling waters filled the vessel, the doctor turned to Anne. "It is ready, Mrs. Wentworth." He reached out his hand to help her to her feet. "The officers and I will tend to your husband in the waters. You may hear the captain scream in pain, but you must not come back in here until I send for you."

"Yes, I understand." She leaned forward to kiss Frederick's feverish lips before she left the room. "Please take care of him." She allowed her hand to linger on her husband's chest; finally, the doctor led her to the door.

"The captain is strong; he will be well." Unconvinced, Anne nonetheless nodded at his words and left the area.

Four of the lower officers entered immediately. Lieutenants Harwood and Avendale began to strip the clothes from the captain's body. "Be careful of opening up his wounds again," the doctor cautioned. "You two, take off your jackets and your shirts. We are all likely to get soaked during this endeavor." Mastermates Langdon and Shipley began to remove their own clothing.

When all five men were bare to the waist, they lifted Wentworth's limp body from the bed. Positioning him as they might a body to lower it into a grave, they began to immerse Frederick's form into the cooling seawaters. "Hold him steady," the physician demanded. "He will fight you when the heat of his body hits the icy water. Do not let him go under completely. We want the water *around* his form, but we do not want it to *cover* his body."

The men all nodded, tightening their holds on Frederick's limbs. The doctor's prediction played out immediately. Still out of his mind with fever, Wentworth twisted and turned, trying to break the hold his men enforced on him. Cries of pain filled the cabin as Frederick cursed their deceit and threatened their safety. Yet, with their combined strength, they held him.

The doctor dipped a cup in the water and poured it over Frederick's body. Again and again, the doctor streamed water over his head and chest and legs, carefully avoiding the bandages around his abdomen. "Aah!" Wentworth gasped. "I will see you rot in hell for this!" Once again he wrenched his arms, trying to free himself, but his men held him in viselike grips. "You will hang for attacking an officer of the British Navy!"

And on it went for nearly three quarters of an hour until the tub water became closer to room temperature. Finally, they lifted him from the water. Drying him quickly, they pulled a nightshirt over his head and placed him back onto the freshly made bed. During this time, Frederick continued to fight them and to mutter curses while emitting moans of pain. The doctor considered all these good signs. He knew the shock of the cold water on the captain's feverish body could cause an apoplexy; Wentworth's fighting meant his body had not given up.

Finally, with the tub and water removed and the bandages checked, only the doctor remained by his side. He watched as Wentworth wrestled his way to consciousness; his eyes fluttered and fought for focus. "Where is Anne?" he mumbled.

"I sent her away so we might tend you. She has been here at the risk of her own health. I will have someone find her now that your fever is down." The doctor checked Frederick's forehead and looked into his eyes for signs of recovery.

Flashes of memory came to Frederick—thoughts of the senseless act that brought him to this point. Now, he knew the answers to all those questions with which Anne had bombarded him. His favorite place of all was a certain small seaside village in Italy. He preferred French wine to British. He hated it when she tickled his feet, but loved it when she kneaded the muscles of his back. So close to losing his life, Frederick could see it all plainly—how to analyze his experiences and know what was good, what *mattered*.

"Will I live?" He licked his parched lips.

"You have a long recovery ahead of you."

A light tap on the door claimed the doctor's attention. "Enter!" he called out.

"Excuse me, Sir," a midshipman reported. "Mrs. Wentworth sends word that she will be here in a moment. She is writing to Captain Harville; she wants word to be sent to him and to Captain Wentworth's family as soon as we make port."

"Thank you, Rogers." The doctor turned back to his patient. "Did you hear, Wentworth?"

"Captain Harville is an old friend," Frederick whispered.

"I remember him well; we all sailed together back in '07 and '08." The physician adjusted the blanket across Wentworth's body. "A pity that his leg wound drove him from the service; we could use such a man right now." The captain gasped with pain as he tried to move in the bed. "Let me give you some laudanum." He supported Frederick's head as he administered the dose. "Rest now," the doctor ordered him.

CHAPTER 4

Each lover has a theory of his own
About the difference between the ache
Of being with his love, and being alone.
—W. H. Auden, "Alone"

"Rest now, Wentworth," Harville reassured him. "You have a ship at last."

"She sure is not much, is she?" Frederick looked around at the condition of the sloop *Asp*.

"She may not be the largest ship on the sea, but the Admiralty found her fit to form part of the line in action. She has thirty guns, Frederick." Harville moved up beside his friend as they surveyed Wentworth's new command.

"What say the orders?" Wentworth asked as he motioned his assistant to store the captain's belongings in his cabin.

When he delivered the news, Harville smiled broadly. "His Majesty desires our attention in the West Indies."

"Who is the new lieutenant?" Wentworth gestured again, this time to his right.

"Harold Rushick." Harville returned the salute offered by the first-rung commissioned officer. "He has much experience with gun divisions in battle and in dangerous boardings, and he is rumored to be most observant in overseeing the watch. We are lucky to have him on board."

"Then I shall extend an invitation to dine with me." Wentworth noted the man's demeanor. "I want him on my side."

The two started to stroll along the deck, each noting the ordinary seamen and landsmen as they loaded the *Asp*'s storage. "Have I told you I asked Milly to wait for me?"

"She is a fine woman, Thomas." Wentworth's thoughts immediately went to Anne Elliot. At least ten times a day, he found himself momentarily lost in thoughts of her. Even after two months, the pain still pierced his being. He never told Thomas Harville about his close encounter with love; Frederick could not bear to speak of the hurt. Each night she came to him in his dreams; Anne professed her love, and they walked hand-in-hand. He swallowed hard and forced Anne's image into the recesses of his mind. "Milly will make you a fine wife. When do you plan to ask her?"

"I need to make my fortune before I can take a wife." Harville paused along the railing, surveying the activities along the dock.

Again, Frederick thought of Anne; his potential was not enough to make her place her trust in him. Her betrayal sucked the air from his lungs. *God, I love her!* He would still win his fortune; he would show her someday what she missed by refusing him. "You will have your chance, Thomas; we will both have our chance." Wentworth stepped up beside his friend. "Now, let us prepare for our journey. The *Asp* is our future!"

★ ★ ★

After nearly six months in the West Indies, Frederick received notice he was to join Higgins and others in an effort to prevent Napoleon from taking the Danish fleet. Frederick called his officers together to share the news. "The British forces will be under the command of Admiral Gambier and General Cathcart." Frederick walked over to refill his glass of brandy. His officers were gathered around the small table in his quarters.

"And the purpose of our mission would be?" Harville asked with feigned nonchalance before shooting Frederick a knowing glance.

"The Danish fleet is superb, but it could fall into Bonaparte's hands if Denmark cannot defend its southern border. If Denmark falls, then my guess is we will be attacking its invaders in Copenhagen by mid-July."

"Will that be all for now, Captain Wentworth?" Lieutenant Rushick asked, steadying his resolve. "If so, Sir, I will see to the men."

"Certainly, Rushick. We will lift anchor when all the supplies are aboard. Gentlemen, you are dismissed."

Once the room had emptied, except for Harville and himself, Frederick turned his attention to his friend. "And your look meant what, Thomas?" he asked as he sipped his drink.

"Something about this mission bothers you, Frederick," Harville asserted as he took a seat. He stretched out his legs, crossing them at his ankles, while folding his arms across his chest.

Wentworth paused to consider his thoughts. "I feel a need to weigh my remarks," he began at last. "In '01 we had a legitimate reason to go up against the Danish. The Armed Neutrality of the North treaty threatened British trade in the Baltic Sea. But this time the Danish are on our side; we are reduced to the point of attacking our allies. The war makes strangers out of friends. Sometimes I wonder if I have the stomach for it." He crossed the room to sit opposite his friend.

Harville uncrossed and recrossed his ankles. "I, too, would like to go home; I do not relish being a pawn in some high-ranking officer's chess game. We came close to counting our own deaths at San Domingo. Duckworth was determined to catch those Frenchies."

"We paid a high price; seventy casualties and nearly three hundred wounded. I admit I enjoy the *spoils* of war—men of my rank have few other ways to make a living—but the loss of life disturbs me. It seems that now we are asked to endanger the lives of good men in a futile battle. Perhaps I am feeling my own mortality." Frederick took another mouthful of brandy and let it trickle down his throat.

"What happened in Somerset?" Harville asked abruptly.

"Why do you believe something happened in Somerset?" He attempted to smile.

"I cannot say for sure, but I know you are different now. You are often somber."

Frederick put down his glass, trying to control the emotions shooting through him. "Perhaps seeing Edward struggle as a curate made me realize how little I have to offer anyone. My father, you

see, was the third son in his family, so he had nothing to leave us."
He could not finish his thoughts without thinking of Anne Elliot;
he would never be good enough for the Elliots. "I suppose I should
be thankful for the opportunity the British Navy gives me; I shall
leave the war with my fortune."

"Once I have made my own fortune, I am headed home to
Milly, and King George can go hang himself. I plan to arrive home
in one piece and raise myself a crop of children." Harville chuckled. "That is what you need, Wentworth—you need a woman to
bring out the best in you. A man was meant to be at a woman's
beck and call," he joked.

Frederick snorted. He realized he would eventually need to
find a woman he could marry. *But what woman,* he thought, *would
want a man with only half a heart to give?* Aloud, he asserted, "My life
belongs to Admiral Gambier and the British Navy."

★ ★ ★

As Wentworth predicted, July found his ship among those gathering along the Danish coastline. The men waited warily, playing cards
to pass the time. Frederick lurked on the periphery, listening to
snippets of conversations. He had learned in the past few years to
judge his men's readiness by how they handled the long hours of
waiting before the battle began.

"You be with Sir Duckworth at Alexandria?" one of the car-
penters asked as he shuffled the cards.

The gunner picked up his hand and began to rearrange it. "We
carted infantry back and forth for days."

"Me hears it was something to see." Both men held warranted
ranks aboard ship, but they had only limited opportunities to attain
commissioned posts. Along with the pursur and the boatswain,
they were part of the standing officers appointed to a ship by the
Navy Board.

The gunner turned his cards over. "We took care of the landies;
that be for sure. Despite high surf, Lieutenant Boxer disembarked
almost seven hundred troops, five field guns, and fifty-six seamen.
They breached the palisades entrenched sometime after nightfall.

The spirits and old Neptune himself be with them that day; that be only way they could have survived the landing. Britain must be the chosen people; Bony may as well give up."

"Chosen people?" Mackenzie, the carpenter laughed loudly. "The chaplain would be disagreeing with you."

"He *cannot* disagree," the gunner asserted. He chuckled as he readied his hand to play. "He be an Englishman also."

Frederick smiled as he moved on. When they spoke of the invincibility of England, that was a good sign. He passed a small group of able seamen, one of whom good-naturedly teased a new landsmen. "You should have been with us in '01 with Nelson," the older sailor boasted. Wentworth peered down at them from his position along the railing. "We had twenty-six battleships and seven frigates in the line. The Danes stood no chance. The only thing *they* had was a sixty-six-gun battery and dangerous shoals, but none of it could stop Horatio Nelson."

Keats, the mast captain, handed the landsman a cup of rum. "Parker panicked when we lost a floating battery and a few other key ships to the shoals, but Nelson had balls. Do you remember what he said, Woods, when old Malcolm told him Parker had ordered a withdrawal?"

Woods guffawed, nearly choking on the spirits they drank to steady their nerves. "You see, Lad, Nelson was blind in one eye. Nelson looked at old Malcolm and said, 'I have only one eye. I do not see the signal.'"

"*That* was a bloody battle," Keats proclaimed.

The landsman looked a bit afraid. It was, after all, his first confrontation. "How bloody?"

"Do not be worrying, Lad. Our captain is nothing like Nelson. The Vice Admiral did not care how many we lost, as long as we won the battle. Nearly one thousand left us that day. Of course, the Danes lost more than twice that many. We learned something in those days. Ye will not be exposed to such carnage."

Frederick strode purposefully toward the men. They started to scramble to their feet, but he motioned for them to remain seated.

"I just wanted to say I am proud to serve with you men. We will engage the Danish by early tomorrow morning. Right now, we are transporting the foot soldiers needed by General Wellesley. Relax as much as you can, but stay alert to changes happening along the Danish line of ships. You each know your job well. If each man attends to his own domain, we will come through this with few problems. Good night, men."

"Good night, Captain," a chorus of voices called as he walked away. "A good man," he heard one of them mutter before he went below deck. Those who were experienced seamen knew how unusual it was for the commanding officer to address them thusly.

★ ★ ★

The smell of gunpowder filled the air; the British fleet continued to bombard the city of Copenhagen. "How much longer can they hold out?" Harville growled as he surveyed the damage with his spyglass.

"Only the Lord knows." Wentworth took the glass from his friend and raised it to his eye. "We sent in at least five thousand rounds last night." He walked to the other side of the upper deck to get a better look. "There are three battleships and one pram sitting dead in the water directly in front of us."

"Our men are boarding them as we speak. Lieutenant Rushick is leading our contingent." Harville squinted down at the lowering of the small boats off the side of the ship.

The appearance of the British transports, making their way toward Copenhagen, obviously, came as a nasty shock to the Danish command. Early on, the Danish had taken a frigate and two brig-sloops. Unlike the weather during the 1801 siege of the city, the high surf and the seas calmed right before the attack. "The latest message from Gambier says Danish General Peymann turned down our offers of capitulation." Harville handed Frederick a message delivered by the communications officer.

"Then we will fight on," Wentworth offered with a shrug of his shoulders, attempting to force tension from his upper back. "There is something rotten in Denmark. At least, the Bard would agree with the Prince Regent." A slight smile turned up the corners of his lips. "At this rate, Thomas, you may marry Milly by year's end."

The night brought no relief from the battle. Frederick made only one trip below in the hours since the battle began. He constantly checked on the conditions above and below deck, assuring himself that his men and his ship had come to no harm. "Get some rest, Frederick," Harville said when he came to check on him. His voice came softly off Frederick's right shoulder. "The men will be fine; they know their jobs."

"Just a few minutes more," Frederick mumbled, searching the horizon for any changes in the siege. The constant bombardment lit up the skyline with explosions; puffy clouds of black smoke followed these as fires sprang up. "The Congreve Rockets appear to be doing their job. Look at the number of fires; the city will never be the same." He stood, riveted to a spot along the railing, not even turning to acknowledge Harville's presence.

"You feel the pain of each battle too intensely, Frederick," his friend concluded with a shake of his head.

"There ought to be a better way of resolving differences. I know I should not want to bite the hand that feeds me, but such destruction—such destruction should not occur. Sometimes I wonder how a God of love can allow it to happen, allow men to make war." Frederick lowered the glass from his eyes.

"Maybe we should let our womenfolk negotiate the resolution of our differences." Harville laughed at his own thought.

"It would be a gentler way." Wentworth turned his attention to his friend. He let down his guard with Harville, who had an unaffected easy kindness of manner, which denoted the feelings of an older acquaintance.

Harville's countenance reassumed the serious, thoughtful expression, which seemed its natural character. "It is the nature of women to seek common ground with others and to lavish attention on, as well as offer protection to friends and family. A woman cannot forget someone she loves."

His words brought Frederick pain although Thomas Harville

was perfectly unsuspicious of inflicting any peculiar wound. "I am sure women might argue that we men have always a profession, pursuits, business of some sort or other, to take us back into the world," Frederick reasoned. "Yet, I will not allow it to be more man's nature than woman's to be inconstant and forget those they *do* love or *have* loved. I believe the reverse. I believe in a true analogy between our bodily frames and our mental; and that as our bodies are the strongest so are our feelings—capable of bearing more rough usage and riding out the heaviest weather."

Thomas took the spyglass from Frederick's hand and began to search the shore for results of their siege. "Songs and proverbs, all talk of women's fickleness. But saying something loudly or frequently doesn't make it so."

Frederick replied, "Both men and women—we each begin probably with a little bias toward our own sex and upon that bias build every circumstance in favor of it which occurred within our own circle; many of which circumstances, perhaps those very cases which strike us the most, may be precisely such as cannot be brought forward. I suspect that men and women are much alike. But because our circumstances are different, we see the world from distinct perspectives."

Harville chuckled and clapped Frederick on the back. "Captain, I, for one, need a few hours of sleep; though you might refuse to take time in your quarters, I will take time in mine." He handed the glass to his commanding officer. "I will see you with the dawn unless you send for me before then."

"Hopefully, with the dawn, this will all be over," Frederick mused. Then his friend moved away into the night, and he was alone. Staring out into the darkness, his thoughts returned to Anne Elliot. He would never find a woman to love the way he loved Anne. He wanted a home with her—wanted children with her— wanted to live out his days with her. But his hopes died when her family convinced Anne Elliot to break their engagement. Silently, he pushed the hurt deeper, feeling it in his gut—in his soul. The hurt had lessened over the past year. Now he could compare it to having a knife plunged deeply into his heart and then twisted; or maybe it was more like a wild animal ripping off his leg at the joint. Swallowing hard, he turned back to the task at hand—trying to leave his love behind. Sometimes he wondered if he should write her to see if she had realized the foolishness of her decision. But he could not bear to be rejected again. Somehow, it was better not to know.

★ ★ ★

Anne Elliot Wentworth sat dutifully by her husband's sickbed; the gauntness of his figure frightened her. The doctor assured her repeatedly that Frederick's recovery seemed inevitable. But Anne's husband was normally a strong, vigorous man, standing feet braced against the swell of the sea. That same man—the man she loved—was now shrunken and feeble.

"Anne?" The soft pleading of his voice brought her attention back to his face. Under the influence of the strong drug, Frederick could not work out how to open his eyes. "Anne," he murmured again. Clouded by the laudanum, Frederick's mind tried to concentrate for more than a few moments at a time; he found himself drifting back into sleep, into nightmares. He dreamed of losing her—*his Anne*—and now he needed to know she was here with him—in this room—guaranteeing the nightmares no longer plagued him. He licked his lips, forcing moisture to his mouth. A flash of memory jolted through his head, and he grimaced with the thought. He spoke her name a third time, and he felt someone sit beside him on the bed.

"I am here, my Love." His eyes were still closed, and he felt warm lips linger enticingly over his and then pull away.

"So nice," he mumbled, and a smile tried to make its way to the corners of his mouth.

Anne's voice held relief. "You are incorrigible," she teased. She felt calmer at hearing his tremulous words. She reached out to take his hand. "May I get you anything?" She spoke close to his ear.

Frederick forced his eyes to flutter open and to focus on his wife's face. "Only you," he managed to say as he searched her countenance. A stray strand of hair hung down loosely along her face. Frederick wanted to reach out and push it behind her ear, but he could not will his hand to respond.

She rested one arm across his chest and leaned over him. Frederick felt the warmth of her body radiate through him; even though he was injured, Anne still had an arousing effect on him.

She smiled. "Concentrate on your recovery," she whispered close to his lips, kissing first the corner of his mouth and then his cheek, his temple, and his ear. Frederick demanded that his body respond; he turned his head to the side to properly kiss her. "You have been here for nearly four days," she explained, and he nodded that he understood. "Rest." She stroked along his cheekbone with her fingertips.

Frederick could only nod once more as he took in her features—features that others might find nondescript—but features, which beset him for years. At first glance, a person might think *his Anne* unexceptional, but on closer observation a man would be a fool not to see her elegance. Her hair changed color with the lamp lighting from a dark chocolate to strands of gold mingled with red within a mahogany forest. Her skin remained a smooth ivory although she had spent the last six months at sea with him, and her eyes sparked with intelligence and amusement. "Your eyes mesmerize me," he choked out. "Pools of strong coffee—a man could get lost in your eyes. I thank God every day they rest only on me."

"Flattery," she whispered, amusement glinting in her eyes.

"Honesty," he muttered. *His Anne* had an utterly feminine presence, which soothed him. She also had a surprising strength of will, honed through years of self-denial. Frederick found himself suddenly very tired again. Knowing Anne would watch over him allowed him to relax back against the pillow. For eight years he took responsibility for everything around him; now, he could give up that answerability. She would tend to him without fail, an intoxicating sensation to say the least. He felt Anne pull the blanket up to his shoulders, careful not to disturb him as he drifted back into oblivion. Suddenly, Frederick forced his eyes open again, wanting to imprint her image on his brain.

She bent to kiss him on the forehead, and her low voice pierced what was left of his consciousness. "Rest and recover. It took us too long, my Love, to find each other again. We promised each other constancy; let us honor our vows."

Frederick groggily interlaced his fingers with hers. "I have missed you." His eyelids drifted closed with the words.

"And I you—more than words can express." She squeezed his hand, and he never felt so totally loved.

"You are mine," his voice barely audible.

Anne touched his lips with hers. "As you well know."

★ ★ ★

As you well know, Frederick,

he read the words out loud from Sophia's letter,

> *Benjamin has long wished to return to Somersetshire and to settle in his own country. Last month we came down to Taunton in order to look at some advertised places in that immediate neighborhood, which, however, did not suit him. Upon accident, we heard from a local innkeeper the possibility of Kellynch Hall being to let. It took Benjamin no time to introduce himself to Mr. Shepherd, Sir Walter Elliot's solicitor. My husband made particular inquiries, and, in the course of a pretty long conference, expressed as strong an inclination for the place as a man who knew it only by description, could feel, and gave Mr. Shepherd, in his explicit account of himself, every proof of his being a most responsible, eligible tenant.*

Frederick took a seat. Sophia's news dredged up memories and stirred up feelings he had hoped were dead.

> *Benjamin did not quibble about the price, as he should have. He let Mr. Shepherd know he only wanted a comfortable home and to get into it as soon as possible—knew he must pay for his convenience—knew what rent a ready-furnished house of that consequence might fetch—should not have been surprised if Sir Walter had asked more. Of course, I asked more questions about the house and terms and*

taxes than the Admiral himself. I even explained to the solicitor my connection to Somersetshire—Edward having lived in Monkford a few years back.

Several weeks later, we toured the manor, and I met the infamous Miss Elizabeth Elliot. I found I often had to keep my tongue in check in order not to offend her sensibilities; yet, we parted with each of us well disposed for an agreement. Benjamin's hearty good humor and open, trusting liberality could not help but influence Sir Walter. The house and grounds and furniture were approved; Mr. Shepherd's clerks were set to work, without there having been a single preliminary difference to modify of all that 'This indenture sheweth.' The Admiral, with sympathetic cordiality observed as we drove back through the Park, 'I thought we should soon come to a deal, my Dear, in spite of what they told us at Taunton. The baronet will never set the Thames on fire, but there seems no harm in him.' The long and the short of it is, my Dear Brother, we take possession of Kellynch Hall at Michaelmas. When you come to us in October, you must return to the area where you spent five weeks with Edward in '06. You are probably more familiar with Kellynch than either the Admiral or I am at this point. I am sure after having spent time in the neighborhood, you already understand what I do not say about Sir Walter or Miss Elizabeth Elliot. Sir Walter must be to Bath to save his reputation and to keep his creditors at bay, but his inability to manage his life gives Benjamin and me a fine home to share with you.

Until we meet, I remain your loving sister,

SC

Frederick let out the breath he had not realized he was holding. He had already made a commitment to visit his sister, but how could he go to Kellynch Hall? For many years the place haunted his dreams. What excuse could he give? Bonaparte was banished to Elba, and as the war dwindled down, Frederick repeatedly let it be known that, barring any new uprisings, he would take his newly made fortune and return to civilian life. Now, Sophia expected him to come to her. How this news trifled with his feelings! His heart was still in Somersetshire; his match with Anne Elliot would not have been the most advantageous match imaginable in the eyes of society, but marriage was not impossible for them. Anne had acted dishonorably by breaking off her engagement to him.

How can I return to Somersetshire? he silently demanded. He searched the letter again, wondering why Sophia did not mention Anne. Could it be that she no longer lived in the area? Had she married at last? It had been eight years, after all. How soon had she married once she broke their engagement? Did Anne have children of her own? Some part of him wished her happy while a more dominate urge wished some form of revenge. A sarcastic laugh escaped his throat. "Is it not revenge that my sister will take possession of Sir Walter's estate house? *My* family was never good enough; now it is *Anne's* family that is found wanting." The thought, although distasteful, consoled him. "Even if Anne Elliot is still in the neighborhood," he shored up his own resolve, "she will soon learn she is nothing to me. I have long since forgotten her hold on me."

CHAPTER 5

No, the heart that has truly loved never forgets,
But as truly loves on to the close,
As the sunflower turns on her god when he sets
The same look which she turned when he rose!
—Thomas Moore, "Believe Me,
If All Those Endearing Young Charms"

"Frederick, you are here at last!" his sister called as she met him in the entrance hall. He handed his hat and greatcoat to the butler before taking her hands in his and lightly kissing her proffered cheek. Finally seeing her eased the chaos that his stomach had endured from the moment his public carriage entered Somerset. "You look well, my Brother." She embraced him again. "Come," she said and took his arm. "Benjamin awaits us in the front parlor."

Sophia Croft, though neither tall nor fat, had a squareness, uprightness, and vigor of form, which gave importance to her person. She had bright dark eyes, good teeth, and altogether an agreeable face; though her reddened and weather-beaten complexion, the consequence of her having been almost as much at sea as her husband, made her seem to have lived some years longer in the world than her real five and thirty. Her manners were open, easy, and decided, like one who had no distrust of herself, and no doubts of what to do, without any approach to coarseness, however, or any want of good humor.

Frederick fought the urge to look around for remnants of Anne Elliot. From the time he had entered the Park, he felt her presence—could nearly visualize her moving through the gardens—entering the house—walking toward the lake to meet him. He shook his head to chase the images away. "You must be exhausted," his sister added as she tightened her grip on his arm. Looking over her shoulder, she turned to the butler, "Mr. Steventon, please have someone bring us fresh tea and refreshments."

"Right away, Mrs. Croft."

"Look at you," Frederick teased, "acting the fine lady of the estate."

Her eyes twinkled. "Who says I am acting?"

Frederick chuckled. "Being the mistress of the house suits you, Sophia. I am pleased to see you well situated."

"It is pleasant to finally have roots rather than seaweeds upon which to stand. Of course, you must not tell the Admiral I made such a bold statement."

He cupped her hand with his. "Your secret is safe with me," he whispered close to her ear. Then he turned his attention toward his brother in marriage and in service. "Admiral," he acknowledged the man rising to his feet, "I am so pleased to see you, Sir."

"No formality here, Frederick." The elder seaman extended his hand in warm welcome. "We have both left our ships behind. I am no longer your superior officer; here at Kellynch Hall, I am Sophia's husband and your brother."

"Thank you, Sir." Frederick took the seat to which the Admiral gestured. "Although I must admit old habits will be hard to break." His sister took the seat next to him on the settee while the Admiral sank back into the wing chair. "How are you feeling, Benjamin?" He noticed immediately the man sat with his leg propped on a close-standing ottoman.

"I am having a bit of difficulty getting my land legs," the older man confessed. "Your sister tends me well, though, and I am sure I will be up and about soon."

"How do you like Kellynch Hall?" Frederick allowed his eyes to circumnavigate the room. Memories of the last time he had sat in this very room flooded his senses.

"It is a fine estate," Sophia mused. "Of course, we are still trying to accustom ourselves to all the room. Benjamin and I are used to much smaller quarters. Were you ever here when you visited Edward years ago?"

"Only once." Frederick's jaw twitched with the strain of not allowing Sophia to see his reaction. "Edward and I dined with some of the local gentry just a week before I left the country."

"Was the master of the house his usual pompous self?" Benjamin asked amusedly.

"It was the only evening Sir Walter and I had a private conversation in the time I resided with Edward." He bit the inside of his mouth to distract himself from the pain of remembering that conversation. "I am afraid Sir Walter did not approve of my bettering my lot in life through the Navy. He was most adamant in his opinions."

The admiral snorted with disgust. "You have no idea how many mirrors I removed from the walls!"

Frederick chuckled. "The man radiated vanity, as I recall."

"That is an understatement." The Admiral shifted his attention to the maid bringing in a fresh tray of tea and cakes. "Thank you, Hilda. We will ring if we need anything else."

"Yes, Sir." She curtsied and left, closing the door behind her.

Sophia poured each of them a fresh cup of tea. Frederick took several sips as he built the courage to ask what he knew he must. "Then the family—the Elliots, that is—have all removed themselves to Bath?"

Sophia settled herself next to him again. "Sir Walter and the eldest daughter, Elizabeth, are there—on Camden Place, I believe I heard Mr. Shepherd say. His widowed daughter, Mrs. Clay, is Miss Elliot's traveling companion." Frederick waited, his heart thumping so loudly in his chest that he thought surely Sophia and the Admiral would hear it. "The youngest daughter married Charles Musgrove and is living at Uppercross. We met them recently. Mrs. Charles is quite insipid, would you not say, Admiral?"

Frederick did not hear his brother's response. All he could do was force himself to take steady breaths. *So Anne married Charles Musgrove.* Frederick had expected as much. More than once he had replayed scenes of Musgrove dancing with her at the assembly.

"Mrs. Musgrove's children," the Admiral's voice penetrated Frederick's musings, "are high-spirited enough; she certainly cannot control them." *Anne had children! Don't be a fool. What did you expect? Certainly she could not remain celibate if she were married.* Yet, the thought of Anne Elliot loving anyone but him seemed a crack in the natural order of things.

"Did you meet the Musgroves when you were here before?" Sophia asked casually.

"Just briefly—I would not recognize the man, I am sure. I am surprised, however, that Anne Elliot married him. From what I remember, he did not have the same fine mind as Miss Anne." It took effort to utter Anne's name.

"Oh, I must apologize, Frederick, when I said the *youngest* daughter married Charles Musgrove," his sister interrupted. "Mrs. Charles was once Mary Elliot; Miss Anne remains unmarried." A lightning bolt shot through him. *Anne, too, has never married!* Surely, it had nothing to do with him. It could not. Just as their failed engagement was not the reason for his bachelorhood. If he chose not to marry, then she could make a similar choice. Having never met her, he had forgotten Anne had a younger sister. *Miss Elizabeth Elliot never married. Why should Anne? Sir Walter probably dashed her hopes with every offer. It would be just like the man to refuse his daughters' suitors so as to keep their affections focused purely on him.* He felt an unexpected twinge of sympathy, centered on Anne's lost dreams, worm its way into his heart. "I assume you knew Miss Anne?" his sister concluded.

"We were in each other's company upon several occasions." He forced himself to control his facial expression.

"I never suspected as much," Sophia replied. "I knew from our conversation when we returned the call at Uppercross some fortnight ago that Miss Anne was familiar with Edward; yet, I did not realize you also made her acquaintance. Had I known, I would have shared your recent success when I told her about Edward's marriage. I am sure she would be interested to know of your moving up in the ranks. You were not yet given your first command, Brother, when you visited Edward all those years ago."

"I assure you Miss Anne would not be interested in my career," Frederick retorted, trying to keep the bitterness out of his words. "Then I assume Miss Anne is at Uppercross with her younger sister?"

"Mrs. Charles is of a delicate nature, or so she prefers to tell anyone who might listen. I suspect Miss Anne is the only one in the family with good sense; she appears to be the only one who can placate Mary Musgrove."

"My wife has immersed herself in neighborhood gossip," Benjamin Croft revealed fondly.

Sophia rolled her eyes before continuing her story. "Miss Anne will travel with Lady Russell to Bath before Christmas. Lady Russell is away in Hertfordshire at the moment. Although she lives in the estate lodge, we have yet to meet the woman. She left the area before we took possession of the house. It is common knowledge that she serves as a confidante to the Elliot family, but you may know that already."

Frederick stiffened with the mention of Lady Russell's name. As much as he blamed Anne for succumbing to her family's advice, he blamed Lady Russell more. Anne trusted Lady Russell to aid her with Sir Walter's objections to the marriage, and the woman sided with Anne's father. He might have overcome the baronet's opposition, but Lady Russell compounded the doubts Anne already held. The knowledge of Lady Russell's absence from the country came as a pleasant surprise; he did not think he could face her without animosity. "Sophia, I suddenly feel very tired; if you would show me to my room, I believe I would like to rest before dinner."

"Of course, Frederick." She rose to lead the way.

"Until dinner, Sir." Frederick offered his brother a slight bow as he stood. The Admiral nodded pleasantly and remained seated as Frederick walked to the door.

"Mr. Steventon arranged for his nephew to serve as your valet while you are here, Frederick. I know you are quite adept at handling your own ablutions, but the man is available if you need him."

"Thank you, Sophia; you are a faultless hostess." He followed her up the staircase to the private quarters. He wondered, as he passed each of the closed doorways, which one had belonged to Anne. For years, Frederick had seen her everywhere he looked. Now he was in her home, or what had been her home; and his memories and his fantasies seemed to be stronger than the present, mundane as it was.

He sat on the edge of the bed; his heart pounding furiously, making him light-headed. He cursed himself for still being susceptible to even the remembered charms of Anne Elliot. Being in Anne's house might prove overwhelming, after all. Why in bloody hell did she still have such a hold on him? "I thought I rid myself of feelings for her long ago," he muttered, catching an image of his demeanor in the reflection of the window and trying desperately for a coherent thought. He moved to take in the view of the garden below, veiled in the last strands of sunlight.

"I'm a fool," he admitted aloud. When Harville had written him of his latest child, Frederick found himself wondering what life with Anne would have held. When his friend James Benwick lost his love Fanny—Thomas Harville's sister—he grieved for both his friends, but he had also grieved for his own loss. When his brother, Edward, had finally married the love of his life, Frederick fantasized about life with Anne Elliot. Each remembrance brought him new pain. "Maybe this is what I need to finally be rid of her— to truly start to live my life again. We will meet, and I will see that she really has no hold on me. I wasted my time loving her. Anne Elliot betrayed me; she ill-abused me." Saying the words, he began to frantically pull at the knot in his cravat. "I will be her puppet no longer. Today I am cutting those strings that once bound me to her." He jerked the shirt over his head and tossed it on the bed. "Yes," he paused before pouring water into the basin. "This is exactly what I need—my chance to finally bid Anne Elliot farewell— on my own terms."

★ ★ ★

With a new resolve, Frederick threw himself into the companionship of his sister and the Admiral. He rode out with them one morning as they took pleasure in examining their lands and holdings. "It is beautiful here," Sophia sighed, and her husband nodded in silent agreement.

One afternoon Frederick and his sister strolled arm in arm through the gardens. "You appear content, Sophie," Frederick remarked.

"I admit I could become accustomed to the serenity that life at Kellynch Hall offers." She smiled up at him. "Benjamin served Britain long enough; it is time he takes care of himself. I wish for the peace to last; I am weary of war."

"Will the Admiral accept his half pension?" Frederick directed her to a bench upon which they could sit.

Sophia glanced furtively toward the house. "I will try to persuade him to do so. My husband might wish to return, but I fear that fate and luck could be against him. My intuition, as well as Benjamin's, tells us he should not return. One cannot sail successfully as often as the Admiral without listening to one's gut feelings. I will use all my powers of persuasion to get him to adhere to what his inclinations already tell him."

Frederick reached out to pat her hand, but before he could respond, a servant interrupted his thoughts. "Pardon, Mrs. Croft," the footman stammered. "Admiral Croft asks that you and Captain Wentworth join him in the front parlor. Mr. Musgrove attends your husband."

"Which Mr. Musgrove?" Frederick asked before he could stifle the words. Only a few days earlier he had believed Anne had married the younger Musgrove.

"The father, Sir." The footman bowed slightly. "The Admiral said to tell you Mr. Musgrove was most interested in meeting you, Sir."

"Thank you, Landon," Sophia acknowledged.

"Yes, Ma'am." He left the area, exiting through the back garden gate.

"Well," Frederick said, turning to his sister, "let us meet Mr. Musgrove."

Frederick followed Sophia into the front parlor as Benjamin and Mr. Musgrove both struggled to their feet to greet her. "My

Love," Croft's eyes lit up when she accepted his hand.

"Mrs. Croft." Mr. Musgrove bowed to Sophia before turning his attention to Wentworth.

Sophia introduced Frederick and the elder Mr. Musgrove and ushered everyone to seats before the conversation began again. Musgrove was in the old English style—a very good sort of person—friendly, not much educated, and not at all cultured. The man cleared his throat, seeming to stall before speaking. "Captain Wentworth, I cannot tell you how pleased I am to finally make your acquaintance," he stated nervously.

"Thank you, Sir." Frederick inclined his head in interest.

"Once Mrs. Croft told us of your return to England, my wife, Mrs. Musgrove, has thought of little else. It appears, Captain, our second son Richard once served under you. Mrs. Musgrove found in his letters where he spoke of his commander, Captain Wentworth. She wishes to thank you for your kindness to our poor Richard when he served under you on the *Laconia*." The words gushed from him, nearly leaving him breathless and quite reddened in the face.

"And how is Midshipman Musgrove?" Frederick inquired. He remembered Richard Musgrove, who was known more familiarly as "Dick," well, having had the ill fortune of adding Musgrove to his crew when he set in at Gibraltar in '09. Musgrove was a troublesome, hopeless man. Obviously, he was unmanageable on shore, and upon reaching his twentieth year, his family sent Musgrove to sea. Wentworth despised anyone who did not pull his own weight on board. In his estimation, "poor Richard" was nothing better than a thickheaded, unfeeling, unprofitable Dick Musgrove, who never did anything to entitle himself to more than the abbreviation of his name.

"Unfortunately, we lost our dear son two years ago, Sir." Mr. Musgrove sounded very out of spirits.

Frederick looked around and caught the Admiral's eye. "Forgive me, Mr. Musgrove; I had no idea."

"Thank you, Captain; we have many other children to fill our home, but we maintain a place in our hearts for Richard. I came here today to invite you to our house to share our table. Mrs. Musgrove insists that she owes you a debt of gratitude for your personal attention to our dear boy."

Frederick fought the urge to roll his eyes. "I assure you, Mr. Musgrove, I did nothing to earn such praise."

"I am afraid, Captain, I will surely have a difficult time convincing my wife of such modesty."

"Then I will meet Mrs. Musgrove and convince her myself; however, I am committed to previous engagements for the next week. Will you and Mrs. Musgrove be kind enough to accept me after that time?" Frederick offered up his best "captain" smile.

Musgrove beamed with delight. "Mrs. Musgrove will be sorry to have to wait so long to make your acquaintance, but the anticipation will enhance the experience. "May we say dinner at Uppercross for you, the Admiral, and Mrs. Croft one week hence?"

While Frederick waited for his sister to respond to the invitation, his thoughts drifted elsewhere. If he called upon the Great House at Uppercross, he would likely come face-to-face with Anne Elliot. How could he bear it? As much as he had told himself that he wanted nothing to do with her, he was not wholly convinced. But his curiosity still loomed. His sister's words penetrated his thoughts. "It would be our pleasure, Mr. Musgrove."

The man scrambled to his feet before the group might withdraw their consent. "I must hurry home," he began, "and give Mrs. Musgrove the good news. She and my daughters will be thrilled." He edged closer to the door. "Thank you for receiving me, Admiral. Mrs. Croft, please know how pleased we at Uppercross are to have you and your husband at Kellynch Hall. This is a most pleasant circumstance indeed."

He was nearly out the door before Sophia could interlace her arm with his and show him to the entranceway. When left alone, Frederick laughed lightly at the absurdity of the scene.

"Mr. Musgrove is an amiable man," the Admiral observed.

"He is," Frederick could not hide his amusement. "To think the

Elliots aligned themselves with the Musgroves is a delightful diversion. Admittedly, I would prefer the company of the Musgroves, however," he replied absently. Yet, his thoughts remained with Anne. *Am I strong enough to see her again? Is she strong enough to see me? Will she see me?*

Croft's eyes danced with humor. "So how bad of a sailor *was* Dick Musgrove? I observed how carefully you chose your words when speaking with his father."

"He was several years at sea, and had, in the course of those removals to which all midshipmen are liable, and especially such midshipmen as every captain wishes to get rid of," he responded succinctly. "Dick Musgrove spent six months onboard the *Laconia*."

"Might you find something positive to say about the man?" Croft slowly got to his feet. "You have a week to think of something." He chuckled as he patted Frederick on the shoulder. "I will see you at dinner; I want to take a look at the ledger book for the preceding month on the estate. I will be in the study if Sophie is looking for me."

"Yes, Sir," Frederick mumbled.

★ ★ ★

"Captain Wentworth!" Mr. Musgrove cried, "It is so good of you to return our call. May I present my wife, Mrs. Musgrove, and our daughters Miss Louisa and Miss Henrietta Musgrove?" Frederick noted the Musgrove parents made a fine pair, both jovial—both well rotund.

Frederick bowed politely. "I am proud to make your acquaintance, Mrs. Musgrove." He saw tears mist her eyes as she took a close look at his countenance while he tried to mask his real feelings. "Misses Musgrove." He bowed formally to her daughters.

Henrietta and Louisa Musgrove were young ladies of nineteen and twenty, respectively, who were brought from a school at Exeter—they possessed all the usual stock of accomplishments, and were now, like thousands of other young ladies, living to be fashionable, happy, and merry. Their dress had every advantage; their faces were rather pretty; their spirits extremely good; their manners unembarrassed and pleasant; they were of consequence at home and favorites abroad.

"Captain, oh, dear Captain, you have no idea how pleased we are to receive you," assured Mrs. Musgrove. "We are anticipating the arrival of our daughter Mrs. Charles and her sister, Miss Anne Elliot. Please have a seat; they will be with us in a few minutes. Miss Anne is newly come from Kellynch Hall." Mrs. Musgrove seated herself on the settee across from his chair.

Hearing Anne's name and realizing within a few minutes he would see her once again, Frederick steeled his composure. After eight years, Anne would be in the same room as he. Sweat formed on his forehead, and, he unobtrusively, wiped it away with his handkerchief. Yet, before he could think further on what he would say or do, a servant rushed into the room. "Oh, Mrs. Musgrove," the woman gasped. "Dear me!"

"What is it, Jemima?" Mr. Musgrove rushed forward. "Is it Charles?"

"Lord, no, Mr. Musgrove," she gulped for air. "It is Little Charles; he fell from a tree. The whole house is at sixes and sevens. Miss Anne sent for the apothecary, informed Master Charles, kept Mrs. Charles from hysterics, and sent me here to inform you. She begs you to forgive their not attending you."

Mrs. Musgrove forgot all about their honored guest. "Father, we need to go immediately."

"Of course, my Dear. Retrieve your wrap. I will have the carriage brought around at once. Forgive us, Captain Wentworth; we must attend to the disturbance at Uppercross Cottage. You will call upon us again on the morrow? Right now I must see to my heir—to Little Charles."

"Naturally, Mr. Musgrove; have no doubt. I will see myself out." Frederick rose quickly to leave. "As far as our engagement, I will wait until I hear from you on your grandson's progress before I call upon you again. Your attention needs to be there, Sir, not with me."

"Thank you, Captain. Now we must leave you. Hurry, girls." So saying, he led Wentworth to the hallway and shook his hand before turning toward his approaching wife.

On the walk back to Kellynch Hall, Frederick brooded. He had come so close to seeing Anne again. He wiped his sweaty palms on his breeches and cursed under his breath, realizing how flushed he felt. A band constricted his chest, and he could barely breathe. "Damn it," he murmured. "What am I to do? I must see her to rid myself of Anne Elliot, but how will I be able to look upon her once more?" He straightened his shoulders and took deep breaths, trying to quiet his troubled heart. "Tomorrow, then," he thought out loud. "One more day will see us together." With a new resolve to be stoic, he continued his walk toward Kellynch Hall.

★ ★ ★

Frederick called on the Musgroves the next evening, having received word earlier in the day of the continued progress of the child. "I must tell you, Captain, I experienced great uneasiness about my heir." Mr. Musgrove took a deep drink of port.

"I was a bit surprised to receive word regarding tonight's entertainment." Frederick let his eyes drift to the others at the table. It amused him to see the Misses Musgrove hang on his every word. If only Anne could see him now! *Pity that she could not be here.*

From the tidbits of conversation he had overheard, Frederick determined that Mary Elliot Musgrove possessed much of the Elliot pride. She was often unwell and out of spirits, although she appeared quite animated on this particular evening. It took him only moments to realize that Mary had not Anne's understanding or temper. While well and happy and properly attended to, she possessed great good humor and excellent spirits; but, evidently, any indisposition sunk her completely; she had no resources for solitude. She had inherited a considerable share of the Elliot self-importance and was prone to add to every other distress that of fancying herself neglected and ill used. In Frederick's opinion, she was inferior to both sisters.

Charles Musgrove was civil and agreeable; in sense and temper, he was undoubtedly superior to his wife, but not of powers of conversation or of discrimination. In Frederick's estimation, a more equal match might greatly improve him, and a woman of real understanding might give more consequence to his character, and more usefulness, rationality, and polish to his habits and pursuits. Musgrove was single-minded in quest of his sport; it appeared he did nothing with much zeal, but sport; and his time was otherwise trifled away, without benefit from books or anything else. Frederick could not imagine a life of such indolence. Yet, the man had very good spirits, which never seemed much affected by his wife's occasional lowness; bore with her unreasonableness; and, upon the whole, though there was very often a little disagreement, they passed for a happy couple.

"The child had a good night," Charles Musgrove confided to Frederick, "and the doctor, Mr. Robinson, found nothing to increase alarm, so I saw no necessity for longer confinement. What can a father do?" Frederick kept his thoughts on the subject to himself.

"I agree, Boy," Mr. Musgrove added quickly. "This is quite a female case, and it would be highly absurd of you, who could be of no use at home, to shut yourself up. Besides I wished you to make the captain's acquaintance."

"Is your sister with the child?" Despite his brooding case of nerves and ill temper, the fact Anne did not arrive with the Musgroves disappointed Frederick. He would like to know how she felt as to a meeting. Perhaps indifferent, if indifference could exist under such circumstances. She must be indifferent or unwilling—unwilling to face him.

Mary joined the conversation. "I told Charles, to be sure, I may just as well come as not, for I am of no use at home—am I?" She turned to her husband for confirmation of what she said. "And it only harasses me. My sister Anne has not a mother's feelings and is a great deal the properest person. She can make Little Charles do anything; he always minds her at a word. It is a great deal better than leaving him with only Jemima."

Anne has a way with children. Of course. How often Frederick envisioned her with a babe in her arms—her child—his child? Pain crept into the pit of his stomach.

"It was very kind of Anne," Charles assured everyone in earshot. "I wanted her to join us in the evening when the child might be at rest for the night. I urged her to let me come and fetch her, but she was quite unpersuadable."

"I am sorry Miss Anne could not join us. We met when I was here before, and it would have been—ah—pleasant to see her again." Frederick felt the necessity of escaping an introduction when they were to meet.

"I never realized you knew my sister!" Mary exclaimed.

"As I recall, you were away at school when I visited Somerset some years ago," was all the explanation he offered before turning his attention to Louisa Musgrove.

The evening continued with music, singing, talking, and laughing; Frederick found it all most agreeable. He forced himself to be charming, leaving his pensive thoughts of Anne in the deep recesses of his mind. He and the Musgroves took to each other quickly; they seemed all to know each other perfectly. "Then you will come for breakfast before we go shooting?" Charles Musgrove confirmed when they said their good-byes.

"Not at the Cottage," Frederick added. Impulsively, he had decided against seeing Anne. If she chose not to let Charles bring her for the evening's end, she, evidently, did not want to see Frederick. He would not force himself upon her. "I would not wish to be in Mrs. Charles's way on account of the child."

"Then we will meet here at the Great House," Charles decided.

"Tomorrow," Frederick confirmed. He bowed, first to the ladies and then to the Musgrove men. He mounted the horse he had borrowed from the Kellynch stables and headed back toward his sister's home.

CHAPTER 6

When we two parted
In silence and tears,
Half broken-hearted
To sever for years,
Pale grew thy cheek and cold,
Colder thy kiss;
Truly that hour foretold
Sorrow to this.
—Lord Byron, "When We Two Parted"

"So beautiful." The words brought Anne's attention to the figure reclining lazily against the pillows. She sat reading a book of poetry as she tended his bedside. "Did you know I fell in love with you the first time I saw you in the mercantile? Your face—those delicately molded features and dark eyes—captivated me immediately. Somehow, I felt that we understood each other. Odd, is it not?"

She smiled tenderly at him. Moving to sit on the edge of the bed, she reached out and pushed the hair away from his forehead. "You did not look away. You charmed me." Anne leaned forward and whispered in his ear. "I saw your eyes darken with something I did not understand at the time." She kissed his temple and his cheek.

Frederick's breath caught in his throat. "I saw the sparkle in your eyes. Suddenly, I had a mad desire to be the only one to make your eyes glow in that way."

"I am thrilled that you are feeling better, my Love. I feared I might lose you."

"Never again. Perhaps even the Angel of Death is deterred by love."

Just then there came a knock at the door, and the ship's doctor announced himself. "Ah, Captain," he called as he entered the room. "It is time to get you up out of that bed." He immediately started checking Frederick's wounds.

"Are you sure, Dr. Laraby?" Anne looked concerned. "Is this not too soon?"

"No, it is not," Laraby firmly denied her words. "He needs exercise, or he will become weaker. And you need to see something other than these four walls for a while. Look at her, Captain; see how pale she is. Your wife has done nothing but tend you, night and day, for nearly five days now. Command her, Wentworth; she ignores me."

Frederick turned his gaze on Anne. Laraby was right; she was white-faced and gaunt, and, if possible, she lost weight. "Anne," he said mournfully, "I am sorry I did not notice."

"You needed me," she said simply.

"I did; I do," he corrected. "But because I need you, my Love, I want you to take care of yourself. Please leave, Sweetheart; go do something special for you." He took her hand in his, bringing her fingertips to his lips for a lingering kiss. "Do not make me give you a direct order, Sweetling." His eyes lit up with amusement.

He watched as she playfully raised an eyebrow in mocked contempt. "Can you spell mutiny, my Love?" she teased.

"M-u-t . . ." Her laughter cut off the end of the word.

She conceded, "I will go, but please note it is not with a willing heart."

"So noted," he quipped. "Now get out of here."

"Aye, aye, Captain." She offered a half-hearted salute before dropping him a quick curtsy.

As she left, Laraby ushered in Lieutenants Avendale and Harwood once again. "We need to get the captain on his feet; I want him walking about the room."

His men supported his every move, allowing him to lean his weight on their shoulders. With his teeth gritted, Frederick made his way haltingly to and fro across the room. Each movement was dizzying, and he periodically paused when the pain became too intense.

"That is enough for now," Laraby declared, and he motioned the sailors to help Frederick to sit on his bunk. "We will have you up again a little later today."

Frederick collapsed to a seated position on the side of the bed. "Thanks for the warning, Laraby," he hissed through the settling pain.

"You know it is best; so quit your complaining." Laraby supported Frederick's shoulders as the captain pivoted on the bed, swinging his long legs up and over the edge. He gasped as he lay back against the pillows.

"Do you need more laudanum?"

"Not just yet," Frederick said as he pushed himself up on his pillows.

Laraby pulled the blanket over Frederick's long frame. "Soon, then. Shall I have a man come in to shave you? That might make you feel better."

"I think I would enjoy that," Frederick agreed. "Mrs. Wentworth would appreciate seeing a shaved face when she returns."

Laraby sent for Wentworth's assistant before saying, "Your wife is devoted to you, Sir. You are fortunate to have earned such regard. I have heard that you two are newly wed. Not wishing to seem rude, Sir, I am surprised some man did not claim her attentions long ago."

Frederick smiled. "Some man did—me." He looked off in space visualizing Anne as he first saw her. "We are indeed newly wed, although we are not in the first blush of youth. I wooed her in '06, but we were young, and things were not to be. I assumed I had lost Mrs. Wentworth until I returned to her home country to visit with my sister Sophia and the Admiral. Then we were thrown together through mutual acquaintances."

"Then you are truly a lucky man," Laraby acknowledged.

Frederick chuckled. "Interestingly, the late Dick Musgrove brought us together."

"Musgrove!" Laraby looked surprised. "*There* was a man who was not cut out to be a sailor, Sir. But how did he bring you and

Mrs. Wentworth together?"

"Dick Musgrove was useless in my estimation also, but his parents thought the world of him. Except for his family, he was scarcely at all regretted once the intelligence of his death abroad worked its way to Uppercross. His parents came to thank me, though, because he had mentioned me positively in a letter home, and I was presented with the pleasant situation of finding *my Anne* in residence with the Musgroves. Mrs. Wentworth's youngest sister is the eldest son's wife. Anne and I took up where we had left off all those years earlier."

The assistant entered at that point and began setting up the shaving tools. Laraby moved to a chair. "It sounds as if God meant for the two of you to be together."

"I like to think so," Wentworth responded, "although the Devil provided us with several twists and turns along the way."

"You will tell me of them sometime?" Laraby asked. "For now, Yates will take care of your ablutions."

The assistant lathered Frederick's cheeks and jaw line with soap. A few minutes later, the captain was clean-shaven once again. Rubbing his palms along his smooth skin, he looked at his reflection in the mirror that Yates offered. "I am glad Anne chose me before I lost so much blood and so much weight. And look at these dark circles under my eyes." Frederick shook his head in disbelief.

"You were never handsome, Captain," Laraby joked. When Frederick snorted, he said, "To be serious, Captain, sleep and exercise will do much to restore your vigor and your looks."

"Exercise?" said Frederick. "You mean pacing a room. And pacing a room is one of my least favorite things."

★ ★ ★

Frederick paced the morning room, waiting for Charles Musgrove to finish his breakfast. The Musgroves thought him eager for the sport of the day. In reality, his thoughts rested on Anne. He and Charles were to return to the Cottage for the dogs; more than likely, Anne would be in attendance. They would meet at last.

"Let us go!" Charles called to Frederick.

Louisa Musgrove strolled into the morning room. "We would join you if you have no objections. Henrietta and I wish to call at the Cottage regarding Little Charles."

Frederick recognized the ruse, but he welcomed it. After all, the Misses Musgrove were two of the most genial young ladies of his acquaintance. "I would be pleased for your company."

They walked to the Cottage, and the Misses Musgrove kept up an animated conversation. Frederick, on the other hand, remained quiet; he felt as if he might be on his way to his own execution. With determination, he steeled himself to face Anne after eight years.

"The morning hours of the Cottage are always later than those of the Great House," Louisa explained as they approached the door. "With the late hours of the party, I suspect Mary and Anne are just beginning their breakfasts."

"Then we will not intrude for long," Frederick insisted. He was grateful for a legitimate reason not to tarry in Anne's presence.

The door opened to the Cottage, and Frederick followed Louisa and Henrietta into the room. Air rushed from his lungs as he stepped forward to greet Mrs. Charles. He bowed, not allowing his eyes to rest on either woman standing by the breakfast sidebar. Although he had not looked at her, his body told him Anne Elliot finally stood before him.

"Mrs. Musgrove," he began, "excuse the intrusion. I came with your husband to inquire on the progress of your son. I pray the morning brings him continued peace."

Gratified by his attention, Mary delightedly received him. "Oh, Captain Wentworth," she gushed. "You honor us."

He heard nothing else; his eyes rested on Anne's face. They were the same features he remembered; yet, she changed. Her eyes met his for the briefest of moments. She nearly blended into the woodwork; Anne appeared used up—defeated by life.

What happened to the woman he had loved so dearly all those years ago? She had allowed life to consume her. It angered him that she never learned to take up her own cause. Perhaps she deserved serving her inane sister and not having a life of her own. He had once thought she was adventurous enough to sail with him around the world; now, he saw her as nothing more than an accessory to her family. How could he have pined for such a woman? How could he have believed that she could spend her days at sea?

A self-conscious silence engulfed him; Mary Musgrove looked at him expectantly. Frederick realized he had not attended to her ramblings; he was just about to make some sort of excuse when her husband appeared at the window. "Come, Wentworth, I have the dogs." He held the leashes of several beagles and pointers.

"If you will excuse me, Ladies," he said with a bow and then turned toward the door, needing to escape the room.

"Let us walk with them to the end of the village," Louisa encouraged her sister.

Mary grabbed her shawl from the back of a chair. "I will go, too."

Frederick paused at the door to allow the women to precede him. Reluctantly, he glanced at Anne to see if she would join them also. Her eyes were still downcast. She curtsied and then stood there, as if rooted to the floor. *Join us,* he wanted to say to her. *Take your life into your own hands.* He tried to will her to move. But she did no such thing. Annoyed, he strode out the door.

He walked silently beside Charles Musgrove, lost in his thoughts. He replayed the scene—her eyes half met his; a bow, a curtsy passed; he talked to Mary, said all that was right; said something to the Misses Musgrove—the room seemed full, full of people and voices—but a few minutes ended it. "It is over! It is over!" he repeated to himself again and again in nervous agitation. "The worst is over!" He had seen her. They had met. They were once more in the same room! Eight years, almost eight years passed, since they gave up on love. How absurd to be resuming the agitation which such an interval had banished into distance and indistinctness! What might not eight years do? Events of every description, changes, alienations, removals—all, all must be comprised in it; and oblivion of the past—how natural, how certain too! It included nearly one quarter of his life.

Alas! With all his reasoning, he found that to retentive feelings, eight years may be little more than nothing. Irritation flooded him—only a few moments in her presence, and he was once again brooding about her.

He turned from his thoughts reluctantly when he heard Henrietta address him. "Captain Wentworth, what did you think of Miss Anne?"

Caught off guard, he responded candidly, "I am sorry to say I found Miss Anne altered beyond my knowledge—so altered I should not have known her again!"

He thought her wretchedly altered, and, in the first moment of appeal, spoke as he felt. He realized he had not forgiven Anne Elliot. She used him ill; deserted and disappointed him; and worse, she showed a feebleness of character in doing so, which his own decided, confident temper could not endure. She gave him up to oblige others. It was the effect of overpersuasion. It was weakness and timidity. He had assumed maturity would have tempered those tendencies; instead, Anne Elliot was but a ghost of the woman she should have become.

He had been most warmly attached to her and had never seen a woman since whom he thought her equal, but he had been wrong. Now, except from some natural sensation of curiosity, he had no desire of meeting her again. He swore her power with him was gone forever.

★ ★ ★

Later that evening, he sat in the drawing room with Sophia and Benjamin. They sipped a fine wine. Staring at the fire in the hearth, Frederick, despite his earlier vow, remained consumed by his continual thoughts of Anne. "The Misses Musgrove are attractive," Sophia roused him from his musings.

Frederick knew where the conversation would lead. "They both offer pleasant company," he said.

"Do not be *evasive*, Frederick," the Admiral admonished him. "Does either of the young ladies interest you? Your sister and I would like to see you as well settled as is Edward."

"I know, Admiral," he conceded. "You and Sophia will be

pleased to know it is now my object to marry. I am rich, and being turned on shore, fully intend to settle as soon as I can be properly tempted. I am actually looking round, am ready to fall in love with all the speed which a clear head and quick taste will allow. I have a heart for either of the Misses Musgrove, if they can catch it; a heart, in short, for any pleasing young woman who comes my way." *Anyone except Anne Elliot,* he thought. This was his only secret exception to his sister's suppositions. "Yes, here I am, Sophia, quite ready to make a foolish match. Anybody between fifteen and thirty may have me for the asking. A little beauty and a few smiles, and a few compliments to the Navy, and I am a lost man. Should not this be enough for a sailor who has had no society among women to make him nice?"

"Frederick, you jest! You just wish me to contradict you," she reasoned. "No woman could ask for a kinder man than you."

He hesitated. "If I were to more seriously describe the woman I should wish to meet," he hesitated, remembering his initial assessment of Anne, "she would possess a strong mind, with a sweetness of manner." He paused again, considering his own words. "This is the woman I want," said he. "Something a little inferior I shall, of course, put up with, but it must not be much. If I am a fool, I shall be a fool indeed, for I have thought on the subject more than most men."

★ ★ ★

From this time, Captain Wentworth and Anne Elliot were repeatedly in the same circle. They soon dined in company together at Mr. Musgrove's, for the little boy's state could not supply his aunt with a pretense for absenting herself; and this was but the beginnings of other meetings.

Frederick grew less fearful of being in the same room with her. He treated Anne as everyone else did; she was a nonentity—she did not exist other than being part of the room decoration. In this manner, he could deal with her presence. Yet, as often as he tried to not let himself think of her, he foolishly succumbed nevertheless. It irritated him to see her treated as an afterthought in the minds of her family. It irritated him to think that she accepted her life as it was. It irritated him that, despite her betrayal, he still had moments when his eyes rested on her and her alone.

"Do you mean to say sailors have private accommodations on board ship?" Louisa asked with surprise one evening after supper. Even her cousins the Misses Hayter, who joined them for the meal, seemed interested in his response.

"Miss Musgrove, we are not barbarians. We officers live quite comfortably. My sister," he said as he nodded toward Sophia, "travels with the Admiral. Obviously, she could not be expected to live in substandard conditions."

"Did you ever hear of such a thing, Anne?" Henrietta turned to her for confirmation.

Frederick, too, turned his attention to Anne. Perhaps she remembered a similar conversation; the thoughts of those pleasant hours with her beside the lake turned up the corners of his mouth with a smile; he noted she held his gaze for a few elongated seconds before looking suddenly away. "I assume, Henrietta, the Crown would not send men off to fight wars in rowboats; it would not be practical. What man would make a career of the Navy if he had to suffer long periods of deplorable conditions?" Her voice painted pleasant ridicule of the Misses Musgrove's flirtations, and it pleased Frederick to see her assert herself.

Frederick started to respond directly to her, but Mrs. Musgrove whispered what appeared to be fond regrets of Dick Musgrove. He watched as Anne suppressed a smile and listened kindly. It was a quality he once admired in her. He considered joining their conversation, but then thought better of it. It was a seductive illusion to which he wanted to succumb; yet, Frederick knew the folly of it.

"Oh, Captain," Henrietta said charmingly, "we sent off for a Navy List. Will you help us find the ships you commanded in it?" She rushed to the mantelpiece to retrieve the book.

"I am sorry, Captain," Mr. Musgrove apologized, "they made me send for it."

Frederick smiled broadly with their regard. "It is quite all right."

"Anne has her own Navy List. Do you not, Anne?" Louisa told

him in passing.

Frederick's eyes darted to her face; he watched a flush overtake her countenance. "I—I am interested in many things, Louisa," she stammered before dropping her eyes to her hands resting on her lap.

"When did you earn your first command, Captain?" Mr. Musgrove asked as he motioned for a servant to refill the wine glasses.

Admiral Croft answered instead. "It was in '06, was it not, Frederick?"

"It was, Sir, shortly after I left Somersetshire. Yes, I was here in '06, visiting my brother, Edward." He watched Anne withdraw into herself with his words.

"Your first was the *Asp*, I remember; we will look for the *Asp*." Louisa pored over the listing.

"You will not find her there.—Quite worn out and broken up. I was the last man who commanded her.—Hardly fit for service then.—Reported fit for home service for a year or two—and so I was sent off to the West Indies."

The Musgrove girls looked all astonishment.

"The Admiralty," he continued, "entertains itself now and then, with sending a few hundred men to sea in a ship not fit to be employed. But they have a great many for which to provide; and among the thousands that may just as well go to the bottom as not, it is impossible for them to distinguish the very set who may be least missed."

"Phoo! Phoo!" cried the Admiral, "what stuff these young fellows talk! Never a better sloop than the *Asp* in her day—for an old built sloop, you would not see her equal. Lucky fellow to get her." He looked sternly at Frederick. "He knows there must have been twenty better men than himself applying for her at the same time. Lucky fellow to get anything so soon, with no more high placed connections than his."

"I felt my luck, Admiral, I assure you." He looked about seriously, planning to make a point with Anne. "I was as well satisfied with my appointment as one can desire. It was a great object with me at the time to be at sea—a very great object. In '06, I wanted to be doing something."

The Admiral got up to stretch his legs, trying to ward off another attack of gout. "To be sure, you did." He spoke more to himself than he did to Frederick. "What should a young fellow, like you, do ashore for an extended period of time?—If a man has not a wife, he soon wants to be afloat again."

Frederick eyed Anne once again. He put special emphasis on the beginning words. "*In '06*, I had no wife to keep me on shore." The words served their purpose; Anne turned a bit away from the rest of the table, her response hidden by shadows. He relished the idea that he could make her think of him; he knew how often over the past eight years he had thought of *her*. It was gratifying in some small way to see his words affect her.

"But, Captain Wentworth," cried Louisa, "how vexed you must have been when you came to the *Asp* to see what an old thing they gave you."

He smiled at her when she lightly laid her hand on his arm. "I knew pretty well what she was before that day. I had no more discoveries to make, than you would have as to the fashion and strength of an old pelisse, which you had seen lent about among half your acquaintance, ever since you could remember, and which at last, on some very wet day, is lent to yourself." Although he did not look at her, he felt Anne's eyes glued to his face. "Ah! She was a dear old *Asp* to me. She did all I wanted. I knew she would . . . I knew we should either go to the bottom together, or she would be the making of me. In reflection, I never had two days of foul weather all the time I was at sea in her, and after taking privateers enough to be very entertaining, I had the good luck, in my passage home the next autumn, to fall in with the very French frigate I wanted. I brought her into Plymouth, and here was another instance of luck."

He focused his attention on Anne's end of the table. She had not looked away during his tale; it was his chance to let her know how successful he had been and how the luck he had known he would have was there. "We were not six hours in the Sound," he continued in a voice that mesmerized his audience, but Frederick's attention rested purely on Anne Elliot, "when a gale came on, which lasted four days and nights, and which would have done in the poor old *Asp*, in half the time; our touch with the Great Nation of France not having much improved our condition. Four and twenty hours later, and I should only have been a gallant Captain Wentworth in a small paragraph at one corner of the newspapers; and being lost in only a sloop, nobody would have thought about me."

Louisa and Henrietta gasped and declared how awful such thoughts were, but Frederick watched Anne for her reaction. She openly shuddered—a shiver shaking her body. Her bottom lip trembled, and although she made no open exclamation of pity and horror, as did the other ladies, he noted tears misting her eyes. Her reaction stunned him—his heart skipped a beat. He only watched her to gleam an idea of whether she regretted her decision in light of the fortune he won, but her obvious distress over his words made him question what to do about her. He told his stories only to boast of his success; yet, his description of how close he came to death moved her—the indication of the fortune he won brought only looks of admiration for his successes, but his near demise affected her in a way he did not expect. He had not considered renewing his addresses to Anne Elliot, but it seemed they would always be connected—their pasts bound him with silver threads to her.

He heard Mrs. Musgrove say something to her son Charles about Dick Musgrove. Frederick knew he would have to think of something positive to say about "poor Dick" soon. He would find a way to ease her pain.

"Come, Captain," Henrietta pulled on his left sleeve. "Help us find the *Laconia* on the List."

He could not deny himself the pleasure of taking the precious volume into his own hands to save them the trouble and to read aloud the little statement of her name and rate and present non-commissioned class, observing over it, that she too was one of the best friends man ever had.

"Ah! Those were pleasant days when I had the *Laconia*! How

fast I made money in her.—A friend of mine and I had such a lovely cruise together off the Western Islands. You remember Harville, do you not, Sophia? You know how much he wanted money—worse than myself. He had a wife.—Excellent fellow! I shall never forget his happiness. He felt it all, so much for her sake. I wished for him again the next summer, when I had still the same luck in the Mediterranean."

His words of the *Laconia* brought Mrs. Musgrove's thoughts once more to her son. The time came for him to console her. After supper, she moved to rest on the same sofa as did Anne. Making his way to her, he allowed himself an indulgence of self-amusement at how many pains he had gone through to be rid of Dick Musgrove. Now he would hide his real feelings from the man's mother. He sat on the same upholstered seat; Mrs. Musgrove separated Frederick and Anne. Even her daughters did nothing to keep Frederick's reaction to Anne in check. Although he fought it, as he entered into the conversation with the elder woman, his real thoughts lay with the petite lady seated to her right. He offered sympathy and attended to Mrs. Musgrove's sighs over the fate of her son. She patted Frederick's hand and thanked him profusely for his kindness. As she did so, he noted the delicate curve of Anne's neck and the slight lift of her chin when she spoke to his sister. A strand of hair worked its way loose from her chignon, and he fought the urge to reach out and touch it.

The Admiral, after two or three refreshing turns about the room with his hands behind him, being called to order by his wife, now came up to Frederick and without any observation of what he might be interrupting, thinking only of his own thoughts, began with, "If you had been a week later at Lisbon, last spring, Frederick, you would have been asked to give passage to Lady Mary Grierson and her daughters."

Lost in thoughts of caressing Anne's neck, Frederick sarcastically turned on his brother. "Should I? I am glad I was not a week later then." Catching himself, Frederick said, "But, if I know myself, this is from no want of gallantry toward them." Eager to correct his blunder, he continued. "It is rather from feeling how impossible it is, with all one's efforts, and all one's sacrifices, to make the accommodations on board, such as women ought to have. There can be no want of gallantry, Admiral, in rating the claims of women to every personal comfort *high*—and this is what I do. I hate to hear of women on board or to see them on board; and no ship, under my command, shall ever convey a family of ladies anywhere, if I can help it." After Anne had broken her engagement with Frederick, he could not bear to think of such intrusions into his domain. If Anne could not travel with him, Frederick wanted *no* woman on his ship.

Sophia took offense at his words. "Oh, Frederick!—But I cannot believe it of you.—All idle refinement!—Women may be as comfortable on board, as in the best house in England. I believe I have lived as much on board as most women, and I know nothing superior to the accommodations of a man of war."

"Nothing to the purpose," Frederick protested. "You were living with your husband and were the only woman on board."

"But you, yourself, brought Mrs. Harville, her sister, her cousin, and the three children round from Portsmouth to Plymouth. Where was this superfine, extraordinary sort of gallantry of yours then?"

"All merged in my friendship, Sophia." Frederick's voice rose in volume, realizing where his sister's argument lay, but he could not concede his *need* to keep women from his ship—a *need* vested in his hurt at Anne's refusal. He knew it was not rational, but reason and love do not always lie together. "I would assist any brother officer's wife I could, but I might not like them the better for that. Such a number of women and children have no *right* to be comfortable on board."

Frederick's stubbornness riled Sophia. "But I hate to hear you talking so, like a fine gentleman and as if women were all fine ladies, instead of rational creatures. We none of us expect to be in smooth waters all our days." He resisted the urge to look at Anne at that moment. Could she have survived on a ship—survived with him?

"Ah! My Dear," the Admiral said as he came to sit beside his wife on the settee, "when he has a wife, he will sing a different tune. When he is married, if we have the good luck to live to another war, we shall see him do as you and I, and a great many others, have done. We shall have him very thankful to anybody who will bring him his wife."

Sophia nodded. "Aye, that we shall."

Frederick could take no more—Anne sat nearby—the Misses Musgrove and their cousins, the Misses Hayter, fawned over him— and all he wanted to do was retreat to the privacy of his room and regain his composure. "Now I have done!" he exclaimed. "When once married people begin to attack me with 'Oh! You will think differently when you are married.' I can only say, 'No, I shall not.' And then they say again, 'Yes, you will.' And there is an end to it." He got up and moved away to the window, staring out into the dying light.

Frederick swallowed hard, trying to steel his nerves. Between him and Anne, they had no conversation together, no intercourse but what the commonest civility required. Once so much to each other! Now nothing! There *had* been a time when of all the large party now filling the drawing room at Uppercross, they would have found it most difficult to cease to speak to one another. With the exception, perhaps, of the Admiral and Sophia, there could have been no two people as much in love. Now they were as strangers— nay, worse than strangers, for they could never become acquainted. It was a perpetual estrangement.

Lost in his thoughts, Frederick barely heard his sister mentioning to Mrs. Musgrove the places to which she had traveled. "Cork and Lisbon and Gibraltar."

Anne's soft lilt caught his attention, and he felt his body come alive with interest. "Did you never suffer, Mrs. Croft, from your time at sea?"

Sophia spoke of her devotion to Benjamin Croft: "The only time I ever really suffered in body or mind, the only time I ever fancied myself unwell, or had any ideas of danger, was the winter I passed by myself at Deal, when the Admiral, Captain Croft then, was in the North Seas. I lived in perpetual fright at that time, and had all manner of imaginary complaints from not knowing what to do with myself, or when I should hear from him next; but as long as we could be together, nothing ever ailed me, and I never met with the smallest inconvenience."

Frederick was struck more by Anne's question than by his sister's answer. *Was that the reason? Was Anne afraid to follow me to sea?* It was something he never considered; he always assumed she did not love him enough to face the hardships together. She was but nineteen in '06. She was larger than life in memory, and he never thought of her as afraid of what he offered. Could she have handled life on a ship? Could she have borne any separations, living alone in a seaport? Sophia had been young when she married Benjamin, but she had not led a sheltered life, and a woman of four and twenty is different from a girl of nineteen. He needed to think; he needed to decide where Anne Elliot fit into his life.

Louisa Musgrove appeared beside him. "Have we said something to offend you, Captain Wentworth?" Her soft eyes told him she would eagerly receive his attentions. Even if he considered renewing his regard for Anne, he could not be sure she would receive him willingly. He would not allow Anne the opportunity to humiliate him again; his heart could not survive such a rebuff. Why not accept what was in front of him? *Why not accept a sure thing?*

"Of course not, Miss Musgrove. I was just taking in the splendor of the evening." He offered her a genuine smile.

"Anne agreed to play for us." Louisa leaned in a bit too close for propriety, but no one, except him, seemed to notice her forwardness. "I hoped you would dance with me, Captain."

He chuckled at her flirtatiousness, remembering another daring young lady, who had asked him to be her supper partner, many years earlier.

"With pleasure, Miss Musgrove," he said. And he offered her his arm.

CHAPTER 7

After great pain, a formal feeling comes—
The Nerves sit ceremonious, like Tombs—
The stiff Heart questions was it He, that bore,
And Yesterday, or Centuries before?
—Emily Dickinson,
"After Great Pain, A Formal Feeling Comes"

Frederick and Louisa moved to the area in the music room cleared for dancing; furtively, he shot a quick glance at Anne as she settled herself on the bench at the pianoforte. She withdrew mentally from the party. *Again*, he thought, *again, she desires nothing but to be unobserved.*

Louisa Musgrove enthusiastically twirled about him in the quadrille, and Frederick could not help but laugh, watching her smiling up at him. "You seem quite happy this evening," he said as he passed her in the form.

"Do I?" She giggled as they came together. "Perhaps it is the company I keep."

Frederick moved away, circling Sophia and Charles Musgrove. When he and Louisa joined hands to move down the line, he leaned toward her and spoke to her hair. "You are very bold, Miss Musgrove."

"I am sure of what I want in my life, Captain Wentworth."

"Interesting, Miss Musgrove." His face did not betray his thoughts. He was thirteen years her senior and, despite his brave words to Sophia and Benjamin, he certainly did not know what he wanted in his life.

After the dance, they joined Henrietta and the Hayter sisters, all waiting patiently for their turns to dance with him. "Do you know how to waltz, Captain Wentworth?" Miss Caroline Hayter, the eldest, asked nervously.

"I do, Miss Hayter. Most officers are familiar with the more popular dances. We find it quite useful when we are required to attend naval functions."

"I wish Mama would allow us to waltz." Henrietta sighed with regret. "She believes it to be a quite scandalous dance. What do you think, Captain?"

Frederick did not know how to answer. Waltzing with the right woman in his arms could be very *stimulating*, but a gentleman did not say such a thing. Instead, he tried to divert their imaginings. "In London, before a lady of the *ton* may waltz, she must be presented at Almack's and receive permission from one of the patronesses there—Lady Jersey, Princess Lieven, or Lady Castlereaugh. The three are quite content to control Society from their lofty perches. It is even rumored they once turned away the Duke of Wellington himself for wearing trousers instead of knee breeches." The girls all giggled at his description of life in London's best parlor rooms. "Will any of you experience a Season this year?"

"Oh, no," Louisa assured him in serious tones, "we will never experience the *ton* and its wicked ways. The Elliots and Lady Russell are the extent of Father's tolerance for the nobility. We will all find matches in the country. Living in London sounds exciting, but Papa would never tolerate the number of soirees and balls in a Season."

It was a merry, joyous party, and Frederick's spirits were high. How could a man not enjoy an evening in which *four* young women vied for his notice? The Misses Musgrove and the Misses Hayter hung on Frederick's every word—his every gesture. At a pause in the music, he moved to the instrument bench to pick out a tune. They crowded around, eager to tease him about his inability to play well.

"Oh, Captain," Miss Hayter vowed, "your playing is perfectly awful!" They all snickered.

He laughed along with them. "Playing the pianoforte is not in the domain of most sailors." Yet, he continued to stroke the keys, aimlessly searching for the right tune, as he spoke.

"Would there be room aboard a ship for my new harp?" Henrietta questioned.

"Of course, there is room for such an extravagance; but I am not sure how the sea air might affect the instrument."

Looking up, he saw Anne approaching the bench. Not wishing her presence to intrude on the vignette he created in his mind where he received the notice of women purely because he was an eligible prospect and where he had no history with Anne, he stood up abruptly, wishing to put the specter of Anne Elliot behind him. "I beg your pardon, Madam, this is your seat." He bowed.

"No, Captain, please, do not let me disturb you." Anne's soft voice betrayed her embarrassment at his studied politeness. She immediately drew back with a decided negative, but he was not to be induced to sit down again.

"I insist, Madam." He offered his arm to Henrietta, and the five of them walked away. Frederick seemed calm on the outside, but that short intercourse changed his reality. When the music began again, he shared the floor with the younger Jane Hayter and then with Sophia, and finally with Henrietta. Throughout, despite his best intentions, his gaze sought Anne; it was impossible for him not to notice her eyes would sometimes fill with tears as she sat at the instrument. He observed her altered features, trying to trace in them the ruins of the face, which once charmed him.

"Miss Henrietta," he asked against his will, "does Miss Elliot never dance?"

"Oh! No, never, she quite gave up dancing. She had rather play. She never tires of playing."

The words shot through him. Anne never danced! How had that happened? Anne lost everything she loved about life. Frederick shook his head in disbelief. His vivacious Anne now found her only meaning in life in being employed for her family's pleasures— her life held no greater promise. Loving him had cost her dearly.

★ ★ ★

"It appears, Frederick, that you no longer intend to leave for

Shropshire to see Edward and his new wife," Sophia teased him.

Frederick's eyebrow shot up in amusement. "Do you wish to be rid of me, Sister dear?"

"You know better. Stay as long as you like. Benjamin enjoys your company; you remind him of his time at sea." She handed him a cup of tea. "Do you call at Uppercross today?"

He took a sip of the strong brew. "I have a standing invitation to do so daily."

"What occupies your time with the Musgroves?" Frederick realized Sophia wanted to know if he considered one of the Musgrove ladies as marriage material, but he made no such decision. For the moment, he simply enjoyed the attractions of Uppercross. There was so much of friendliness, and of flattery, and of everything most bewitching in his reception there; the old were so hospitable, the young so agreeable, that he could not but resolve to remain where he was, and take all the charms and perfections of Edward's wife upon credit for a little longer.

"Charles enjoys his sport; we often hunt or shoot. I walk out with the Misses Musgrove; we walk into the village or visit at the Cottage. One sunny day we spent the afternoon at croquet—another at archery. The days are pleasant with such amiable company." He paused before adding, "Their cousin Charles Hayter of Winthrop joined us for supper last night."

"Really?" Sophia mused. "How did you find the curate?"

"His disquiet seemed out of place on such a homecoming. From what I understand, Hayter was away a fortnight. The Musgroves seemed pleased that he might discharge his curacy duties soon at Uppercross itself as Dr. Shirley's assistant. I wish Edward could have experienced such opportunities early on."

"He seems well situated now," Sophia noted as she refilled her teacup. "I suppose you dine at Uppercross again this evening?"

Frederick smiled to himself. "I believe I will. He stood and returned his empty cup to the tray. "I will take my leave, Sophia, as soon as I change my waistcoat." She tilted her head up to receive the kiss he bent to bestow upon her cheek. He tapped her nose tenderly with his index finger. "And if I were to choose one or another of the Musgroves for my wife, you would be the first to know." He winked at her and then strode from the room.

★ ★ ★

"The ladies are all at the Cottage," Mrs. Musgrove told him when he presented himself at the Great House. "You are welcome to wait, Captain, but if I know my daughters, it will be some time. Mrs. Charles received a new book of fashion plates. I am sure Henrietta and Louisa are making plans for creating the latest fashions for their holiday dresses."

"Perhaps, Ma'am, I will walk to the Cottage and offer my services upon their return." He bowed to excuse himself.

"That is an excellent idea, Captain Wentworth." She chuckled as she picked up her embroidery. "I have no doubt your presence will delight Henrietta and Louisa."

Less than a quarter of an hour later, Frederick presented himself to the servant who answered the door at the Cottage and was immediately shown into the drawing room. He stopped short, finding only Anne and Little Charles in the room. Little Charles, still recovering from his fall, lay on the sofa; Anne sat next to him.

"Fred—" she blurted out and caught herself. "Captain Wentworth—welcome, Sir." She stood and curtsied.

Her near use of his Christian name deprived his manners of their usual composure: He started and could only say, "I thought the Misses Musgrove were here—Mrs. Musgrove told me this is where I might find them." Surprised at being almost alone with Anne Elliot, he walked to the window to collect himself and to feel how he ought to behave. He clasped his hands behind his back and focused his attention on the withered flowers of the garden.

Anne too stammered in embarrassment. "They—they are upstairs with my sister—they will be down in a few minutes, I dare say."

"Aunt Anne," Little Charles's voice called her to his side. "May I have some water?"

She busied herself with bringing the boy his water, cradling his head as he held his lips to the glass. "Let me rub your arms and legs; lying still so long is nearly as tiring as being outside, is it not, Sweetheart?" She began to gently massage the boy's arms, working her way slowly down his limbs, offering the comfort of her touch and her attention.

Frederick remained at the window, but he knew good manners demanded he say something. He turned to face her. "I hope the little boy is better." His words brought Anne's eyes to his; she smiled and nodded. Anne caressed the boy's cheek with the palm of her hand. The picture of the two of them together brought images of Anne with her own children—with *their* children. It was a vision that had haunted him for years.

The sound of some other person crossing the little vestibule made Frederick pray to see Charles Musgrove. Instead, Charles Hayter stepped briskly into the room.

Anne looked up from where she tended the child. She stood to offer the visitor a welcoming greeting and a curtsy. "How do you do?" she mumbled. "Will not you sit down? The others will be here presently." She looked tentatively at Frederick. "I believe you know Captain Wentworth." She gestured to where Frederick stood and then turned her attention once more to the child.

It did not take Frederick long to determine Charles Hayter was probably not at all better pleased by the sight of him, than Frederick was by the sight of Anne. However, Frederick forced himself away from the window and bowed. "How do you do, Sir? It is pleasant to see you again."

Hayter bowed and responded coolly, "Captain Wentworth." Turning to Anne, he inquired, "Miss Elliot, is Little Charles better?"

"I believe so," she answered from her seated position.

Then Hayter strode to a wing chair next to a side table and picked up the newspaper lying there, ignoring everyone else in the room. Frederick could not decide whether he found Hayter's actions offensive or amusing. Having lived for many years in close quarters with other men, he sometimes forgot how rude landlubbers could be. He shrugged his shoulders and returned to the window, wondering how much longer he would have to wait for the Misses Musgrove. He suspected the ladies would make the gentlemen wait at least a quarter hour. It seemed to be the way of ladies, and secretly, Frederick enjoyed the ploy.

Deep in such thoughts, the arrival of the youngest Musgrove child took him by surprise. Evidently, someone opened the door for the boy. He scrambled to where Anne sat beside young Charles. "Aunt Anne," he called as he ran toward the sofa, "I am hungry."

"I am busy with your brother," she explained in an even voice. "Please ask Jemima to prepare you something, Walter."

The use of her father's name for the child piqued Frederick's curiosity, and he turned to take a look at the boy, Sir Walter's namesake. He was a remarkably stout, forward child of two years, and Frederick thought the boy would never be handsome. *How ironic that will be for Sir Walter!* he thought, chuckling with the idea. *The man will blame the mix of the Musgrove heritage for any inadequacies the boy possesses.*

"But I want *you* to get it, Aunt Anne." The child began to pull at her hands to try to get her to leave his brother.

She worked his chubby hands free from her sleeve. "You must wait, then, Walter, until I finish helping Little Charles."

"I want to play," the boy whined. "Come play with me." Again, he latched onto her arm and pulled with all his might. Anne had to catch her weight with her hand or be pulled over.

"Walter, that is no way to get me to play with you. If you wait until your mother comes down with Aunt Henrietta and Aunt Louisa, I will happily take you outside to play, but I cannot leave your brother unattended." She spoke close to the child's face.

The boy stamped his feet, demanding that she do as he said. Frederick thought the child looked like Sir Walter after all. "I want to play now!" he ordered while hopping onto her back.

"Get down, Walter," she insisted, pushing him successfully away.

Just as she turned back to the invalid, Little Walter had the great pleasure of getting upon her back again. "Get up, Horsey," he called close to her ear as he kicked Anne in the side. His arms clutched about her neck.

"Walter," she said more determinedly, "get down this moment. You are extremely troublesome. I am very angry with you."

"Leave her alone, Walter," Little Charles warned from his position. "Papa will be mad at you if you do not get down."

"Walter," cried Charles Hayter, "why do you not do as you are bid? Do you not hear your aunt speak? Come to me, Walter; come to cousin Charles."

Frederick waited for Charles Hayter to take some sort of action; after all, he was family and could step in to discipline the child if necessary. The boy obviously hurt Anne, as he continued to kick her in the side, pretending she was a pony to be ridden. She pushed at the child, ordering him to let her go. Hayter watched her struggle for a few moments and then returned to the paper. Frederick wanted to throttle the man. He did not know who needed a thrashing more—the child or Charles Hayter.

Anne bowed with the boy's weight upon her back and the strength of his grip about her neck. She struggled to remain upright, but the child's continued high-spirited wrangling forced her to her hands and knees. Frederick could take no more; he would not watch her fight the humiliation of what life held for her.

Before he thought what he did, he caught the boy by the nape of the neck with one hand, while prying away his arms from Anne's neck with the other. He spun around and forcibly placed the boy in a nearby chair. A warning stare told the child not to even consider moving. Then he advanced quietly to where Anne rested on her knees. Silently, he leaned down and offered his hand. Unsteadily, she placed her delicate fingers in his gloved hand and rose to her feet. She never raised her eyes to him nor did she thank him; it was not necessary between them. He had witnessed her mortification; Frederick would not amplify that with his words of concern. She nodded slightly and returned to her place by the boy on the sofa. A silence as thick as overstuffed upholstery hung between them.

Frederick moved a chair next to Little Walter. Using the tone he might use to demand obedience from his crew, he leaned down to look in the child's face. "A gentleman *never* hurts a lady."

Hayter lowered his paper and reprimanded the boy also. "You ought to have minded *me*, Walter; I told you not to tease your aunt." With an obvious look of regret that Frederick did what he ought to have done himself, he buried his face behind the paper once more.

Frederick saw the boy's face twist in a pretense of crying. Whispering to the child, he kept up his warning: "Do not cry, Boy, unless you are truly sorry for what you do. A man must protect the women in his house; they will love and protect him in return." He gave a level, cautionary look to the boy. "I would be most displeased to know you hurt your Aunt Anne again. Do you understand me, Walter?"

"Yes, Sir," the child's lower lip trembled, and he squirmed uncomfortably in his chair.

"Before you go to bed this evening, you will apologize to your aunt. Do I make myself clear, Child?" His words were spoken so softly anyone watching them would think he shared secrets to a buried treasure with the boy.

"Yes, Sir."

Clearing his throat audibly, Frederick took the child's hand. "Let us find your nurse," he said loud enough for the room to hear. "She will find you something to eat while you wait for your mother to come downstairs." He walked the child to the door and motioned for his nurse to take him. That done, Frederick returned to the silence of the window. Anne's soft song to the child as she massaged his legs underlined the regret they all felt.

A few minutes later, Mary Musgrove and her husband's sisters swept into the room. "Oh, Captain Wentworth," Mary called as he bowed, "we did not realize you waited upon us, did we Henrietta?" Mary was discreetly maneuvering the girl toward Frederick when she spotted Charles Hayter rising from the chair in the far corner of the room. "Cousin Charles," she said as she flicked a wrist in his direction, "you are here, too." Hayter greeted them all while eyeing Henrietta. "Please have a seat, Captain. Let me send for tea." Mary seated herself close to the hearth, where she could rule over the room. Henrietta looked divided—she knew not to whom she should show her notice. "Henrietta, tell the Captain what we decided to do for the holiday wardrobes."

Henrietta turned to speak to Frederick. As she did, Hayter moved forward to interrupt. "Henrietta, might I speak to you privately?"

"Of—Of course, Charles," she stumbled through the words. Then she turned to leave the room, and he followed her toward the garden.

"Well," Mary said with disgust. "I never saw such rudeness! But what is one to expect from those at Winthrop! He did not even pay proper due to those of us in the room."

"Mary," Anne interrupted Mary's censure of Charles Hayter, "I will leave Little Charles in your care and check on Walter." Without waiting for her sister's agreement, she slipped from the room.

Frederick's eyes followed her. Like a child picking at a sore place, he needed to know she did not suffer from her predicament. "I came to walk you back to the Great House, Miss Musgrove." He forced a smile to his face as he finally turned to Louisa.

"Thank you, Captain." Louisa stepped forward to take his proffered arm. She smiled up at him with anticipation. "You will join us for dinner, will you not?"

"It would be my honor, Miss Musgrove." After the histrionics of the past few minutes, Frederick allowed his body to relax into his quickly developing familiarity with Louisa Musgrove's flirtation. "If you are ready, we will set off."

"Indeed, I am, Captain."

★ ★ ★

"Should we let him stretch his legs?" Dr. Laraby asked as he swung into the cabin, making his morning call on Frederick Wentworth.

Anne Wentworth laughed lightly. "I am not sure the man appreciates our efforts." While the doctor busied himself opening his bag, she turned her head and murmured to Frederick, "You spoke to Louisa in your dreams." An amused smile flitted across her face. She watched distress creep into his demeanor.

"I never thought of Louisa like that," he whispered so only she could hear. Anne moved to sit on the edge of his bed, leaning close to him. "I love only you, Anne."

"I know that, Frederick. I did not think you regretted our union. You allow me to be me—all my insecurities—all my strengths. You accept them all and love me for them. A man who gives such freedom to a woman does not dream of another."

"I dreamed of finding *you* again; that is why I spoke to Louisa in the dream. But she and James were meant to be, as were you and I."

Anne smiled and said more loudly, "I will leave you alone with the doctor."

"Do not be gone long." He grabbed at her hand as she started away. "I miss you when you are not near."

"You cannot be rid of me that easily," she teased again. "You may count on that, my Love."

"I always count on your affections, Anne." He leaned back heavily against the pillow.

"Then do what the doctor suggests. Come back to me; I need you as you need me." She squeezed his hand before slipping out of the room.

Laraby took her place by Frederick's bed. "Let me see this wound," he murmured as he moved Frederick's nightshirt aside. "I believe we might need to drain this one—the exit wound on the side. Infection seems to be a possibility." He worked the bandage loose. "You must be rubbing it somehow as you sleep; it looks raw." He pushed against the opening, forcing the skin together and squeezed the pus from around the stitches while Frederick gritted his teeth. "I will clean this with soap and water when we are finished. A tincture should heal it up soon enough. We will use leeches if we need to—if the circulation becomes a problem."

"None of those nasty things if you please," Frederick protested. "How uncivilized are you, Laraby?"

"You may think the use of some ancient ways uncivilized, Wentworth, where I see medicine from the ancient cultures the basis of civilization. I have seen the healing ways of leeches and snake venom and Chinese ginseng and many other folk remedies. I will use any restorative that cures my patients without regard to what propriety says is proper." Laraby began to rebind the wound, making sure the bandages were tighter than before. "I do not want you pulling this open when you walk today. I will call Avendale and Harwood. They are becoming quite adept at handling your bulk as you maneuver across this room."

"When might I go up on deck? This room and this bunk seem to have shrunk since my men carried me in here." Frederick pushed up on his forearms before pivoting his legs to hang off the edge of the bed.

"Not for a few more days," Laraby cautioned him. "First you must get rid of the infection."

"This room has become my prison, Laraby," he said heavily. "But I will follow your orders." Frederick planted his feet soundly on the floor and stood on his own. Yet, he waited for his crewmen before he attempted a step forward. He no longer clung to their shoulders or dragged his feet along the worn boards. Now, he used their arms for balance, and he lifted his feet gingerly.

★ ★ ★

"Making progress, I see," Anne said cheerfully as she posed in the door of his cabin.

"I weave about almost as much as Benjamin driving a gig," he complained.

She stepped into the room. "I recall you once placed me in Benjamin's gig and left me to his care." Anne straightened the bed linens as he made his last tour of the room.

He looked over his shoulder at her. "You were exhausted, and you staggered as much as I do now. It was either Benjamin's gig, or I would have had to carry you the last mile to Uppercross Cottage. At the time, Mrs. Wentworth, it would have scandalized your family and friends."

She laughed and moved the blanket back as he made his way to the bed. Moving to the far side of the room, she pretended to straighten the items on his dresser while the men helped him prop himself up in bed.

"We will return later, Captain Wentworth," Laraby called as he followed the men from the room.

"Tomorrow," Frederick said, leveling a look at the doctor.

Laraby hesitated and then nodded. "Tomorrow morning." Then he was gone.

She remained still, running her fingers over his brush and the leather strap. "Anne?" His voice came softly behind her.

She did not turn to look at him. "Yes, Frederick?"

"Lock the door, my Love, and come lie next to me."

His words sent a shiver of excitement down her back. She turned to face him, worry in her eyes. "Frederick, we cannot. It is too soon."

"It is never too soon to hold my wife—the love of my life—in my arms. I need you next to me, Anne. I will rest better with your lying alongside me where I might feel the heat of your body radiating through me."

"Frederick," she gasped, blushing profusely.

He laughed lightly. "How nice it is to see my words still affect you, my Dear." Then he suddenly quieted, revealing his lack of confidence. "You will lie with me, Sweetling?"

She smiled and moved to lock the door. "I will lie with you, Frederick." Her eyes darkened with a passion he recognized only as being for him.

"Only your chemise, Anne." She reached back to undo the buttons of her gown, never taking her eyes from him. She let it drop from her shoulders to the floor before stepping out of it. Then she slipped under the blanket and turned into his embrace. He kissed the top of her head as he reached for the pins holding her hair. "You are beautiful, my Love." He cupped her chin and brought her mouth to his for a long, lingering kiss.

"I should chastise you, Frederick." She snuggled in closer to him. "You accused me once of not being a good walker. I was offended then. I remain offended." Her voice taunted, but her fingertips stroked his jawline.

"But I never said any such thing!" he protested. "I simply wanted to protect the woman I loved. At any rate, my Darling, that was a long time ago." He kissed her again, this time with more fervor.

CHAPTER 8

When in disgrace with Fortune and men's eyes,
I all alone beweep my outcast state,
And trouble deaf heaven with my bootless cries,
And look upon myself and curse my fate.
—William Shakespeare, "Sonnet 29"

"*Why* do you suppose I am not a good walker?" Mary bemoaned the obvious ruse of Louisa and Henrietta to be rid of her.

"We will take a *long* walk—a very *long* walk."

"I should like to join you very much; I am exceedingly fond of a long walk." Mary insisted. Anne tried to dissuade Mary from going, but in vain; and that being the case, thought it best to accept the Misses Musgrove's much more cordial invitation to herself to go likewise.

About the same time, Frederick and Charles Musgrove returned from their hunt. They took out a young dog, who spoilt their sport, and sent them back early.

"I wonder of what Mary complains," Charles grumbled upon hearing her shrill voice from the entranceway.

"I cannot imagine why they should suppose I should not like a long walk!" she complained to Anne as they made their way up the stairs. "Everybody is always supposing I am not a good walker! And yet they would not be pleased if we refused to join them. When people come in this manner on purpose to ask us, how can one say no?" She continued her lament as Charles and Frederick entered the passageway leading to the private quarters.

Frederick watched as Charles and Anne glanced at each other and discreetly rolled their eyes before moving away to their own diversions. Surprisingly, Frederick found himself jealous of the private moment and of the intimate understanding they shared.

98

"Captain Wentworth," Louisa called when she spotted him through the Cottage's open window. "It is such a very fine November day," she said as she approached, "that Henrietta and I propose to take a long walk. Would you consider joining us?"

"What do you say, Charles? Do you have the time and the strength and the spirit to accompany the ladies on their journey?" Frederick noticed Anne's countenance changed, as if she wished to retract her agreement to walk out with them. *Does she wish not to be in my company?* He tried to read her reaction. He wanted to see her eyes; they spoke the truth even when her words did not.

"I believe I am exactly ready for this walk," Charles Musgrove added quickly. With that, all six set forward together in the direction chosen by the Misses Musgrove, who evidently considered the walk as under their guidance.

Frederick walked with Louisa and Henrietta, but his thoughts dwelled on Anne. As always, she lagged behind the others, placing herself in a subservient position, allowing the others to take precedence over her. In reality, he should be walking with her; as the elder Elliot, she was the highest-ranking woman in the party and should assume her rightful place. His hand still burned from touching her; it was a week, but he could still feel it in his fingertips and his palm. Instinctively, he started to raise his arm to look at his hand, to discover the source of the sensation still lingering there, but, instead, he clenched it, fisting it at his side. To him, the fist represented the pain of their separation and the anger he felt at her rejection. It also represented his anger with her for allowing her own degradation. Heaven help him, he could not stand by and see her suffer so.

Louisa prattled on about inconsequential things as she walked beside him. He remarked to himself how quickly they all moved to an intimate footing. He wondered whether he should continue to pursue these relationships. Frederick considered himself to be emotionally damaged. If he were to choose one of the Musgrove girls as his wife, he would periodically be thrown together with Anne. Treating one of the Misses Musgrove with respect and regard as his wife, while Anne looked on, no longer seemed appealing. *Could I hurt her that way? Could I even bring myself to touch another woman with Anne so much on my mind?* Maybe if she chose another, his conscience would be clearer—but, no; that would not make him happy either. Perhaps he should move up the date when he would leave Kellynch and move on to visit Edward and his brother's new wife. He needed to remove himself from Anne. He needed to be away from her and decide what he must do about her. *Sorry* was the hardest word he knew, and lately sorry was all he felt. They were beyond talking about their situation. Neither of them, he was sure, could muster the desire to examine what they had once had.

Louisa put forth for his notice once again. "It is a beautiful day, is it not, Captain?"

He looked about, forcing his attention to the scenery and to the girl walking beside him. "What glorious weather for the Admiral and my sister!" he responded. "They meant to take a long drive this morning; perhaps we may hail them from some of these hills. They talked of coming into this side of the country. I wonder whereabouts they will upset today. Oh! It does happen very often, I assure you—but my sister makes nothing of it—she would as lieve be tossed out as not."

"Ah! You make the most of it, I know," cried Louisa, "but if it were really so, I should do just the same in her place. If I loved a man as she loves the Admiral, I would be always with him, nothing should ever separate us, and I would rather be overturned by him, than driven safely by anybody else." She blushed prettily after her speech.

He knew she only said what she thought he wanted to hear; women placated to men in such a way. *Yet, why not continue the flirtation?* he thought. *What else is there for me here?* "Had you?" cried he, catching the same tone. "I honor you!" Unfortunately, Louisa's words brought him back to Anne; she had allowed others to *separate* them. *Anne Elliot weighs entirely too much on my mind.*

"Is not this one of the ways to Winthrop?" he heard Anne ask; but nobody else heard, or, at least, nobody answered her. Her insignificance reigned; no one except him attended to her musings; and he had no idea whether Winthrop was near or not, nor did he wish to discuss the question with her. At the time, he knew not whether Winthrop was the predetermined destination of the Miss Musgroves, but after another half mile of gradual ascent through large enclosures, where the ploughs at work, and the fresh-made path spoke the farmer, counteracting the sweets of poetical despondence, and meaning to have spring again, they gained the summit of the most considerable hill, which parted Uppercross and Winthrop, and soon commanded a full view of the latter, at the foot of the hill on the other side. Winthrop, without beauty and without dignity, was stretched before them—an indifferent house, standing low, and hemmed in by the barns and buildings of a farmyard.

He heard Mary exclaim in disgust, "Bless me! Here is Winthrop—I declare I had no idea!—Well, now I think we had better turn back; I am excessively tired."

Frederick felt the tension that gathered in the air upon Mary's exclamation. A family drama was about to play out in front of him. He turned his back on the scene, trying to distance himself from the emotions. He noticed, out of the corner of his eye, that Anne, too, seemed to hold back. Perhaps she wanted to say something sensible to her younger sister, but she stared off at the view.

"No," declared Charles Musgrove to his wife's avowal.

Louisa pulled Henrietta aside before she added her own, "No, no."

"We are this close," Charles pleaded, "and I will do what is proper—what is my duty—and call upon my aunt. Mama would be terribly upset if I did not. You will accompany me, Mary." The statement came out as a plea for her acquiesces.

"I will not go, Charles." Her audience strengthened Mary's resolve.

"You may rest at Winthrop for a quarter hour while I pay my respects," her husband reasoned.

Mary spoke regally, "Oh! No, indeed!—Walking up that hill again would do me more harm than any sitting down would do me good. I will not go."

After a little succession of these sorts of debates and consultations, Charles and his sisters decided that he and Henrietta, should just run down for a few minutes to see their aunt and cousins, while the rest of the party waited for them at the top of the hill. Frederick disapproved of how easily Charles Musgrove gave in to his wife's lamentations. Personally, he would not tolerate such silliness from the woman he married.

At first, it appeared Louisa would accompany her siblings to the estate house, but she soon turned back to where he stood. Frederick allowed himself a moment of relief, having panicked at being alone with Anne and her sister and having to make conversation in the absence of the others.

Only Mary was serene. Finally settling herself on a comfortable seat on the step of a stile, she took the opportunity of looking scornfully around her and of saying to him, "It is very unpleasant, having such connections! But I assure you, I have never been in the house above twice in my life!"

Mary Elliot Musgrove treated the Hayters the way Sir Walter had treated him—and the way she—the way they all—treated her own sister. All he could offer her was an artificial assenting smile, followed by a contemptuous glance, as he turned away. If he spoke to her at that moment, Mrs. Charles Musgrove would know his wrath.

Luckily, Louisa reached him at that time. "Captain, let us glean some nuts in the hedgerows while we wait." As he walked away, he heard Anne trying to soothe Mary's discontent. How he hated Anne being in such a position! It gnawed at him excessively.

Yet, he tried to give Louisa the attention she deserved. Forcing his conversation, he acknowledged, "That was quite a scene of *domestic tranquility.*"

"My brother Charles is too kind to his wife," she noted as she reached for a low-hanging branch. "Mary lords her heritage over all of us. It riles me to see her trying to supplant Mama in her own house by taking Mama's seat at the table."

"I assume your sister planned to come here today." The reasons for Charles Hayter's disdain became clearer.

"Henrietta and Cousin Charles have a long-standing affection for each other. Of late, there was some doubt on both their parts. We resolved that she would speak to him today." Frederick smiled. It seemed Henrietta Musgrove had given Frederick over to her sister; Frederick now understood the lay of the land.

They walked on in silence for a few minutes, pausing occasionally to pick the hazelnuts still remaining on the trees. Frederick finally noted, "It appeared for a few minutes that your sister would acquiesce to Mrs. Charles's demands."

Louisa looked at him incredulously. "I made her go, you know. I could not bear she should be frightened from the visit by such nonsense. What!—Would I be turned back from doing a thing I was determined to do, and I knew to be right, by the airs and interference of such a person?—Or, of any person I may say. No—I have no idea of being so easily persuaded. When I make up my mind, I make it. And Henrietta seemed entirely to make up hers to call on Winthrop today—and yet, she was as near giving it up, out of nonsensical complaisance!"

Frederick remembered how Anne had turned to Lady Russell for counsel, and how that woman destroyed his hopes for marriage to Anne by not supporting her godchild. Would his life have been different if Anne had a sister possessing Louisa's sensibilities? He mused aloud, "She would have turned back then, but for you?"

"She would indeed. I am almost ashamed to say it." Louisa met his eyes and gave him a bold triumphant look.

Moved by his thoughts of what might have been with Anne, Frederick spoke from his heart. "Happy for her, to have such a mind as yours at hand!—After the hints you gave just now, which did but confirm my own observations, the last time I was in company with him, I need not affect to have no comprehension of what is going on. I see more than a mere dutiful morning visit to your aunt was in question—and woe betide him, and her too, when it comes to things of consequence, when they are placed in circumstances, requiring fortitude and strength of mind, if she have not resolution enough to resist idle interference in such a trifle as this. Your sister is an amiable creature, but *yours* is the character of decision and firmness, I see. If you value her conduct or happiness, infuse as much of your own spirit into her, as you can. But this, no doubt, you have always done. It is the worst evil of too yielding and indecisive a character, that no influence over it can be depended on.—You are never sure of a good impression being durable. Everybody may sway it; let those who would be happy be firm." He was wrapped up in his fervor—all the memories of how Anne had dashed his plans by succumbing to Lady Russell's advice occupied his mind. It did not occur to him that his words would encourage Louisa's regard. He praised her for her resolve, not for herself, but as an example of what he wished for Anne.

He was on a roll—he had kept these thoughts secret for so long—he could not hide his passion. Frederick finally had a chance to speak his regrets out loud. "Here is a nut," said he, catching one down from an upper bough. "To exemplify—a beautiful glossy nut, which, blessed with original strength, outlived all the storms of autumn. Not a puncture, not a weak spot anywhere.—This nut," he continued, with playful solemnity, "while so many of its brethren fell and were trodden underfoot, is still in possession of all the happiness a hazelnut can be supposed capable of." Then returning to his former earnest tone, "My first wish for all, whom I am interested in is they should be firm. If Louisa Musgrove would be beautiful and happy in her November of life, she will cherish all her present powers of mind."

Finished, he waited for Louisa to respond—waited for her confirmation or her refutation of what he said, but he remained unanswered. She reacted to the serious warmth of his tone, but Frederick realized she did not have much depth of understanding of the analogy he made. If he chose Louisa as his companion, it would mean a life where no one would challenge him—no one would *see* him. Louisa would see only his role, his place in society, his accomplishments, and his wealth. Could such an existence bring him satisfaction? He dropped the nut to the ground and, not knowing what else to do, Frederick offered her his arm.

Louisa smiled up at him charmingly, and she and Frederick circled the hedgerow. They walked on in silence before they spotted Mrs. Charles sitting under a shady tree. Louisa nodded toward her brother's wife, letting her dismay show through her words. "Mary is good-natured enough in many respects, but she does sometimes provoke me excessively, by her nonsense and her pride—the Elliot pride. She has a great deal too much of the Elliot pride." Frederick silently agreed. "We do so wish Charles married Anne instead.—I suppose you know he wanted to marry Anne?"

Her words shot through Frederick. Nightmares where Anne and Charles walked away from him hand in hand had haunted him for years after the separation. He cleared his throat, and after a moment's hesitation, said, "Do you mean she refused him?"

Loving gossip, Louisa chattered on. This was a subject upon which she could speak with authority. "Oh! Yes, certainly!"

He did not want to ask the question, but he could not resist the temptation. "When did that happen?"

Louisa smiled; she was in her element. "I do not exactly know, for Henrietta and I were at school at the time; but I believe about a year before he married Mary. I wish she accepted him. We should all like Anne a great deal better; and Papa and Mama always think it was her great friend Lady Russell's doing, that she did not—they think Charles not to be learned and bookish enough to please Lady Russell, and that, therefore, she persuaded Anne to refuse him."

Lady Russell again, Frederick thought. *The woman, obviously, played a role in Anne's current state.* Frederick was now under the persuasion to believe that in the name of love, she single-handedly ruined Anne's chances of happiness on two separate occasions. How could the woman refuse Charles Musgrove as a legitimate suitor? He was amiable and kind, and, more importantly, he could give Anne a fine estate in the country. The Musgroves lacked the Elliot lineage, but they were still a dominant element in the local society. Although he hated to admit it, Charles Musgrove would have been a caring husband for *his Anne.* Perhaps—an idea ricocheted through him—perhaps it was not Lady Russell's decision.

Perhaps—Anne—*his Anne*—had refused Charles Musgrove because of Frederick. She would have been one and twenty by then. She would have been of age. *Is it possible?* He had often wondered whether, if he had come to her in '08, before he took the *Laconia,* if she would have left with him then. These facts suggested that perhaps—perhaps she would have.

He needed time alone to consider this possibility, so Frederick was happy to see their whole party being immediately afterwards collected and once more in motion together. Charles Hayter, as expected, returned with Musgrove and Henrietta. This time he shook hands with Frederick—evidently, there was a withdrawing on the gentleman's side and a relenting on the lady's, and they were now very glad to be together again. They were devoted to each other almost from the first instant of their all setting forward for Uppercross.

As he had been spending time with both ladies equally, Henrietta's silent declaration for Charles Hayter left everyone to assume Louisa now marked him for her own. *Nothing can be plainer to them all, including Anne,* he thought. How could he renew his addresses to Anne if she thought he favored another? And did he want to renew his addresses? He walked beside Louisa, but his heart took another path. Suddenly, every fiber of his being became aware of Anne. She was tired enough to be very glad of Charles Musgrove's arm, and Frederick wished it was he to whom she turned.

They crossed a long strip of meadowland—forming distinct parties: Charles Hayter and Henrietta, he and Louisa, Anne and Mary and sometimes Charles Musgrove. Louisa continued to chatter on about the things that interested girls, but her words meant little to him. He responded automatically, allowing her to think as she would. He should distance himself, but that was impossible now; it would have to wait until the next time.

"Catch me!" Louisa demanded as usual, once she climbed to the top of the stile. He did so, but tried to set her some distance away from him when her feet touched the ground again. She purposely clung to his lapels longer than necessary, and he gently removed her hands before offering her his arm. Before, he had welcomed her interest, but now he saw how he must find a way to curtail her ardor.

The long meadow bordered a lane, which their footpath, at the end of it, was to cross. When the party all reached the gate of exit, they heard a carriage advancing in the same direction and looked up to see Admiral Croft's gig. Benjamin and Sophia had taken their intended drive and were returning home.

"How far did you walk, Frederick?" his sister inquired once they stopped.

He added casually, "The nearly two miles to Winthrop and back, I suppose."

"Two miles!" Sophia exclaimed. "Please let us offer one of the ladies a ride back to Uppercross."

"My sister will share her seat with any lady who might be particularly tired," Frederick announced to the group.

Henrietta would not leave Charles Hayter. "It is less than a mile," she pointed out brightly.

Louisa asserted, "I am not tired in any way!"

"I am fine," Mary said, a little sullenly.

Frederick knew Sophia had offended Mrs. Charles by not asking *her* to ride before any of the *others*. He overheard Louisa whisper close by to Hayter, "Mary would not make a third in a one-horse chaise. It is not grand enough for her."

At that moment, Frederick saw Anne struggling over the stile between two fields. Without thinking, he walked quickly to the carriage; he leaned in to speak to his sister before he could change his mind.

"What is it, Frederick?" Sophia looked around at the walking party crossing the lane and clamoring over an opposite stile.

"Take Miss Anne," he whispered in her ear.

Sophia shot him a look of concern. "Are you sure, Frederick? You will center your attention on her?" She spoke so softly no one could hear.

"I have never been more sure of anything." They kept their counsel close and secret.

Sophia nodded and then raised her head to call out, "Miss Anne, I am sure *you* are tired. Do let us have the pleasure of taking you home. Here is excellent room for three, I assure you. If we were all like you, I believe we might sit four.—You must, indeed, you must."

Anne was still in the lane and instinctively started to decline. "I assure you, Mrs. Croft, I am well."

"Please, Miss Anne, humor an old man. You must let us be of service to you." The Admiral's kind urgency came in support of his wife's.

"That is very kind—" Frederick heard Anne begin, but he did not let her finish. He turned to her and quietly obliged her to be assisted into the carriage. One hand rested at the small of her back, and the other held hers tightly as he directed her to the gig and helped her up the step. Beside it, he turned her to him and placed his hands at her waist.

"Frederick?" her mouth moved to say the word, but no sound came out.

A slight smile turned up the corners of his mouth. "Anne," he whispered close to her hair as he lifted her to the seat. Quickly, he looked away to lessen the attention of his actions. He watched his family compress themselves into the smallest possible space to leave her a corner. He did it. She was in the carriage, and he placed her there; his will and his hands did it. He had recognized her fatigue when the others did not, and he had resolved to give her rest. This little circumstance seemed the completion of all that had gone on before. He understood her. He could not forgive her—but he could not be unfeeling. Though condemning her for the past, still he could not see her suffer without the desire of giving her relief. It was, he told himself, the remainder of former sentiment; it was an impulse of pure, though unacknowledged, friendship. Emotions of compounded pleasure and pain still prevailed.

"Walk on." The Admiral clucked his tongue to encourage the

horse. Frederick stepped to the side to let them pass, and then he walked back to where the others stood. He chose not to turn around and acknowledge the pull Anne's presence had on him. If he looked back, he would likely chase down the gig, take her in his arms, and demand she love him once again. Instead, he fell into place beside Louisa to finish their walk to Uppercross Cottage. Maybe when they arrived, he would see Anne again before he returned to Kellynch. Maybe he could speak to her at last without the hurt crowding his heart.

★ ★ ★

"What happened today, Brother?" Sophia asked as they sat together in the library after supper. "With Miss Anne, that is." He knew she would ask eventually and wondered why she waited so long.

Frederick looked up from his book and feigned disinterest. "There is nothing to explain; Miss Anne appeared exhausted; I recognized her need." He turned his attention to the military history volume he grasped loosely in one hand.

Sophia paused before adding. "I observed your exchange with Miss Anne. The others could not see because they were on the far side of the road, but I saw, Frederick."

"Leave it, Sophia," he warned.

"Benjamin and I thought you to be interested in the Misses Musgrove," she mused. His only response was a raised eyebrow; otherwise, he did not even raise his head. "The Admiral told Miss Anne of our abbreviated courtship, claiming that is the way of sailors."

That captured his interest. "What was Miss Anne's opinion of your conjectures?"

"She spoke little, but she made herself clear. The woman holds you in some regard. How long have you loved her?"

He frowned. "I shall not honor that question with a response."

Sophia laughed out loud. "That long, eh?"

"Please do not vocalize your unfounded theory, even to the Admiral. Rumors spread quickly in country society." Frederick closed his book and walked to the fireplace, leaning his arm and forehead on the mantel as he stared into the flame.

"I do not wish to see you hurt, Frederick," she observed with a sigh. "But I will leave your heart to its own devices."

"Then you need to look the other way, Sophia. My heart is fairly bruised and battered already." With that, he strode from the room, leaving her to imagine the worst.

★ ★ ★

Mr. Steventon, the estate butler, tapped on the door of the morning room. Upon entering, he presented a silver salver to Frederick. "A letter for you, Captain."

Frederick took the thickly folded missive from the tray. "Thank you, Mr. Steventon," he murmured.

"Who is it, Frederick?" the Admiral called from his end of the table.

Frederick turned the bundle over in his hand, looking at the post. "The letter has been to Plymouth and back," he said. "It is from Captain Harville."

"Open it, open it, Man; tell us where he has settled," the Admiral said impatiently.

Frederick broke the wax seal to open the three pages that were from Harville but written in Milly's hand. He sat quietly for a few minutes, perusing the first page. "Thomas has settled with his family at Lyme for the winter."

"Really?" Sophia commented. "That is not far from here."

Frederick spoke his thoughts aloud. "How far, do you suppose?"

Sophia looked to Benjamin for specifics. "I would say a little short of twenty miles—by the sea—Lyme is a great port; Harville will like it there."

Frederick's eyebrows contracted as he frowned. "What is it, Dear?" Sophia asked.

He still held the letter in front of him. "Milly Harville wrote a few lines regarding Thomas's deteriorating condition. He has not been in good health since receiving that severe wound to his leg two years ago." His jaw took on a hard line. He stood quickly and announced, "I believe I will go upstairs and pack a bag; I will ride to Lyme today if neither of you have an objection to my borrowing one of the horses again."

"Of course not, Frederick," the Admiral assured him. "Stay a day or two with your old friend."

"Friends," Frederick corrected him. "It seems Captain James Benwick has taken up residence with the Harvilles. He still grieves for Fanny Harville, no doubt, and finds solace in her brother's home."

The Admiral stepped into the hallway, and Sophia caught Frederick's hand before he left the morning room. She spoke in a low voice. "Being away from Uppercross for a few days—placing distance between yourself and those in attendance there—is probably for the best—it will give you time to think."

"It will be what it will be, Sophia. I cannot manipulate it through my own will." He leaned down to kiss her cheek. "I will see you in a few days, my Dear."

CHAPTER 9

He who binds to himself a joy
Does the winged life destroy;
But he who kisses the joy as it flies
Lives in Eternity's sun rise.
—William Blake, "Eternity"

Milly Harville opened the door to her cottage. "Frederick Wentworth, as I live and breathe!" she said as she embraced him. "Do come in," she said, ushering him into a living room. "Thomas will be delighted to see you; he longs for your company. You received his letter?"

"I did." Frederick shot a quick look about the room, taking in its sparse furnishings.

She followed his eyes with hers. "It is not much, but I insisted we economize until Thomas can find steady work." She gestured toward a comfortable chair while taking his hat and greatcoat.

"There is no need to explain, Milly." Frederick took the seat to which she indicated.

"I do not mind. You are Thomas's closest friend." She seated herself across from him. "Thomas will arrive at any moment, and you should know how things are before he does."

"I am your servant, Milly." Frederick took a second, longer look at their surroundings. "Tell me what I need to know; you must not stand on ceremony with me."

"Things have gone poorly for Thomas; a bad investment took a large chunk of his savings, plus his leg injury keeps him from productive work." Her words struck Frederick as if something had sucked the air from his lungs. "Of course, Thomas's generous nature did not keep him from denying family and friends their loans. We are not destitute, but unless things change we could soon be."

"But Thomas took nearly ten thousand pounds with him when he left the service!" The concept of his friend losing so much astounded Frederick.

"I understand your dismay," she spoke softly. "Thomas never admits his weaknesses."

Before they could say more, they heard male voices in the entryway. Both stood to greet the men. "Thomas," Milly said as she rushed forward to take her husband's hand and to discreetly offer him steadiness as he stepped into the room, "look who came to visit!"

"Wentworth!" he exclaimed. "You were in my thoughts lately, and now you are in front of me." Harville embraced his old friend.

"Your letter found me, at last." Frederick teased with a grinned. "Actually, I am with Sophia and the Admiral in Somerset—twenty miles from here."

"You are so close!" Milly grabbed at his hands. "I did not realize."

Harville stepped to the side to allow the other man access to his guest. "Hello, Frederick," James Benwick said as he stepped forward.

"Benwick, I did not realize you were with Thomas until I received his letter."

James Benwick shot a quick glance at Harville. "Thomas shows me a great kindness."

They shook hands as Milly began to hustle them into the room. "Come now," Milly encouraged, "let me find us all some tea and cakes. Thomas, would you check on the children before you sit down?" She rushed toward the kitchen.

"I will see to the children," Benwick supplied. "Join Wentworth by the fire, Thomas."

"Thank you, Benwick."

Thomas Harville slowly lowered his bulk into a nearby chair, balancing his weight on the cane he held in his left hand. Frederick waited, anticipating Thomas's need for support, before he resettled himself in an accompanying chair. "I am so pleased to see you at last, Wentworth," Harville sighed deeply with relief as he settled his limbs into the comfort of the cushions. "I have missed your dry wit. Benwick is not much of a conversationalist; what attracted my sister Fanny to him I will never understand."

"Love is not to be understood," Frederick mumbled in response. "Benwick has an intellectual attractiveness, and as I recall your dear Fanny could masquerade as a bluestocking if she came from more austere roots. She read voraciously; Fanny and James found a companionable peace in each other," Frederick remarked. "That is a rare thing."

Harville looked off, as if seeing Fanny's face in his memory. "She possessed such a joy for living. Sometimes it is hard for me to believe she is no longer with us." With a slight shake of his head, he slowly returned his attention to his friend.

"How goes it with Benwick?" Frederick asked, letting his voice drop in case the man was close at hand.

Thomas glanced toward the door leading to the second story. "His sadness is intense." Harville searched for the right words. "He was always so bookish—depending on someone else's words to express his emotions so he does not say much. Milly and I agreed he should be with us. I feared, at first, that he might try to find a watery grave and join Fanny for an eternity. I see some improvement since he came to us—I think the children bring him a quiet joy—but he needs so much more than what we can give him. He needs to find an occupation or a hobby or an interest to distract his mind—something besides the volumes of poetry he reads incessantly."

Frederick nodded. "When I delivered the news of Fanny's passing, I never saw such anguish in a man's face. For two days, Benwick sat at a table—unmoving. No words—no tears—no anger—nothing! He turned everything inward—his grief filled him. He took to his bed for days; and then one day he took a step back to life. James returned to his duties, but even a casual observer could see he did so out of routine; his passion left him."

"He privately shared that he would not have survived the news if you had not been with him." Harville shook his head.

"A man like Benwick—a thinking man, a reading man—does not soon forget the woman he loved." Wentworth whispered, as images of Anne Elliot crept into his psyche. Even with all the years, he could not erase her from his mind.

"Nature surely played a foul trick on him and my sister." Harville stretched out his leg to relieve the stiffness seeping into his joints. "It was ironic that just as Benwick earned enough money to give Fanny a life of leisure, the good Lord took her away."

"Indeed." Frederick thought about the fortune he now possessed and realized, like Benwick, *he* did not have his love in his life. Anne owned his heart. Perhaps she always would. Could he consider moving on with someone else? Should he try to rekindle what they once had? If he knew she would welcome his attentions, he might be able to forgive her. But he was not certain he could survive if she turned him away again. Maybe he should begin to show her his true feelings in little ways, like he did with the Admiral's gig the other day, and see how she responded. If positive, he would risk it all—he would make Anne his.

"Are you enjoying your stay with your sister and the Admiral, Wentworth?" Thomas asked.

Frederick smiled. "Sophia and the Admiral are excellent hosts. Except for the occasional hints about marriage, it has been a pleasant sojourn. I still plan to visit Edward and his new wife in Shropshire soon."

"Your sister believes all naval men to be like the Admiral." Thomas chuckled. "Not all are as needy as he."

Frederick laughed lightly. "The Admiral is an astute military man, but he concedes other points in his life to Sophia. They complement each other well."

"Does Sophia wish you to return to the love you left behind in Somerset eight years ago?" Harville watched Wentworth's face for a reaction.

"*Nothing* happened in Somerset eight years ago!" Frederick said with a little more frustration than he cared to display.

"That is what your words always say, Wentworth, but your face tells another story. However, you are entitled to keep your secrets. How long can you stay? Please tell me it will be an extended visit."

"I am to disappoint you then; I have previous engagements at the end of the week, but your letter compelled me to come immediately. I return to Kellynch Hall late tomorrow."

Thomas looked dissatisfied. "I suppose we will make do."

Milly Harville entered the room at that instant, carrying a tray of teacups and a plate of finger cakes. "I hope you stay for supper, Captain Wentworth," she offered as she placed the tray on a low table.

"I will, Milly." Wentworth smiled up at her. "But I insist the Harville family and Captain Benwick be my guests at the inn. It will be my pleasure to give you an evening away from the kitchen."

"That will not be necessary, Captain," she protested.

"Milly, I did not say it was *necessary*. I said it would be my *pleasure* to entertain you for a change." Frederick turned to his friend. "Tell her, Thomas—remind your wife how often over the years she took care of you and me when we were deep in our cups. She deserves an evening without waiting on the two of us."

Thomas Harville let his eyes drift slowly over Milly, caressing her with his smile. "The man is right, my Love." A note of sadness entered his words. "You deserve more from life. Let the captain thank you for being devoted to your family and friends."

Milly handed Thomas a cup of tea and spoke affectionately, "Life gave me you and the children, Thomas. I could not ask for more."

"Excellent!" said Frederick. "We will be a lively party. Let me visit the innkeeper, so he can prepare for us properly. I shall return shortly." Wentworth stood and quickly moved to the door. He looked back just in time to see Thomas Harville intertwine his fingers with his wife's and pull her onto his lap for an embrace. The domestic picture increased Frederick's loneliness—what he would not give to know Anne as his friend knew Milly.

Returning to the Harvilles' dwelling after supper, Frederick sat up late with Thomas, sipping weak ale, which he found tolerable only because of the company. "You have been quite industrious in making this place a home," Wentworth offered up a compliment. "Benwick pointed out the shelves you fashioned for his volumes of poetry; he praised you profusely for it. I see fruits of your labors spread throughout the house—a chair, a table, new netting needles and pins, the fishing net in the corner, toys for the children." Unconsciously, Frederick picked up a Jacob's Ladder left behind by Harville's daughter when Milly carried the child to bed. Instinctively, he examined the workmanship—the way the wood segments turned within the colorful grosgrain ribbon strips in an inexplicable illusion of simplicity. "I never understood how these things work," he said as he shoved the toy across the table to his friend.

Harville chortled. "You no longer possess a child's imagination, my Friend. Here, try the Bilbo Catcher instead." Thomas playfully tossed the ball attached to the string and adeptly caught it on the end of the spindle, balancing it there before releasing it to spin once again.

"You made all these?" Frederick moved to the wooden crate in the corner of the room. He took out toy after toy, laying them on the floor in front of the box, displaying a variety of cup-and-ball toys, dice games, tabletop ninepins, a whip top, solid wood grace hoops, a hammered-lead musket ball whirligig, and several peg games.

"I spoil my children the only way I can." Harville offered up a sheepish grin. "I take scraps of wood and give them a new life."

Frederick spun one of the wooden hoops on his finger before placing everything carefully back into the box. "They are incredible, Harville."

"The joy on my children's faces when I finish another design is priceless. Children are God's hope come to life—something set free—a fledgling—a seed drifting and taking roots." Harville saluted his friend with his tankard as Frederick returned to his seat. "Someday I hope to see you blessed with children, Wentworth."

Frederick picked up his drink and gulped down the last of the bitter brew. "With that," he began as he wiped his mouth with the back of his hand, "I will bid you a good night." Wentworth located his greatcoat and beaver.

"You will break your fast with us before you return to your sister's home?" Harville asked as he struggled to his feet to show

Frederick to the door.

"It would be my honor, Thomas." Having donned his outerwear, Frederick turned to his friend. They clasped hands. "I will see you early, my Friend."

"Until the morrow, then."

The next morning, Frederick reflected on his brief visit with Thomas Harville as he rode to Somersetshire. "He is blessed," he murmured as he remembered the happiness he saw in the faces of his friend's family. Contentment spread through him as he thought of finally having his own home—his own wife—his own children. Where would Anne fit into that picture? He never imagined anyone but her in his bed—at his side when he entered a room—taking meals at *his* table. Even after eight years, only *she* stirred his soul. "I must first distance myself from Louisa Musgrove. Anne must see my withdrawal for herself; otherwise, she will think I ill-used the girl to make her jealous. She must see I was never truly interested in Louisa Musgrove as a potential mate. Anne would never tolerate such abuse," he reasoned aloud.

His thoughts returned to Harville's financial straits. A seed of an idea began the previous evening as he lay on the lumpy mattress of the inn's four-poster bed. Harville's craftsmanship had been evident in each piece of furniture he had built and each toy he had made. Frederick had a plan, but he would tell no one until everything was in place. If he was right, Thomas could make a fair living with his hands. Frederick would send off a letter of inquiry as soon as he reached Kellynch.

* * *

"Wentworth," Charles Musgrove exclaimed as Frederick entered the drawing room of the Great House, "you were missed, Sir!"

"I am sorry if I caused anyone at Uppercross a moment's concern." Frederick offered his new friend a polite bow.

"I am glad to see you again," Musgrove added quickly. "I am sure the ladies will be pleased to see you as well. They are all at the Cottage. Come along." He hastened the captain toward the door. "They will have my head if I let you get away without their receiving your call."

They walked the quarter mile to the Cottage, with Musgrove prattling on about a new gun he hoped to purchase soon from a dealer in Bath. Frederick only half listened to the man. Truthfully, as much as he enjoyed Charles Musgrove's company, some days the man's obsession with hunting bored Frederick completely.

Obviously, someone in the Cottage had noted their approach because the Misses Musgrove met them in the foyer. "Captain, for shame," Louisa chastised him as she helped him to remove his coat. "You sent us no word of your withdrawal."

"I apologize for any offense, Miss Musgrove." He moved past her in his urgency to see Anne again. He could not explain it even to himself, but after viewing Thomas Harville's domestic bliss, Frederick needed to see that Anne was still there at Uppercross.

"Mrs. Musgrove," he acknowledged Mary; Anne should not feel her sister's ire because he turned to her first. Then his eyes fell on her. "Miss Anne," he said huskily as his gaze bid her eyes to meet his. "It is pleasant to see you remain at Uppercross." He could say no more, but Frederick relished the slight blush overtaking her face as she stammered her thanks.

"Have a seat, Captain." Mary gestured to several chairs grouped near the fireplace.

Frederick paused just long enough to determine where Anne planned to sit, and then he took one close to her.

"Will you tell us where you have been?" Louisa demanded as she poured tea for him.

Wentworth laughed. "My manners were poor, and I ask all of you to forgive me." He took the cup passed to him by Anne, allowing his fingers to briefly touch hers. "My closest friend sent me a letter, and I rushed off to greet him."

"One of your Navy friends?" He heard Anne's soft voice ask the question before she looked away in embarrassment.

"Captain Harville served with me for nearly eight years; he was my second in command on both the *Asp* and the *Laconia*. His letter tracked me to Plymouth and then finally to Kellynch. He is living in Lyme with his family and with another compatriot, a Captain James Benwick, who some time ago was first lieutenant of the *Laconia*. You may remember my mentioning them the night we dined with the Admiral and my sister."

"Was it not Harville's family who sparked your sister's rebukes about women aboard a ship?" Charles teased him.

"It was indeed." Wentworth made a point of catching Anne's eye. "Obviously, there was a time, I believed that women should not travel aboard a ship, but now—just a short time later, I know—I thoroughly understand how a man needs his wife with him." He hoped Anne would recognize his sincerity and would understand that his words served as a reminder of when they planned for her to sail with him as his wife; he also hoped—without much reason for the hope—that Louisa did not misinterpret his words as being meant for her.

"So you went to Lyme?" Henrietta asked as she reached for one of the apple tarts brought in by a servant.

"I did, Miss Henrietta." Frederick turned toward her. "You see, Thomas Harville suffered a leg wound in a skirmish two years ago; he continues to languish from his wound although he never complains about his fate. I went to see for myself what I could do for my friend. He lost part of the fortune he accumulated along the way; I will not allow him to withdraw from society, and I will not tolerate his decline."

"Really, Captain Wentworth, you are to be praised for your loyalty," Louisa insisted. "Yet, you must realize that Captain Harville's fate is not your responsibility."

Frederick bristled at her words; she did not understand him at all. He started to respond, but Anne found her voice first. "Louisa, I believe Captain Wentworth conveys the feelings of many men in the military. As we would rush to help someone in our own family, so would most soldiers and sailors help one another. In times of war, they learn to depend upon one another—very much like a family. Besides, as the ship's commander, and as he did with your brother, I am sure Captain Wentworth feels responsible for all those who served under him." Frederick forced the smile from his lips. He always knew Anne would comprehend his need to serve others. *God!* He wasted so many years hating her when he could have been building a family with her.

"What is Lyme like, Captain?" Henrietta asked brightly.

"It is a port city. Holiday travel to the shale beach slacks off this time of year, but I found the Cobb breathtaking in its wildness. It makes one feel very insignificant."

"I would love to walk along a beach," Louisa interjected. "It would be very adventurous to have the sea roll in around my feet." She turned to her older brother. "Charles, why do we not go to Lyme for a day trip? All of us could go, could we not?"

"How far is it to Lyme?" Henrietta questioned.

Charles Musgrove seemed to like the idea. "It is only seventeen miles—a few hours of travel—we could go in the morning and return at night. What do you say, Wentworth? Should we all go to Lyme together?"

"We would be honored to meet your friends, Captain." Louisa looked hopeful, obviously thinking his friends could be her friends some day.

"I do not like the sea," Mary grumbled. "I am sure the sea air will exacerbate my recent head cold."

"Then remain at Uppercross." Louisa's boldness silenced Mary for the time. "I am ready for a holiday; are you not, Anne?"

Anne looked away quickly. "I—I should remain behind," she stammered. "Lady Russell shall return soon, and we travel to Bath after Christmas."

"That is nonsense, Anne," Henrietta insisted. "Tell her, Charles; she must come with us."

"Of course, you must, Anne. You have done nothing but help Mary and tend to Little Charles since you came to visit. I will not hear of your remaining behind."

"It is not necessary—" she began, but Charles Musgrove would brook no dissent. Frederick let out a jagged breath. If Anne did not go to Lyme, neither would he.

Charles took charge of the arrangements. "I will arrange to use Papa's carriage for you ladies, and Wentworth and I may use the curricle."

"When shall we leave?" Louisa asked, looking pleased with herself.

Musgrove thought about what his days might hold. "I plan to shoot with Anderson tomorrow; he has a new bitch, and he wishes to see how she trees. The season is nearly over, and I do not want to miss the chance to go with him. We could go right after an early breakfast the day after tomorrow. How does that sound?"

Henrietta and Louisa loved the idea; Frederick mused that it was a good idea, but carried a large element of emotional risk. He would have a chance to speak to Anne more privately, to gauge her reaction to a renewal of his attentions. Sophia seemed to think Anne held him in some regard; he wanted to see that for himself. He would exploit every opportunity on this trip to approach Anne—to determine if she could accept him this time. If not, Frederick would be leaving for Shropshire soon; he would not offer for Louisa Musgrove.

★ ★ ★

Their first heedless scheme was to go in the morning and return at night, but to this Mr. Musgrove, for the sake of his horses, would not consent; and when it came to be rationally considered, a day in the middle of November would not leave much time for seeing a new place, after deducting seven hours, as the nature of the country required, for going and returning. They were consequently to stay the night there and not to be expected back until the next day's dinner. This was felt to be a considerable amendment; and though they all met at the Great House at rather an early breakfast hour and set off very punctually, it was so much past noon before the two carriages, Mr. Musgrove's coach containing the four ladies and Charles's curricle, in which he drove Captain Wentworth, were descending the long hill into Lyme.

"Will we never reach this God-forsaken place?" Mary moaned as the ladies' coach drew up beside her husband's two-wheeled carriage and paused before descending into the city.

Frederick heard Anne reassure her. "Not much longer; I could see the city as we circled around that last bend in the road."

Entering upon the still steeper street of the town itself, it was evident they would not have more than time for looking about them before the light and warmth of the day were gone.

"Finally," Mary grumbled as Charles helped her from the coach.

Luckily, for Frederick, he accepted first Henrietta and then Anne on his arm as they entered the inn. The innkeeper rushed forward, surprised to see Frederick again so soon. "Captain!" he cried, "you returned and brought friends." He bowed low.

"I did, Mr. Morris. I assume you can accommodate us for the evening?"

"It will be my honor, Sir. How many rooms might you require, Captain?"

Frederick quickly conferred with Charles. "Four rooms, Mr. Morris. Let us register, and then you may send your man to bring in the luggage and to tend to the horses."

"Excellent, Captain." The man ushered them forward. "If you desire anything else, you have only to ask."

"We will walk down to the beach before we lose the light, but first, we shall order supper for later. Possibly, we could have a light dinner before our walk. I am sure the ladies would enjoy some tea." Frederick beamed throughout this exchange. In reality, Mr. Morris should placate to Charles and Mary, but, he, obviously, saw Frederick as the superior member of the group. Even better, both Henrietta and Anne rested on his arms throughout the exchange. He could feel his chest fill with pride as he glanced down at Anne's soft lashes, shadowing the crest of her cheeks. Did she realize how much he still admired her and how right she felt on his arm?

After securing the accommodations and ordering their dinner, the next thing to be done was unquestionably to walk directly down to the sea. They were come too late in the year for any amusement or variety which Lyme, as a public place, might offer; the assembly rooms were shut up, and the lodgers almost all gone, scarcely any family but of the residents left—and, as there is nothing to admire in the buildings themselves, the remarkable situation of the town, the principal street almost hurrying into the water, the walk to the Cobb itself, its old wonders and new improvements, with the very beautiful line of cliffs stretching out to the east of the town, are what the stranger's eye will seek; and a very strange stranger it must be, who does not see charms in the immediate environs of Lyme, to make him wish to know it better.

The scenes in its neighborhood, Charmouth, with its high grounds and extensive sweeps of country and still more its sweet bay, backed by dark cliffs, where fragments of low rock among the sands make it the happiest spot for watching the flow of the tide, for sitting in unwearied contemplation—the woody varieties of the cheerful village of Up Lyme, and, above all, Pinny, with its green chasms between romantic rock, where the scattered forest trees and orchards of luxuriant growth declare that many a generation must have passed away since the first partial falling of the cliff prepared the ground for such a state, where a scene so wonderful and so lovely is exhibited as may more than equal any of the resembling scenes of the far-famed Isle of Wight: These places must be visited, and visited again, to make the worth of Lyme understood.

The party from Uppercross passing down by the now deserted and melancholy looking rooms, and still descending, soon found themselves on the seashore.

"It is so windy and so damp," Mary complained as they walked to the sea's edge. She refused to go near the water.

Louisa and Henrietta chased the tide in and out, just as small children might do. They giggled and laughed with joy of the novelty—as they would never experience a Season in London, their parents saw no reason for the girls to travel about the countryside. Charles Musgrove walked out on one of the rocks littering the shoreline and pretended to cast a line from a rod into the sea. His sisters encouraged him to pull in a great whale on his imaginary line, and he bent to indicate the weight of the catch. The waves lapped about his high boots, keeping him safe from the water.

Frederick watched with some amusement. Then he turned to find Anne, who stood alone on a rocky promontory. Anne closed her eyes and inhaled deeply; she leaned into the power of the ocean—allowing it to draw her into its grasp and hold her. Unlike the rush of water surrounding the others, the waves lapped at Anne's feet, never touching her slippers, but kissing her feet, nevertheless. She opened her eyes and smiled.

Frederick stood mesmerized by her beauty and by her demonstration of the effect the sea had on her. He understood Anne's feelings well, having experienced it on more than one occasion. The sea became a part of a sailor's soul, taking him into its depths and bringing him back once again to the land. He saw that on Anne Elliot's face when he looked at her, and Frederick now knew, without a doubt, Anne could survive as his wife, accepting the dangers the sea offered, but never allowing a natural fear of the sea to rule her. Frederick found himself trying to quiet the thud he heard resounding from his chest. "Not yet," he mumbled in warning to himself, anxious to right the wrong in his life. "Soon," he mouthed the word as he turned to the others.

"Let us walk to the Cobb before we lose the light completely," he called to gather them once more and to quell the anxiety building in his chest.

They proceeded toward the stone breakwater wall bordering the harbor. "The sea will claim the wall one day," he added as they gaped wide-eyed at the structure. "It will allow nothing to stop its flow."

"May we walk along the top, Charles?" Louisa persisted.

He easily conceded, wanting to experience the power of the ocean himself. "At least part of the way." He escorted the group to the steps leading to the top of the sea wall.

Wentworth pulled Charles to the side to speak to him privately. "If you do not mind, I will leave you for a few minutes. I wish to let Captain Harville know I have returned."

"Of course, Wentworth, take as long as you need. If we finish before you complete your visit, we will meet you back at the inn."

"I shall not be long." With that, they watched as Frederick turned into a small house near the foot of an old pier of unknown date. The others walked on with the assurance that he was to join them on the Cobb.

CHAPTER 10

I ne'er was struck before that hour
With love so sudden and so sweet,
Her face it bloomed like a sweet flower
And stole my heart away complete.
—John Clare, "First Love"

"Wentworth, you returned!" Harville called out to his friend as he hobbled into the room, having been summoned by his wife.

"I have, Thomas." They shook hands. "My new acquaintances, upon hearing my description of Lyme, wished most earnestly to experience it on their own. We came for a day trip, which will extend into tomorrow morning, so we might properly rest the horses."

"And where are these *new* acquaintances?" Thomas tried to peer over Frederick's shoulder, expecting to see strangers on his doorstep.

"They are walking along the Cobb."

Milly joined them, having checked on the children first. "How many are in your party, Captain?"

"There are six, counting myself. Four ladies and two gentlemen."

"Ladies?" She looked happy with the news.

"My Milly misses the companionship of other women," Thomas informed him. "I fear Benwick and I bore her with tales of the *Laconia*." He gestured toward their permanent houseguest.

Milly Harville slapped her husband on the arm, feigning being insulted. "That is so untrue," she protested, but a grin quickly overspread her face. "I love hearing you two speak of your time together—even if you share it for the twentieth time."

"I believe you wound me, my Dear." Thomas caught her hand and brought the back of it to his lips. "Come, Wentworth." He chuckled as he turned back to his friend. "I must find an audience for my retellings who would more appreciate them."

"We will all go." Milly reached for her cloak.

Wentworth asked, "You, too, Benwick?"

"Of course." James Benwick rose to join them.

The Uppercross party walked nearly to the end of the Cobb before turning back toward the inn. They discovered Captain Wentworth leading three companions, all well known already by description. Meeting at last, Wentworth made the appropriate introductions. People talked over one another in their eagerness to become acquainted. Milly bubbled with excitement, especially enjoying the enthusiasm of the Misses Musgrove.

Frederick watched carefully as the group interacted. Charles, Henrietta, and Louisa Musgrove gushed with meeting the Harvilles and Benwick. Less focused on class, they welcomed the connections because of Wentworth's warm praise of each of them. Mary Musgrove acknowledged the trio, but made little effort to get to know them.

Frederick noted all their exchanges, but it was upon Anne his attention rested. She seemed to struggle against the meeting, and that bothered him. Of course, he expected Mary to disdain the group, but he did not anticipate a like action from Anne. Yet, as she stood there, Frederick watched her withdraw from the group. *Why?* he thought. If they had married, these would have been all her friends. Anger crept into his heart. *How dare she judge them?* Less than an hour earlier, he had considered renewing his attentions; now, he was having second thoughts. He started to turn away from her, but, unpredictably, Anne lifted her chin, and Frederick gazed into her eyes—pools misted over—eyes blinking back tears. Anne dropped her chin, letting her bonnet hide what only Frederick had seen. He froze. *Why does she cry?* Did Anne, like him, realize this could have been their life—a seaport—his comrades—other naval wives? Frederick swallowed hard, fighting to keep his emotions in check.

"Please, you must come to our home," he heard Milly Harville offer the invitation.

"That would be most pleasant," Anne said before turning to Musgrove. "I am sure Mary would like a few moments to warm up, do you not agree, Charles?" Wentworth smiled at her diplomacy, the way she would not allow Mrs. Charles to speak disparagingly about the arrangement.

"Of course, Anne—an excellent idea." Charles began to usher everyone along. "Follow Mrs. Harville."

Stepping into the space, Frederick wondered what the others must think. Only those who invite from the heart could think rooms so small capable of accommodating so many. Yet, he listened as Anne, Louisa, Henrietta, and Charles all commented on the pleasanter feelings evoked by the sight of all the ingenious contrivances and nice arrangements of Captain Harville to turn the actual space to the best possible account, to make up for the deficiencies of lodging-house furniture. Milly praised Thomas's ingenuity in the varieties in the fitting-up of the rooms, where the common necessaries provided by the owner, in the common indifferent plight, were contrasted with some few articles of a rare species of wood, excellently worked up, and with something curious and valuable from all the distant countries Frederick and Thomas had visited.

"My Thomas is quite talented!" Milly Harville boasted as she set up a tea tray for everyone.

"Look at these," Wentworth said, indicating the toy chest. "Harville made all these." He handed a few of them to Anne and Louisa.

Louisa immediately tried to catch the ball in the cup while Anne examined the craftsmanship found in the Jacob's Ladder. "These are exceptional, Captain Harville," she emphasized as she returned the toys to the box.

Thomas looked a bit uncomfortable with all the praise. "My injury prevents me from taking much exercise, but I have a mind to be useful, and a bit of ingenuity furnishes me with constant employment. If I find nothing else to do, I mend that large fishing net in the corner."

"Your talent, Sir, is remarkable," insisted Charles Musgrove.

The group enjoyed their tea, and then the time came for them to return to the inn. "Are you sure, Captain, that we cannot convince you and your party to join us for supper?" Milly Harville asked as she busied herself by collecting the teacups and plates.

"We could not so impose, Mrs. Harville," Mary responded with polite disdain.

Frederick forced himself to not show his own contempt for Mrs. Charles's behavior. "We ordered supper, Milly. Mrs. Morris would be upset if we declined to eat at the inn after putting her to so much trouble."

"Of course." Her disappointment showed.

Frederick touched her hand. "We will see each other tomorrow before we leave for Uppercross."

"I shall come for a visit after supper," Thomas added, "if that is acceptable to all. I still have many stories to tell about Wentworth!"

"Please do, Captain," Louisa encouraged. "We all want to be regaled with tales of the captain's adventures." She crossed the room and took his arm as if he offered it to her. "The Captain has quickly become one of our *favorite* people."

Frederick felt his skin crawl with Louisa's touch. He wanted to put distance between them—to reestablish a connection to Anne. He forced a smile to his face; he would walk with Louisa to the inn, but he would take more care not to be caught in her attentions again.

★ ★ ★

"So tell us, Captain, what is the story with James Benwick? He is so very melancholy." Louisa nearly snarled her nose in remembrance.

Frederick put down his knife and fork. "I believe I told you previously Captain Benwick lost his fiancée. He was engaged to Captain Harville's sister and now mourns her loss. They were a year or two waiting for fortune and promotion. Fortune came, his prize money, as lieutenant, being great—promotion, too, came at *last*, but Fanny Harville did not live to know it. She died last summer while he was at sea. I do not believe it possible for a man to be more attached to a woman than poor Benwick was to Fanny Harville or to be more deeply afflicted under the dreadful change. His disposition is as of the sort that must suffer heavily—uniting very strong feelings with quiet, serious, and retiring manners and a decided taste for reading and sedentary pursuits. The friendship between him and the Harvilles seems if possible, augmented by the event, which closed all their views of alliance. Captain Benwick now lives with them entirely. I believe the quiet solitude of Lyme in winter is exactly adapted to Captain Benwick's state of mind."

"Oh, the poor man!" Henrietta spoke her thoughts aloud.

Louisa conceded recalcitrantly, "I suppose he has a right to his sadness."

Frederick nodded in agreement. "He is young, and, I believe, Benwick will rally again and be happy with another, although it will be some time. Because he never had an opportunity to renew his addresses to Fanny, he will eventually seek another, but I cannot imagine his doing so at the moment." His attention rested on Anne's face. *What would I do if I returned to Somerset to find Anne had passed away?* He often thought of losing Anne to another, but Frederick never considered she would not survive something as common as a fever. A shiver ran down his spine as he reflected on the time he wasted.

Anne remarked, "I doubt Captain Benwick will join us this evening; he has all the appearance of being oppressed by the presence of so many strangers."

The words had no sooner escaped her lips than Captains Harville and Benwick appeared in the doorway of the private dining room. Charles Musgrove greeted them loudly, so that no one else would speak of Benwick. The group split, allowing the two newcomers a chance to take center stage.

At first, both men sat with the entire group, but as the evening progressed, Frederick watched James Benwick withdraw both physically and mentally from the gathering. To Frederick's chagrin, the very good impulse of Anne's nature obliged her to begin an acquaintance with Benwick. She seated herself beside him and devoted her conversation to him. Frederick wanted her to hear of *his* exploits—*his* successes—to appreciate how close *he* had come to death and how hard *he* had worked to achieve respectability.

"Did you tell them about Copenhagen?" Captain Harville asked as he launched into another story of their service together. Frederick shook his head in the negative, but his eyes and ears still searched the corner where Anne sat with Benwick.

He strained to hear what they shared. Their heads bent together in quiet conversation; Frederick noted Benwick's shyness and his disposal to abstraction faded as the engaging mildness of her countenance and the gentleness of her manners soon had their effect, and his response repaid Anne the trouble of her exertion. Despite twinges of jealousy, Frederick could not help but smile with the knowledge *his Anne* could reach the unreachable. Frederick picked up snippets of what they said to each other.

"Miss Anne, it is a pleasure to speak to someone who loves poetry as much as you. I feel less alone in my sadness when I read a tragic poem." Benwick's shyness existed on a different level now.

Anne smiled. "I agree, Captain; but I remind you of the duty and benefit of struggling against affliction."

"Oh, Miss Anne, a man could not feel such remorse in your presence." Benwick said the words with such passion that Anne blushed. That jealous pang shot through Frederick again, and he forced the ache from his throat. Looking back at them, Frederick took some delight in watching the redness spread even if it came from another man's attention. A woman in a full blush was exquisite, and he recalled speaking words of endearment to Anne simply to achieve that same reaction. The thoughts brought him an "unusual" contentment.

"Did you really eat caviar three times a day?" Louisa's words pulled Frederick into the conversation at hand.

"Every man on board developed a taste for fish eggs," Frederick declared. "The French love the dish, but, personally, I quickly tired of its novelty."

"What other French foods have you tasted?" Louisa inquired sweetly.

Harville answered for him, and Frederick only half heard the gasps as Thomas described escargot.

"Snails!" Mary Musgrove said with distaste.

What Benwick said to Anne captured his attention again. "Do you prefer Sir Walter Scott's 'Marmion' or 'The Lady of the Lake'?"

Anne laughed lightly. "Obviously, 'The Lady.'"

"A romantic." Benwick's gentle gaze rested on Anne's face, and Frederick felt the green-eyed monster all over again. The tenor of his friend's voice softened as he began to repeat Scott's words:

> Hark! as my lingering footsteps slow retire,
> Some Spirit of the Air has waked thy string!
> 'Tis now a seraph bold, with touch of fire,
> 'Tis now the brush of Fairy's frolic wing.
> Receding now, the dying numbers ring
> Fainter and fainter down the rugged dell;
> And now the mountain breezes scarcely bring
> A wandering witch-note of the distant spell—
> And now, 'tis silent all!—Enchantress, fare thee well!

How dare he? Frederick thought. The man repeated love poetry to *his Anne,* the only woman he had ever loved! He had once saved Benwick's life, and he was the one who had given the man comfort when Benwick found out about Fanny Harville. *And what of Fanny?* Would he push her memory to the side and welcome Anne into his heart?

"You captured Scott's tenderness, Captain." Anne offered him an enchanting smile. "And what of Lord Byron? Do you prefer 'Giaour' or 'The Bride of Abydos'?"

Again, Benwick fell into the rhythm of the poem.

> Burst forth in one wild cry—and all was still.
> Peace to thy broken heart, and virgin grave!

Ah! Happy! but of life to lose the worst!

That grief—though deep—though fatal—was thy first!

Anne looked concerned. "Captain, you must not let the hopeless agony consume your thoughts. May I recommend a larger allowance of prose in your daily study?"

He smiled sadly. "I loved Fanny Harville, Miss Anne. You cannot know my pain—my despair."

Anne pulled herself upright. "I preach patience and resignation, Captain, because I, too, suffered the pains of lost love, and I wish most desperately that someone had offered me such advice."

Had he heard her correctly? Frederick felt his heart would break; his departure had hurt Anne as much as it had hurt him. He knew she spoke of *their* love, for, without a doubt, Anne had once loved him. When he left that day eight years ago, she still desired him as much as he desired her. After that, Frederick heard nothing either group said. He was lost to his own thoughts. Finally, Louisa Musgrove and the others demanded his undivided attention. For once, Frederick was happy to divine her with his tales; he did not want to think anymore about Anne Elliot and their lost love. All he really wanted was to escape to his own room and replay every word spoken and not spoken today.

★ ★ ★

"Captain." Louisa snuggled into his arm. "I thought we might take a stroll before breakfast."

"Should we not wait for the rest of our party?" Frederick purposely stepped away from her, pretending to look toward the stairway to see if Anne or the others might be about.

"Henrietta wanted to speak to Anne privately about pleading for Lady Russell's help in securing a position for Cousin Charles. They left a quarter hour ago, and, of course, Mary will not be up for at least another hour." She smiled winningly.

"Then maybe we should find them." Frederick started toward the door, avoiding offering her his arm. He would walk with Louisa, but he would not encourage her unduly. During the night, he thought it best to make Anne aware of his constancy. Somehow he must find a way to speak again of his love.

They walked less than a quarter mile down to the sea, where they met Henrietta and Anne, who were returning from their walk, one where the women went to the sands to watch the flowing of the tide. Frederick regretted not joining them. He would have liked to tell Anne about the tide—how a fine southeasterly breeze was bringing it in with all the grandeur, which so flat a shore admitted. He would teach her to praise the morning, to glory in the sea, to sympathize in the delight of the fresh-feeling breeze—and to be silent, just as she was yesterday—and let the world come to her.

Breaking his concentration—his thoughts of Anne—Louisa exclaimed, "I wanted to buy a new fan for Mama! We must go back to town. After breakfast we will be leaving, and there will be no time."

"Certainly," Anne added quickly. "Mrs. Musgrove will be quite pleased with your thoughtfulness."

Frederick watched as Louisa beamed with praise, playing the grown up role bestowed upon her by Anne. Crossing the last of the shoreline, they prepared to climb the steps leading upwards from the beach to the top of the seawall and the path into town. Just as they reached the steps, a gentleman at the same moment preparing to come down, politely drew back and stopped to give them way. He wore an armband, indicating he observed a period of mourning. They ascended and passed him, and as they passed, Anne's face caught his eye, and he looked at her with a degree of earnest admiration.

Frederick, having gone up the steps first, stood braced near the top, waiting to help each of the ladies over the last step and to safety. Louisa, always taking precedence, waited for the others, and Frederick held Henrietta's hand to steady her footing when he saw the man's intense interest in Anne. Frederick followed the man's eyes. She was looking remarkably well; her very regular, very pretty features, having the bloom and freshness of youth restored by the fine wind, which had been blowing on her complexion, and by the animation of her eyes, which it also produced.

It was evident that the gentleman, completely a gentleman in manner, admired her exceedingly. Frederick quickly summed up the situation. If he did not make a move soon, Anne would assume he intended to declare himself for Louisa and take up with someone else. *I cannot lose her again!* he thought, although as quickly as the thought came, he amended it—knowing at the moment Anne Elliot was not his to lose. What was worse was Anne took note of the man's interest, and she gifted him with a beguiling smile. Frederick wanted to grab the cad's cravat and throw him from the steps into the sea. Finally, Anne reached him, and as Frederick took her hand to steady her way as he did the others, he could not resist giving hers a gentle squeeze and stroking the inside of her wrist with his index finger. A slight blush radiated from her, and Frederick basked in her heat. She refused to make eye contact with him, but he did not care. He elicited a response from Anne, and she repaid his effort.

They soon reached the town and, after attending Louisa through her business and loitering about a little longer, they returned to the inn. Frederick noted upon their return that the gentleman in question was also staying at the inn. A well-looking groom strolled about the area, and, like the man on the steps, the servant was in mourning. The knowledge that Anne might see the stranger again vexed Frederick; he could not risk their forming an acquaintance. Feeling a bit overwhelmed with how quickly things changed and how little control he had over the situation, Frederick resolved to make an immediate move. He would ask to speak to Anne privately, and he would explain he was foolish in thinking he could forget her. He would explain he would not want to hurt Louisa Musgrove or affect Anne's relationship with the Musgrove family, so he would travel to Shropshire and spend time with Edward in order to weaken the girl's expectations. He would reason that with Anne's returning to Lady Russell's home, it might not be best for him to call upon her at this time, but he would seek her permission to do so when she retired to Bath with her family. He would let her know he hoped to regain her regard.

Happy with the decision, Frederick waited impatiently in the main hallway for Anne to come down to breakfast. Finally, he heard her light tread on the landing. Blood rushed to his ears, and he could briefly hear only the beat of his own heart. Then a heavy thud—one of a door closing nearby—mixed with the approach of Anne's footsteps. The voices rang clear as he moved into the shadows.

"Pardon me," the man responded to Anne's small gasp of surprise. Then an elongated silence told Frederick they partook of each other's countenances. There was a moment of silence, and then the man spoke again. "It seems, Miss, I am to plague you with my presence." Frederick knew instantly it was the man from the beach, and Frederick stifled a moan of disbelief.

"It is perfectly all right, Sir," Anne replied pleasantly. "You simply frightened me momentarily; my heart you gave a start."

"My apologies." Frederick imagined the gentleman doffed his hat with these words. "I would not have you fear me in any way. May I say it is rare to meet such a delicate rose in winter?"

"You *are* too bold, Sir," she replied. "Now, if you will excuse me." With that, Frederick heard her step away from the guest. Before she could see Frederick there in the shadows, he moved quickly away. *My timing is off. Damnably off.* He could not approach her so soon after the stranger's unwelcomed way. He would wait until they prepared to load the coaches; in the midst of the chaos of packing so many bags, he would take her into the private dining room and plead his case. Trying to appear casual, he was at the sidebar filling a plate when Anne entered the dining room.

★ ★ ★

They had nearly finished breakfast when the sound of a carriage, almost the first they had heard since entering Lyme drew half the party to the window. Henrietta noted, "It is a gentleman's carriage—a curricle—but it is only coming round from the stable yard to the front. Somebody must be going away.—Look, it is driven by a servant in mourning."

"A curricle, you say?" Charles Musgrove jumped up, hoping to compare the one outside to his own.

By now, they all stared out the window at the carriage. Frederick had no intention of spying, but when Anne moved to the window, he moved, too. He thought the curricle must belong to the stranger. He reasoned there would not be two gentlemen in mourning staying at the same inn. By the time the owner of the curricle issued forth from the door admidst the bows and civilities of the household and took his seat to drive off, the six of them collectively stared out the window.

Wentworth half glanced at Anne. "Ah, it is the very man we passed." He waited to see Anne's reaction, but she turned away to the sidebar once more before he could ascertain her feelings.

"I believe you are right, Captain," Henrietta confirmed and then kindly watched the man as far up the hill as she could.

"I wonder who he is," Mary Musgrove mused as she sat down again.

At that moment, the waiter came into the room. "Pray," said Wentworth, "can you tell us the name of the gentleman who is just gone away?"

"Yes, Sir, a Mr. Elliot, a gentleman of large fortune—came in last night from Sidmouth—daresay you heard the carriage, Sir, while you were at supper—going on now for Crewkherne, in his way to Bath and London."

"Elliot!" Louisa gasped.

Charles returned to the window for a second look. "Did he say Elliot?"

"Bless me!" cried Mary. "It must be our cousin—it must be our Mr. Elliot; it must, indeed!—Charles, Anne, must not it? In mourning, you see, just as our Mr. Elliot must be. You recall that disgraceful first marriage of his. How very extraordinary! In the very same inn with us! Anne, must not it be our Mr. Elliot, my father's heir?" Turning to the waiter, she continued, "Pray, did not you hear—did not his servant say whether he belonged to the Kellynch family?"

"No, Ma'am, he did not mention no particular family, but he said his master was a very rich gentleman and would be a baronet someday."

"There! You see!" cried Mary, in an ecstasy. "Just as I said! Heir to Sir Walter Elliot! —I was sure that would come out if it were so. Depend upon it—that is a circumstance, which his servants take care to publish wherever he goes. But, Anne, only conceive how extraordinary!" Mary clutched at Anne's arm. "I wish I looked at him more. I wish we had been aware in time, who it was, that he might have been introduced to us. What a pity we should not have been introduced to each other!—Do you think he had the Elliot countenance? I hardly looked at him; I was looking at the horses, but I think he had something of the Elliot countenance." She jumped up and paced the floor, trying to organize her thoughts. "I wonder the coat of arms did not strike me! Oh!—the great-coat was hanging over the pannel and hid the arms; so it did, otherwise, I am sure, I should have observed them and the livery too; if the servant had not been in mourning, one should have known him by the livery."

"Of course, we all would have," Charles assured his wife.

"*We* saw him briefly on the steps to the beach," Louisa wanted desperately to be a part of the action.

When she could command Mary's attention, Anne quietly observed, "Mary, Father would not wish us to renew an acquaintance with Mr. Elliot. Father and Mr. Elliot have not for many years been on such terms as to make the power of attempting an introduction at all desirable."

Frederick spoke with an edge of sarcasm: "Putting all these very extraordinary circumstances together, we must consider it to be the arrangement of Providence, that you should not be introduced to your cousin."

Mary Musgrove ignored Frederick's snide remark. "Of course," said Mary to Anne, "you will mention our seeing Mr. Elliot the next time you write to Bath. I think my father certainly ought to hear of it; do mention all to him."

"Mary, I will not bring such news to our father; you may write him if you choose, but I shall not be the bearer of such tidings. You were away at school through much of Father's dealings with Mr. Elliot. I know the offense offered our father, and I suspect Elizabeth's particular share in it. The idea of Mr. Elliot always produces irritation in both."

"Do not be silly, Anne!" Mary cried. "Prior to the man's arrival at an assembly or a holiday soiree, Father would want news of Mr. Elliot's appearance in Bath if our cousin truly plans to travel there."

Anne avoided a direct reply. Arguing with Mary would be fruitless.

"Well, all that can be decided when we return to Uppercross," Frederick offered. "We promised Captain and Mrs. Harville a final walk about Lyme. We ought to be setting off for Uppercross by one."

CHAPTER 11

Are flowers the winter's choice?
Is love's bed always snow?
She seemed to hear my silent voice,
Not love's appeals to know.
—John Clare, "First Love"

Breakfast was not long over when Captain and Mrs. Harville and Captain Benwick joined them. As a group of nine, they started to take their last walk about Lyme. Frederick noted how quickly Benwick sought Anne's attention; evidently, their conversation the preceding evening did not disincline him to see her again. He walked beside her, talking as before of Mr. Scott and Lord Byron.

"Your Miss Anne was most kind in speaking so long to James," Harville confided as he and Frederick walked along together. "She did a good deed in making that poor fellow talk so much. I wish he could have such company oftener. It is bad for him, I know, to be shut up as he is, but what can we do? We cannot part."

"Then you should tell her so." Frederick nodded in Anne's direction. "It does not surprise me, though; Anne Elliot is the kindest woman I have ever known. The man who receives her affection is blessed indeed."

Frederick's words sparked Harville's interest. "How long have you known Miss Anne?" His curiosity flamed into being.

Frederick still watched Anne as she spoke to James Benwick. "Nearly eight years," he mumbled.

"Eight years?" Thomas's voice rose with anticipation. "When you were in Somerset with Edward?"

Frederick's attention snapped back to his friend. "I understand the implications, Thomas, but you are mistaken. Miss Anne's family is the only aristocratic one in the area. Of course, my brother would be familiar with them."

"Anything you say, Wentworth." However, his tone told Frederick that Harville did not believe him.

"Get on with you." He laughed as he lightly shoved Harville in Anne's direction.

They continued on for some time, each pair engrossed in their conversations. Eventually, Milly Harville became concerned for her husband's leg injury, and she insisted they return home. The group would accompany them to their door and then return to the inn and set off themselves. By all their calculations there was just time for this; but as they drew near the Cobb, there was a general wish to walk along it once more.

"We really must," Frederick heard Louisa beg Charles.

"Louisa," he tried to reason with his sister, "we must be off. Late November days are short of light, and Mama will worry so if we do not return home by dinner."

"Be patient with me, Charles," she nearly whined. "How long would it actually take us to walk the length of the Cobb? I may never get a chance to see the ocean again. Do not deny Henrietta or me that pleasure."

Her words softened Musgrove's resolve; the man had little backbone when it came to making decisions regarding his family. Frederick thought it ironic Louisa spoke so poorly of the manipulative ways of Mrs. Charles; from his point of view, Louisa incorporated the same techniques into her dealings, as did Mary Musgrove. She whined and cajoled until she got her way, and Louisa always "demanded" to be the center of attention. *Poor Charles! He lives a life of constant compromise!* thought Frederick.

"What is a quarter hour, give or take?" Charles assured the others in a loud voice.

"We depart from you here, Wentworth." Harville turned to take his leave of his friend. "You will no longer be a stranger to us; we insist that you return soon."

"Wild horses could not keep me from seeking your hospitality."

He took Milly's ungloved hands and brought each to his lips. "You are charged with keeping this rascal in line," he teased as he lightly kissed her knuckles. "I leave him in your able hands." With those words, he took Harville's hand and placed Milly's in it.

Thomas interlaced his fingers with hers. "Only my Milly could have such control over me. As you recall, Wentworth, I do not take orders very well."

"Neither of us does, my Friend," he said, and he bowed to Milly.

So with all the kind leave-taking and all the kind interchange of invitations and promises, which may be imagined, they parted from Captain and Mrs. Harville at their own door, and still accompanied by Captain Benwick, who seemed to cling to them to the last, proceeded to make the proper adieus to the Cobb.

"My, it is very windy today!" Mary noted as she grasped her bonnet to keep it from blowing away. "Should we not turn back, Charles?"

"What do you think, Anne?" Like everyone else in the group, Charles constantly sought Anne's confirmation when it came to dealing with her sister.

Anne's cloak whipped around her. She stood steady, allowing the wind to dance about her, rather than to fight its force. Anne offered her brother-in-law a slight smile, knowing Charles would suffer if the group did not agree with Mary's request. "The wind seems especially powerful today. I am sure that now you know the beauty of this place, you will return in the *spring*, when it is more lively in its entertainments."

"I agree." Charles nearly laughed with having the decision taken from his hands. He would neither want to disappoint his sisters nor to meet his wife's wrath. "Let us turn back."

"May we at least walk along the shoreline?" Henrietta asked quietly.

Charles jumped at the idea of appeasing everyone. "What a good compromise, my Dear." He turned to the others. "Let us get down the steps to the lower."

As he did previously, Frederick preceded the others down so he could help the women on the narrow steps. Charles and Benwick remained at the top as Mary, Anne, and Henrietta descended the tapered path. All were contented to pass quietly and carefully down the steep flight.

"I need no one's help," Louisa assured her brother, pulling her hand from his. "I would prefer to stay up here; the wind is of no consequence to me."

"Please, Louisa," Charles Musgrove murmured.

She hissed, "You give in to Mary too often!"

Charles whispered, "I made my bed years ago, and although you do not understand now, soon you will realize a man must pick his battles. This is not one I choose to fight."

"Then go on," she admonished him. "I will make my own way."

Frederick remained at the bottom of the steps, waiting for Louisa's descent. The others, on safe footing, began to regroup and move away. Charles came past Frederick, grinning sheepishly for his part in the disagreement, followed closely by Benwick.

Louisa was nearly three-fourths of the way down the steps when she called out to Frederick, "Catch me!" In all their walks, he had had to jump her from stiles; the sensation delighted her.

"Louisa, be careful," Frederick cautioned, as he quickly moved to prepare for her leap. The hardness of the pavement for her feet made him less willing to play her game upon the present occasion; he did it, however. Catching her at the waist, Frederick sat Louisa decisively away from him.

Louisa smiled flirtatiously; then she broke away from his grasp, and, instantly, to show her enjoyment, ran up the steps to be jumped down again. "Once more," she teased as she climbed several steps higher than before.

"Louisa, no!" he warned her. "It is too high! The jar will be too great!"

Having let her go, Frederick turned momentarily away to pick up his hat and gloves, which he had discarded to catch her the first time. But before he could turn back to properly station himself, she smiled and said, "I am determined. I will."

He put out his hands; she was to precipitate him by a half second. Louisa's body floated through the air in slow motion; her skirt tail and cloak spread out like angel wings. Frederick saw the horror overtake her face when she realized he could not catch her, and her body braced for the impact. The thudding sound reverberated as she fell on the pavement on the Lower Cobb and was taken up lifeless.

"No!" Frederick's words, as well as the sound of Louisa's crash turned the rest of the party in their direction. Frederick hovered over her. "Louisa—please, Louisa!" He reached for her hand. There was no wound, no blood, no visible bruise; but her eyes were closed, she breathed not, her face was like death.—The horror of that moment froze all who stood around. Wentworth, who caught her up, knelt with her in his arms, looking on her with a face as pallid as her own, in an agony of silence.

"She is dead! She is dead!" screamed Mary, catching hold of her husband, her words contributing to his own horror and making Charles immoveable. In another moment, Henrietta, sinking under the conviction, lost her senses too and would have fallen but for Captain Benwick and Anne, who caught and supported her between them.

"Is there no one to help me?" Frederick cried out in a tone of despair, as if all his own strength left him.

"Go to him. Go to him!" cried Anne. "For heaven's sake go to him. I can support her myself. Leave me, and go to him. Rub her hands; rub her temples. Here are salts—take them, take them!"

Captain Benwick obeyed, and Charles at the same moment, disengaging himself from his wife, were both with Frederick. They raised Louisa up and supported her more firmly between them. They did Anne's bidding—rubbing her extremities and placing the smelling salts under her nose—but in vain.

In horror, Frederick staggered backward, clinging to the wall for support. He exclaimed in the bitterest agony, "Oh, God! Her father and mother!"

"A surgeon!" said Anne.

Frederick caught the word; it seemed to rouse him at once, giving him hope and a purpose. "True, true, a surgeon this instant!" he called and started to dart in the direction of the town.

"Wait!" Anne's words caught him in mid stride. "Captain Benwick! Captain Benwick! Would not it be better for Captain Benwick? He knows where a surgeon is to be found."

Everyone capable of thinking felt the advantage of the idea, and in a moment—it was all done in rapid moments—Captain Benwick resigned the poor corpse-like figure entirely to Charles's care and was off for the town with the utmost rapidity.

"Louisa, talk to me." Charles patted her face gently, trying to coax his sister back to consciousness.

Mary kept up her laments. "Dead—she is dead! Oh, what will we do? Help me, Charles, I feel so weak!"

Charles looked up from his sister.

"Mary, be quiet!" Anne ordered. "You are not helping." Then she turned to the sagging Henrietta. "Louisa will be fine; she just took a bad spill. The surgeon will be here in a moment." Henrietta nodded.

Frederick looked on—the dreadful tableau playing out before his stare. The only thing he could comprehend was Anne would make it right; she would know what to do.

"Anne, Anne," cried Charles, "what is to be done next? What, in heaven's name, is to be done next?"

Wentworth's eyes also turned toward her. Her shoulders shifted, as if shrugging off the weight of the situation. "Had not she better be carried to the inn?" she said with all the calm possible. "Yes, I am sure, carry her gently to the inn."

"Yes, yes, to the inn," repeated Wentworth, comparatively collected and eager to be doing something. "I will carry her myself. Musgrove, take care of the others."

By this time the report of the accident had spread among the workmen and boatmen about the Cobb, and many were collected near them, to be useful if wanted, at any rate, to enjoy the sight of a dead young lady, nay, two dead young ladies, for it proved twice as fine as the first report. To some of the best-looking of these good people they consigned Henrietta, for, though partially revived, she was quite helpless; and in this manner, Anne walking by her side, and Charles, attending to his wife, they set forward, treading back with feelings unutterable, the ground, which so lately, so very lately, and so light of heart, they had passed along.

They were not off the Cobb before the Harvilles met them. Captain Benwick had flown by their house, with a countenance, which showed something to be wrong, and they had set off immediately, informed and directed, as they passed toward the spot.

Shocked as Captain Harville was, he brought senses and nerves that could be instantly useful; and a look between him and his wife decided what was to be done. "Take her to our house!" Harville ordered.

Without a second thought, Frederick trusted his old friend's advice. He turned in at the Harville's door, and the others followed. "Upstairs!" Milly directed him. "Place her in my bed."

"Oh, no, we cannot take your bed," Charles protested, although it was a weak effort on his part, having his attention divided by his still sobbing wife and the need to care for both of his sisters.

"Nonsense," Milly admonished. "Do as I say, Frederick." Wentworth quickly disappeared through the entranceway and just as quickly conveyed Louisa's limp body to the waiting bed. "I will tend her until the surgeon arrives. Go back down and help Thomas."

"Th-Thank you, Milly," he stammered. "You and Thomas . . ." he began, but he could not finish the thoughts. Ducking his head to clear the doorframe, he made his way slowly down the stairs, needing to digest the ramifications of what just happened, his face pale as death.

At the bottom, he met the surgeon hurrying up the steps. "I guess we wait," Anne said softly as she helped Captain Harville pour restorative drinks for all who needed them.

After a quarter of an hour, the surgeon reappeared in the Harvilles' sitting room. Both Charles and Frederick rushed forward to meet him. "Tell us, Doctor," Charles pleaded. "Will my sister live?"

"Your sister will likely recover. Her head received a severe contusion, but I have seen people recover from greater injuries. I do not deem the situation hopeless. In fact, the young lady opened her eyes momentarily, although she did not regain consciousness. I take that as a good sign." A sob was heard from one of the ladies, and several people sighed with relief. "I do not regard your sister's condition as desperate, but I cannot say how quickly she will convalesce; the brain has its own schedule for recuperation."

"Thank God," Frederick heard himself say. Then he collapsed into a nearby chair. Leaning over a table—his hands folded and his face in shadow—overpowered by emotion, he offered a silent prayer for Louisa's speedy recovery.

It now became necessary for the party to consider what was best to be done, as to their general situation. They were now able to speak to each other and consult. That Louisa must remain where she was, however distressing to her friends to be involving the Harvilles in such trouble, did not admit a doubt. Her removal was impossible. The Harvilles silenced all scruples, and, as much as they could, all gratitude. They looked forward and arranged everything, before the others began to reflect. Captain Benwick must give up his room to them and get a bed elsewhere—and the whole was settled. They were only concerned the house could accommodate no more; and yet perhaps by "putting the children away in the maids' room or swinging a cot somewhere," they could hardly bear to think of not finding room for two or three besides, supposing they might wish to stay; though, with regard to any attendance on Miss Musgrove, there need not be the least uneasiness in leaving her to Mrs. Harville's care entirely. Mrs. Harville was a very experienced nurse; and her nursery maid, who had lived with her long and gone about with her everywhere, was just such another. Between those two, Louisa could want no possible attendance by day or night. And all this was said with a truth and sincerity of feeling irresistible.

Charles, Henrietta, and Frederick were the three in consultation, and for a little while it was only an interchange of perplexity and terror. "Uppercross—the necessity of someone's going to Uppercross—the news to be conveyed—how it could be broken to Mr. and Mrs. Musgrove—the lateness of the morning—an hour already gone since they ought to have been off—the impossibility of being in tolerable time."

At first, they were capable of nothing more to the purpose than such exclamations; but, after a while, Wentworth, exerting himself, said, "We must be decided and without the loss of another minute. Every minute is valuable. Some must resolve on being off for Uppercross instantly. Musgrove, either you or I must go."

"I cannot leave my sister," Charles emphasized. "I will sleep in a chair if necessary, but I cannot leave Louisa in such a state."

Henrietta declared, "I need to stay, too."

Charles reached for his younger sister's hand. "I love your resolve, my Dear, but we both know you are not even able to be in the room with Louisa without crying."

"But I *must*, Charles," she protested.

"Miss Henrietta," Frederick reasoned, "you could help Louisa more if you brought comfort to your mother and father. Neither I nor Miss Anne nor Mrs. Charles could offer them what you can."

"Wentworth is right, Henrietta."

"You are correct. I need to be with Mama; she will need me, will she not? When do we leave?"

"Then it is settled, Musgrove," cried Frederick. "You will stay, and I will take your sister home. But as to the rest—as to the others—if one stays to assist Mrs. Harville, I think, it need be only one.—Mrs. Charles will, of course, wish to get back to her children; but, if Anne will stay, no one is so proper, so capable, as Anne!"

Charles added quickly, "I concur."

Henrietta nodded her agreement. "If not for Anne, where would we be now?"

Frederick rose to greet Anne when she entered the room. "You will stay; I am sure; you will stay and nurse her." He turned to her and spoke with a glow, and yet a gentleness, which seemed almost restoring the past. She nodded, and he recollected himself and moved away. A thought ricocheted through his head. He had just begged the woman he loved to tend the girl with whom he had flirted outrageously for a time.

"I would gladly stay with Louisa," she began with a gentle assurance. "It is just what I was thinking. If Mrs. Harville would make up a bed on the floor of Louisa's room, it would be sufficient for me."

"Musgrove, we should leave your father's carriage here. You will need it in the morning to send an account of Louisa's night to your parents. I will rent a chaise or a curricle at the inn to take your wife and sister home."

"Agreed." Charles turned immediately to the task of informing the others, and Frederick hurried off to make the arrangements.

Less than half an hour later, Frederick returned to see Charles attending his sister and Captain Benwick walking beside Anne. Musgrove, it transpired, had once again given in to his wife's demands; the man put peace in his household above peace of mind for his sister. If it were Sophia lying in the Harvilles' bed, nothing and no one would sway Frederick. He would want Anne to nurse her. Mary, he was sure, would soon find any tasks she took on onerous.

Frederick knew arguing with Mary would be futile. And so without delay, he handed Henrietta and Anne into the carriage and placed himself between them. Full of astonishment and vexation, Frederick maneuvered the curricle out onto the road.

Through the early part of the drive, Frederick devoted most of his energy toward Henrietta, trying to support her view—raising her hopes and her spirits. In general, his voice and manner were studiously calm. To spare Henrietta from agitation seemed the governing principle. Frederick knew not what to say to Anne. He knew what he *wanted* to say to her—he wanted to renew his attentions. Now, it was too late. He could not speak words of affection for Anne with Louisa lying unconscious in Harville's house.

Henrietta leaned against his shoulder as he guided the carriage toward Uppercross. She looked up into his face before speaking. "I wish that we had never gone to Lyme—never seen the Cobb." Her voice was flat.

"Please—do not talk of it—do not talk of it!" he cried. "Oh,

God! That I had not given way to her at the fatal moment! Had I done as I ought! But so eager and so resolute! Dear, sweet Louisa!" As he said the words, Frederick recalled the conversation he had with Louisa about universal felicity and the advantage of firmness of character. Now, he wished he had encouraged her to realize that, like all other qualities of the mind, independent thinking should have its proportions and limits. He now felt a persuadable temper might sometimes be as much in favor of happiness as a very resolute character.

As they neared Somersetshire, Henrietta slumped against him, having succumbed to the rhythmic swaying of the horses' gait. "Take the reins for a moment," he whispered in Anne's ear.

She took the straps he laid in her palm. "Hold them easy," he instructed, and she nodded. Turning slightly, he eased Henrietta's limp form back against the seat. "Thank you," he spoke quietly as he reached once more for the reins. Their fingers touched for a moment, and Frederick knew real regret. He spoke on impulse, "Anne, I need to tell you—"

"Do *not* say the words, Captain," she interrupted.

She was correct. Frederick knew he had no right to speak frankly; Anne could not be his now, no matter what he desired. He nodded silently. A few minutes later, he spoke of another matter, "We will be at Uppercross soon." In a low, cautious voice, he continued, "I was considering what we had best do. Henrietta must not appear at first; she could not stand it. I was thinking whether you had not better remain in the carriage with her, while I go and break it to Mr. and Mrs. Musgrove. Do you think this is a good plan?"

"That seems prudent," she said thoughtfully. "Mrs. Musgrove will be distressed and would likely send Henrietta into new hysterics. You calm down the mother, and I will instruct Henrietta on what to do to be of service to her parents."

They rode the rest of the way in silence, both deep in thought of what could be. As they turned into the gates leading to the Great House, Anne placed her hand on top of his and gave it a squeeze. "You will do the honorable thing," she whispered, "because that is the kind of man you are."

"I will return to Lyme tonight as soon as the horses are baited." He did not turn to look at Anne; his heart would stop if he did, but Frederick concentrated deeply on the feel of her hand on his—memorizing the beauty of the moment.

He disembarked as soon as the carriage came to a halt, and, without looking back at Anne, strode to the house. After rapping twice, a servant finally opened the door. Frederick waited impatiently for Mr. Musgrove in the yellow drawing room. He reflected on how often over the past month he had sat in that same room, making small talk with the Misses Musgrove, but especially with Louisa. He cursed the fact he could have been calling on Anne at the Cottage. "*How foolish I was,*" he chastised himself. "*Anne was there for the taking, and all I wanted was revenge.*"

Mr. Musgrove interrupted his musings. "Captain Wentworth? Is something amiss? You have returned without my family."

"Your son and Mrs. Charles are still in Lyme with Louisa," Frederick began. "I regret that I must bring you bad news."

Mr. Musgrove demanded, "Tell me quickly, Man!"

"Louisa—Louisa fell from the seawall. She has a severe contusion and is at present unconscious. The surgeon feels strongly that she will recover, but there are no guarantees. Your son remains behind to help tend her."

"Where is Henrietta?"

"Miss Henrietta is in the carriage with Miss Anne. I wanted the opportunity to speak to you and Mrs. Musgrove first; Henrietta is a bit distraught. I did not want to upset her further."

Mr. Musgrove stepped past Frederick and reached for the brandy decanter. He poured himself one and tossed it off before refilling the glass. "How did it happen? I need to know everything before I tell Mrs. Musgrove." He stood with his back to Frederick, his shoulders hunched, trying to ward off reality.

"It was *my* fault, Sir. I encouraged Louisa to be adventurous. She jumped from the seawall. I tried to catch her, but I was too late. It was purely my fault. I know not what else to say, Sir."

Mr. Musgrove started past him. "I will tell Mrs. Musgrove—if you would be so kind as to bring Henrietta in? I am sure that Mother will want to assure herself of Henrietta's safety." He patted Frederick's shoulder.

"I will return to Lyme this evening, as soon as I refresh the horses and retrieve some clothing from Kellynch. If you wish to send anything to Charles or Mary or Louisa, I will gladly take it with me." Frederick stood in supplication. "I beg your forgiveness, Sir."

"There is nothing to forgive, Captain." Mr. Musgrove moved dejectedly toward the stairs.

Frederick returned to the carriage, where Henrietta and Anne sat. "Your parents need your help, Miss Henrietta," he said without emotion as he helped her from the carriage.

"Thank you, Captain." She rushed up the steps and through the door, still being held open by the footman.

Frederick turned to help Anne. "If you could see that the Musgroves gather some items for your sister and Charles, I would appreciate it. I will look to the horses. When they are fed properly, I am to Kellynch and then back to Lyme."

"I shall take care of it; a footman will bring out the items." She paused, obviously, not wanting to part from him; Frederick, too, lingered.

"Thank you, Anne. If not for you, today would have been even worse. Thank you for your good counsel."

"I did no more than anyone else, and a good deal less than some."

Again, silence prevailed. So much needed saying, but neither of them had a right to speak the words. "I suppose, then, that this is farewell," he said as he took the bridle of the nearest horse to lead it away.

"Good-bye, Captain." She gave him one last look and then hurried up the steps and into the mansion.

"Good-bye, my Dearest Anne," he whispered to her retreating form.

Frederick stopped at Kellynch to give Sophia and Benjamin the news and to gather some of his belongings. He sent Ned Steventon to prepare his clothes, anticipating a lengthy stay in Lyme.

Reluctantly, he entered one of the bedrooms in the east wing. He knew exactly which one it was, having innocently asked Ned several weeks ago. Sophia refused to use this wing of the house—it was where the Elliots lived. Frederick closed the door quietly behind him, before taking the candle and holding it high. This had been Anne's room, and although most of her personal items were no longer evident, Frederick felt he needed to be there, where she had once slept.

Setting the candle on the nightstand, he sat gingerly on the edge of the bed. He looked about him, envisioning Anne moving around the room—dressing behind the screen—writing letters at the desk—standing by the window—observing the garden below. She would never be his; he knew that now. Lying back, he stared up at the canopy above his head. *His Anne* had slept in this very bed, and Frederick found himself grasping the pillow to his chest, trying to smell the lavender she always wore. A pain shot through his heart; happiness eluded him. A quarter hour passed in this way. Then he resolutely shook off the despondency filling his whole being. "I had best return to Lyme," he said out loud. "I must finish what I started."

★ ★ ★

Returning to the Harvilles' house, Frederick joined those gathered in the downstairs sitting room. As expected, Charles had taken the latest news of Louisa's recovery to his parents that very day. Frederick had barely arrived in Lyme before Musgrove was on his way to Uppercross. When Frederick showed up at the house, Musgrove greeted him and said wearily, "Mrs. Harville is exceptional. She has handled everything. Mary had a fainting spell, and so she and I returned early to the inn last night. Mary was hysterical again this morning, but Captain Benwick was kind enough to walk out with her. I wish I had sent her home last night. She is of no use to Mrs. Harville; Anne would have been of service."

"Anne is uncommon," is all Frederick could get out before Charles took his leave.

When Musgrove returned to Lyme in the early evening, he brought with him the family's old nursery maid. Mrs. Musgrove thought the woman would speed Louisa's recovery; the nursery maid had a reputation for coddling her charges, and she had less to do since Harry, the Musgroves' youngest, had gone off to school.

For the next two days, Frederick spent most of his time sitting quietly in the Harvilles' parlor. Everyone assured him the intervals of sense and consciousness were stronger; Louisa's recovery had begun in earnest. He took solace in the news. God had answered his prayers—at least, his prayers for Louisa.

★ ★ ★

A few days later, Frederick was thankful for the assignment of returning to Uppercross to retrieve some of Louisa's personal belongings and bring them back to Lyme. It got him out of the parlor; he did not know how much longer he could sit in that room and wait. As a man of action, such indolence drove him mad.

Riding into the circle at Kellynch, he slid easily from the saddle as the groom took the animal to the stables. Sophia was out the door before he could reach the steps. "Oh, Frederick!" she caressed his face. "You look pale. You are not sleeping, and I can tell you are not eating properly. Look how much weight you have lost!" She wrapped her arm through his as they walked to the house. "You must spend the night."

"I must return to Lyme," he said automatically.

"You will not," she insisted.

Frederick looked at her with hollow eyes. "I have no choice, Sophia. I came here first to pick up some more of my own clothes. I am to call at Uppercross and have the Musgrove maid gather some of Miss Musgrove's trinkets and personal belongings. There is hope such remembrances will speed her recovery."

"Then the girl is improving?" she asked. The Admiral joined his wife and Frederick in the foyer.

Frederick seemed lost in his thoughts. "Miss Musgrove is awake for longer periods each day. She converses with Milly Harville and the family's nursery maid." He headed to the staircase.

"Have you not spoken to her?" Sophia asked as she followed him up the first few steps.

He turned back to her. "Sophia, it would not be proper for me to enter Miss Musgrove's bed chamber." A part of Frederick thanked the rules of propriety for such behavior. He had no desire to encourage Louisa's affections any more than they might already be in place.

"Of course, of course," she added quickly. "Learning everything secondhand must be maddening."

"Yes." Frederick took several steps before casting a glance back over his shoulder at her. "Would you ask the groom for a fresh horse while I take care of a few things in my room?"

"Naturally, Frederick. I shall see to it right away, and I will send a tray up for you." His sister headed to the servants' entrance, and Frederick took the remainder of the steps two at a time.

Less than an hour later, he reappeared in the drawing room, a satchel under his arm. "You are off again?" Sophia asked with regret. "When will we see you next?"

"I have no intention of quitting Lyme until this is settled." Frederick was resigned to his fate. He walked to the window, not really seeing the garden view. Pausing, he debated before asking his next question. "Sophia, have you seen Miss Anne? I assume she returned to Kellynch Lodge with Lady Russell."

"I have not seen her, but she and Lady Russell sent a note with an intention to call here tomorrow."

Frederick sighed; he could not turn around and look at his sister. He would give anything just for a glimpse of Anne. "Would you convey my respects to Miss Anne and tell her I hope she is none the worse for what happened at Lyme. She was the stalwart throughout those initial moments. The exertions were great, and I pray she did not suffer unduly." He would love to leave her word of his constancy—to tell her how much he still admired her, but those words would never be spoken.

"Perhaps you would like to leave Miss Anne a note. I am sure she is eager to receive information on Miss Musgrove's progress,"

Sophia suggested.

"An excellent idea, Sophia. I will do so before I leave." Frederick crossed to the desk, took out a piece of foolscap, and scribbled Anne a message. He did not allow himself the liberty of saying anything personal or even to sign the paper. He knew Sophia would convey that information directly to Anne. In an impetuous move, he kissed the corner of the folded page before he sealed it with wax. His kiss would touch her fingertips as she unfolded the paper to read his message. Closing his eyes, he envisioned his lips caressing Anne's fingertips in a playful seduction. It was all he could do not to groan as the vision played across his mind.

"I believe that is it," he said before placing the note on a side table. "I am back to Lyme once I retrieve Miss Musgrove's belongings. I shall send you word every few days to let you know how things progress."

Sophia walked out with him. "You are in my prayers, Frederick."

"Thank you, Sophia. Pray for us all, please." He swung up into the saddle and rode away.

★ ★ ★

Thomas Harville slid into the chair next to him. Frederick had sat at the table for three hours, shuffling a deck of cards he did not play—staring off into space, lost in his thoughts. "The girl will recover," Harville assured him.

"What? Yes—yes, I know she will with time. It has not been a fortnight, after all." Frederick sipped on a cup of cooled tea, now several hours old.

Harville hesitated and then spoke: "Louisa Musgrove will make you a fine wife, Frederick."

Frederick rolled his eyes heavenward in supplication. "Do I have a choice?" Frederick asked rhetorically.

"Obviously, her family expects a proposal when she recovers; it seems you have paid the young lady with your attentions for several weeks. Mrs. Charles, and even the nursery maid, indicated as much. I understand her mother and father and Miss Henrietta will arrive in Lyme tomorrow." Thomas leaned back in the chair to watch carefully his best friend's reaction.

"I was so foolish, Thomas!" Bitterness laced his words. "I allowed Louisa Musgrove the liberty to think I would choose her, even though my heart has belonged to another for many years. Now, if she recovers, I am obligated to ask for her." Frederick stared off into the distance once again. "What else can I do? It is the only honorable thing." In the back of his mind, he heard Anne telling him the same thing—her words from the last time they were together.

"Perhaps you should withdraw and see how things go once Miss Musgrove recovers. She is young and possibly it would be a matter of out of sight, out of mind. Should you not visit Edward, after all?"

Frederick looked at Thomas. What his friend suggested gave him a faint hope. "I would only be in the way here, would I not?" he said slowly, as if he needed to digest the idea himself. "Louisa has her whole family to tend to her, and you could send me word if I needed to return because of her illness. I should be off to Plymouth for a time to oversee the dismantling of the *Laconia*, and Edward has a new wife whom I must really meet." He searched for permission to leave.

"If absence makes her heart grow fonder, I will send you word immediately. Take your leave early tomorrow morning."

"Thank you, Thomas. You have seen what others have not."

"Go with God, Frederick."

CHAPTER 12

Nothing in the world is single,
All things by a law divine
In one another's being mingle—
Why not I with thine?
—Percy Bysshe Shelley, "Love's Philosophy"

"Is that better, Sir?" Lieutenant Avendale asked as he helped Frederick to a chair. It was the first time Frederick was on deck since the fateful day they had overtaken the French sloop.

Frederick took a deep breath, filling his lungs with sea air. "It is near perfect—thank you, Lieutenant Avendale." The journey from his quarters to this chair propped against an outside wall had taken nearly ten days, but, at last, he could feel the mist on his freshly shaved face.

"I am to wait with you until Mrs. Wentworth comes. I believe she went back for a blanket." The officer transferred his weight from one foot to another.

Frederick chuckled. "Women are the practical ones, are they not, Avendale?"

"I believe they are, Sir. At least, my Maggie seems to always know what is best." The man smiled with his recollection.

"Is Maggie your wife?" Frederick asked, glad to hold a normal conversation with one of his men.

"I hope to make her my wife when we put into port. My term is up, and I will be going home."

"We will be losing a valuable member of the crew when you leave us."

"Thank you, Captain." Avendale dropped his eyes. "The sea is not my life; I thought it would be, but I am not meant for this constant pull of Nature."

"What will you do?"

Avendale stared off for a moment. "I would like to take my orders; I studied at the university. My father wished me to pursue a military career, but the life of a country curate would serve me quite well. My father will be disappointed, but a man must define his own life. Do you not agree, Captain?"

"For those not firstborn or for those whose family can offer their sons little, I am a firm believer in the power of choice. My brother, Edward, chose the clergy and is very happy, whereas I could think of little but the sea and the adventure. The Navy gave me opportunities I would never have otherwise."

"Does your brother have his own parish?"

"My brother toiled for many years as a curate, but he, at last, took a position in Shropshire, near Shrewsbury. He married and will welcome his first child soon."

"Then he is happy?"

Frederick nodded. "When I saw him last, he was. His calling serves him well, as I am sure it will you."

"When we reach Plymouth, I will meet Maggie there; she travels from Bristol. I hope to make her my wife—and then I hope for a position near Hull." Avendale stood as he saw Anne Wentworth approach. "Your wife approaches, Sir. When you are ready to return to your quarters, it will be my honor to assist you."

"I will send for you."

After Avendale saluted and left, Anne took the seat next to Frederick, but only after spreading a light blanket over his lap. "Is not the sea air glorious?" she whispered.

Frederick turned his head to look at her. "You love it as much as I do."

"A ship is nothing like what I imagined. When I saw the sails from a distance, I thought a ship moves silently upon the waves; I was surprised that the canvas sails roar and snap in the wind, the hull breaks water like an explosive thunderclap, and the guns roll with a volcanic eruption. I was more surprised that in the mix of all this noise, there is a peace—a faceless gentleness that creeps into my soul—into my veins." Her voice trailed off. There was silence for a few companionable minutes, and then Anne said, "What do you ponder, Captain?"

"Hmm? Oh, I was thinking of Plymouth. The last time I spent more than a few days there, I was trying to forget the chaos of my life just after Louisa's fall and trying to come to terms with my undying need for your love." Frederick reached out and took her hand in his. He placed a kiss on the pulse of her wrist.

"What did you do in Plymouth? I know so little about what you did before you came to Bath."

He chortled. "Do you mean before I threw myself at your feet and begged you to marry me?"

"First, you did not beg," she began to protest, but then stopped suddenly. "Why do you enjoy teasing me so?"

"Because I cannot live without that spark of passion I see in your face when your emotions are engaged." He traced his fingertips from her temple to her jaw line. "You mesmerize me; when you are near, I am spellbound—enthralled—captivated—just pick a word because none of them completely describe what I feel." Love and need held them as they memorized each other's features. After longing moments only those who truly love understand, he cleared his throat, needing also to clear his thoughts of Anne's heat-laden eyes. Looking straight ahead, he began, "I have been to Plymouth many times."

★ ★ ★

Walking along George Street, Frederick mused at the many changes he had witnessed in the Plymouth landscape over the years. When he had first made port there, back before his sailing to the Americas, George Street had been strictly residential. Now, the Theatre Royal II anchored a development, which also included the Royal Hotel. Between 1811 and 1813, every time he sailed into port, he made a special trip to the area, intrigued by the construction.

The theater boasted a special vestibule, private boxes, a pit, and a gallery; it had once been isolated, but now the town met the site. Frederick had been in attendance for the opening program—*As*

You Like It and a farce titled *Catherine and Petruchio*. Some members of the unruly audience had interrupted portions of the performance. The building itself was something of an anomaly, using cast and wrought iron for fireproofing. Seeing the structure from a distance, he smiled with the remembrance.

He walked past the theater and took a room at an inn on Cornwall Street. Frederick had come to Plymouth because he was heartsick and anxious; he wanted nothing more than to escape the scenario playing out in Lyme. If Louisa Musgrove did not recover completely, he would be obligated to make her an offer of marriage. She had placed her trust in him, and he could not turn from her if she continued to suffer from her fall. He prayed daily for her full recovery; admittedly, this was partly an act of self-interest. Frederick hoped that with the distance, Louisa would forget her feelings for him. It was an act of a desperate man, and one of which he was not proud; but he could not control the dread he felt when he considered making Louisa his wife.

In town for just three days, Frederick spent his time walking the streets of Plymouth, visiting with clothiers and auctioneers. He purchased a new watch as a gift for Edward and several packets of seeds and bulbs for Christine, Edward's wife.

He stood along the shore one day and watched for hours as barge after barge made its way from the quay at the Breakwater Quarry out to the sea, dropping stones and cable to form the Breakwater. The Breakwater was located at the mouth of Plymouth Sound, between Boyisand Bay on the east and Cawsand Bay on the west, and would eventually be one thousand yards in length and ten feet above the low water.

He recalled coming into the Sound the first time. The port was dangerous because Plymouth Sound was open to storms from the southwest, creating anchorage problems. On that particular entrance, he had stood on deck as a lieutenant, gritting his teeth as the crew navigated past a previous wreckage on the Boyisand coast.

One late afternoon, he drifted toward the shipyards in hopes of meeting some former crewmates. Shipbuilding and repair establishments sprinkled the shores of Hamoaze, and Frederick sought familiar faces. Amazingly, he had been in town for nearly a week, and he had seen no one whom he knew, a testament of how much the war had changed the port city. As he turned toward the harbor off Exeter Street, however, he heard someone call his name. "Wentworth! Say, Wentworth!"

Frederick turned in the direction of the sound. He saw a man broad of shoulder, but also broad of hip, hurrying toward him. He had an iron jaw and intense eyes. "It that you, Hawker?" Frederick asked as the man drew near.

"What brings you to Plymouth?" Hawker said. He shook Frederick's hand. "Is not your ship already in dry dock?"

Frederick could not explain his real reasons for being in town. "I came on business on behalf of Thomas Harville. He is struggling a bit right now."

"I see." John Hawker turned to acknowledge another acquaintance. In 1810, although it was apparently drying out at every spring tide, John Hawker had taken over the Sutton Pool. When the Prince Regent miraculously gave a ninety-nine-year lease to the Sutton Pool Company, Hawker went from fool to astute businessman. "Do you have plans for dinner? I would enjoy catching up."

Frederick hesitated and then said, "I have no definite plans."

"Then please join our party," Hawker cajoled.

Frederick became suspicious. "Who else will be in the group?"

Hawker looked about sheepishly. "Several business investors, of course, and Lord Grierson will be in attendance."

Frederick rolled his eyes in exasperation. "I assume Lady Mary Grierson and her daughters will be among the party."

"I would imagine," Hawker said, trying to sound innocent.

"I thank you, Hawker, for the invitation, but I will decline."

"Must you? I am sure Her Ladyship would approve of your company."

"Although Her Ladyship is most pleasurable company, I will still decline. You might mention to Her Ladyship that I intend to make an offer of marriage soon." It was not a lie; if Louisa did not recover or even if she did and still expected a proposal, she would receive his offer; and if he were fortunate enough for Louisa to look elsewhere, he would seek out Anne once again.

Looking about as if he suddenly remembered a prior appointment, Hawker questioned, "Marriage? Really? Well, I will tell Her Ladyship, and I will wish you happy, Wentworth. I would be honored to meet your future wife some day." With that, Hawker made a quick bow and took his leave.

Frederick snorted with the irony of the situation. Lord and Lady Grierson wanted Frederick to pursue one of their daughters, but Sir Walter Elliot had found the prospect of Frederick marrying Anne to be degrading to her. Frederick shook his head. If worse came to worse, he could turn to the Griersons in order to squelch Louisa's plans. If he must marry someone whom he did not love, marrying one of the Grierson daughters would be financially advantageous, and no one would criticize his withdrawal from Louisa Musgrove for such a prestigious alliance. *What am I thinking? I don't want a Grierson daughter! Nor do I want Louisa. I want Anne— for eight years, I have wanted Anne Elliot.*

On the seventh day of his stay, his mail caught up with him, having been forwarded to him by Sophia. Actually, Frederick had nearly forgotten about sending a letter of inquiry on Thomas's behalf. It seemed a lifetime ago when he had sent it off—in reality, it was only a little more than three weeks. He opened the reply and read what he expected. Aloud he said, "Well, I guess I will call at Lyme and stay at least long enough to speak to Milly and Thomas. If only I can find a way not to see Louisa or her family!"

★ ★ ★

The public carriage rolled into Lyme in the late afternoon. Instead of seeking out the better accommodations that Mr. Morris offered at the Wooden Lion, he took a substandard room at the posting inn. It was out of the way, and he was less likely to meet any of the Musgroves along the post road. They stayed in town, close to the Harvilles' home. He planned to stay only one night; he would be on his way to Shrewsbury and Edward's new home the next day.

"Say, Boy," he called to one of the stable hands hanging around the inn. "Would you take this message to Thomas Harville? I wrote the directions on the back. Do you read, Boy?"

"Yes, Sir." The youth looked at him. "Should I wait for a reply, Sir?"

"No—that will not be necessary." He slipped two shillings into the boy's hand. "Give the message only to Thomas Harville or to Mrs. Harville—no one else. Do you understand?"

"Yes, Sir—it will be done, Sir." The boy disappeared across the road, heading along an open orchard on his way to the town center.

Frederick waited, knowing it would be after supper before his friend would appear. He took his meal in his chamber, avoiding the public rooms, in case someone recognized him. It was well after dark when he heard a light tap on the door. He opened it to find both Thomas and Milly.

"Welcome," he said as he hustled them into the room. "Did you have any trouble getting away?" He carried another chair to the table, bringing a bottle of brandy and two glasses with him. "Let me send for some tea, Milly." Frederick stepped to the hallway and, luckily, found one of the maids. He gave her the order before returning to his friends.

"How was Plymouth?" Thomas asked as he poured himself a drink.

"Tolerable." Frederick seated himself across from them. "I saw Hawker; he tried to hook me into joining him and Lord and Lady Grierson for dinner."

"I am sure the daughters were not far behind," Harville said sarcastically. "If they want to rid themselves of those two mousey, colorless women, they will need to increase the size of their dowries." He laughed at his words. "Neither has any personality—no redeeming qualities whatsoever."

"They are amiable and biddable if a man was so inclined," Frederick added without looking at either of his friends. He would not let them know that just yesterday he had briefly considered the Griersons as a way out of his current situation.

Milly reached for his hand. "I am sorry, Frederick, that you feel you must hide from the Musgroves; I find them to be very pleasant people."

"And I would thoroughly agree with you." He patted the back of her hand before reaching for the brandy decanter. "I just do not choose to become part of their family if I can avoid it."

"So, do you wish to know the latest on Miss Musgrove?" Thomas became his second in command again—roles with which they were both familiar.

"Please."

"Miss Musgrove is able to sit up for significantly longer periods of time; although more subdued, she has no problem in recalling details. In fact, Charles and Mary Musgrove return to Uppercross tomorrow. Mrs. Charles thoroughly enjoyed her holiday—she walks about the town with Benwick, she shops, and she reads—just about anything other than tending her sister."

"That does not surprise me; at Uppercross, she pawned off her boys on Miss Anne or on their grandmother." Just the mention of Anne caused Frederick to flinch. "How long do you expect to tend Miss Musgrove?"

Milly answered. "Mr. and Mrs. Musgrove leave at the end of the week; they take our children with them—the youngest Musgroves will be home for the holidays at that time—the children will be able to celebrate together. Miss Henrietta remains with us for as long as it takes for her sister to recuperate. The doctor says at least another month."

"*That* long." Frederick sighed.

The maid brought the tea tray, and all conversation stopped until she exited the room. When she left, Thomas turned to Frederick. "Your note said you had something of importance to tell us."

Frederick nodded. "Actually, Thomas, I bring some *news* for you. In fact, if I did not deem it important, I would never stop in Lyme on my way to see Edward."

"Then tell us," Milly encouraged.

"When I was here the first time, your craftsmanship impressed me.

"Yes, I recall. What of it?"

"When I returned to Kellynch, I sent a letter of inquiry. Do you remember Harold Rushick?"

"Certainly, he was a damn fine lieutenant; I hated the fact that he left us to return to civil life." Thomas took a sip of his drink. "What does he have to do with all this?"

"On the ride home, I remembered something important about Rushick. His family owns a novelty and furniture business outside Brighton; he left us to take over the business when his uncle died. I wrote him about the toys and the chairs and the hammock. Here is his response." Frederick slid the letter across the table to his dearest friend.

Thomas picked it up and read it quickly. "What does it say?" Milly asked impatiently. Her husband passed the note to her, his pride warring with his need to support his family.

"Oh, Thomas!" she exclaimed. "This is like a prayer come true." Tears misted her eyes as she turned to Frederick. "Bless you." She shook her head in disbelief.

"Why?" Thomas looked questioningly at Frederick.

"Why did you help the Musgroves, people whom you did not know? Because we are friends, Thomas. We served together in a brotherhood that no one else can understand. I found you an opportunity—you must take advantage of it. It is not charity; Rushick will expect you to perform well. That is how he approaches work; you know that."

"Thomas," Milly pleaded, "you can make furniture, and Lieutenant Rushick will sell your items on commission. The letter says that wooden toys are selling quickly in the Americas. You can create your pieces. In May, when our lease is up, we can move closer to Brighton; you will still be near the sea there."

"Brighton is quickly becoming the new Bath. Visitors will be eager to buy something of quality," Frederick encouraged. "Think about it; I will say no more. If you want to deal with Rushick, his directions are in the letter."

Thomas let a smile turn up the corners of his mouth. "Milly

and I will discuss it and see what is possible. Thank you, my friend."

Frederick allowed himself to take a deep breath at last. He knew Harville's pride, and he had feared his friend would reject the idea before hearing it out. Thankfully, his need to provide for his family had overpowered his misplaced independence. "Someday I will say I was one of the first to own a Harville original," Frederick teased.

"We should get back." Thomas took the lead, after shaking Frederick's hand. "I borrowed Musgrove's curricle; we told everyone Milly needed to call on a sick friend."

"Should I cough now, so that your explanation was not a lie?" Frederick said. He stood to bid them farewell.

"We will keep your secret." Milly gave him a quick hug of gratitude. "I will write to you in care of Edward and keep you abreast of Miss Musgrove's progress."

"Thank you, Milly," Frederick said. "You know, I do not wish Louisa ill. Quite the contrary. I wish her happiness—with someone other than me."

★ ★ ★

Three days after Frederick met with the Harvilles, the public carriage rolled into Shrewsbury, and Frederick alighted at last. It had been a bone-jarring ride, plagued by snow and rain for two of the days. The driver tossed down his bag, and Frederick spun around, trying to get his bearings, but found himself in his brother's happy embrace. "Thank God." Edward laughed with relief. "I am so glad you are here; I thought you would never come."

A smile spread across Frederick's face; he had forgotten how much he needed Edward's presence in his life. He loved Edward not only as a brother, but also as a trusted friend. Frederick could count on Edward not judging him.

"You have changed, Edward," Frederick half mocked as he took a close look at his brother. "You look positively contented."

"When you meet my Christine, you will understand why. Come." He pulled Frederick toward a waiting chaise and four. "Lord Calderson, my patron, loaned me his carriage to bring my brother home—no more poorly sprung carriages for you today."

"Thank Goodness for that." They stored his gear in the luggage compartment and climbed in. "I am thrilled to be here, Edward; I need your counsel when we find time for some privacy."

"I would be pleased to help you. Let us return home, and later we will sit together—just like old times."

★ ★ ★

"Christine, he is here!" Edward called as they entered the vicarage bestowed upon him as part of the Calderson's living. Frederick looked around, taking in the simple décor. Some of the furniture showed wear, but the house offered large rooms, a great improvement from Edward's previous lodgings.

Christine Wentworth came quickly to answer her husband's call. Frederick took in her presence—tall and thin and aristocratic in her posture, she, at first glance could make a man think haughty, but her fair hair framed a face sporting a faint smile and a demure downward glance at her messy apron. She evidently had been cleaning one of the fireplaces and was now covered in soot.

Edward laughed, "My cinder maid." He bestowed a quick kiss on the end of her nose and used his fingertips to remove a smudge from her cheek before pulling her close to him. "Meet my own version of the Cinderella story," he told Frederick. "This is your new sister—my wife, Christine."

Frederick bowed and approved, "Christine, welcome to the family. Do not let this cad tease you, my Dear. Edward was always more of a frog than a prince." He shot her a knowing smile.

She returned her own amused one. "We are pleased you are finally here, Captain. I apologize for my appearance; I foolishly tried to clear the flue in the guest room—something I asked my 'prince' to do yesterday, in fact." It was Edward's turn to look embarrassed. "Now, if you will excuse me, I will freshen my clothing." She looked at Edward. "Please have Sadie bring in some tea. I will ask Cal to finish sweeping out the ashes before you show your brother his room."

"I am at your beck and call, my Lady Love." Edward gave her an exaggerated bow.

"I have never seen you so carefree," Frederick noted as he took the seat to which his brother gestured.

"Christine is remarkable." Edward gazed at the doorway through which his wife had exited. "She gives me a new purpose; Christine brings me contentment. The woman actually knows me better than I know myself sometimes. I really cannot explain it."

"Love." The word hung in the air as if it explained everything.

Edward smiled again. "Marriage to Christine has been the exciting—the satisfying—experience God intended it to be."

"Now I am jealous," Frederick declared. "Both you and Sophia have placed the bar high. How will I ever measure up?"

Edward's countenance sobered. "I assume you wish to speak to me about love. Did your heart survive its encounter with Somersetshire? I cringed when I realized Sophia and the Admiral planned to take over the Elliot estate. Did you ever tell her about Anne Elliot?"

"*No one* knows about Anne—no one but you." Frederick shifted uncomfortably in his chair.

"Is Miss Anne still in the area? Have you seen her?"

Frederick snorted. "I have seen Miss Anne Elliot repeatedly over the past two months. She stays with her younger sister at Uppercross Cottage."

"Yes, I recall now. Mary Elliot became Mrs. Charles Musgrove only a few months before I left the area. There were rumors Musgrove asked for Miss Anne first, but she refused him. I relished in the news on your behalf although I dared not tell you at the time." Edward took a tray from the pretty housekeeper, and he began to pour them both some tea.

"Yes, I heard as much. It was quite a *revelation*. I became friends with the Musgroves when I arrived in the area. Ironically, one of Musgroves' sons served under me."

"Dick Musgrove?" Edward exclaimed. "I should have made the connection. Oh, Frederick, he was a trouble to his family; I hope he served you better than he did them."

"Unfortunately, no." Frederick chuckled, "But his parents have fond memories of their son's worth."

Edward nodded, as if to say such was a common occurrence. "How did you handle seeing Miss Anne after all these years? I know how you suffered with the parting."

Frederick paused, reflecting on how the foolishness of his actions gave him little amusement. "At first, I relished the idea of seeing Miss Anne treated poorly by her family; they speak of her as an afterthought. I wanted to see her brought down—see her Elliot pride dragged through the dirt. But she does not deserve that, Edward. Anne is still the kindest, most intelligent woman I have ever known. She possesses a silent strength; a man would be blessed to hold her in his arms. I was a fool, Edward. I should have returned to Somerset and renewed my offer to her in '08. She would have been of age by then, but I feared rejection."

"Why not renew your proposal now? Do you believe Miss Anne is indifferent to you?" Edward leaned back in his chair. He knew to let Frederick tell his story at his own pace.

"I created a quagmire. When I first went to Uppercross, I purposely entertained the attention of Miss Musgrove. I needed Anne to see how *others* wanted me, even though *she* did not. I played games for which I now must pay. Lately, I decided I still wanted Anne, but I knew I had to distance myself from Louisa Musgrove, before I could plead my case with Miss Anne."

"That seems a logical sequence," Edward said drily.

Frederick frowned, bringing the lines of his brows together. "Oh, Edward, I wish it were that simple. I was in Lyme with Harville, and the Musgroves, as well as Anne; we traveled there together."

"I see," Edward said cautiously.

"Throughout my relationship with Louisa Musgrove, I encouraged her to demonstrate her independence. I did it as part of my revenge on Miss Anne; I was of the opinion that Anne possessed a *too-persuadable* nature. Louisa flirted with me by climbing on stiles and high steps and having me catch her when she jumped. In Lyme, she jumped from the seawall steps. The first time, I caught her and set her apart from me. My thoughts were on Anne at the time. Captain Benwick and a stranger—who, we later realized, was her family's estranged cousin—both paid her attentions. I was desperate to win her heart before one of them did. Louisa must have sensed my withdrawal, for she climbed the steps a second time, taking on a greater height. Although I tried, I could not catch her. She sustained a blow to her head and was unconscious for a prolonged period. In short, her family expects an offer because I showed her so much attention. I cannot, in good conscience, withhold that proposal. Yet my heart does not belong to Louisa Musgrove. Even if I marry her, she will never be Anne—no one will."

Edward seemed confused. "What do you do now? Should you not be in Lyme?"

"Harville suggested I put distance between Louisa Musgrove and myself. He believes she is young and consequently might forget the flirtation. If she does not, then I will do the honorable thing and make her my wife."

Edward let out a low whistle; he finally leaned forward. "What if Miss Anne moves on before this is resolved? Did you not say she attracted the attention of two men in less than a day? What of her cousin? Is this the same cousin—the future baronet?"

"Evidently." Frederick grimaced, remembering Mr. Elliot's forwardness in speaking to Anne at the inn.

"If I recall, the man snubbed the Elliots' advances previously. Now that he is older, he may see the advantage of such a marriage. Sir Walter wanted Mr. Elliot for his Elizabeth, but I am sure the baronet would be just as pleased if the heir apparent chose Miss Anne. If so, her father's family would keep control of Kellynch Hall. Our family, of course, would be looking for another residence."

"For me, it could be no worse. Back in Lyme, when we discovered who Mr. Elliot was, the waiter disclosed that the gentleman's servant had mentioned going to Bath soon. Sir Walter and Miss Elliot are in Bath, and Anne is to travel there with Lady Russell. I had hoped to renew my attentions to Anne once she arrived in Bath. Now, I must wait for my fate back in Lyme while Mr. Elliot is likely to move in the same circles as the Elliots and have free access to Anne." Frederick nearly growled with thoughts of such a development. "Even if Louisa recovers and chooses someone else or chooses to end our relationship, I may be too late to earn Anne's regard again."

"You are right—*quagmire* is an appropriate term." Edward shook his head in disbelief. "So I am to entertain you while you wait. Great! A caged animal in my house! Does Sophia know what she sent me? If so, I will plot my retaliation."

"Our sister is innocent this time," Frederick insisted. "Sophia discerned my regard for Anne about a week before our fateful trip to Lyme. It surprised her, as she believed Louisa Musgrove to be my choice."

"Our sister thinks she understands us," Edward observed. "Unfortunately, she thinks you and I would choose someone like her. Obviously, my Christine is not like Sophia. The Admiral could not survive civilian life without our sister, where Christine complements my existence after so many years as a bachelor."

Frederick sighed. "What you said a moment ago was correct; I am a caged animal."

Edward stood and clapped him on the shoulder. "Never mind. I have a long list of projects that need more than two hands. Hard work will take your mind off your troubles."

"The Wentworth men together again! Look out Shrewsbury, you are in for a treat." Frederick gave his brother a full smile. "Thank you, Edward—thank you for understanding my need to be here."

"You are my brother. No matter what your troubles, you may always find a home under my roof. Now, let us get you settled. Tomorrow, we begin your visit in earnest." Together they climbed the stairs, laughing and jostling all the way.

CHAPTER 13

"Let us not speak, for the love we bear one another—
Let us hold hands and look."
She, such a very ordinary little woman;
He, such a thumping crook;
But both, for a moment, little lower than the angels
In the teashop's ingle-nook.
—Sir John Betjeman, "In a Bath Teashop"

Over the next few weeks, Frederick became Edward's shadow.
Rarely separated from his brother, he willingly did all the things
necessary to ease Edward's way in the community. He helped Edward prepare the land for Widow Leverton's garden, removing
rocks and weeds despite the hardness of the winter soil. Frederick
spent a night in one of the estate cottager's main rooms, tending to
the family's small children, while Edward administered to the needs
of a dying parent. He used his physical strength and natural agility
to make repairs around the vicarage, and he sat with pride beside
his sister Christine as Edward delivered soul-searching sermons to a
packed village church.

Regularly, he received reports from Harville as to Louisa's
recovery. Evidently, the Musgroves had returned to Uppercross,
and, as Milly indicated earlier, they had taken the Harville children
with them. The last letter revealed the fact that Louisa would return
home before her brothers and sisters left for school, presumably
right after the start of the new year. Frederick nearly panicked with
the news; his fate awaited him. Would Anne be a part of his future?
Nightly, he dreamed of her—the dreams even more real now than
they were had been when they first parted years earlier. In his
favorite dream, Frederick played out the many ways he would

greet her if Anne should appear before him again—everything from dropping to his knees immediately and begging her to accept him to taking her in his arms and kissing her until she could think of nothing but him to clasping her hand in his and slowly bringing her delicately gloved fingers to his lips. He preferred the kissing her crazy idea best, but, no matter what, Frederick knew he would never walk away from her again. He would stay in her life until Anne Elliot accepted him. Thoughts of such pleasure brought a warm smile to his face.

On Christmas Eve, Frederick helped Christine down from an open carriage. As they entered the vestibule, she lightly placed her hand on his arm. "Frederick," she whispered, as they started up the aisle. He turned his head to look down at her, noting how she glowed. "How would you feel about being an uncle?"

Frederick froze, pulling her to a quick halt and nearly causing the family behind them to crash into their backsides. Christine smiled up at him and urged him on. He leaned down and murmured as he helped her into a pew, "Did I misunderstand you, my Dear?"

She leaned so close that their heads nearly touched. "You did not. I was just thinking what a great uncle you will be to our child."

"Does Edward know?" He nearly laughed.

Christine's eyes drifted to where her husband stood greeting parishioners. "He will tonight." She blushed and looked away quickly.

"Edward will be ecstatic!" Frederick took her hand in his and kissed her cheek.

"Do you believe it to be so?" Suddenly, his self-assured sister in marriage seemed to ask for advice on how to handle his brother.

Frederick's gaze found his older brother in the throng gathering at the back of the church. "Edward says a Wentworth man waits until his future is secure before he marries, and then he marries for love; he loves you, Christine. And I am certain that he will love this child."

Christine smiled. "I will tell him this evening. You will keep my confidence?"

"You know I will, my Dear."

Christine squeezed his fingers. "May the upcoming year bring you happiness, Frederick. I pray you at last find the love you seek."

"Edward has told you?" he asked in a low voice.

"No, Edward said nothing to me. A woman sees such things in a man's eyes, and *your* eyes, Frederick, say you have an unrequited love."

Frederick cleared his throat. "I have but one prayer on this Christmas Eve: I hope to find the happiness my brother has found with you."

Listening to Edward's words regarding a child being born and bringing happiness to the world took on special meaning that evening.

★ ★ ★

After six weeks in Shropshire, the weekly reports from Harville became redundant; and when one came late in the afternoon, Frederick did not open it. Reluctantly, Frederick took it to the table for the midday meal, leaving it lying conspicuously next to his setting while he filled a plate from a sidebar piled high with food.

"You have another letter from Harville?" Edward noted as he filled Christine's plate; he took a protective stance since learning of his wife's first pregnancy. Christine had adopted several unusual eating habits of late; for example, she seemed to desire herring and chocolate, not always as separate dishes. Frederick tried not to observe what might be her latest culinary concoction.

"I am sure it is very much as always—filled with praises for the Musgroves' continued kindness. Louisa slowly improves," Frederick recited in a mocking tone. He dug into the boiled potatoes as soon as Edward offered his blessing for the meal.

Christine insisted, "You must read it, Frederick; I have a feeling about this." She shrugged, indicating she could not explain her words. "It will—I know it will—give you what you want."

Frederick smiled at her; in the past few weeks, his very sensible sister had become a good deal less rational and more emotional. "For you, my Dear," he offered, and he broke the seal on the letter. Harville addressed the envelope, but Milly had written the letter,

176

and Frederick relaxed, expecting a more detailed accounting of the situation.

> *1 February 1815*
> *My dear Frederick,*
>
> *Both Thomas and I pray this letter finds you well. As your last missive brought us the news of Christine and Edward's upcoming arrival, we know that all is happy with the Wentworths in Shropshire.*
>
> *We are still in residence at Uppercross, although Thomas insists we return to Lyme; we will do so on Friday. Thomas says he must refocus on creating pieces for Mr. Rushick, but I know otherwise. My husband does not choose to be at Uppercross now that others join our party.*
>
> *I suppose I need to tell you, Frederick, that things with Louisa Musgrove have changed dramatically.*

Frederick's hand began to shake, and Christine ungraciously kicked her husband's ankle to get his attention. "What is it, Frederick?" Edward's voice rose in concern.

As he thumbed to page two, Frederick pushed his apprehension down by wiping his forehead with his linen. "Mrs. Harville says things have changed."

"What things?" Christine gasped before she could stifle the words.

Edward touched his brother's shoulder. "Why do you not read it out loud, Frederick? We would like to share whatever it is."

Frederick nodded and shuffled the pages in his hands. He cleared his throat, trying to stall for as long as possible, before reading.

> *As you know, while in Lyme, Miss Musgrove spent several weeks with us. We tried, as your friends, to care for her, as we knew you would if you were here. Once the young lady began to recover, we all—including her loving family—spent hours reading to her and trying to entertain Miss Musgrove—to help her remember what she might have forgotten.*
>
> *However, as her family felt the need to return to Somerset, the extended hours assisting Miss Musgrove fell completely in our laps. You know Thomas is not a reading man, and sitting quietly for hours*

would certainly not appeal to him. Plus, he felt the need to provide Mr. Rushick with many offerings to prove his worth and to secure our children's futures.

So when James Benwick offered to sit with Miss Musgrove, we were thrilled to relinquish some of our duties to him. Captain Benwick recited beautiful verses to Miss Musgrove; I often heard his resonant tones as I completed my household tasks.

Here is how the situation has changed drastically. Captain Benwick comes to Uppercross today, for he has asked Miss Musgrove to marry him. The good captain sent a letter to Mr. Musgrove via Thomas, and his plight was accepted. The happy couple will make a formal announcement with his arrival. Thomas does not know how to respond to all this; he is relieved for your benefit—it is as he predicted: Once you were out of Miss Musgrove's sight, you were out of her mind. Yet, Thomas feels betrayed—on Fanny's account. Deep down, my Thomas knows Captain Benwick could not be expected to never find another love, but the fact that Fanny's death came less than a year ago creates a quandary for him. Therefore, we will wish the couple happy and then return to our home.

I am sure this letter brings you relief, and that is its purpose. Both Thomas and I pray you will be able to return to us soon; I believe my husband could use your sensibility in dealing with the change in our home situation.

As always, we remain your friends.

MH

Frederick looked up in disbelief to see tears streaming down Christine's face. "You were right," he whispered.

"Oh, Frederick!" she exclaimed.

Edward half laughed. "I suppose this is the end of your visit?" He slapped Frederick on his shoulder. "You are one lucky man, my Brother!"

"Can it be true?" Frederick still held the letter, afraid that if he moved, all his hopes would be dashed. "I must write to Sophie." He turned wide-eyed to stare at his brother.

Edward's smile grew by the moment. "Yes, write to Captain Benwick and offer him your congratulations. Send Thomas Harville words to ease his consternation, and then write to our sister. By the way, you do recall that Sophia and the Admiral traveled to Bath so that he might take the waters for his gout?"

The significance of what Edward said dawned on Frederick. "Benjamin's gout? They are in Bath!" He started to laugh hysterically. Getting up and dancing around the room, he swept Christine out of her seat. "Sophia is in Bath," he chanted as he twirled her around the furniture.

"Easy, Frederick," Edward cautioned. "Those are my goods you swing about the room."

Frederick spun his brother's wife around once more. Bowing to her, he said, "I have so much to do." Then he headed toward the door.

"What about your meal?"

"I will take it with me." Frederick grabbed his plate from the table. "I can breathe again, Edward!" he nearly shouted on his way out of the room. "I can breathe at last!"

Christine sat down on Edward's lap and snaked her arms around his neck as he adjusted her in his embrace. She laid her head on his shoulder. "Someday," she said dreamily, "you will explain to me what just happened?"

"If things go the way I suspect, the next time we see my younger brother, he will introduce you to the love of his life." He lifted her chin. "Frederick's love will meet my love."

★ ★ ★

Frederick Wentworth strode down the busy street, secure in the knowledge that he would see Anne Elliot soon. He arrived in Bath only the day before, nearly a week from the day he had received Milly Harville's note—the longest week of his existence. In his letter, he had not told Sophia he planned to join her in Bath, even though Frederick knew she would be thrilled when he returned to her household. He simply told her of the developments at Uppercross.

Today, he would meet some acquaintances; if he were fortunate, he would learn the latest gossip about the Elliots. Later, he would ask Sophia to help him meet Anne again. Sophia and the Admiral called on the Elliots previously, and Benjamin spoke of how often they saw Anne about town. In fact, the Admiral had escorted her home only three days earlier. If nothing else, he could make a call of respect on her to see how she fared. After spending so much time in each other's company at Uppercross, such an act would be appropriate.

A little below Milson Street, he met his party, having agreed the previous evening to spend time with Lieutenant Harding, the younger son of the Marquis of Brookstone; his sisters, Ladies Amelia and Caroline; as well as their cousin Lady Susan Lowery. Yesterday morning, Frederick had encountered Buford Harding quite unexpectedly at a posting inn twenty miles north of Bath. They had agreed to meet for today's outing. Frederick might have declined the offer, but he knew Harding's family would move in the same circles as did Anne's. He hoped to see Anne Elliot again without seeming to pursue her.

"Ah, Wentworth!" Harding called out as he approached. Frederick offered the group a bow. "Let me introduce you, Captain," he said, clarifying the connections by explaining to his family that Captain Wentworth was the personal friend of Captain Benwick, under whom Harding recently served.

"Our brother tells us Captain Benwick recently became engaged," Lady Amelia hinted for information.

"Only a fortnight ago," Frederick assured her, "if my source was reliable." They started walking toward Molland's, a fashionable confectioner's shop often patronized by members of the *ton*. Frederick assumed he could ask his companions about the Elliots soon enough.

"Do you know his betrothed?" Lady Amelia asked.

Frederick guarded his words, unsure what she might have heard. "The young lady is quite pleasant; Miss Musgrove should soften Captain Benwick's need for solitude, and the Captain should allow Louisa Musgrove to develop a deep love of learning. They are well matched."

"My brother admired Captain Benwick," Miss Amelia added quickly. "I do not believe I know the Musgroves."

Frederick thought, *This lady wants to know the latest gossip.* He paused before answering. "The Musgroves are a wealthy family in Somerset. Their son once served under me, but Richard Musgrove passed away several years ago."

"Ah, so they have no title?" Lady Amelia asked disdainfully.

Frederick could not resist, having felt the sting of such judgments before. "Perhaps I should withdraw. You should not be seen in my company, Lady Amelia. Like the Musgroves, *I* am among the untitled."

"Oh, Captain," she said and giggled, "I meant no offense."

"None taken," he muttered, but the lady's words so incensed him that when his party stepped into Molland's, and he found the one person in the world he most wanted to see, every word he had planned to say upon finding Anne Elliot flew out of his mind. He stood there transfixed, feeling himself turn quite red. God! She was more beautiful than he remembered, and it was all he could do not to shout for joy at being in her presence once again. Obviously equally struck by seeing him, Anne took a slight step back, and Frederick, automatically reached out to steady her. Just touching her sent a shock through him. All the overpowering, blinding, bewildering, first effects of strong surprise were over for her, but Frederick still could not conquer his sensibilities. It was agitation, pain, pleasure, a something between delight and misery.

"Miss—Miss Anne!" he stammered.

Still a bit confused by the sight of him, Anne managed to curtsy. "Captain Wentworth." A smile turned up the corners of her mouth as Frederick searched her face.

"Miss Anne," Lady Susan interrupted their conversation, "it is pleasant to see you again. May I inquire as to the health of the rest of your family?"

"My father is well, thank you, Lady Susan." Then Anne gestured toward one of the tables. "My sister and her companion, Mrs. Clay, as you see, are with me. We took refuge from the rainy weather." Lady Susan and Elizabeth acknowledged each other with a nod.

"I assume with your cousin Lady Dalrymple's patronage of the arts, your family will be in attendance for Madame Tresurré's premiere concert performance?"

Anne shifted her weight. "My family shall attend."

"Then we shall see you there." Lady Susan and her cousins started to move away, and, after a nervous bow, Frederick followed suit. He neared the table Harding had located for them before he realized he just walked away from Anne—the one thing he swore he would never do again. For nearly two months he prayed daily for the opportunity to rekindle Anne's desire for him, and he just walked past her to sit with Lady Amelia, a woman who not three minutes ago made him so angry he reacted in a very non-gentlemanlike manner. "Excuse me," he said to his group and went back to where Anne still stood, looking out at the street.

"Miss Anne," he spoke softly as he stepped up beside her, "I am happy to see you well."

"Thank you, Captain, and are you well? I understand from the Admiral that you were with your bother in Shropshire?"

"I could do little in Lyme to help the situation, so I took the opportunity to visit with Edward and his new wife. He took a living with Lord Calderson and is very productive." Frederick barely noted his own words; he simply wanted to be there in her presence and to look into Anne's eyes.

Anne lifted her chin to engage his stare. "Then Mr. Wentworth has his own congregation? I am ashamed to say I lost track of him after he left the country. It gives me pleasure to know he is doing well."

"His story is even better than that. Edward and his wife, Christine, will welcome their first child in mid-summer."

"Indeed!" Her eyes sparkled. "Your brother is blessed to find such happiness at last. Please convey my best wishes to both Edward and Mrs. Wentworth."

Emboldened, Frederick said, "I would be pleased to do so. I have not asked of your own family, Miss Anne. Are they in health?"

Anne motioned toward where Elizabeth sat. "My family does well in Bath, Sir."

Frederick caught Elizabeth Elliot's eye and nodded, but the woman turned away with unalterable coldness. Momentarily stunned by her casual cruelty, Frederick pretended to be indifferent to the social cut, saying, "I was—I was concerned—concerned for how the situation at Lyme affected you." He gazed into her eyes.

"I knew agitation for several hours when Louisa first suffered her injury, but I cannot compare my angst with what you endured," she said softly.

"I am deeply sorry to be a part of any affliction Miss Musgrove met that day. I, foolishly, in my pride and conceit, paid her too much attention; she, obviously, misinterpreted the extent of my interest. Miss Musgrove's desire to act impulsively—to act in an independent manner—led to her accident, but it was I who often encouraged her free spirit," he said somberly. He looked down at the floor and took a deep breath. Looking up at Anne, he said, "And I am pleased that Miss Musgrove has now found happiness with Captain Benwick and he with her. He has known grief at its lowest depth, and if Louisa Musgrove gives him a new focus in life, then things have worked out better than any one of us could have imagined."

"I wondered if the change would affect your relationship with Captain Benwick. I hoped you would not feel ill used by your friend. I should be very sorry that such a friendship as has subsisted between you and Captain Benwick should be destroyed, or even wounded, by a circumstance of this sort."

Frederick smiled and shook his head. "Miss Musgrove is a pleasant companion, and any man would be blessed to have her in his life, but I believe she chose the man who is best for her. She is an affectionate, outgoing girl, and her warm heart will heal James Benwick, as is proper."

A servant in Dalrymple livery interrupted their exchange.

"The Lady Dalrymple's coach for the Misses Elliot," he called in a clear voice.

Elizabeth Elliot haughtily stood. Meanwhile, her companion scrambled to retrieve their packages. Seeing Elizabeth and the woman exit, Frederick offered Anne his arm: "May I escort you to your carriage?"

Anne dropped her eyes in embarrassment. "I am much obliged to you, but I am not going with them. The carriage would not accommodate so many. I walk." She added quickly, "I prefer walking."

Frederick realized that nothing had changed for Anne; her family still treated her worse than they would treat a poor relative. He looked out the window and exclaimed, "But it rains!"

"Oh, very little. Nothing that I regard," she assured him.

After a moment's pause he said, "Though I came only yesterday, I have equipped myself properly for Bath already, you see." Frederick pointed to a new umbrella. "I wish you would make use of it, if you are determined to walk; though, I think, it would be more prudent to let me get you a chair."

"Please, no, Captain. I am much obliged for your kindness, but I need no cover from the elements, and the rain will come to nothing." Looking away, she added, "I am only waiting for my cousin, Mr. Elliot. He will be here in a moment, I am sure."

Just then, Mr. Elliot walked in. Frederick recollected him perfectly. There was no difference between him and the man who stood on the steps at Lyme, admiring Anne as she passed, except in the air and look and manner of the privileged relation and friend. He came in with eagerness, appeared to see and think only of her, apologized for his stay, was grieved to have kept her waiting, and anxious to get her away without further loss of time, and before they walked off together, her arm under his, Anne sent Frederick a gentle and embarrassed glance, and a "good morning to you."

Frederick stood frozen for a few moments, confused by how quickly Mr. Elliot had whisked Anne away. He returned to his party and reluctantly joined them as they watched Anne and Mr. Elliot make their way across the busy street. As soon as they were out of sight, the ladies of his party began talking of them. "Mr. Elliot does not dislike his cousin, I fancy?" Lady Caroline said dreamily.

Lady Susan leaned across the table as if to share a prime piece of gossip. "Oh! No, that is clear enough. One can guess what will happen there." A shiver shot up Frederick's spine. "He is always with them—half lives in the family, I believe. What a very good-looking man!" Frederick's breath became shallow.

"Yes, and Miss Atkinson, who dined with him once at the Wallises, says he is the most agreeable man she ever was in company with." Lady Amelia motioned for the wait staff to bring another pot of tea to the table. She poured a cup for Frederick and refreshed the others' cups before adding, "She is pretty, I think; Anne Elliot—very pretty, when one comes to look at her." Lady Amelia shot Frederick a knowing glance, but he barely registered the words she spoke. "Of course, it is not the fashion to say so, but I confess I admire her more than her sister."

"Oh! So do I," Caroline declared vehemently.

Lady Susan giggled, enjoying the idle talk on a rainy afternoon. "And so do I. No comparison." Then she began to tease her cousin, "But the men are all wild after Miss Elizabeth Elliot. Anne is too delicate for them. Is that not right, Buford?"

Buford Harding cleared his throat before offering up a defense. "Miss Elizabeth Elliot has a certain charm. In her own way, she is attractive. Would you not say so, Wentworth?"

"Hmm? I am sorry, Harding, I missed what you said last."

"I just commented on how Miss Elliot possesses a certain charm."

"Oh, I think," his oldest sister put aside her brother's opinions, "from what we have observed in the past few minutes, Captain Wentworth would barely look at Elizabeth Elliot."

"Oh, really?" Lady Susan encouraged tauntingly. "Whom do you prefer, Captain—Elizabeth Elliot or Anne Elliot?"

A thousand thoughts rushed through him. How could he stop the rumors these three would gladly carry forth? He spoke slowly. "I have known the Elliot family for many years—from before the time I received my first ship. My older brother began his clerical career in Somerset, and, at present, my sister and Admiral Croft are letting the Elliots' estate. Our families are not intimate, but we have a long-standing acquaintance—nearly a decade. Miss Anne is the most agreeable of the three Elliot daughters, if that is of what you speak, Lady Susan."

"Three?" Lady Amelia interrupted. "I understood there were only the two."

Frederick smiled. "Oh, no," he said, savoring the moment. "The youngest sister, Mary, is now Mrs. Charles Musgrove—the same Musgrove family into which Captain Benwick will marry. Her husband will inherit the Musgrove estate at his father's passing. The younger Musgroves reside less than three miles from Kellynch Hall. In fact, I spent much of October and November in the company of all the Musgroves and Miss Anne. Mrs. Charles suffers from a number of maladies, and Miss Anne tended her sister. I became a regular guest of the Musgroves because their son Dick served under me before his passing."

"So you know the family well," Lady Amelia questioned. She looked a trifle deflated.

"I traveled to Lyme with the Musgroves and Miss Anne for a day trip in late November, so that they might meet my old friends Captain Harville and his family. It was on that trip that Captain Benwick, who had taken up temporary residence with the Harvilles, first met Louisa Musgrove. Miss Anne and I were just now discussing the happy news of Captain Benwick and Louisa Musgrove's engagement."

Buford Harding reprimanded his family. "I am afraid, Captain Wentworth, that my sisters have vivid imaginations. I apologize if they pried into your personal affairs. It appears Bath does not offer them enough distractions to entertain them sufficiently."

"It is of no consequence, Harding. I am not ashamed of my admiration for Anne Elliot, nor would I ever speak poorly of her." Frederick pretended a calm he did not feel. He sipped his tea before changing the subject. "What will you do now, Lieutenant, with Napoleon on Elba? Will you stay with the service or seek a buy out?"

Frederick sat back and feigned an interest in Harding's schemes for bettering himself. He satisfactorily stifled the prattle of three mildly vicious young ladies—protecting Anne's reputation. Nearly thirty minutes later, he excused himself, claiming a prior engagement with Admiral Croft. He wanted nothing more than to escape to his room at Sophia's residence and regroup. Winning Anne Elliot would be his greatest reward—what did he care if he had to move a few mountains in order to do so? Frederick was up to the task—all he needed was a way of seeing her again—a way to be in Anne's company. He would leave the rest to fate.

CHAPTER 14

In secret we met—
In silence I grieve,
That thy heart could forget,
Thy spirit deceive.
If I should meet thee
After long years,
How should I greet thee?
With silence and tears.
—Lord Byron, "When We Two Parted"

Frederick spent a restless night, but in the morning he left Sophia's house on Gay Street with a new resolve. He hated that Mr. Elliot had made inroads with Anne while he languished in Shrewsbury, but Anne was not *promised* to the man, so Frederick still had a chance. Plus, he thought it positive that she risked her family's censure by speaking to him—to actually leave her table and seek him out for private conversation. Likely, she had spotted him prior to his entrance with the Hardings and stood near the door, waiting to talk to him.

In addition, the situation at Lyme had not unduly distressed her. Anne knew a level of apprehension for Louisa's recovery, but she also demonstrated a concern for him. She cared whether Louisa's engagement destroyed a long-standing friendship.

Finally, when she had left yesterday, reluctance showed on Anne's face. She wanted to remain with him. At least, that was what Frederick preferred to believe.

The only time Frederick saw Anne that day was on Pulteney Street. He spoke to some of the Admiral's naval cronies before starting up the right-hand pavement, heading toward the main shopping district. "There she is," he murmured. Anne sat in an upscale coach. Seeing her there, Frederick began walking in the same direction the coach traveled. Regularly, he turned his head to glance at her, while pretending to observe the busy street commerce. He wondered for a moment if he could wave down the coach—until he recognized Lady Russell's livery. At first, he thought Lady Russell must have seen him also, her eyes being turned exactly in direction for him, of her being in short intently observing him, but he noted the woman pointing to one of the houses along his side of the street. Anne nodded to her godmother in response. Perversely, Frederick stepped to the street at the intersection, striking a pose of interest in the local architecture. He hoped Anne would see him clearly; he prayed she would recognize his smile of approval. Frederick stood his ground, seeking Anne's face for as long as the coach remained in sight, then he turned once more toward Gay Street.

★ ★ ★

Unfortunately, Frederick did not see Anne anywhere—a day or two passed without producing anything. The theater and public rooms where he was in attendance were, obviously, not fashionable enough for the Elliots, whose evening amusements, according to the society pages, were solely in the elegant stupidity of private parties.

His encounter with Anne at Molland's told Frederick where he would find her this evening, though. Despite the dumbfounding surprise of encountering her that day, he did recall Lady Susan asking specifically about a special concert scheduled for this very night. It was a concert for the benefit of a person patronized by Lady Dalrymple, one of the Elliots' relatives. As he dressed, Frederick reasoned aloud, "The concert was really expected to be a good one, and I am very fond of music." If he could only have a few minutes of conversation with her again, he fancied he should be satisfied; and as to the power of addressing her, he felt all over courage if the opportunity occurred.

Attired in his full dress uniform, Frederick took a deep breath and settled his nerves before the door opened for him, and he strode into the octagon-shaped room, to be met immediately by a vision of the Elliot family—Sir Walter, two of his daughters, and Miss Elliot's companion—stationed by one of the fires. A satisfied smile crept across his face, and he slowed his pace, trying to figure out a way to approach them in order to speak specifically to Anne. He could pay his sister's respects to the family. The Elliots would disdain his familiarity, but speaking to Anne was what was important. But a look of contempt from Miss Elizabeth Elliot made him question his choice, and he prepared only to bow and pass on.

To his pleasure, however, Anne, nearest to him, made yet a little advance and placed herself directly in his path. Despite the formidable father and sister in the background, Anne instantly spoke, "How do you do?"

Frederick touched her arm and led Anne out of the straight line to stand near her before responding. "Miss Anne, I am pleased to see you. I am well. May I assume that you are, too?"

"I am, Captain." Looking furtively over her shoulder at her family's glare, she said softly, "I was not sure you would remember my conversation with Lady Susan regarding the concert."

Frederick felt a rush of happiness. "I believe I told you years ago, Miss Anne, there is little about you of which I take no note. Plus, you remember my fondness for great music."

"It should be very entertaining, Captain," she assured him. "Lady Dalrymple is a connoisseur of Italian opera."

"Then I shall be most pleased, Miss Anne." He smiled down at her. "I experienced many such performances in Mediterranean port cities; from tonight's program, I noticed some with which I became familiar in Romola, Italy, in the region of Tuscany."

"It sounds so beautiful! *Romola*. Do you not simply adore the sound of the word?" She laughed lightly before looking off wistfully. "At least, you were able to come unarmed for Bath's weather. It is to be a star-lit evening."

"My hand will seem empty," he teased. Standing before her, Frederick had a full view of her family over Anne's shoulder. "I assume that your family is in health," he said when he could think of nothing else.

Sir Walter must have heard the inquiry because Frederick suddenly became aware of a whispering between her father and Elizabeth, and, to his surprise, Sir Walter judged so well as to give him a simple acknowledgment of acquaintance while Elizabeth Elliot offered a slight curtsy. This, though late and reluctant and ungracious, was better than nothing, and Frederick dutifully made a distant bow in return. Their actions seemed to raise Anne's spirits.

After talking of the weather and of Bath and of the concert, the conversation began to flag, but Frederick was in no hurry to leave her. Just seeing her renewed his hopes. With a little smile—a little glow, he said, "I have hardly seen you since our day at Lyme. I am afraid you must have suffered from the shock, and the more from its not overpowering you at the time."

She assured him, "Captain, what I felt was concern for all involved, nothing more."

"It was a frightful hour," he said, "a frightful day!" Frederick passed his hand across his eyes—the remembrance still too painful. Forcing calmness, he added, "As we previously discussed, the day produced some effects—had some consequences, which must be considered as the very reverse of frightful."

"I should hope it would be a very happy match. There are on both sides good principles and good temper."

"Yes," said he, "but there I think ends the resemblance. With all my soul I wish them happy and rejoice over every circumstance in favor of it." The resentment he had held for eight years crept into his words. "They have no difficulties to contend with at home, no opposition, no caprice, no delays.—The Musgroves are behaving like themselves, most honorably and kindly, only anxious, with true parental hearts, to promote their daughter's comfort. All this is much, very much, in favor of their happiness, more than perhaps some."

Riled by years of frustration, Frederick nearly allowed himself to be carried away, but a sudden recollection gave him some taste of that emotion, which was now reddening Anne's cheeks and fixing her eyes on the ground, and he stopped—feeling her pain. Needing to protect her even from himself, he cleared his throat before proceeding thus, "I confess I do think there is a disparity, too great a disparity, and in a point no less essential than the mind.—I regard Louisa Musgrove as a very amiable, sweet-tempered girl, and not deficient in understanding, but Benwick is something more. He is a clever man, a reading man—and I confess I do consider his attaching himself to her, with some surprise. Had it been the effect of gratitude, had he learned to love her, because he believed her to prefer him, it would be another thing. But I have no reason to suppose it so. It seems, on the contrary, to be a perfectly spontaneous, untaught feeling on his side, and this surprises me. A man like him, in this situation! With a heart pierced, wounded, almost broken! Fanny Harville was a very superior creature; and his attachment to her was indeed attachment. A man does not recover from such a devotion of the heart to such a woman!—He ought not—he does not."

Frederick stopped abruptly and looked at Anne. Suddenly, everything else—the various noises of the room, the almost ceaseless slam of the door, and the ceaseless buzz of persons walking through—faded away. He watched her chest rise and fall with quick breaths.

Finally, Anne found her voice. "You were a good while at Lyme, I think."

Frederick focused his energies in order to respond intelligently. "Almost a fortnight. I could not leave it until Louisa's doing well was quite ascertained. I was too deeply concerned in the mischief to be soon at peace. It was my doing—solely mine. She would not have been obstinate if I was not weak. The country around Lyme is very fine. I walked and rode a great deal; and the more I saw, the more I found to admire."

"I should very much like to see Lyme again," said she.

"Indeed!" he exclaimed. "I should not suppose you could have found anything in Lyme to inspire such a feeling. The horror and distress in which you were involved—the stretch of mind, the wear of spirits!—I should think your last impressions of Lyme must be strong disgust."

"The last few hours were certainly very painful," replied Anne. "But when pain is over, the remembrance of it often becomes a pleasure. One does not love a place the less for having suffered in it, unless it was all suffering, nothing but suffering—which was by no means the case at Lyme. We were only in anxiety and distress during the last two hours; and, previously, there was a great deal of enjoyment. So much novelty and beauty! I have traveled so little, that every fresh place would be interesting to me."

To think I once debated whether Anne would take to my nomadic life.

She continued, "But there is real beauty at Lyme." She reddened with a faint blush at some recollection, and Frederick smiled with delight. "In short, altogether, my impressions of the place are very agreeable."

"Anne," he stammered wanting to speak the long-lost words, "I need to say . . ." Before he could finish, the entrance door opened again, and the very party appeared for whom they were waiting.

He heard a footman calling out, "Lady Dalrymple, Lady Dalrymple," and to Frederick's deep disappointment, with all the eagerness compatible with anxious elegance, Sir Walter and his two ladies stepped forward to meet her. Lady Dalrymple and her daughter Miss Carteret, escorted by Mr. Elliot and his friend Colonel Wallis, advanced into the room. The others joined them, and it was a group in which Anne found herself also necessarily included, sweeping her from Frederick—dividing them.

Frederick stood glued to the spot; their interesting, almost too interesting conversation broken up, but slight was the penance compared with the happiness! He had learned, in the last ten minutes, to feel hope.

Frederick strolled into the concert room. He stood in the back, not sure where the Elliot party would sit. He saw nothing, thought nothing of the brilliancy of the room; his happiness was from within. He thought only of the last half hour: their choice of subjects, her expressions, and still more her manner and look. Anne still felt something for him; on that, he would bet everything. Anger, resentment, avoidance were no more, being succeeded, not merely by friendship and regard, but by the tenderness of the past—yes—some share of the tenderness of the past. *Could she learn to love me again?*

Leaning against one of the columns, he smiled when Anne entered the room. Her eyes were bright, and her cheeks glowed. He watched as she searched the crowd; hopefully, she looked for him. Once she was settled, he would move closer. He noted with some concern that Lady Russell had joined their group; someday he might be able to forgive Sir Walter—the man was hopelessly ignorant about all manner of things—but he was not sure that he could ever forgive Lady Russell. At nineteen, Anne had turned to the woman for guidance, and her godmother had betrayed the trust, destroying their chance for happiness Her party divided, sharing two contiguous benches: Anne was among those on the foremost. To Frederick's chagrin, Mr. Elliot, with the assistance of his friend Colonel Wallis, maneuvered the seat by her.

Frederick moved to the right-hand wall. From his new position, he could see Anne's face, and he delighted in watching her abandonment to the music. Anne sat mesmerized by the chords—lost in the melodic strains; it reminded him of her reaction to the sea.

As the first act came to a close, Mr. Elliot made a point of moving in closer to Anne, and they whispered together. Frederick watched Anne flush with color. Whatever Mr. Elliot said to her, she found intriguing, and then she flipped back and forth through the concert bill. Mr. Elliot's words had piqued her interest. She questioned him eagerly, but the man would not comment further. Frederick heard him tease, "No, no—some time or other perhaps," leaving Anne visibly disappointed.

Her intimate conversation with Mr. Elliot made Frederick wonder, *What games does Anne Elliot play?* Not half an hour earlier, her attitude toward *him* had his heart singing; now *Mr. Elliot* brought a flush to her face. The man was an obvious rake; he feigned regard with a practiced ease. Could Anne not recognize those qualities in him? Of course, she was an innocent—not used to the ways of a depraved soul; but she should listen to her intuition! He knew her to be intelligent. Why could Anne not see what was clearly in front of her? *Perfection is not achievable in a man, nor in a woman,* he reminded himself. Could she not remember how Mr. Elliot had snubbed the family when they sought his alliance years earlier? *A tiger does not change its stripes.*

Watching the scenario playing out in front of him, Frederick hated the liberties the man took with Anne—with *his* Anne. Elliot sat too close—laughed too loudly at her wit—touched her hand or her arm or her shoulder with too much familiarity.

Engrossed in his brooding, at first Sir Walter Elliot's words did not penetrate Frederick's thoughts.

"A well-looking man," said Sir Walter, "a very well-looking man."

"A very fine young man indeed!" said Lady Dalrymple. "More air than one often sees in Bath.—Irish, I daresay. Do you know him?"

"No, I just know his name. A bowing acquaintance. Wentworth—Captain Wentworth of the Navy. His sister married my tenant in Somersetshire—Admiral Croft, who rents Kellynch."

Frederick's body turned first hot with anger and then cold with humiliation. Sir Walter did not even do him the courtesy of remembering him, the man who had asked for his daughter's hand.

His heart raced with anger—first at Sir Walter and then at Mr. Elliot, and then even at Anne for not accepting him years earlier. Trying to quiet his contempt, Frederick joined a cluster of men standing a little distance away. He seethed from the insults and from the uncertainty. *Maybe I should just walk away—accept the fact the barn door is closed.* He looked over at Anne, but she still spoke with Mr. Elliot.

The next few minutes saw a reshuffling of positions. The performance was recommencing, and the cluster of men restored their attention to the orchestra, so Frederick moved away. The first act was over, and he tried to decide what to do. After a period of nothing amongst the party, some of them did decide on going in quest of tea. Anne was one of the few who did not choose to move. She remained in her seat, but so did Lady Russell. How could he approach Anne with Lady Russell close by?

When the others drifted back in, some further changes occurred as they resettled. Colonel Wallis declined sitting down again, and Elizabeth and Miss Carteret invited Mr. Elliot to sit between them. Eventually, Anne placed herself much nearer the end of the bench than she was before—much more within reach.

Now! he told himself as he moved forward a bit at a time; he did not make a direct line to where Anne sat. Frederick tried to look grave and seem irresolute, as by very slow degrees, he came at last near enough to speak to her. With the others nearby, he would, he knew, find it hard to express himself with the same freedom they had enjoyed in the octagon room. The difference was strikingly great.

Before he could speak, she spotted him. "Are you enjoying the concert, Captain?" Anne searched his eyes, but although he chastised himself for doing so, he met her with the same gravity he had offered when at Uppercross.

"In truth, Miss Anne, I am disappointed.—I expected better singing. In short, I must confess I should not be sorry when it is over."

"I am sad that you feel so, Captain; I thought it quite good, especially the Italian arias at the end, but I expect that, having heard the pieces in Italy, you have a different perspective."

Anne always touched his heart. His countenance softened. "You are a true diplomat, Miss Anne."

"Do you think so, Captain Wentworth?" She gave him a beguiling smile. "Should I apply to the Central Office for Naval Affairs?" she joked.

"May I offer you a letter of reference, Miss Anne?"

"Ah—a letter from a naval officer! I am indeed lucky."

Frederick looked down toward the bench, seeing a place on it well worth occupying. Just as he started to move and be with her despite everything, a touch on her shoulder obliged Anne to turn around.

"Miss Anne," Mr. Elliot said as he leaned in close—*too* close—"I beg your pardon, but you must explain the Italian again. Miss Carteret is very anxious to have a general idea of what is next to be sung."

"Certainly." Anne nodded to Frederick and turned toward her extended family.

Noting their motioning to him, Frederick took a few steps to the left and held a stilted conversation with Lieutenant Harding and Lady Susan. Although they invited him most earnestly to join them, he declined. *Every time*, he thought. His gut twisted. *Every time I think we have escaped their pull, Anne's family drag her back in.*

As quickly as possible, he excused himself from his friends, promising to join them at the theater one day in the coming week. He could take no more of this evening. He noted that Anne had finished her translations, so he took his leave of her. "I wish you a good night, Miss Anne. I am going.—I should get home as fast as I can; Sophia will be expecting me."

"Must you, Captain?" she asked. "Is not this song worth staying for? It is an Italian love song."

"No!" he heard himself say curtly. "There is nothing worth my staying for, even an Italian love song." He bowed and left the room.

"Why, with my luck, it will be raining," he grumbled as he retrieved his hat. Frederick turned up the collar of his jacket against the wind before starting to pull on his left glove. Suddenly, he stopped. *Why am I so upset with Anne? Did she seek out Mr. Elliot?* Slowly, he pulled on his right glove. *What did you expect her to do? Ignore her family?* Frederick looked back at the concert hall he just left. *Should I go back in and apologize to her?* He stood still for a moment, lost in thought.

He made a decision. "I will call on her tomorrow at Camden Place. I have embarrassed myself enough for one evening." He would go home and construct a proper apology—an earnest pledge. He would extend to Anne Elliot his sincere regrets for tonight—for Lyme—for Uppercross—and for leaving her, eight years earlier.

★ ★ ★

Frederick and Anne completed their first circuit of the deck. Today he walked without assistance; although he was a bit slow, he relished finally being on his own.

"Dr. Laraby says we should be in port sometime between late tomorrow afternoon and early the next morning, depending on the weather." Anne held her husband's arm more for his sake than for him to give her support. She watched as he took each step, a tentative move followed by a solid planting of his foot. "I will be happy to have you on dry land again." She squeezed his arm. "Will it not be nice to have some solitary time together?"

"I must admit that I look forward to resting in your arms." Frederick's words caressed her ear, just loud enough to bring a flush to Anne's cheek.

"You, Sir," she half-heartedly reprimanded, "might be beyond reform."

"I am definitely beyond reform. And you love me that way," he whispered softly—a wicked grin spreading across his face. "In fact, you love me very well. I am married to the most beautiful wife that a man could have."

"Why do you tease me so? You know false platitudes work only with my father and sisters," Anne argued.

Frederick pulled her hand in closer to his side, holding her tightly to him. "I apologize, my Love. I suppose I am a man hopelessly in love. Come, Anne, let us make another turn around the deck."

They walked a third of the way on the starboard side before he said anything else, but again Frederick spoke only loud enough for his wife's ear. "For you, my Dear, to think of yourself as not deserving of praise—of every declared compliment—would be a blasphemy against nature. Some others might think your sister Elizabeth the beauty in the family, for she truly has a handsome face, but one need spend only a minute in her company before one sees that there is nothing there but porcelain skin and striking features." Frederick paused before finishing; he cupped her hand with his. "However, your face is pure beauty because your loveliness comes from an inner charm—a goodness of spirit. Look at how quickly James Benwick came under your spell. Not to mention your cousin Mr. Elliot, who obviously preferred you to your sister Elizabeth. You caught the man's attention before he even knew who you were. As much as I despise him for his deceit, I cannot fault his taste in women."

Anne smiled and again they walked in silence; no words needed to be spoken. Finally, Anne lifted her chin and spoke: "I am surprised, my Love; you actually said something positive about my cousin."

"Do not expect it to happen very often," he warned. "From the moment I saw Mr. Elliot look at you in Lyme, I wanted to introduce him to a set of chains in a rat-infested cargo hold."

Anne looked amused. "I appreciated your display of jealousy at the concert. The gratification was exquisite. My only concern was how to quiet such jealousy and how, in all the peculiar disadvantages of our respective situations, you would ever learn my real sentiments. It was misery to think of Mr. Elliot's attentions.—Their evil was incalculable."

"I have been reliving our romance since my injury. It began with the laudanum-induced sleep, but it has continued throughout my recovery." Anne nodded, surprised by his words. "Last night I dreamed of finally winning your regard, but it was not how it actually happened. It was quite extraordinary, though. I am not sure I do not prefer it to the actual event."

"How so?"

"For one thing, I was out of my misery the day after the concert instead of having to wait three more days to know my fate." He smiled down at her.

"Tell me about your dream," she demanded. "I would enjoy your version of how everything *should* have been resolved."

"Only if you will lie in my arms again when we return to my quarters." His voice became husky.

Anne nodded her agreement.

"I am becoming tired," he said loud enough for those close by to hear. "If you do not mind, Mrs. Wentworth, we will retire to my quarters."

CHAPTER 15

Your open heart,
Simple with giving, gives the primal deed,
The first good world, the blossom, the blowing seed,
The hearth, the steadfast land, the wandering sea,
Not beautiful or rare in every part,
But like yourself, as they were meant to be.
—Edwin Muir, "The Confirmation"

The candle burned down, leaving distorted shadows dancing in every corner. Anne snuggled against her husband's chest as he stroked the silkiness of her hair spread out across his arm.

"Now, my Love, I want to hear how things *should* have been between us." She caressed Frederick's jaw line with her fingertips.

He kissed her forehead as he pulled her closer to him. "You might find this amusing," he cautioned.

"I will not scoff at or make light of what you say. Actually, I am most interested; I used to devise scenarios of how we would rediscover each other."

"My Darling." He raised her chin with his fingertips and kissed her gently.

"*Tell* me," she demanded once he withdrew.

"Yes, Sweetling," he said dutifully before settling her in his arms once more. "Well, if you recall, you visited Mrs. Smith at Westgate Building the morning after the concert. She kindly warned you about Mr. Elliot, but, of course, I had no idea that you had left her apartment altogether in a confusion of images and doubts—a perplexity, an agitation of which you could not see the end."

Anne sighed audibly and snuggled in closer. She kissed the underside of his jaw line before leaning back to lightly stroke the muscles of his chest. Frederick held her tightly to him, unwilling to release her closeness. "Oh, Anne," he groaned as he tried to force the desire away.

"I am *waiting*," she whispered.

Unwilling to control his need, Frederick rolled her to her back and repeatedly drank of Anne's lips. "I love you." His mouth rested just above hers. "You are everything to me."

Anne nibbled on his lower lip. "I suppose I will never hear your story's ending," she joked.

"Oh, you will hear it," he whispered in her ear, "but not for many minutes. I have a different story to tell you—one about a man who loves his wife beyond reason."

Anne snaked her arms around his neck, lacing her fingers through his hair. "I believe I have heard this story before." She giggled as he kissed the sensitive spot between her neck and shoulder. "But," she gasped as his lips traced a line from her ear to the base of her neck, "I believe—it needs—retelling."

★ ★ ★

Some time later, Anne sat tailor-style in the middle of the bed, her hair draped prettily over her shoulders. "So I knew about Mr. Elliot. But *you* did not know how I *felt* about him," she prompted him.

Frederick leaned against the backboard; pillows propped up his upper body. He took Anne's hand and pulled her into closer proximity, lacing their fingers together.[1]

"Here is my dream. While you were speaking to Mrs. Smith about Mr. Elliot, I heard another version of the story from my sister and the Admiral. The Admiral had heard from one of his cronies, who also attended the concert, that at the end, Mr. Elliot declared himself—and you accepted. I did not know what to believe; I could not accept the Admiral's words as the truth, but I knew how Mr. Elliot touched you with a familiarity that I was no longer allowed."

"I—I am sorry," Anne stammered.

---

[1] The canceled chapters of *Persuasion* were written from July 8, 1816, to July 18, 1816. According-
ing to all accounts, Austen rewrote them, thinking the originals "tame and flat." The original draft is on display at the British Museum. This dream sequence is based on Edith
Lank's translation found on the *Republic of Pemberley*'s website.

Frederick squeezed her hand. "It occurred to the Admiral that you and Mr. Elliot might want to return to Kellynch, and he and Sophia could speak of nothing else. My heart knew such pain, and my family did not recognize it. After I heard the story, I hid in the study, pretending to read, but envisioning the worst.

"Somehow, the Admiral and you met on the street. That part of the dream was not very clear. I suppose I just needed an excuse for your appearance at Gay Street. Anyway, I hid in the study, but—much to my horror—I heard Benjamin outside the door.

"'I cannot stay' said the Admiral, 'because I must go to the Central Office for Naval Affairs, but if you will only sit down for five minutes, I am sure Sophie will come.—You will find nobody to disturb you; there is nobody but Frederick here.' The Admiral opened the door as he spoke.

"There was no time for recollection! For planning behavior or regulating manners!—There was only time to turn pale before you passed through the door and met my astonished eyes. I was sitting by the fire, pretending to read and prepared for no greater surprise than the Admiral's hasty return from his errands. Equally unexpected was the meeting, on each side. There was nothing to be done, however, but to stifle feelings and be quietly polite.

"The Admiral wanted to know the truth of the rumors, so he began to question you. 'Why, Miss Anne, we begin to hear strange things of you.' Benjamin smiled nicely while I cringed, awaiting your response. 'But you have not much the look of it,' the Admiral teased, 'as grave as a little judge.' His words brought a blush to your face, which, to Benjamin, confirmed his suspicions. 'Aye, aye, that will do. Now, it is right. I *thought* we were not mistaken.' His words ripped a hole in my soul. 'My Sophie will be very happy to see you. Mind—I will not swear that she has not something particular to say to you—but *that* will all come out in the right place. I give no hints. Please sit down, Miss Anne. Mrs. Croft will be down very soon.' You moved to one of the wing chairs and sat on the edge, obviously very nervous. I assumed from my observations that you simply did not know how to tell me the truth. 'I will go upstairs and give Sophie notice directly.'

"You sprang to your feet. 'Please, Admiral, do not interrupt Mrs. Croft. I will call another time.'

"'I will not hear of it,' the Admiral said in his best military tone, and, like every man who ever served under Benjamin, you followed orders and reseated yourself. Then the Admiral bowed and offered his excuses once again—taking his leave. You and I were to be left alone to deal with our quandary. However, at the door, he turned back to me and said, 'Frederick, a word with *you*, if you please.'"

"That sounds so like Benjamin," she observed. "What happened next?"

"I had no choice but to attend him. As Benjamin might do, he began the conversation before we were out of your hearing. 'As I am going to leave you together, it is but fair I should give you something to talk of.' I managed to close the door, because I knew where Benjamin's words would lead and because I did not wish to give you pain.

"Benjamin continued, 'I must know, so if you please, I need you to speak to Miss Anne.'

"I pleaded, 'I cannot do this, Sir. Please do not ask me.'

"However, the Admiral's agitation could not be contained. 'We have a lease for Kellynch, but Sir Walter has an option to end it on proper notice.'

"'Have you not signed the lease?' I asked.

"'Yes—yes, of course, but I hate to be at an uncertainty.—I must know at once.—Sophie thinks the same. If Miss Anne is to marry, Sophie and I will remove to another property.'

"The thought of asking if you were to marry Mr. Elliot nearly brought me to my knees, but Benjamin was oblivious to my feelings. I begged to be excused from the task; however, the Admiral was determined. 'Phoo, Phoo,' he shamed me. 'Now is the time. If *you* will not speak, I will stop and speak myself.'

"I agreed, although a firing squad would have been more welcome. I no more said, 'Yes, Sir,' than he opened the door leading back to you. There we were—alone—trying to overcome the impossible. I knew you must have heard part, if not all, of my conversation with Benjamin. He spoke without any management of voice, although I tried to check him."

"Poor Frederick," she cooed. "You actually dreamed such an awful state of affairs for yourself?"

In feigned seriousness, he spoke, "I am a real trooper."

Anne laughed lightly at his false bravado—a tender, romantic gesture. "You are a saint, my Husband."

"Anyway," he began again, "I walked immediately to a window, irresolute and embarrassed. I longed to be able to speak of the weather or the concert. I stood looking out at nothing for, at least, a half minute. Then I forced myself to walk to where you sat. In a voice of effort and constraint, I followed the Admiral's orders. 'You must have heard too much already, Madam, to be in any doubt of my having promised Admiral Croft to speak to you on some particular subject—and this conviction determines me to do it—however repugnant to my—to all my senses of propriety, to be taking so great a liberty.—You will acquit me of impertinence, I trust, by considering me as speaking only for another, and speaking by necessity.—The Admiral is a man who can never be thought impertinent by one who knows him as you do.—His intentions are always the kindest and the best; and you will perceive he is actuated by none other, in the application, which I am now with—with very peculiar feelings—obliged to make.'

"I knew I made little sense—rambling on—but when you refused to look at me, I could barely think. I stopped—merely to recover my breath—not expecting an answer. I proceeded, with a forced alacrity. 'The Admiral, Madam, was this morning confidently informed you were—upon my word I am quite at a loss—.' Again I took a deep breath to settle my nerves and finished by speaking quickly. 'The awkwardness of *giving* information of this sort to one of the parties—you can be at no loss to understand me.—It was very confidently said that Mr. Elliot—that everything was settled in the family for a union between Mr. Elliot—and yourself. It was added that you were to live at Kellynch—Kellynch was to be given up. This, the Admiral knew, could not be correct.— But it occurred to him that it might be the wish of the parties— and my commission from him, Madam, is to say if the family wish is such, his lease of Kellynch shall be canceled, and he and my sister will provide themselves with another home, without imagining themselves to be doing anything which under similar circumstances would not be done for *them*.—This is all, Madam.—A very few words in reply from you will be sufficient.—That *I* should be the person commissioned on this subject is extraordinary!—And, believe me, Madam, it is no less painful.—A very few words, however, will put an end to the awkwardness and distress we may both be feeling."

Wentworth heard Anne gasp. "Oh, Frederick, tell me I said something *intelligible* at this juncture! Please say I was not as *tongue-tied* as I usually am."

"I am afraid, my Love, that I dreamed you as you really are—perfect—but often afraid to give offense to anyone." He continued his tale as Anne stared silently at him.

"Before you could answer, I added, 'If you only tell me that the Admiral may address a line to Sir Walter, it will be enough. Pronounce only the words, *He may*.—I shall immediately follow him with your message.'

"I stood transfixed, waiting for you to speak the words, which would doom me to a life of loneliness. Finally, you found your voice. 'No, Sir—there is no message.—You are misin—the Admiral is misinformed.—I do justice to the kindness of his intentions, but he is quite mistaken. There is no truth in any such report.'

"There we were—hearts beating madly—held in a moment of exquisite agony. I was a moment silent, and then you turned your eyes toward me for the first time since my reentering the room. I saw all the power and keenness that no other eyes possess. '*No* truth in any such report!' I repeated.

"You gave me an amused smile. 'No truth in any *part* of it?— None.'

"I collapsed in the chair I was standing behind, enjoying the relief of what you said. I drew a little nearer to you. We looked at each other with expressions that were silent but still a very powerful dialogue. On my side there was supplication, on yours, acceptance. Then I took your hand and said, 'Anne, my own dear Anne!'"

With this, he pulled her hand to his lips and kissed the inside of her wrists. "Was that the end of the dream?" She barely got the words out. He had taken her breath away.

"Not entirely." Frederick's eyes lit up with mischief. "You, of course, ended up in my arms."

Anne rolled her eyes.

"We kissed passionately until Sophia finally made an appearance in the study. I am afraid that my sister quite understood the situation even without our explanation. Your lips were swollen from our ardent kisses." Frederick chuckled in remembrance. "Beautifully swollen, in fact."

"You would enjoy embarrassing me so!" she chastised him.

Frederick pulled her even closer. "I enjoyed holding you in my arms. You were finally mine. How could I not kiss you blind?"

"Then what?"

"Well, it began to rain, and my sister astutely invited you to stay to dinner. A note was dispatched to Camden Place—and you stayed—stayed with me until ten at night. Sophia contrived for her and the Admiral to be frequently out of the room together. Nature, or fate, took its course. The rest of the dream is very much like what happened in reality. I told you of my love, and we found each other—so rationally, but so rapturously, happy as any two people could be."

"I agree." Anne fell into his embrace. "Your version is nearly as romantic as the real thing." She smiled mischievously. "Now, I was wondering if you would care to demonstrate how well you kissed me during this romantic dream?" Her lips came near to his. Wordlessly, he complied.

CHAPTER 16

Love, faithful love, recalled thee to my mind—
But how could I forget thee? Through what power,
Even for the least division of an hour,
Have I been so beguiled as to be blind
To my most grievous loss?
—William Wordsworth, "Sonnet"

Frederick knew he could not escape Sophia's close examination when he returned, but he honestly wished he could simply slink off to lick his wounds and regroup for a new assault on Anne's regard. He handed his hat and coat to a waiting servant before heading upstairs to the Admiral's study.

"Frederick, you are home early," the Admiral noted as Frederick stepped through the open door. "I thought you might join some friends after the concert."

Frederick walked to where Sophia sat, bending to kiss his sister's upturned cheek. "I left before the concert ended." He crossed to the window to peer out at the darkness. *Just get through the civilities, and then you can withdraw,* he told himself.

"Was the concert not entertaining?" Sophia watched him to see his reaction.

Frederick clasped his hands behind his back. "I was disappointed—the singer was lacking."

"Really?" His sister sounded surprised. "I would have thought that Lady Dalrymple would never lend her name to any entertainment that was less than stunning."

Frederick paused before answering, not wanting to rehash the evening with his sister. "Some found the performance adequate."

"But *you* did not?" Benjamin seemed as surprised as his wife.

"Miss Anne says that it is probably because I heard the arias while I was in Italy. These were poor imitations."

Sophia set down her book. "You spoke to Miss Anne at the concert?"

"Indeed. Lady Dalrymple is a relative of the Elliots, and, of course, Sir Walter would want to preserve the connection. The whole Elliot clan was in attendance."

"I see," Sophia mused. "Were you received by the family?"

He turned to face them. "Only Miss Anne. The rest treated me only as a bowing acquaintance, although Sir Walter thinks I am a 'very well-looking man.'" Sarcasm dripped from his every word. "And even though Lady Dalrymple agreed, she believes I have the air of an Irishman!"

The Admiral guffawed, nearly choking on his port, while Sophia stifled her smile. "That is better than being the best-looking sailor he ever met," Benjamin countered.

"When one puts it that way, I suppose I prefer my compliment to yours." He begrudgingly took the seat across from his sister.

"I am sure Miss Anne did not treat you poorly." His sister spoke the words softly, not sure whether Frederick wanted to hear them. "Miss Anne is not as anxious about class as the rest of her family."

"No, she is not," Frederick allowed at last. His time with Anne this evening had been superb; surrounded by concertgoers, he remembered none of them—only he and Anne existed in those moments.

"If the two of you do not mind, I think I will make it an early evening. After spending six weeks with Edward, I am accustomed to country hours." He rose to his feet before offering them a quick bow. Then he headed to the door; he needed time—time to figure out how to fix the mess *he* had created.

★ ★ ★

The night seemed endless—little sleep came, and Frederick took some relief at leaving his bed, having had a thorough battle with the linens and pillows throughout most of the time he spent stretched out across it. Part of the time he thought it best to abandon Anne to Mr. Elliot. As much as he despised the man, Mr. Elliot could offer Anne things of which Frederick could only dream. If Anne married Mr. Elliot, she could assume her mother's position as the mistress of Kellynch Hall. She would be Lady Elliot—call Kellynch her home again—her home forever. Mr. Elliot was to inherit everything.—Anne deserved *everything*.—Frederick thought there would be every possibility of their being happy together. A most suitable connection everybody must consider it—but he thought it might be a very happy one also.

Yet, the thought of Anne sharing her life with anyone but him seemed to rip his heart from his chest. Anne—*his Anne*—was incomparable—beautiful—intelligent. His fascination with her had begun years ago, and it never waned, even though he had tried repeatedly to put her behind him. *Am I just a wishful fool—hoping against hope that something will change before Anne accepts Mr. Elliot's troth?*

★ ★ ★

Frederick spent the day after the concert walking about Bath in hopes of a sighting Anne. He visited the Pump Room, Victoria Park, the Royal Crescent, the shops, and Sydney Gardens; yet, Anne could not be found. Panic set in!—Could Mr. Elliot be applying for Anne's hand while Frederick searched fruitlessly for her? *I was foolish—damnably foolish—yesterday evening. I left her in the company of Mr. Elliot, although she, obviously, wanted me to stay—to join her, even, on the bench. She asked me to listen to a love song, and I refused. "There is nothing worth my staying for." What idiotic words! I should have told Anne she was worth staying for and then seated myself next to her. But I allowed her family to turn me away—to question my own worth—to retreat before being snubbed. What do I care if the likes of Lady Russell or Lady Dalrymple or Sir Walter Elliot do not approve of my relationship with Anne? Evidently, more than I thought! How could I let them ruin my chances to see Anne or to call on her again?*

That evening, he took a tray in his room, unable to hold a conversation with his sister or Benjamin. His head throbbed, and he felt a prickling along his neck and spine, telling him that time was short. If he did not reconnect with Anne Elliot by the next afternoon, he would call, unannounced, at Camden Place and plead for her to receive him. He would immediately pledge his love for her and ask Anne to make him the happiest of men.

He knew that he could not rely on the inspiration of the moment; he needed to carefully construct what he would say to Anne. He had missed a golden opportunity at the concert; now he must formulate a plan. He would prove himself to her. This gave him a focus for the evening—a way to pass the hours until he could search for Anne again.

★ ★ ★

"Wentworth!" Frederick turned quickly to search the faces rushing by him on the busy street. Finally, he saw the smiling countenance of Thomas Harville, who was followed closely by Charles Musgrove.

"I say, old man." Charles laughed lightly as he extended his hand in friendship. "I never expected to find you on the streets of Bath."

"Nor did I," Harville joined in the greeting, "but I am pleased to see you, Frederick. You are looking well. How long have you been in Bath?"

"Only for a week." They stepped to the side to let the pedestrians pass them by. "I came to join Sophia and the Admiral; he is here to take the water for his gout. What brings you two to Bath?"

Charles supplied the answer, "Captain Harville wanted to come to Bath on business."

Thomas interrupted, "I wanted to see some of the offerings at the better shops—to inspect the workmanship. It would give me an idea of what Rushick might need." Frederick nodded his understanding.

"Anyway," Charles continued, "Harville began to talk of it a week ago; and by way of doing something, as shooting was over, I proposed coming with him, and Mrs. Harville seemed to like the idea of it very much, as an advantage to her husband; but Mary could not bear to be left, and made herself so unhappy about it that, for a day or two, everything seemed to be in suspense, or at an end. But then, Papa and Mama took up the cause. Mama has some old friends in Bath, whom she wanted to see; it was thought a good opportunity for Henrietta to come and buy wedding clothes for herself and Louisa; and, in short, it ended being Mama's party, making it easier on the captain here. Mary and I came, too—Mary to help Henrietta with the shopping."

Frederick looked pleased to see them. "When did you get in?"

"Late yesterday evening," Thomas added as he shifted his weight to his cane hand.

"You must come say hello to Mama," Charles insisted. "She would have my hide if I let you slip away without her renewing the acquaintance. You know, you are as good as family as far as my parents are concerned."

"That is very kind of you." Frederick looked at his best friend. "Milly's last letter gave me the impression that you were to return to Lyme."

Thomas met Frederick's eyes; they would have a conversation in front of him to which Charles would not be privy. "I assumed we would travel," he stressed the words, "but the Musgroves were insistent that we stay. Plus, the children have developed friendships with Charles's youngest siblings. Milly stays behind with *all* the children and Mr. Musgrove. Of course, James tends Miss Musgrove."

"I see," Frederick said with a touch of amusement. "How *fortunate* for all of you!"

"Come," Charles encouraged, ushering them forward. "We took a suite of rooms at the White Hart." He led the way for the two friends. "Mary and I called on her father earlier today. Miss Anne came back with us; she may still be with Mama. Have you seen her since you came to Bath, Wentworth?"

"We spoke at a concert recently," Frederick said, his heart leaping with the news. He would see Anne today! But now, with the possibility, he found his resolve faltering. *Maybe I should observe how she reacts to me—make sure I did not misconstrue her feelings the other evening. If she seems the same today, I will approach her with my pledge.*

"Good—good," Charles replied. "It will be just like last autumn—all of us together again."

They walked the few streets needed to take them to the White Hart. Charles hustled both of his friends into the room. "Mama, look who we found!" he called.

The wrinkles in Mrs. Musgrove's face increased as she laughed with pleasure. "Captain Wentworth! For heaven's sake, how perfect is it to have you among us again! You were sorely missed, Sir."

Wentworth bowed to Mrs. Musgrove and the rest of the room, and then took Mrs. Musgrove's outstretched hands in his. He brought one set of chubby knuckles to his mouth and grazed them with his lips. "Thank you, Ma'am, for receiving me."

Mrs. Musgrove teased him about his formality, and then led Frederick into the center of the room. Frederick had not looked directly at Anne since coming through the door, but his whole body knew she was there, even before Charles led them across the portal. Although he had prepared himself for the prospect that she might be among the party, the surprise of his first look at Anne, after pining intensely for her, took his breath away. *Stay calm. Observe.* He made a quiet comment or two to the group at large and then took up a position behind one of the more imposing wing chairs scattered across the room.

Frederick tried not to make it obvious that he watched Anne, but try as he might, his eyes remained on her. He attempted to be calm and leave things to take their course, trying to be rational. He thought, *Surely, if there be constant attachment on each side, our hearts must understand each other ere long.* And yet, a few minutes afterward, he felt as if their being in company with each other, under their present circumstance, could be exposing them to inadvertencies and misconstructions of the most mischievous kind.

Mary's call to Anne broke Frederick's concentration. Standing close to the window, Mrs. Charles seemed pleased to announce to the whole room, "Anne, there is Mrs. Clay, I am sure, standing under the colonnade, and a gentleman with her. I saw them turn the corner from Bath Street just now. They seem deep in talk. Who is it?—Come and tell me." But before Anne could obey, Mary gasped, "Good heavens! I recollect.—It is Mr. Elliot himself."

"No," cried Anne, and Frederick watched as she blushed. "It cannot be Mr. Elliot," she offered in explanation. "I assure you he was to leave Bath at nine this morning and does not come back until tomorrow."

How does Anne know Mr. Elliot's traveling plans? he wondered. *How intimate are they?* The questions vexed him greatly. He hated the uncertainty.

Mary, resenting she should be supposed not to know her own cousin, began talking very warmly about the family features, and protesting still more positively it was Mr. Elliot. She called for Anne to come and look herself.

Anne would not accede to Mary's wishes. He prayed she refused for his sake, but those moments of hope vanished on perceiving smiles and intelligent glances between two or three of Mrs. Musgrove's friends, as if they believed themselves quite in the secret. It was evident the report concerning Anne and Mr. Elliot had spread; and the short pause succeeded in ensuring it would now spread further.

Reluctantly, Anne moved to the window to satisfy all the eyes now falling upon her. Frederick cringed as she stepped forward and drew back the drape. "Yes, it is Mr. Elliot certainly," she announced to the room. "He changed his hour of going, I suppose, that is all— or I may be mistaken; I might not attend." Frederick's eyes followed her back to her chair. Anne seemed composed, and it irritated him to think others in the room thought she must acquit herself to them.

After a few more excruciating minutes, Mrs. Musgrove's friends finally departed. Frederick took the opportunity to find a seat. Then Charles revealed, "Well, Mother I did something for you while I was out today that you will like. I went to the theater and secured a box for tomorrow night. Am not I a good boy? I know you love a play, and there is room for us all. It holds nine. I am sure we can engage Captain Wentworth, and Anne will not be sorry to join us, too. We all like a play. Have not I done well, Mother?" *This could be just the opening that I need*, thought Frederick.

"Charles, how thoughtful," Mrs. Musgrove began. "I do so love a play, and it would be a wonderful evening if Henrietta and all the others could join us. You will come, will you not, Miss Anne?"

Mary interrupted the exchange, delivering a reprimand to her husband with a large dose of Elliot pride. "Take a box for tomorrow night! Have you forgotten we are engaged to Camden Place for the same evening? We were most particularly asked on purpose to meet Lady Dalrymple and her daughter and Mr. Elliot—all the principal family connections—on purpose to be introduced to them? How can you be so forgetful?"

Frederick and Thomas Harville traded a knowing look—they both held the same opinion of Mary Musgrove. *No wonder Charles spends so much time out of the house.* Frederick thought Charles would happily turn back the clock and press Anne harder if he could.

His pride wounded, Charles Musgrove had no choice but to be contrary, declaring his renewed intentions. "Your father might have asked us to supper if he wanted to see us. You may do as you like, but I shall go to the play."

Thus began a heated discussion on both sides. Frederick had witnessed more than one of these arguments during his time with the Musgroves. In the beginning he had found them amusing, but now he thought it a pathetic situation. It came from marrying without love—marrying without respect. If he did not win Anne, he might never marry; he did not believe he could tolerate such a life just for the sake of an heir. He could leave his fortune to Edward's children.

"Please, Charles, there was always such a great connection between the Dalrymples and ourselves," Mary pleaded. "We are quite near relations, you know—and Mr. Elliot too, with whom you ought so particularly to be acquainted! In time, he will be our nearest neighbor. Every attention is due to Mr. Elliot. Consider my father's heir—the future representative of the family."

"Do not talk to me about heirs," cried Charles. "I am not one of those who neglect the reigning power to bow to the rising sun. If I would not go for the sake of your father, I should think it scandalous to go for the sake of his heir. What is Mr. Elliot to me?"

Frederick became even more alert, looking and listening with his whole soul. The last words brought his inquiring eyes from Charles to Anne. *Will Mr. Elliot be Charles's new brother? Tell me, Anne. Deny your connection to the man!* He tried to will her to bring their love together.

Finally, Mrs. Musgrove interceded. "We better put it off. Charles, you had much better go back and change the box for Tuesday. It would be a pity to be divided, and we should be losing Miss Anne too, if there is a party at her father's; and I am sure neither Henrietta nor I should care at all for the play if Miss Anne could not be with us."

Frederick realized that Mrs. Musgrove wanted Anne to attend to serve as a buffer between Mary and everyone else. The woman provided Anne with the opportunity to set everyone's assumptions straight. *Say it, Anne*, he silently pleaded.

Frederick listened intently as, trembling noticeably, Anne spoke, "If it depended only on my inclination, Ma'am, the party at home, excepting on Mary's account, would not be the smallest impediment. I take no pleasure in that sort of meeting and should be too happy to change it for a play and with you. But, it better not be attempted, perhaps."

Frederick let out his breath. *Anne did it!* She had made it clear that she wanted nothing to do with the stuffy way of life to which her family clung. As if in a dream, he moved from his seat to the fireplace, pretending to warm his hands with the flame before taking a station with less barefaced design by Anne. As the others continued to speak of the pros and cons of the party and the play, Frederick spoke directly to her: "You have not been long in Bath," said he, "to enjoy the evening parties of the place." He demanded she confirm what he hoped to be true.

With a beguiling smile, she turned her full beauty on him, and Frederick felt his knees go weak. "Oh, no! The usual character of them has nothing for me. I am no card player."

A smile of his own turned up the corners of Frederick's mouth; he seemed to hear the strings of a love song. "You were not formerly, I know." *I know you better than anyone does.* "You did not used to like cards, but time makes many changes." Their words spoke of cards, but their hearts spoke of love.

"I am not yet so much changed," she protested, and then she stopped.

Frederick feared she did not want him to mistake what she said, but he could no longer contain the emotions coursing through him. As if it were the result of immediate feeling, he declared, "It is a period, indeed! Eight years and a half is a period!"

Before Anne could respond, Henrietta interrupted their private moment, totally unaware of the magic building between them. Frederick felt the air sucked from him; he still had no answer—strong suspicions—but no answer; and he watched in dismay as Anne, obviously reluctant, spoke of being perfectly ready to retire the room.

Even more vexing was the entrance of Sir Walter and Miss Elliot. Having moved away unwillingly from Anne, Frederick noted the general chill hanging over the room. Anne, disquieted by her family's grand entrance, appeared oppressed, and wherever he looked, he saw symptoms of the same. The comfort, the freedom, the gaiety of the room was over, hushed into cold composure, determined silence, or insipid talk, to meet the heartless elegance of Anne's father and sister.

"We came to issue everyone an invitation for tomorrow evening," Elizabeth declared. Then she turned to Frederick, offering him not only an *acknowledgment* but a flirtatious smile. "Oh, Captain Wentworth, I especially hope that you will be available to join us." A shiver shot down his spine. *What was Anne thinking with the change of situation?* He often wished for such acceptance but never at this cost. "Tomorrow evening," he heard Miss Elliot saying the proper nothings, "to meet a few friends, no formal party."

It was all said very gracefully, and the cards which she provided herself, the "Miss Elliot at home" were laid on the table, with a courteous, comprehensive smile to all, and one smile and one card more decidedly for Frederick. A definite twist in his stomach sent his earlier meal rising to a sickening awareness. He fought back the urge to run from the room. *Lord knows,* he thought, *no such alliance would satisfy me!* Elizabeth pointedly slid her card across the table to Frederick before she and Sir Walter disappeared.

He knew that all eyes fell on him, and although Frederick saw the offering as atonement for all the insolence of the past, he knew only surprise rather than gratitude—polite acknowledgment rather than acceptance. He held the card in his hand after they left, peering at it as if it held the answers to all his questions. He seriously considered accepting the invitation, but never for Elizabeth. If he ever entered Sir Walter's drawing room, it would be to claim Anne as his own.

The interruption was short, and ease and animation returned to most of those they left, as the door shut the Elliots out. Frederick stepped to the side, deep in contemplation, wondering how Anne perceived all that had just happened.

Mary moved to her sister's side and audibly whispered, "Only think of Elizabeth including everybody! I do not wonder Captain Wentworth is delighted! You see he cannot put the card out of his hand."

Frederick felt a momentary urge to toss the card into the fire, as if it were a live spark burning his fingertips. Anne caught his eye, and he felt his cheeks glow with embarrassment. His mouth formed itself into a momentary expression of contempt before he turned away in embarrassment and frustration.

"Wentworth, Harville and I plan to check out some of the shops in the trade district. We would be pleased if you joined us." Charles picked up his hat.

"Cer-Certainly, Musgrove," Frederick stammered, although he would have preferred to stay behind in hopes of speaking to Anne. "Are you ready, Harville?" Thomas grabbed his cane and followed the other men out.

Both he and Thomas remained quiet, deep in their own brooding. Musgrove rattled on about the possibility of taking up falconry or some other such sport, but neither of the other two men heard much of what he said. When they reached the trade shops, they agreed to separate for a while. Frederick then joined Harville, claiming his friend might need his help in maneuvering the crowded stores.

"You must be put out by all this," Frederick noted as they stepped through the doorway of a cramped furniture shop.

"What brings you to say that?" Harville stopped to look carefully at the intricate carving on a grandfather clock.

Frederick chuckled lightly. "You did not object when I used your injury as an excuse to avoid Musgrove right now. You would never accept any such offer otherwise."

Harville stopped short, leaning heavily on his cane. "Do you have any idea what Benwick requested of me?" Anger hung on every word.

"Tell me," Frederick's lips barely parted—his jaw clenched in anticipated contempt.

"That pretentious ass wants me to commission a portrait of him—for Louisa Musgrove! He gave me this to use as the model." Harville thrust a small miniature painting into Frederick's hand. "Damn him! He had it made for Fanny—remember, at the Cape—he met with a clever young German artist at the Cape, and in compliance with a promise to my poor sister, sat to him, and was bringing it home for her. And I have now the charge of getting it properly set for another!" And with a quivering lip he wound up the whole by adding, "Poor Fanny! She would not have forgotten him so soon!"

Frederick stared at his best friend. "You should not be in this position; I brought my folly upon your home."

"I do not hold you responsible any more than I do James. Who else is there for him to employ? Yet I cannot easily accept this. Fanny was my dearest sister—the playmate of my childhood." Harville walked away, needing to distance himself from his own words.

After a long moment, Frederick followed. "Leave it to me," he told Harville. "I will take care of the commission. That is the least I can do for you. You must cherish Fanny's memory.—I will not have it tarnished."

Harville muttered, "Thank you, my Friend."

Frederick did not acknowledge the thanks—no need existed between them. A person cannot stand beside another in times of war and not develop a deep, unspoken connection—a brotherhood in arms. Instead, he pointed to the elaborate design of a nearby table. "Do you suppose you can duplicate such artistry?"

"I expect I can; I made some preliminary drawings. Seeing all these pieces gives me some ideas of how I can make my mark." With his fingertips, Thomas reached out and traced the edges of a small table. "I love the feel of the wood," he confided. "The smell of the oil as it stains the grain." For a brief moment, he existed in another realm. "I know all that probably sounds fanciful."

"It sounds sincere." Frederick clapped him on the back. "It is time to meet Musgrove—let us hear more about shooting and sport."

Harville laughed—a deep belly laugh. "He does go on, does he not?" They started for the shop's door.

Frederick spent the evening with the Musgrove party. He would not abandon Thomas to the group's continual talk of James Benwick and Louisa Musgrove and wedded bliss. Secretly, he hoped that Anne might rejoin them, but she did not come, although Mrs. Musgrove relayed how she had earnestly begged Anne to return and dine—to give them all the rest of the day, but Anne promised to come again for breakfast on the morrow. Frederick vowed he would be there; he and Anne would finish this.

CHAPTER 17

Yes, yours, my love, is the right human face,
I in my mind had waited for this long.
Seeing the false and searching for the true,
Then I found you as a traveler finds a place
Of welcome suddenly amid the wrong.
—Edwin Muir, "The Confirmation"

Anne did *not* keep her appointment to break her fast with the Musgroves. Of course, the weather had taken an unfavorable turn, and Frederick knew she would walk to the hotel, but it did nothing for his state of mind. The rest of the party feasted on hearty fare; Frederick ate little of what he placed on his plate. He hungered for something totally unrelated to food; only Anne's acceptance could fill him.

In the late morning, she made her way to the proper apartment, and Frederick breathed at last. The aura of the room glowed from the moment Anne walked through the door, and her arrival signaled a clearing from the earlier downpour.

Their eyes met immediately. Being close to the door, having positioned himself to greet her upon her arrival, Frederick stepped forward and took her proffered hand and raised it to his lips in greeting; then he forced his legs to move, placing himself at the desk and beginning to separate the papers and prepare the pen.

"Ah, Miss Anne," Mrs. Musgrove ushered her forward toward a chair at the table, "we are so glad you came. Henrietta and Mary feared that you would not—what with the weather and all. The ladies could not wait once the sky began to clear, but they will be back again soon. They gave strict injunctions before they left; I am to keep you here until they turn back."

Out of the corner of his eye, Frederick noted how outwardly composed Anne appeared, and he wondered how he must look to the others. The moment *she* walked into the room, he felt himself plunged at once into all the agitations which he had merely antici-pated tasting a little before the morning closed. There was no delay—no waste of time. He was deep in the happiness of such misery or the misery of such happiness, instantly.

Clearing his throat and trying to sound disinterested, Frederick spoke to his friend, "We will write the letter, Harville, of which we spoke, if you will give me the materials."

"They are on the side table." Thomas gestured to a small table to Frederick's left. With materials all in hand, he went to it, and nearly turning his back on the gathered party, Frederick tried to appear engrossed by writing.

His sister, Sophia, spoke to Mrs. Musgrove, and he listened carefully to their conversation, trying to hear any words spoken by Anne. Mrs. Musgrove informed Sophia about the changes taking place at Uppercross, and his sister heartily agreed that young people should not dwell in long engagements. Frederick found himself agreeing in principle with Sophia's sentiments. He knew that she spoke from experience; she and the Admiral had married a little more than a month after their meeting. As he pretended to draft the letter, which he had composed in his head the night before, Frederick thought about how quickly he could marry Anne after she accepted him. He would not be willing to wait any longer than necessary.

Sophia declared, "To begin without knowing that at such a time there will be the means of marrying, I hold to be very unsafe and unwise. Couples should not delay their coming together."

His pen ceased to move, his head raised, pausing, listening, and he turned around the next instant to give a look—one quick, con-scious look at Anne. She flushed with the recognition, but neither of them looked away. The two ladies continued to talk—to urge again the same admitted truths and enforce them with such exam-ples of the ill effect of long engagements as had fallen within their observation, but Frederick heard nothing distinctly; it was only a buzz of words in his ear, and his mind felt the confusion. Finally, Anne looked away at Thomas Harville, who motioned her to join him by the window.

Frederick pushed the longing back down and returned to the task at hand. He began writing the letter in earnest.

Scratching out the order for the artist he would commission, Frederick heard Thomas talk to Anne about the miniature. His friend explained to her why Frederick took up the charge of the letter. He thought it ironic that Thomas spoke so openly to Anne when he refused to share his frustration with anyone else in the party besides Frederick. When their words turned to a light-hearted debate on which sex loved better, Frederick heard only *their* musings; his sister's conversation no longer existed. Every nerve in his body remained attuned to Anne—only *she* existed in *his* world, and he *must* know how she felt.

"It would not be the nature of any woman who truly loved," she protested against Harville's assertion that, unlike a woman, a man never forsook a woman he loved. Frederick would never forsake Anne—of that he was sure. Her soft voice brought him back. "Yes, we certainly do not forget you so soon as you forget us. It is, per-haps, our fate rather than our merit. We cannot help ourselves. We live at home, quiet, confined, and our feelings prey on us. You are forced on exertion. You have always a profession, pursuits, business of some sort or other, to take you back into the world immediately, and continual occupation and change soon weaken impressions."

Frederick stopped breathing for a moment. *Was that how it seemed to Anne? Does she believe that I did not suffer from our separation? She must think that because I threw myself into my work, I forgot her—that I did not leave my heart behind in Somerset. I must tell her; only her love has ever given me comfort.*

Needing to respond immediately, he took another sheet of foolscap from the desk drawer and addressed her passionately:

I can listen no longer in silence. I must speak to you by such means as

are within my reach. You pierce my soul! I am half agony—half hope.
Tell me not that I am too late, that such precious feelings are gone
forever. I offer myself to you again with a heart even more your own
than when you almost broke it eight years and a half ago. Dare not
say that man forgets sooner than woman, that his love has an earlier
death. I have loved none but you.

Anne's voice now spoke with a fervor, and Frederick jerked his head up and clumsily knocked over the blotting jar, sending it scattering dust across the carpet. His pen followed. He quickly retrieved the items, embarrassed at being so obvious in his intent.

"Have you finished your letter?" called Captain Harville.

Frederick stammered, "Not-Not quite, a few lines more. I shall have done in five minutes."

Harville smiled at Anne. Frederick should have known Anne would win Thomas's loyalty; he and Harville both understood the qualities of a fine woman. "There is no hurry on my side," his friend shared. "I am only ready whenever you are.—I am in very good anchorage here—well supplied and wanting for nothing.— No hurry for a signal at all."

As Frederick rearranged the items on the desk, he heard Harville lower his voice to speak to Anne further. They talked of inconstancy, and Frederick's heart went out to his friend as Thomas spoke with compassion and with insight into how a sailor feels about the woman he loves. "I speak, you know, only of such men as have hearts!"

"Oh!" cried Anne eagerly; "I hope I do justice to all that is felt by you and by those who resemble you." She offered his friend empathy, and Frederick smiled, knowing it to be her true nature. "I believe you capable of everything equal and good in your married lives. I believe you equal to every important exertion, and to every domestic forbearance, so long as—if I may be allowed the expression, so long as you have an object." Frederick leaned forward, hanging on Anne's every word. "I mean, while the woman you love lives and lives for you. All the privilege I claim for my own sex is of loving longest when existence or when hope is gone."

Out of the corner of his eye, Frederick watched as Thomas put his hand on her arm quite affectionately.

Hearing his sister speaking to someone behind him, Frederick returned to his letter:

> *Unjust I may have been, weak and resentful I have been, but never inconstant. You alone brought me to Bath. For you alone I think and plan.—Have you not seen this? Can you fail to understand my wishes?—I had not waited even these ten days, could I read your feelings, as I think you must have penetrated mine. I can hardly write. I am every instant hearing something which overpowers me. You sink your voice, but I can distinguish the tones of that voice, when they would be lost on others.—Too good, too excellent creature! You do us justice indeed. You do believe there is true attachment and constancy among men. Believe it to be most fervent, most undeviating in*
>
> FW

"Here, Frederick you and I part company, I believe," Sophia spoke loudly enough to recall him from his task. "I am going home, and you have an engagement with your friend.—Tonight we may have the pleasure of all meeting again at your party." She directed her last thought to Anne. "We had your sister's card yesterday, and I understand Frederick had a card, too, though I did not see it—and you are disengaged, Frederick, are you not, as well as ourselves?"

As she spoke, Frederick scratched out his postscript:

> *I must go, uncertain of my fate; but I shall return hither, or follow your party, as soon as possible. A word, a look will be enough to decide whether I enter your father's house this evening, or never.*

He managed to answer his sister, although a bit incoherently. "Yes, very true; here we separate, but Harville and I shall soon be after you, that is, Harville, if you are ready, I am in half a minute. I know you will not be sorry to be off. I shall be at your service in half a minute."

Sophia nodded her farewell to each of them, and he and Thomas began to make their leave also. Frederick sealed his letter with great rapidity. Having made the decision to write it, he wanted the words in Anne's hands; Frederick needed to be finished with this part and to start his life with Anne—if she would have him.

He slid Anne's letter under the blotter pad, having sealed it and marked it with her initials. "Let us be off, Harville," he encouraged. Frederick picked up his gloves—laying them purposely to the side of the desk—and then his hat before walking to the door. He could not speak to Anne—nor even look at her. His impatience to be gone created a hurried air as he exited the room.

Frederick heard Thomas offer a kind "Good morning. God bless you," to Anne.

He regretted not being able to speak his good-byes—the agitation too great, but if Anne was to refuse him, he wanted no pity from those who saw their departure.

He and Thomas made it to the outside door before Frederick spoke again. "Harville, wait for me a moment; I seemed to have left my gloves in the Musgroves' quarters."

"It is no problem—I shall remain here." Harville shifted his weight, allowing the cane to support him.

Making his unexpected return, Frederick said, "I apologize, Mrs. Musgrove," as he crossed the room, "I left my gloves behind."

Mrs. Musgrove stood by the window, looking out for the rest of their party. "It is quite all right, Captain Wentworth." The woman did not even turn around.

However, Anne stood close by, and she watched his every move. Stepping beside the desk, Frederick purposefully slid his fingers along the edge of the blotter paper. He locked eyes with Anne and then he drew out the letter and placed it on the desk. With the slightest of nods, he hastily collected his gloves and was again out of the room—the work of an instant!

His future was now in her hands. Frederick found Harville where he had left him, and they started toward the portrait studio to meet with the artist. They walked two blocks in complete silence—Frederick's vexation clearly evident.

"Do you want to tell me who will receive the second letter?"

Thomas asked softly, never looking at his friend.

Frederick hesitated. "You saw that?"

"Obviously," Thomas taunted. "Was it a love letter for Miss Anne?" Then he guffawed at his own joke. His friend chuckled some more at seeing Frederick flinch, but when Frederick did not answer, Harville gasped a little too loudly, "It was a love letter for Miss Anne!"

Barely audible, Frederick acknowledged, "Yes—yes, it was for Anne."

"Anne?" Thomas responded with disbelief. "How long has she been *Anne*?"

"From the first day I laid eyes on her—"

"In Somerset more than eight years ago," Thomas finished the sentence for him. "I knew it, you sly fox!" He slapped Frederick on the shoulder.

Obviously distressed, Frederick countered, "Do not congratulate me, Thomas; I know not my fate. The letter professes my love, but will Anne accept a renewal of my regard?"

Thomas took pity on his old friend. "May I ask why you are with me? Give me the miniature and the letter; I can well do this without you." Frederick started to protest, but a wave of Thomas's hand stopped him short. "Go—go back to the White Hart and win the woman you love. Do not leave there until *she* is *yours!*"

"Dare I risk it?" Frederick looked back the way they had come; he was unsure what to do.

Thomas grinned. "Do you truly love this woman?"

"Most wholeheartedly," Frederick insisted.

"I never knew you, my Friend, to allow anything to keep you from what you most desired. This would be a first."

"No." Frederick shook his head. "It would not be a first." His anxiety increased as he looked away once more. "I must go—I am sorry, Harville, but I must go!" As he strode away, he heard Thomas chuckling.

Turning the corner at Bath Street, he noted that Anne and Charles Musgrove had crossed to Union. He quickened his step to catch up, but when Frederick reached them, he paused. Knowing that within a few minutes he would speak what was in his heart, he froze—irresolute whether to join them or to pass on, saying nothing, after all. He stared at her, wondering what to do, each heartbeat infinitely long. Then Anne, sensing his approach, turned suddenly; she blushed—the cheeks, which were pale, now glowed, and the movement, which hesitated, was decided. Frederick stepped up beside her, and they were lost to each other. Eyes danced in happiness, and they were as before—united—hearts interlocked, needing no words to declare their love.

"Say, Wentworth," Charles implored him. "Which way are you going? Only to Gay Street or farther up the town?" Charles appeared most anxious to leave.

Frederick did not take his eyes from Anne's face. "I hardly know," he replied.

Charles continued, oblivious to the lovers. "Are you going as high as Belmont? Are you going near Camden Place? Because if you are, I shall have no scruple in asking you to take my place and give Anne your arm to her father's door. She is rather done for this morning and must not go so far without help. And I ought to be at that fellow's in the marketplace. He promised me the sight of a capital gun he is just going to send off; said he would keep it unpacked to the last possible moment, that I might see it; and if I do not turn back now, I will have no chance. By his description, a good deal like the second-sized double barrel of mine, which you shot with one day, round Winthrop. What do you say, Wentworth?"

Frederick tried to stop smiling, but he gave up the effort when he saw a like smile on Anne's face. "It is fine, Musgrove. Go see the gun. I will be most honored to escort Miss Anne home; she will be safe with me."

"That is superb news! I am in your debt," Charles added quickly. Then he disappeared, hurrying along Union Street.

"Which way, Miss Anne?" Frederick's voice remained husky with emotion.

"Some place quiet, Captain—you may choose." Anne placed her

hand on his proffered arm, and Frederick pulled her close to his side. Relief rushed through him as they turned away from the crowd.

As they entered the park, Frederick led her to a nearby bench. "May we sit for a time?" They spoke little over the last few blocks other than small talk about the weather and such. When he properly seated himself beside her, Frederick took her hand in his, clutching it to his chest. "Anne," he whispered, "my heart beats again because of you—with the hope that you will receive me—that you understand how ardently I adore you." He brought her palm to his lips and planted a kiss on the inside of her wrist. "Please say that I am not too late."

Anne released her hand from his, but she did so to trace the outline of his lips. "Yours is the face I see every time I close my eyes. It has been so for eight years—nothing you could say or do would ever change that."

Frederick suddenly felt quite warm. "May I be so forward as to presume there is hope for us?"

"There is more than hope, Frederick. I give you my assurance." She did not look away. "I am no longer that foolish green girl; I am not so persuadable. If God gives us a time once more, I will never turn from you. You will be my life if that is truly your desire." She raised her chin to look him directly in the eyes. "I love you, Frederick Wentworth; I have loved none but you."

Frederick's fingertips traced the line of her cheek from her temple to her jaw. "You have no idea," he began, "how much I love you." He took her hand once more and pulled Anne to her feet. "Come, my Dear, let us walk. It would not do for me to take you in my arms in the midst of this busy park, and I fear if we sit here any longer, I will ruin your reputation with that or more."

Anne laughed—a light tinkling of bells drifting on the breeze. "You would never break with propriety, Captain," she teased.

He leaned towards her, letting his breath tickle her ear. "Do not tempt me, Miss Elliot," he taunted in return. "When it comes to you, I have little control."

Redness spread across her chest and warmed Anne's face. "I

recall vividly," she murmured.

Frederick knew instantly he liked the more mature Anne. She still blushed with his words, a fact in which he took great delight, but she, too, spoke more boldly and accepted his *seductive* ways. "I plan to give you new memories," he whispered.

They retired to the gravel walk, where the power of conversation would make the present hour a blessing indeed. There they exchanged again those feelings and those promises, which once before seemed to secure every thing, but which were followed by so many, many years of division and estrangement. There they returned again into the past, more exquisitely happy, perhaps in their reunion, than when it was first projected: more tender, more tried, more fixed in a knowledge of each other's character, truth, and attachment; more equal to act—more justified in acting. And there, as they slowly paced the gradual ascent, heedless of every group around them, seeing neither sauntering politicians, bustling housekeepers, flirting girls, nor nursery maids and children, they could indulge in those retrospections and acknowledgments, and especially in those explanations of what directly proceeded to the present moment, which were so poignant and so ceaseless in interest. All the little variations of the past week were gone through, and of yesterday and today there could scarcely be an end.

"Admit it; you were jealous," Anne suggested.

They walked into a secluded area; a row of hedges blocked their view of the finely worn path. Instinctively, he pulled Anne to him, taking her into his arms; she snuggled into him—her head resting on his chest. Frederick glanced down at her. "Were you trying to make me jealous, Sweetling?"

Anne tilted her head back to look up at him. "If I did, you deserved it, you know." A smile turned up the corners of her mouth, and Anne's eyes twinkled with enjoyment.

Frederick outlined her lips with his fingertips, pulling gently on her bottom one. His smile matched hers—his being lost to her closeness. "I believe, Sweetling, I did; but you have no idea how I suffered this past week."

"I would think that you would know me well enough to realize that Mr. Elliot was not to my liking."

"Oh, Anne, you do not know the doubt—the torment. It is not pleasant to speak of." Frederick held her to him until he heard someone approaching at a distance. "We should walk again, my Dear."

"Frederick," she began softly as she fell into step beside him. "I would like for us to be honest with each other. When we were together before neither of us spoke the whole truth. For me, it was because I did not want to disappoint; I so desperately feared losing your love. I suppose it was my age or my lack of life experience; I had no idea of what I should expect.—Sometimes, the feelings were so foreign to me, and I wondered if other women felt as I did. For you, I believe you tried to protect me. Unfortunately, because I did not know what to expect, my fears surfaced too quickly."

"I do not understand, Anne. What do you desire of me?"

"I would like for us to speak what is in our hearts, whether it is jealousy, love, or fear. I want the same type of relationship I observe in your sister and the Admiral."

"Then you wish to know of my anguish?"

"I would never ask of you to do so, especially if it was a painful experience; yet, if we are to really know each other, we must speak our hearts." Anne looked up at him, trying to explain the unexplainable.

Frederick nodded. "Your words make excellent sense. Over the past few months, I have observed couples: my brother and Christine, Thomas and Milly, and Sophia and Benjamin. Seeing them, I realized I could not settle for anyone other than you.

"I came to Bath to win your regard, and when I saw you in the company of Mr. Elliot, I regret to say that I lost reason. Jealousy began to operate in the very hour of first meeting you in Bath; it returned, after a short suspension, to ruin the concert; and it influenced me in everything I said or did or omitted saying and doing in the past four-and-twenty hours. It gradually yielded to the better hopes, which your looks, or words, or actions occasionally encouraged; it was vanquished at last by those sentiments and those tones which reached me while you talked with Captain Harville. Listening closely and feeling so much, I knew I must respond."

"It was a beautiful letter," Anne maintained. "I was in awe."

"Every word was true," he insisted. "I have loved none but you; no one could supplant you in my life; I never saw your equal. I tried to forget you and believed it to be so; I imagined myself indifferent when I was simply angry at your actions. Because I suffered from our separation, I tried to deny your merits; but your character is perfection itself. Only at Uppercross did I learn to give you justice, and only at Lyme did I understand myself."

They returned to the main courseway, and Frederick led her to another bench. "When Mr. Elliot gazed at you admiringly on the steps at Lyme, I wanted to throw the man into the sea; I had no right, but I admit to such violent thoughts. You mesmerized me as I watched you on the Cobb—the way the ocean played at your feet; you were like a water sprite. Your superiority shone through at the Harvilles' home, when you showed empathy for Benwick. And I have nothing but respect for the calm, confident way you handled Louisa's accident on the beach."

Anne dropped her eyes and pretended to straighten a seam on her dress. Frederick took her chin in his palm and raised it once more. "Anne, I am a foolish man—very foolish. I wanted to punish you for not loving me enough." Anne started to protest, but he silenced her with a touch of his finger to her lips. "I know you love me—I knew it then, but my pride would not let me admit it, so I tried to attach myself to Louisa Musgrove, although I soon realized we had nothing upon which to build a relationship. At Lyme, I tried to distance myself from her; I planned to approach you before we boarded our coaches to return to Uppercross, but fate twisted those plans. Louisa's mind could never compare with the excellence of your mind or the perfect, unrivaled possession it has over mine. At Lyme, I learned to distinguish between the steadiness of principle and the obstinacy of self-will. I deplore the pride, the folly, and the madness of resentment, which kept me from trying to regain your love the moment I returned to Somerset and found you unattached."

Anne responded slowly, "It was a terrible time for both of us. I knew we could still be friends from the moment you took Little Walter from the room; I believed you no longer hated me when you secured the Admiral's carriage for my comfort." She slid her hand under his cupped one, and Frederick tightened his grip, guaranteeing she could not change her mind and withdraw. "Of course, I would have preferred not to listen to the Admiral speculate on which Musgrove you would marry."

Frederick chuckled. "Do I detect a bit of jealousy in your tone? I would relish in knowing so."

"Then fancy yourself satisfied, Sir. I wanted you for myself, and as much as I esteem Louisa Musgrove, I could never picture you with her." Anne's voice did not falter.

"I was so pleased when Louisa began to recover, thinking I could wait a reasonable amount of time and then present myself to you. I no sooner began to feel alive again, than I began to feel, though alive, not at liberty. I found Harville considered me an engaged man! Neither Harville nor his wife entertained a doubt of Louisa's and my mutual attachment. I was startled and shocked. To a degree, I could contradict this instantly; but when I began to reflect others might have felt the same—her own family, nay, perhaps herself, I was no longer at my own disposal. I was hers in honor if she wished it. I was unguarded. I had not thought seriously on this subject before. I had not considered that my excessive intimacy must have its danger of ill consequence in many ways; and I had no right to be trying whether I could attach myself to either of the girls, at the risk of raising even an unpleasant report, were there no ill effects. I was grossly wrong and must abide the consequences.

"In short, at precisely the time I became fully satisfied that I did not care for Louisa at all, I regarded myself as bound to her, if her sentiments for me were what the Harvilles supposed. Therefore, I chose to weaken whatever feelings or speculations existed by removing myself to Shropshire, meaning after a while to return to

Kellynch and act as circumstances might require.

"I was six weeks with Edward and saw him happy. I could have no other pleasure. I deserved none. He inquired after you particularly—asked even if you were personally altered, little suspecting to my eye you could never alter." Anne squeezed his hand and offered a little smile. "I remained in Shropshire, lamenting the blindness of my own pride until at once released from Louisa by the astonishing and felicitous intelligence of her engagement to Benwick.

"Here," said he, "ended the worst of my state; for now I could, at least, put myself in the way of happiness; I could exert myself; I could do something. But waiting so long in inaction was dreadful. Within five minutes I said, 'I will be at Bath on Wednesday,' and I was. Was it unpardonable to think it worth my while to come? And to arrive with some degree of hope? You were single. It was possible you might retain the feelings of the past as I did; and one encouragement happened to be mine. I could never doubt you would be loved and sought by others, but I knew to a certainty you refused one man, at least, of better pretensions than myself in the form of Charles Musgrove, and I could not help often saying, 'Was this for me?'"

"Yes, I overheard Louisa tell you about Charles's proposal." She added, "Charles is very amiable, and as much as I respect him as my sister's husband, the thought of spending my life with a man who rarely reads or who prefers sport above all else was not tolerable. Besides, my heart was elsewhere." She offered him a flirtatious smile.

"You are even more beautiful when you smile." Frederick stroked the inside of her wrist with his thumb.

"You, my Love, are giving me more reasons to smile."

Frederick spoke again, more seriously now. "Your presence in Molland's confectioner's shop was exquisite torture. You were in front of me—all I saw was you, but horror in the guise of Mr. Elliot broke that splendor. Then you stepped forward in the octagonal room to speak to me, and my heart was again yours. No one else existed at that moment. But again, your family whisked you away."

"I turned back to speak to you after acknowledging Lady Dalrymple's entrance—but you were gone!" she protested.

"I did not suspect," he muttered. "It was such a time—to see you," cried he, "in the midst of those who could not be my well-wishers, to see your cousin close by you, conversing and smiling, and feel all the horrible eligibilities and proprieties of the match! You could be Lady Elliot, just as your mother was! To consider it as the certain wish of every being who could hope to influence you! Even, if your feelings were reluctant or indifferent, to consider what supports would be his! Was it not enough to make the fool of me, which I appeared? How could I look on without agony? Was not the very sight of the friend who sat behind you, was not the recollection of what had been, the knowledge of her influence, the indelible, immovable impression of what persuasion had once done—was it not all against me?"

"Oh, Frederick," Anne sympathized, "I am sorry you suffered because of me. I assure you that from the beginning, there was a sensation of something more than immediately appeared in Mr. Elliot's wishing to reconcile with my father. In a worldly view, he had nothing to gain by being on terms with my family. In all probability, he was richer, and the Kellynch estate would as surely be his hereafter as the title. At first, I thought it to be for Elizabeth's sake."

"How could any man consider your sister Elizabeth once he met you?" Frederick asked rhetorically as he leaned back against the seat. "I am sorry to speak poorly of your sister, Anne, but from our first day in the mercantile, Miss Elliot held no sway over me; my thoughts were only of you."

Anne looked around quickly, as if worried that someone might overhear. "I cannot explain everything at this time, but believe me when I say that Mr. Elliot's intentions were not simply to seek my regard. He was more concerned with preventing my father from taking up with Mrs. Clay. Mr. Elliot has spent a great deal of his time of late trying to convince me of Mrs. Clay's *supposed* intentions to become the next Lady Elliot."

"*Now* I see," replied Frederick, leaning forward. "If your father would have another child—a boy—Mr. Elliot would not gain the title."

Anne confirmed, "Exactly."

"Yet, I had no idea at the time. All I could see was the benefit of your connection to your cousin and my fear of being too late!" he exclaimed.

"You should have distinguished," replied Anne. "You should not have suspected me now; the case so different, and my age so different. If I was wrong in yielding to persuasion once, remember that it was to persuasion exerted on the side of safety, not of risk. When I yielded, I thought it was to duty; but no duty could be called in aid here. In marrying a man indifferent to me, all risk would be incurred, and all duty violated."

"Perhaps I ought to have reasoned," he replied, "but I could not. I could not derive benefit from the late knowledge I acquired of your character. I could not bring it into play: it was overwhelmed—buried—lost in those earlier feelings, which I smarted under year after year. I could think of you only as one who yielded, who gave me up, who anyone, rather than by me, influenced you. I saw you with that very person who guided you in that year of misery. I had no reason to believe her of less authority now.—The force of habit was to be added."

"I should have thought," said Anne, "that my manner to yourself might have spared you much or all of this."

"No, no! Your manner might be only the ease, which your engagement to another man would give. I left you in this belief; and yet—I was determined to see you again. My spirits rallied with the morning, and I felt I had still a motive for remaining here."

Anne laughed lightly. "We certainly misconstrued each other!"

Frederick stood at last; he reached out his hand to her. "Yes, we did, but no more. There will be no more misperceptions—and no one else will come between us." Anne took his hand and allowed him to pull her to her feet. "You must know, Anne, that it is my intention that we will be married as soon as the banns can be read. I will not spend one more minute than necessary without you in my life." He held both her hands grasped tightly to his chest, where she might feel his heart beating for her. "Although we do not need his permission any longer, if you will agree, I will speak to your father this evening after the party. I have fortune enough for us to live comfortably, and I have plans for ways to secure your future. Please say you will be my wife."

"I have been *yours* since we met all those years ago. Yes, address my father, but I will be your wife no matter what my family may say. We will make our plans tomorrow."

Frederick brought one of her gloved hands to his lips. "Tomorrow," he murmured. "I suppose that I must see you home," he said after a long pause, "although my heart hates the idea of leaving you even for a few minutes."

"But you will accept *Elizabeth's* invitation for the evening?" she teased.

"I never realized, Sweetling, that you were such an *evil* woman; I may need to rethink my offer." They turned toward the park entrance. "Should I give your sister my attention this evening?"

"Only if you wish to be alone on your wedding day," she warned.

"I will be with *you*, my Dear, tonight—and on our wedding day—and on every day for the rest of our lives. Is that understood?"

"Giving orders so early on, my Captain?" she mocked.

"As if," he laughed, "you would allow me to order you about or you would allow me to think you would obey. I expect from this moment on, I will contentedly walk the plank daily for you."

Anne tightened her hold on his arm. "I promise it will be a pleasant walk."

Frederick cupped her hand in his. Leaning in, he whispered, "I can barely wait for it to begin."

CHAPTER 18

My face in thine eye, thine in mine appears,
And true plain hearts do in the faces rest;
Where can we find two better hemispheres
Without sharp north, without declining west?
Whatever dies, was not mix't equally;
If our two loves be one, or thou and I
Love so alike that none can slacken, none can die.
—John Donne, "The Good Morrow"

Back on Gay Street with Sophia and Benjamin, Frederick found it difficult to contain his happiness, but he and Anne had agreed that they would not announce their engagement until he had spoken to Sir Walter. Even though they no longer needed her father's permission, Frederick felt it best to, at least, inform Anne's father of their intentions. He anticipated less resentment on Sir Walter's part this time, but he still assumed the worst in dealing with the man—prideful vanity could be unpredictable.

"Your sister says that Miss Elliot personally gave you her card," Benjamin noted as they took a light meal prior to the Elliots' party.

"She did," was Frederick's brief response.

The Admiral continued, "Are we then to presume that our family now meets the Elliots' standards? It would be pleasant to be referred to as something more than a *tenant*. It is not as if Sophie and I are simple cottagers on the estate. The man lives off the money I pay him for the use of his house."

Frederick put down his spoon. "If I were to conjecture about Miss Elliot's attentions to me, I would suspect that she has been informed that I possess a certain amount of prize money. After all, Miss Elliot served as Kellynch's mistress for years; she contributed to Sir Walter's current financial loss of status. Even if I were interested,

I cannot imagine I would have enough funds to satisfy Miss Elliot's need to spend; I would soon find myself without financial soundness, and, unlike Sir Walter, I may not live off my aristocratic name. However, I do not attend tonight with any desire to earn Miss Elliot's attentions. She is handsome, but rather long in the tooth."

Sophia looked up with his last words. "One might say the same of Miss Anne."

Frederick attempted to sound calm. "Anne Elliot is three years younger than Miss Elliot, and I think you will agree that a comparison between the two is without merit. Anne is far superior to either of her sisters in intelligence and character."

Sophia smiled at him with her "I thought so" attitude before saying, "The man who earns Anne Elliot's hand, I suspect, will be remarkable. Do you suppose she is really intended for her cousin Mr. Elliot? He seems a bit too perfect to be true, if you ask me."

"I have no idea of Mr. Elliot's plans." Frederick realized his sister wanted to know why his mood changed so suddenly today; Sophia suspected his feelings for Anne, but he wanted everyone to be surprised by their announcement. "I promised Thomas I would call on him before the Elliot party; I will bring him along with me."

"Then we will see you there," Benjamin declared, laying his napkin on the table before standing. "Come along, Sophie. We *tenants* should not be late."

★ ★ ★

Frederick swore Thomas to secrecy, knowing that his friend would be happy with the outcome of the evening. Frederick had little time for an explanation with the entire Musgrove party around, but he managed to tell him not to say anything just yet. So when they stepped into the Elliots' drawing room, Frederick's nerves reached a peak. All those who only a few nights earlier would oppose his pledge to marry Anne—Sir Walter, Lady Russell, and Mr. Elliot— sat before him; the difference was the look on Anne's face. He gained confidence just looking at her laughing eyes, which reminded him the evening would include exchanging compliments with a pack of self-absorbed, overdressed aristocrats. The thought was laughable—actually ludicrous,—and Frederick could not help but return her smile with one of his own. A frisson of excitement coursed through him as he finally stepped in front of her.

"Miss Anne," he said courteously as he raised her offered hand to his lips. Their eyes spoke of the desire—created by the touch of a hand and a pronouncing of a name.

"Captain Wentworth," she said in a low voice, "we are pleased you could join us for the evening. May I show you to one of the tables or perhaps offer you some refreshment?"

Frederick looked around the room; he would be unable to concentrate on a card hand this evening. "A drink would be nice, Miss Anne," he said loudly enough for others to hear.

"This way, Captain." Anne motioned to a table with port, wine, lemonade, and champagne. Frederick followed her there; it was the closest he would come to being alone with her for the next few hours. "Champagne, Captain?" she said as she handed him a glass and took one for herself. "To us," Anne mouthed the words.

Frederick turned his back to the room, blocking her view and preventing the others from observing their exchange. "You are exquisite, Sweetling," his voice barely audible. "Such beauty easily unmans me."

"Frederick," she laughed softly, before taking a sip of the bubbly mixture. "You are such a flirt."

"It is not flirting, my Dear, if I speak the truth." He took a sip from his glass and leaned in as close as he dared without raising suspicion. "Are you as happy as I?"

Anne smiled up at him. "Ecstatic."

"Excellent, Miss Anne," he said. "A very fine champagne." Again, he spoke for the room and not for her ears alone. He offered her a crisp bow and moved away to where Thomas and Charles Musgrove held a discussion over glasses of port. Musgrove spoke of the gun he had rushed off to see that day, but a preoccupied Frederick heard only bits and pieces of the conversation.

The planned evening—a card party—was a mixture of those who met before and those who met too often—a common place business, too numerous for intimacy and too small for variety. Frederick's gaze followed Anne as she made her way around the room. Glowing and lovely in sensibility and happiness, she had cheerful or forbearing feelings for every creature around her. Judiciously, she avoided Mr. Elliot, sparing Frederick any possible pain. She displayed restrained amusement with Mr. Elliot's friends, the Wallises, and with her cousins Lady Dalrymple and Miss Carteret. Anne also avoided Mrs. Clay, who she long suspected used her sister Elizabeth to move up in the world and who proved of late she might be part of Mr. Elliot's diversions. After all, with her own eyes, she had seen them on the street together outside the Musgroves' hotel.

With the Musgroves, there was the happy chat of perfect ease; with Captain Harville, the kind-hearted intercourse of brother and sister; with Lady Russell, attempts at conversation, and with the Admiral and Sophia, everything of peculiar cordiality and fervent interest.

She was making her way toward him, and he pretended not to anticipate her approach. Frederick turned slightly away, but not before hearing Miss Elliot reprimand her, "Do not monopolize Captain Wentworth, as you always do. Others would like his company, too."

"I believe the Captain is capable of choosing his own company, Elizabeth. I will not avoid him because it is your wish that I do so." Anne gave her sister a curt nod and moved on.

He moved to the far side of the room and pretended to admire a fine display of greenhouse plants. Sensing her approach, Frederick turned to meet her. "I wondered when you would make your way back to me," he whispered.

"I felt your eyes on me, Sir. Did you not *will* me to return?"

Frederick chuckled at her boldness. "I did indeed. You are a vixen in disguise as a demur lady. How could I not take note of such before?"

"It is odd." Anne shook her head as if to clear it. "With my family—with everyone—I take the role as the quiet, unassuming sister, but when I am with you, my tongue says things I never realized were part of my thoughts."

"It is because, my Love, I see you differently from the others. With me, you are the other half of my heart. There is little you could say that would offend me. In reality, I rejoice in seeing you allow me such insights."

He watched as she bit her lower lip; then she looked back to the gathering before speaking, assuming a serious tone. "I was thinking—thinking over the past and trying impartially to judge of the right and wrong, I mean with regard to myself; and I must believe I was right, much as I suffered from it; I was perfectly right in being guided by the friend whom you will love better than you do now. To me, she was in the place of a parent. Do not mistake me, however. I am not saying she did not err in her advice. It was, perhaps, one of those cases in which advice is good or bad only as the event decides; and for myself, I certainly never should, in any circumstance of tolerable similarity, give such advice. But I mean, I was right in submitting to her, and if I did otherwise, I should suffer more in continuing the engagement than I did in giving it up, because I should suffer in my conscience. I have now, as far as such a sentiment is allowable in human nature, with which nothing to reproach myself; and if I mistake not, a strong sense of duty is no bad part of a woman's portion."

Frederick looked at her, looked at Lady Russell, and looking again at Anne, replied, as if in cool deliberation, "Not yet. But there are hopes of her being forgiven in time. I trust to being in charity with her soon, but I, too, was thinking over the past, and a question has suggested itself, whether there may not have been one person more my enemy even than that lady? My own self. Tell me if, when I returned to England in the year '08, with a few thousand pounds, and was posted into the *Laconia*, if I then wrote to you, would you have answered my letter? Would you, in short, have renewed the engagement then?"

"Would I?" was all her answer, but the accent was decisive enough.

"Good God!" he cried, "you would! It is not that I did not

think of it or desire it, as what could alone crown all my other success. But I was proud, too proud to ask again. I did not understand you. I shut my eyes and would not understand you, or do you justice. This is a recollection which ought to me forgive everyone sooner than myself. Six years of separation and suffering might have been spared. It is a sort of pain, too, which is new to me. I was used to the gratification of believing myself to earn every blessing I enjoyed. I valued myself on honorable toils and just rewards. Like other great men under reverses," he added with a smile, "I must endeavor to subdue my mind to fortune. I must learn to brook being happier than I deserve."

"We will speak no more of this," Anne declared. "We—you and I—knew sadness in our separation, but we will let no such impediment keep us apart ever again."

"For you, my Dear, I will temper my dislike for the lady." He glanced around the room again. "Anne," he spoke softly for only her ears, "I want nothing more than to spend the rest of my days with you by my side and the rest of my nights with you in my arms. After tonight, you may be sorely plagued by my presence, but I will not hear of our parting ever again."

"That would please me, Frederick."

Their conversation ended, as Elizabeth insisted that he join the group to whom she would show the house. The group included Mrs. Musgrove, Henrietta, Captain Harville, the Admiral, and Sophia. Bowing to Anne, he reluctantly followed the others to the hallway.

When Sir Walter briefly stepped from the drawing room to offer his own anecdotes, Frederick took the opportunity to approach the man. "Sir Walter," he said, "may I speak to you for a moment, Sir?"

Sir Walter looked a bit annoyed at losing his audience to his daughter, but he accepted the interference with as much graciousness as he was known to extend to anyone. "Certainly, Captain." He gestured toward an open door. "Perhaps the library will do." Frederick followed the man into a dimly lit room. The number of books on the shelves surprised Frederick. Other than Anne, he felt confident that none of the Elliots regularly opened a book for pleasure. However, the two huge mirrors hanging on opposing walls did not surprise him. "Well, Captain," Sir Walter's voice brought him to the moment at hand, "what may I do for you?"

Frederick cleared his throat nervously. "Today, I renewed my proposal to your daughter Anne, and she accepted my offer."

Sir Walter looked shocked. "But-But there is Mr. Elliot," he stammered.

"I understand your surprise, Sir, but I assure you Miss Anne does not take Mr. Elliot's attentions seriously. We will marry; Anne is of age, and we no longer need your permission or your blessing, although I pray for the sake of family accord, you will not withhold either. As I told you eight years ago, the Navy allows a man to make his fortune in the world. I have accumulated nearly thirty thousand pounds to date. I plan to purchase an estate, so Anne may be the mistress of her own home. She will want for nothing as long as I live."

"Captain, your continued devotion to my daughter amazes me, especially considering the fact Mr. Elliot is in the picture." Frederick flinched with the words. "If Anne chooses to attach herself to you, then I have no objections. Even the Prince Regent prizes the accomplishments of men such as you. It would be well for my family to align itself with a man of service to our country. Anne will receive her share of ten thousand pounds upon my death."

Frederick nodded. *The more things change, the more they remain the same.* Sir Walter valued Anne only as a means for her father to advance his own place in society. Frederick was now esteemed quite worthy to address the daughter of a foolish, spendthrift baronet, who had not principle or sense enough to maintain himself in the situation in which Providence had placed him. Sir Walter, indeed, though he held no affection for Anne to make him really happy on the occasion, was very far from thinking it a bad match for her. "We would like to announce our engagement this evening, Sir, as we have both family and friends in attendance. Would you do the honors, Sir Walter?"

"I hear the others returning, Captain. Why do we not join them? We may address this before people begin to retire for the evening." The baronet ushered Frederick toward the door. "Do you know, Captain, my cousin Lady Dalrymple found you to be a very fine young man."

"Really?" Frederick feigned surprise. "Then I hope Her Ladyship will approve of our connection."

"I am positive that she will." Sir Walter instinctively stepped in front of Frederick, checking his appearance in the nearest mirror.

When they reentered the drawing room, Anne, who stood beside Sophia, looked up in anticipation. He smiled at her as he strode across the room and took her hand in his. He heard Sophia gasp in delight as Sir Walter cleared his throat loudly enough to draw attention to himself as he stood by the open door. "My friends and family," he began in his most pretentious tone, "it is with pleasure that I announce that our modest card party has become a momentous occasion. My daughter Anne has this day accepted the proposal of Captain Wentworth, and they wish you to share in their happiness."

The room was silent for a heartbeat, and then Frederick and Anne were surrounded by well-wishers. Sophia, with tears of happiness streaming down her face, hugged Anne tightly to her.

Harville, who had moved behind Frederick during Sir Walter's speech, was the first to reach him. He gave his friend a hug and pounded him on the back. "You did it!" he congratulated him. "I knew *nothing* could stop you once you put your mind to it. At last, you will be happy; you will have the one thing you missed."

"The one thing I always needed," Frederick assured him before the others interrupted.

"Miss Anne!" Mrs. Musgrove caught her at Sophia's release. "How you kept us all in dark! None of us suspected that you and Captain Wentworth had developed an affection for each other these past few months."

Frederick wanted to set the record straight; he would not let it appear Anne had accepted Louisa Musgrove's castoffs. "Mrs. Musgrove, I am sure you are not aware that I lived in Somerset for a short time with my brother years ago. I fell in love with Miss Anne at that time, but she was too young. Although I tried to forget her, when I returned to the area, I found she still owned my heart."

"How romantic," Henrietta emphasized; her eyes were misty. Thankfully, no one reminded him that for a while it appeared that his sights were set on Louisa.

Lady Russell made her way to them, and with his hand resting lightly on her back, ready to offer her protection, he felt Anne stiffen. "My dear Anne," the older friend took both of Anne's hands in hers, "let me wish you happy."

"Thank you," Anne murmured. Then she added, "Will you not acknowledge my future husband?" Her remarks, demanding recognition for him, surprised Frederick.

Lady Russell's jaw twitched with something he suspected to be disdain; she hesitated, but then she graciously turned to him. "Captain, you won a jewel; cherish her and protect her as such."

Frederick offered her a polite bow. "I will do nothing less, Lady Russell." With that, she stepped to the side to allow others their moment with them.

He noted, out of the corner of his eye, that Mr. Elliot and Mrs. Clay conversed intimately on the far side of the room, nearly unseen behind a large palm. Anne, he was sure, did not observe how, shortly afterward, Mr. Elliot took his leave. Neither he nor Mrs. Clay offered them words of congratulations.

For Frederick, the rest of the evening was perfection. He walked about the room with Anne on his arm, sat with her on a secluded settee for nearly an hour, and openly declared his affection for her. At one point, Anne motioned to Sophia to join them. "Mrs. Croft," Anne began, "I have a boon to ask of you."

"Of course, Miss Anne, how might I serve you?" Sophia shot a look of approval at Frederick.

Anne slipped her hand into Frederick's before speaking. "Your brother and I wish to marry as soon as the banns can be called. Although I am sure Mary and the Musgroves will wish to assist me, their party will return to Uppercross soon. Would you, I wonder, go with me to a modiste to secure my bride clothes? I would not know to whom to turn in Bath."

"Oh, Miss Anne, what a delight! I know *just* the person. Plus, it will give us time to learn more of each other. I have always wanted a sister. Did you hear, Frederick?" Her voice was breathy with excitement.

"I believe my future wife has given you the perfect excuse to spend more of the Admiral's money," he teased her lovingly.

"Phoo, phoo!" cried Sophia. "What a notion!"

More seriously, Frederick offered, "I will be pleased to escort the two of you if you wish."

"Let us say, the day after tomorrow, if that is acceptable to you, Mrs. Croft," Anne added quickly.

"It is most acceptable. And please call me Sophia. May I call you Anne?"

"I would prefer that."

"I will leave you two for now," Sophia said. "The Admiral is signaling to me."

They were alone again. Anne leaned against Frederick's shoulder for a few brief seconds. "It is all so sudden, and it just occurred to me I will be part of a different family—one with new brothers and new sisters."

"The Wentworths are very close," he warned her. "Sometimes you may wish they did not want to know your business, but you will find no stronger allies."

"Unfortunately, the Elliots are not so devoted to their loved ones." Anne's face fell with the disclosure.

He assured her, "I have the *best* of the Elliots; the others are insignificant to me."

"You deserve better than what I offer you. You give me a family and friendships in which to share." She finally met his gaze with hers.

"I *deserve* nothing, but I *need* you." He kissed her fingertips. "Let us return to our wedding plans. Do you suppose Edward could officiate?"

"Do you want to marry out of Bath or out of Uppercross?" she asked.

Frederick smiled with the question. "It would be best if we did so in Bath. As much as it would please me to marry you in the chapel on Kellynch, the place where this all began, it would be awkward for your father and sister and Lady Russell to celebrate our union there. Let us choose some place here where Edward might be part of the service. I will make it my mission to find such a church tomorrow. I will ask your father for the nearest services."

At that moment, Sophia returned, bright-eyed. "I had inspiration. May I see if the Pump Room Assembly Hall is available for the breakfast? I did not attend Edward's joining with Christine because the Admiral and I were still at sea. This will be a pleasure to help plan."

"Yes," said Anne. "Thank you, Sophia." She said in a low tone, "I think my sister might choose a location that is a bit—how shall I say it—too formal. I would like my guests to be comfortable."

"We will, of course, include Bath's high society. And Frederick's fellow officers!" Sophia's excitement continued to grow.

"Definitely," Anne confirmed. "I wish to meet Frederick's friends."

"Then it is settled," Sophia authorized. "I will call on you tomorrow, and we will come up with a tentative list. This is most exciting!" She took several steps in retreat.

"Make it before noon," Frederick called to his sister. "I plan to spend the afternoon with Anne."

Sophia turned to say, "Anne, we will wait until Monday and spend time together. That way, you and Frederick may attend services together and speak to the vicar about calling the banns. I will send a note around tomorrow to confirm." With that, she was gone, leaving a faint trace of rose perfume behind her.

★ ★ ★

Happy to recognize the union of a member of the aristocracy in his parish, Mr. Osgood readily agreed to share the services with Edward Wentworth. Although a bit rushed, the first reading of the banns occurred that day; the official announcement would appear in the society pages the next morning.

"Can you believe this is happening—at last?" Anne sat beside him as Frederick addressed a note to Edward and Christine, telling his brother of his plans and asking him to participate.

Although a chaperone should have been with them, they had been left to their own devices; Frederick assumed Anne's impeccable reputation offered no one any qualms or maybe her family still saw her as insignificant. He preferred the former explanation. Frederick leaned toward her and brushed his lips across hers. "Nothing matters but our union; I am afraid I have become quite singular in my thoughts. We have waited long enough for this. If I could convince you to leave with me for Gretna Green, I would; but I cannot, so I am putting all my energy into planning our ceremony here."

"May we call on my friend Mrs. Smith this afternoon? I wish to share my news with her; she is a widow now."

"Who is Mrs. Smith, my Dear?" Frederick sealed his letter with wax and wrote the directions on the outer side.

Anne placed her hand lightly on his knee, and Frederick forced himself to breathe. Her touch sent heat radiating through him, and without realizing what he did, he placed his free hand behind her neck, pulling her mouth to his. This time he tasted her lips fully, quickly deepening the kiss before releasing her—with the sounds of the servants in the hall. She sat, staring at him, eyes glazed over with desire, and he chuckled before moving back. Despite finding it more than a bit distracting, he left her hand on his leg; it was a splendid sort of torture. "Mrs. Smith?" he repeated, his voice a bit husky.

Anne felt the torture, too. "Mrs.-Mrs. Smith," she stammered. "Mrs. Smith is my old school friend Miss Hamilton. I told you of her years ago; she was my most dear friend when I attended school here after my mother's death."

Frederick nodded in recollection. "And she is in Bath now?"

"She lives in Westgate Building. She is a widow with little means. Mrs. Smith suffers from rheumatic fever and cannot go about." Anne continued to sit too close for propriety, but she innocently took no note of it. With Frederick every thing seemed so natural she took and allowed liberties she would never consider with anyone else.

"Is it important to you that we see her today?" Frederick asked in all seriousness.

If anyone else asked Anne whether the visit might be postponed, she would consider doing so, but with Frederick, Anne knew he would not judge Mrs. Smith's condition or lack of connections. "I would like for you to meet her." Anne could not explain it to him—would not say the words because they were too personal. She felt her own inferiority keenly.

Frederick saw the sadness on her face. "What is it, Sweetling? Is it something to do with Mrs. Smith? You may tell me anything."

"I need for you to meet Mrs. Smith; it was she who warned me about Mr. Elliot, but that is not my concern. I have no words to make this sensible."

"Whatever it is, Anne, we can address it together."

"My—My Love," she spoke haltingly, "I am—I am ashamed how little I bring to our union." Frederick wanted to disagree with her, but he listened quietly. "I spoke of it before; it is a real concern for me. I do not speak of the disproportion in our fortunes—although great, it does not give me a moment's regret, because you would have it no other way. But to have no family to receive and esteem you properly—nothing of respectability, of harmony, of goodwill to offer in return for all the worth and all the prompt welcome, which met me in your brothers and sisters, is a lively pain. I have but two friends in the world to add to your list: Lady Russell and Mrs. Smith."

"As I said yesterday evening, I will do my best with Lady Russell; I have decided that I will not dwell on her former transgression, but will judge her based on the here and now." He took her hand from his knee, which now burned with an erotic energy, and squeezed it gently. "And as for Mrs. Smith, if she helped turn you from Mr. Elliot's attentions, then she is in my favor already."

"Oh, Frederick, I cannot comprehend what my cousin did to

Mrs. Smith. It is so terrible! I am horrified that he is our relation!" she exclaimed.

Frederick felt her anxiety. "Tell me what you know. Is there some way we may help your friend?"

"Mr. Elliot was an associate of the late Mr. Smith," she began to explain. Frederick leaned back in his seat. "Because of that, Mr. Elliot knew much about me—my friend spoke often of our times together. He had taken a dislike to my father and sister years ago, but with me, he had a new 'in' with our family, and he had a double motive to his visits: Mrs. Clay gave a general idea among my father's acquaintances of her meaning to be the new Lady Elliot, and, unfortunately, despite my warning months ago, my sister was blind to the fact. Mr. Elliot returned to Bath to fix himself here for a time, with the view of renewing his former acquaintance and recovering such a footing in the family, as might give him the means of ascertaining the degree of his danger of losing the title and of circumventing the lady if he found it material."

"What of your friend? How did Mr. Elliot betray her?"

"As I said earlier, Mr. Elliot and Mr. Smith were long-standing friends. The Smiths often loaned him money prior to Mr. Elliot's marriage. His wife was wealthy—but from the trade class—and wealth was the basis of Mr. Elliot's wooing game. Even after my cousin's marriage, they were as before, always together, and Mr. Elliot led his friend into expenses much beyond his fortune.

"From his wife's account of him, Mr. Smith was a man of warm feelings, easy temper, careless habits, and not strong understanding, much more amiable than his friend, and very unlike him—led by him, and probably despised by him. Mr. Elliot, raised by his marriage to great affluence and disposed to every gratification of pleasure and vanity which could be commanded without involving himself, and beginning to be rich, just as his friend found himself to be poor, seemed to have no concern at all for that friend's probable finances, but, on the contrary, prompted and encouraged expenses, which ended in the Smiths being ruined.

"The husband died just in time to be spared the full knowledge of it. It was not until his death that the wretched state of his affairs became fully known. With a confidence in Mr. Elliot's regard, more creditable to his feelings than his judgment, Mr. Smith appointed him the executor of his will; but Mr. Elliot refused to act, and the difficulties and distresses, which this refusal heaped on Mrs. Smith, in addition to the inevitable sufferings of her situation, brought on anguish. I find myself *quite* indignant!

"She told me she had applied to Mr. Elliot for assistance many times, and she showed me return letters, which displayed his hard-hearted indifference. In my opinion, no flagrant, open crime could be worse! Mrs. Smith related incident after incident, creating a dreadful picture of ingratitude and inhumanity."

Frederick thought out loud. "It is beyond reprehensible that a man—a gentleman, no less—should treat a woman as such!"

"There was one circumstance," Anne continued, "in the history of her grievances of particular irritation. She has good reason to believe some property of her husband's in the West Indies, which was for many years under a sort of sequestration for the payment of its own encumbrances, might be recoverable by proper measures, and this property, though not large, would be enough to make her comparatively rich. But there was nobody to stir in it. Mr. Elliot did nothing, and she can do nothing herself, equally disabled from personal exertion by her state of bodily weakness and from employing others by her want of money. She has no natural connections to assist her even with their counsel, and she cannot afford to purchase the assistance of the law. She really ought to be in better circumstances! Just a little trouble in the right place might do it! I fear the delay might be even weakening her claims, and that is hard to bear!"

"Anne," he said as he squeezed her hand, "I may be able to help Mrs. Smith."

"How, Frederick?" She sat now on the edge of the seat.

His smile grew larger by the second. "I did not serve twice in the West Indies without connections. If your friend's property claim is legitimate, I know to whom to apply for retribution. She may sell the property, for there are many in the Americas seeking such land opportunities, or we may secure the proper overseer to handle it for her. I will help Mrs. Smith find out to whom to write; if she will permit it, I can act for her and see her through all the petty difficulties of the case."

Before she thought what she did, Anne threw herself into Frederick's arms, and he instinctively pulled her onto his lap. "Oh, Frederick," she cackled with glee, "I knew you would make it right! You always do!" Her arms went around his neck, and Anne gave him a kiss on the cheek. Then she sprang up. "Let us go see Mrs. Smith now." But Frederick pulled her back onto his lap.

"In a moment, my Love," he whispered. "Let me hold you while I can. These moments will have to sustain me until our wedding day." He held her tightly to him, and Anne rested her head on his shoulder. "I love you more than life," he whispered softly. He twisted a strand of her hair around his finger. "Your hair is like silk," he murmured against the side of her face as he kissed her temple. "I dream of it down and spread across my pillow."

Anne sat up straight, lifted her arms, and pulled pins from the loose chignon. When she released her hands, her auburn locks fell over her shoulders and down her back.

Frederick laced his fingers through her hair, twisting handfuls of it and releasing it to repeat the action. "I need to adjust my dreams," he said in a raspy voice. "They do not come close to your beauty in reality." Frederick kissed her lightly; then he kissed her in earnest. It was a dream of eight years: her slightly parted lips, the silky texture of her hair, the lavender emanating from her every pore. The kiss began sweetly and gently, taking more effort at self-control than he imagined. His embrace tightened when her body arched toward him. He deepened the kiss, tasting Anne's sweetness.

Suddenly, Anne broke away abruptly from the kiss; she was breathing heavily. When she had regained her breath, she said, "It is only a few more weeks, Frederick. I wish our first time to be perfect—with no regrets."

Frederick said in a strained voice, "You are right, my Love." He paused for a moment to catch his breath. "We have known one another for so long that it seems natural to be in each other's arms. But we will do this properly."

Anne spoke softly as she pinned her hair up, "Maybe we should go to see my friend."

Frederick touched her lips with his fingertips. "Sweetling, you are quite beautiful when you have been thoroughly kissed," he teased her.

"I feel quite beautiful, and I never felt as such before," she whispered.

"Then our taste of sweetness was not insignificant. We learned we are strongly suited, and you saw something in yourself I saw from the first day in that mercantile years ago. Now, my Love, let us straighten our disheveled appearances and go see your friend Mrs. Smith."

Frederick sat her on her feet beside his chair and then stood himself. Anne smoothed the wrinkles in her skirt, as Frederick did the same with his waistcoat and jacket. Frederick moved to the door. At the portal, he turned and extended his hand to her. "Come, Love, I believe we both need a long walk and the company of other people."

"Yes," she murmured, "the company of other people." Trance-like, she moved to him, taking comfort in the feel of his hand around hers.

Frederick brought the back of her hand to his lips. "I love you, Anne Elliot," he said boldly, loud enough for anyone nearby to hear.

"And I love you, Frederick Wentworth," she responded just as brazenly. Then she took his proffered arm, to leave the study behind.

★ ★ ★

Frederick, Sophia, and Anne worked assiduously on wedding plans and the invitation list in the Admiral's study on Gay Street. The trio decided to move their planning to the Crofts' house to avoid the cold and unconcerned looks Elizabeth Elliot now gave her sister.

"Father will want Lady Dalrymple and Miss Carteret on the list." Anne and Sophia dutifully recorded the names.

"What of Mrs. Clay?" Sophia asked.

Anne looked surprised. "Have you not heard?"

Frederick confided, "I did not want to spread rumors."

"Sophia is your sister, Frederick," Anne reprimanded him. "She will be my new family, and I see no reason not to tell her."

"Your point is cogent. Please tell my sister."

Anne said with some embarrassment, "The announcement of our engagement deranged Mr. Elliot's best plan of domestic happiness—his best hope of keeping my father single by the watchfulness a son's rights would give him. He quitted Bath, and Mrs. Clay did likewise. Because Frederick observed them talking intimately at the party, and earlier my sister Mary observed them as such on the street, we assume they are together, even now." Anne delivered the news with some perverted delight. "At least, that is how your brother sees it."

"No," he protested, "I simply noted that if Mrs. Clay could not fulfill her wish and become Lady Elliot by marrying your father, then possibly she could still become Lady Elliot by marrying Sir Walter's heir."

"You are just happy not to have to welcome Mr. Elliot to our celebration," she said definitively.

"That is where you err, my Love," he taunted. "It would give me great pleasure to see your cousin's face when I make you my wife. The agony I felt the past few weeks would be displayed on his face, and I would take comfort in that."

Anne chastised him, "You are unforgiving, Frederick Wentworth!"

Frederick smiled wickedly. "And you are beautiful when you are angry, Sweetling."

Anne blushed with the intimacy of his words in front of his sister, but Sophia did not look at either of them. She seemed engrossed in adding names to her list. Frederick started to offer her an apology for his teasing, but before he could express his feelings a distraught-looking Benjamin Croft interrupted them.

"Admiral!" Anne called and was immediately on her feet, but Frederick got to his brother before her. He supported the man to the nearest chair. Anne rushed to a table for a glass of water, while Sophia knelt at her husband's feet.

"Benjamin?" Sophia patted his hand and stroked his face. "What is it? Tell me, Sweetheart."

"I am afraid, Sophie, that I—I bring bad news," he said haltingly.

"What do you mean?" she coaxed, as Anne moved into Frederick's embrace.

The Admiral looked up at Wentworth. "Frederick, my boy, you are being ordered back into service. You must be in Plymouth in ten days."

"What-What?" Frederick stammered. "I do not understand, Sir."

The Admiral forced himself to his feet. "While we were all enjoying the blessings of the Lord yesterday, Bonaparte escaped the island of Elba."

Sophia gasped and cried, "How?"

"The French!" His thoughts now animated the Admiral. "They barely guarded the man! He assembled several hundred followers and a flotilla of seven vessels. He appears to be headed for Cannes!"

"No!" Anne protested, burying her face into Frederick's chest. He pulled her tightly to him.

Frederick demanded, "Admiral, how do you know I am to be called back up for service?"

"I went to get a paper to see your wedding announcement in print." The Admiral paced the room, trying to organize his thoughts. "The papers are full of speculation on the French emperor, so I went to the Central Office to learn more. That is when I found out they were organizing those to be recalled."

"How do you know I have only ten days?" Frederick prodded him.

Glancing back at his brother in marriage, the Admiral stopped in his tracks. "I do not know for sure, Frederick, but you will have ten days, at most, from the time they find you. Did you not report to the Central Office when you came here?"

"Yes, Sir." He stroked Anne's back, trying to comfort her.

"Then it is only a matter of time before you receive orders. It may be you have twelve days instead of ten, but it will not be three weeks. I am sorry, Frederick." The man sank into the nearest chair.

"But the wedding?" Sophia pleaded.

Anne raised her head to look at Frederick. "What will we do?"

"I do not know, my Love. We do not even have time to go to Gretna Green." He began to think out loud.

"A common license?" Sophia suggested.

Benjamin reasoned, "Frederick has not lived here long enough to qualify for such consideration. What of you, Miss Anne?"

"I have been in Bath long enough if the archbishop will allow it. Usually, he prefers it to be the man's residency rather than the woman's, but we can try."

"Even securing a common license may take too much time. I could be made to report before the end of the week. We need to marry immediately."

"What of a special license?" Anne followed suit.

Frederick reminded her, "I am not an aristocrat."

"But *I* am," she protested, "and so is my father and so is Lady Russell and Lady Dalrymple. *Surely* their names can help us."

Frederick traced the outline of her face with his thumb. "As you said moments ago, we will try," he assured her.

"You and I will go to see my father immediately." She moved to find her things. "I will not let you leave without me."

"Anne." Frederick did not move. "We must realize our plans may not come to fruition."

She turned on him angrily. "I will not hear of it, Frederick Wentworth! I will not let Fate bring us together again and then pull you away! I will not have it!" It was her turn to collapse into the nearest chair, an overstuffed one, where she wept loudly. Sophia and the Admiral slipped from the room.

Frederick sat on the arm of the chair. "Sweetheart," he coaxed her as he dabbed her tears with his handkerchief, "please let us figure out what we must do."

Anne took the handkerchief and wiped her eyes and cheeks. Still sniffling, she declared, "I will go with you even if we are not married." She raised her chin in determination.

"Anne, I cannot allow you to risk your reputation by taking

you with me. I will not brook such an idea. Come, let us sit together on the sofa." He led her to a seat and sat down next to her. Taking her hand in his, he spoke seriously, "If I must leave before the banns are called the third time, I will be gone only a few months—a year at most. We can wait."

"Frederick, I want children. Do you not want children, too? I am near eight and twenty; another year and I may not be able to bear a child!" Tears began to stream down her face again.

Frederick closed his eyes; images of Anne holding their child came easily to him. "Of course, I want children—*our* children, but I want you more than even the possibility of a child. If I do not marry you, I will not marry at all." He kissed her lips lightly. "If I must leave before we marry," he began again, "I will send for you before the first time we make port. You will need to be wherever it is for a fortnight before I arrive; I will have Sophia travel with you, and as soon as I make land, we will marry. It will be only a matter of months at most."

"May we, at least, ask my father for help?" she pleaded. "I have never asked for such preferential treatment before; I am sure he will make things right."

"Anne, your father agreed to our marriage because Prinny is all aglow with praise for the military. I am sure the Prince Regent will not be happy to have the resurgence of this war thrown in his face. Your father may choose to distance himself from our union. It is a fact, my Love, that we must face."

"That may be, but I insist we try." She began to release her hand from his clasp. "Will you come with me?" she asked as she stood.

"Of course, I will come with you." Frederick followed her to his feet.

★ ★ ★

"Captain!" Sir Walter called out as soon as Frederick and Anne entered the room. "How will the latest development with the French affect your plans?"

Frederick led Anne to a nearby chair before answering. "I cannot say, Sir Walter; the Admiral believes I will be called to command a new ship, as the *Laconia* was to be dismantled."

"We are unsure, Father," Anne interrupted, "how soon that will be."

Lady Russell, who sat to the left of Sir Walter's desk, spoke up, "Maybe this is Providence's way of saying this union is not meant to be."

"Do not—do not let me hear you say such a thing again if you expect to remain in my favor," Anne warned her long time companion.

"Anne, I am sorry if I upset you; but Fate may be speaking to you," Lady Russell repeated softly.

"Lady Russell, when I turned to you for advice years ago, I did so with love for a surrogate mother. But now, I question your motives. If I leave, what will be your connection to this family? Do you worry that you will no longer be needed? Is that why you bid me to deny Frederick and later Charles Musgrove?"

"Anne," the woman flustered, "I always wanted to protect you from your overly romantic heart."

"Do not protect me, Lady Russell. I am a grown woman." Anne took Frederick's hand as he stood beside her chair. "I need you to help me marry the man I love." Anne held the woman's gaze, challenging her to do the right thing.

Sir Walter rejoined the conversation, "What do you expect us to do, Anne?"

"We wish to marry before I leave for Plymouth," Frederick explained. "It is definite; I must return to service before the third time the banns are called. If we are to marry, we will need a special license. We considered a common license, but even that may take too long."

"That may be a problem," Sir Walter observed. "The bishop is particular about to whom he issues such privileges. Plus, a baronet is not a peer of the realm; the title is purely hereditary."

"We know that, Father. That is why we are here to beg for your assistance."

Sir Walter stammered, "*My—My* help? You expect *my* help with this? I am afraid, Anne, that your request is impossible. I will not allow the public to think you *must* marry. Besides, this match is still with a man of no connections. The Captain has risen admirably in society, but if you were the first daughter, rather than the second, I would not consider the match acceptable."

"Then why, pray tell, did Elizabeth flirt so blatantly with Frederick prior to our announcement? Would you have accepted him then? Would all his money have been enough for acceptance in this family?" she challenged.

Sir Walter held his ground. "At the time, we thought you were to marry your cousin. None of us expected such a turn of events. If you married Mr. Elliot, the title would stay in the family, and Elizabeth would have a husband with money. It was an acceptable solution."

"Anne." Frederick's resonant voice broke into the confrontation. "I should take my leave. It is as we suspected—a moot point—we will receive no help here. I will see what else the Admiral learned and call for you later. We are to dine with the Musgroves this evening."

"I will go with you now." She stood and hooked her arm through his.

Sir Walter stood. "It would be best, Anne, if you did as the Captain suggested."

"That is the difference, Father; Frederick makes *suggestions*; he does not demand *obedience*. There are a few things you should consider over the next few hours. First, I will marry Frederick, or I will not marry. I have already turned down Charles Musgrove and Mr. Elliot—that is money *and* a title. If I do not marry, you will have two spinster daughters. What will that say about Sir Walter Elliot? You never considered Mary's match appropriate. You, Sir Walter Elliot, will have three daughters—none with a match you would want to recognize." Frederick saw Sir Walter clutch the edge of his desk in anger. "What will you write of the Elliot family in the Baronetage, Father?"

Lady Russell warned, "Anne, that is enough!"

"No, it is not enough!" She left Frederick's side, and he suddenly felt naked. He would never have suspected Anne had so much mettle. It was as if she had saved up all her frustrations and now finally gave full vent to them. She leaned across her father's desk. "Either you help us get a special license and weather the gossip of how we anticipated our marriage *or*," and at this she paused and waited for her father's full attention, "we *will* anticipate our marriage. How will you explain a grandchild that is less than nine months in the womb, Father? Or perhaps I will simply leave with Frederick without the sacrament of union."

"Anne!" Lady Russell exclaimed. "You cannot mean what you say! See what an evil influence this man has over you!"

Frederick started to object, but this was Anne's show—her step to freedom, and he savored every moment. She would make him a splendid wife; how he ever thought otherwise amazed him, so he swallowed his words. *His Anne*—flexible, accommodating Anne—had a backbone of steel.

"That is where you are in error, Lady Russell." She turned to face Frederick. "This man is honorable; he has said he will not ruin my reputation, but I will do my best to change his mind because I will have him above all others. Even if he keeps his honor, I will swear I lost mine, and you, Father, will have no choice but to protect me and help us purchase a special license to salvage what is left of my reputation. We will return early for your decision." She turned on her heel and headed toward the door. "Are you coming, Frederick?"

He smiled. "Yes, my Love." Frederick offered her father and Lady Russell a proper bow and strode from the room. He caught up with her in the foyer just as she accepted her cloak from the waiting servant. "You were *magnificent*," he whispered to her as he put on his greatcoat.

"Perhaps." Anne's trembling voice caught Frederick by surprise. "But if you could see how my legs wish to buckle, you would offer me the support of your arm immediately." She began to slump, and Frederick pulled her to him. He laughed and then twirled her around under his arm before stepping into an impromptu waltz. "What are you doing?" she gleefully gasped.

"I am celebrating our upcoming marriage." He said as he maneuvered her around a table and back into the main entranceway.

"Then you believe it will happen?"

Frederick slowed their steps where they just swayed together. "My Dear, you left your father no choice." He pulled her to him. "And me no choice."

"Frederick, do you mean?" she murmured.

"Anne, I will have you as my wife and as my lover." Even though several footmen lurked in the shadows, he kissed her briefly. "Now, you are thoroughly compromised, my Love. Before we return to Gay Street, half of Bath will hear of how I held you too close, waltzed you around the floor, and kissed you shamelessly before your household staff. You will have to marry me."

She laced her arms around his neck. "May I be just as shameless?"

"We are a perfect pair." With that, she returned his earlier kiss and then walked purposely out the door. He smiled with the knowledge he unleashed a passion no one knew was there.

CHAPTER 19

Then you rose into my life
Like a promised sunrise.
Brightened my days with the light in your eyes.
I've never been so strong,
Now I'm where I belong.
—Maya Angelou, "Where We Belong: A Duet"

It was not Bath Abbey; however, Frederick paced the front of the church, waiting, as patiently as possible, for Anne's appearance. Dressed in his full military regalia, he cut a fine figure. The morning had crept by slowly, but in a few minutes, Anne would be his.

After Anne had delivered an ultimatum to her father, things changed quickly. Lady Russell overcame her initial shock and then the woman began her own campaign on Anne's behalf, enlisting the help of Lady Dalrymple, a powerful member of high society. With Lady Dalrymple's stated approval, Sir Walter's determination to ignore Anne's demand melted. And for a tidy sum, the needed license was procured.

Anne found it all humorous and found the feeling of being powerful—for a change—quite an intoxicating one. But Frederick felt like a puppet—strings tangled in a knotted mess. Neither he nor Anne intended to follow through on her threats, a few intimate kisses were the most they shared. Frederick respected her too much to possess Anne without the bonds of marriage; his orders would force them to wait—and wait they would.

It was a week of "what ifs" for both of them. What if the church could not be secured? What if Edward and Christine did not arrive in time? What if the Musgrove party at Uppercross did not arrive in time? What if Anne's dress was not finished in time? Somehow, with Sophia's tenacity and the Admiral's charm, even the surly manager at the White Hart was able to accommodate them, and they booked the wedding breakfast in the hotel's large dining room after finding out the Pump Room Assembly Hall would not be available. This wedding would happen.

The stain-glassed windows fractured the early spring sun streaming through the color prisms, every face highlighted with flecks of the rainbow. Somehow they were all there—family and friends. Besides Benwick and the Harvilles, the Admiral managed to locate many of the officers with whom Frederick had served over the years. Those seasoned sailors filled the pews of the church—most of them amazed to see their captain, a man of decision and of action, obviously anxious.

"Relax, Wentworth," Thomas Harville leaned in to whisper his admonition. "Miss Anne will be here."

"Probably her father," Frederick grumbled. "Heaven forbid that my future wife should outshine Sir Walter on her wedding day."

Thomas chuckled before observing, "He is quite a dandy."

A stir at the rear of the church brought their attention immediately to the small group gathered there. A bevy of females started making their way down the aisle, many of them already dabbing away tears. Among them were Mary Musgrove, Lady Russell, and Mrs. Musgrove. Elizabeth Elliot, looking surprisingly young in a dark green gown, entered with Lady Dalrymple and Miss Carteret. He noted how several of his fellow officers openly admired Miss Elliot's beauty.

A sharp breath escaped his chest when Frederick finally saw her—*his Anne*—coming toward him on Sir Walter's arm. Surprisingly, her father had toned down his appearance for the occasion, choosing a more traditional look, except for his lace-trimmed cravat and sleeves. Then Sir Walter turned, and there was Anne, beautiful in white with rubies at her neck and dangling from her ears. She carried deep red roses and white lilies, streaming with ribbons. His eyes rested on Anne's countenance. A short veil blocked his view of her returning gaze, but Frederick could see the full smile creating dimples in her rosy cheeks. Suddenly, he felt calm, as if he had prepared for this day all his life.

When she reached him, Frederick vaguely heard Sir Walter announce that he would give Anne's hand in marriage, and then, even though it was gloved, he felt the warmth of her hand as it slid into his. Anne gifted him with a dazzling smile, and the hectic pace of the past four days melted into insignificance.

Behind him, he heard Milly shush one of the Musgrove children, probably Little Walter, as Edward delivered the opening lines of the service: "Dearly Beloved, we are gathered here in the sight of God to join this man and this woman in the bonds of Holy matrimony."

When it came time for him to pledge his love and devotion to Anne, Frederick had to clear his throat before finding his voice to repeat his vows. Then he slid the ring, a symbol of their never-ending love, upon her finger.

Before he knew what had happened, Edward, who had stood silently as the local vicar read the ceremony, delivered the final line: "With Mr. Osgood's blessing, as well as mine, I pronounce that Frederick James Wentworth and Anne Gabriella Elliot be man and wife together, in the name of the Father, and of the Son, and of the Holy Ghost. Amen."

Frederick turned her to him so he might lift the veil, rolling it back to drape over the brim of her bonnet. *If I had a choice, Anne would be in my arms right now.* But it was not his choice, so instead he placed her hand in the crook of his arm and led her up the aisle and into the vestibule, where the registry lay waiting for their signatures.

"Are you happy?" he whispered near her ear as Anne wrote her name with a flourish.

Wide, bright eyes met his. "Absolutely—intensely happy."

"Then are you ready, Mrs. Wentworth?"

The words brought tears to Anne's eyes. "I thought I would never hear those words," she gasped. "I am Anne Elliot Wentworth now!" She laughed nervously.

He gently pulled her hands to his lips and kissed them. "You most certainly are Anne Gabriella Elliot Wentworth—forever—

that will be your name, my Love."

"Then let us meet our well-wishers, my Husband." She laughed again, watching him fill in his signature next to hers. "Husband," she repeated. "I believe that is the most beloved word in the world."

"Next to the word *wife*," he teased, before leading her outside to a cheering crowd, which was waiting in the churchyard to pelt them with rose petals.

"Run for it," she cheerfully ordered him as she turned her head to avoid a mouthful of petals, thrown with accuracy by Harry Musgrove, the youngest of Mr. and Mrs. Musgrove's brood.

Frederick wrapped his arm around her and began to hustle Anne toward their waiting coach. She lifted the skirt of her dress, trying to match his long strides, as they made their way to the bow-decorated carriage. He lifted her easily into the waiting landaulette.

"From where did this come?" she asked, noticing the lushness of the finely upholstered seats.

"It is yours," he said, climbing up beside her. "It is your wedding present, my Love."

"Frederick—you did not!" she exclaimed as she lightly ran her fingertips across the thickly padded cushions.

"My *wife*," he emphasized the word, "will have the best I can afford."

She wrapped her arms through his, clutching tightly to him. "It is not necessary." Her eyes rested on his face.

"You, Anne, are my beloved; you touched my heart in a way no one else can. Love is *necessary*—your love is necessary for my survival." He leaned down and kissed her gently, much to the delight of the gathering throng. "Let us make it through the wedding breakfast. I plan to spend the night showing you how much I love you and how very essential you are to me." As he expected, his words made Anne blush, but Frederick also saw something else in Anne's eyes: a desire to know him as intimately as he wished to know her. "Do I embarrass you, my Love?" he asked as he picked up the reins.

Anne flushed again with color, but her voice held a calmness he had not expected. "In my heart I waited for this night; I am afraid of the unknown, but I welcome it just the same." She raised her hand to his cheek, and he turned his lips to kiss her palm. "I love you, Frederick James Wentworth."

"I am not sure I can wait until this breakfast is over," he said seductively.

Anne looked up at his laughing eyes. "Just a few more hours." She rested her hand on his. "Let us go before we become even more distracted." With that, he flicked the reins, lunging forward into their future.

Hand-in-hand, they entered the large dining room to thunderous applause and even a few catcalls. Voices and laughter followed as everyone pushed forward to either shake his hand or to kiss Anne's cheek. "You make a beautiful bride, Mrs. Wentworth," Lady Susan Lowery praised her as she stepped in front of the couple.

"Thank you, Lady Susan," Anne responded automatically, her new name somehow already familiar.

"And you, Captain," she spoke louder to be heard over the din, "my family sends its regards and wishes you happy."

"Are your cousins not here, Ma'am?" He steadied Anne's stance by edging slightly behind her.

"No, Captain, I am afraid they are not. My cousin Lieutenant Harding received his orders. He is to report to Bristol today, but he sends his undying devotion to you and Mrs. Wentworth. Buford regretted missing an opportunity to meet Captain Benwick's betrothed."

"You may present the lieutenant's regards to Benwick." Frederick paused in contemplation. "Lieutenant Harding will be safe; Napoleon cannot hope to succeed," he asserted.

Lady Susan displayed a courageous smile. "Listen to us; this is a day of *happiness!* I am pleased to be found right all along, Captain. You *did* favor Miss Anne."

Frederick looked down at the profile of the woman he loved. "Yes, despite all my protests to the contrary, I have been found out."

"It will gratify me to send my family word of the day and all the beauty and love found in this room." She moved on as the last of the well-wishers nearly crushed the couple in their eagerness to wish them many years of contentment.

Sophia clapped her hands loudly, bringing some order to the celebration, and everyone found a place at one of the tables, while Anne and Frederick made their way to the central setting. As much as he hated such formal occasions, Frederick took a perverse pleasure in knowing that Anne's family would be expected to offer their blessings in a very public way.

Once everyone was seated, Edward rose to his feet. "I am Edward Wentworth and will represent our family this morning. With this marriage, my brother Frederick expands our family circle. Our Sophia found love with her husband, Benjamin. I am blessed with my Christine." He gestured to his beautiful wife, who sat next to him. "Now, Frederick finally has the love of his life. Raise your glasses, please, and with me wish Frederick and Anne much happiness."

"Hear! Hear!" was heard about the room, and to recognize his brother's sentiments, Frederick raised Anne's gloved hand to his lips and kissed the back of it.

Sir Walter Elliot stood next, and the room fell quiet. Frederick leaned back, content to be amused by watching the man say what he did not wish to say. "The Elliot family is an ancient and respectable one, first settling in Cheshire and being listed as part of the nobility by Sir William Dugdale in 1675 and honored by Charles II with a baronetcy. Today, it gives me great pleasure to write this into the Baronetage by my daughter Anne's name: Married 3 March 1815, Frederick, son of Edward and Cassandra Wentworth of Herefordshire, Captain and war hero, the British Royal Navy." Her father paused before going on. "Captain," Sir Walter addressed him, "our Anne will undoubtedly make you an excellent wife." He lifted his glass in a salute to his daughter and Frederick, and then took his seat on Anne's right.

The toasts continued for nearly half an hour, many of them coming from the men with whom he served on various expeditions. Their words of genuine devotion to him as their leader in moments where death came close to claiming them spoke of his character, and Frederick found himself choked up with more than one declaration. Although on another day, words of war might seem inappropriate for a wedding, Bonaparte's influence on the British public invaded their celebration. It seemed natural because without the resurgence of the war, Frederick and Anne would wait, but duty called many of these men back to their fleet, and to acknowledge that life awaited them—love awaited them seemed ever important.

"I am sorry our special day was colored by the war," he whispered close to Anne's ear after Thomas Harville's toast.

Anne turned her head slowly to look at him. A single tear cascaded down her cheek. He used his thumb to wipe it away. "Do not be afraid that stories of your bravery will ruin my day, my Love. How could they? They speak of the man I have loved for nearly a decade—a compassionate man of determination. I was thinking how much you changed the lives of these people and countless others, and although we suffered in our separation, God needed you where you were, because without your leadership, many men in this room would not be among the living. God knew we would find our way back to each other after you did what you must for others." She laid her head on his shoulder. "I am honored to be your wife."

Frederick stopped breathing for a moment; nearly overwhelmed by her words, he kissed her forehead. "Why do we not circulate about the room and greet our guests?" he spoke softly, trying not to let her hear the emotion in his voice. She nodded and they stood to move to the various tables of family and friends.

After greeting Lady Dalrymple first, as well as several other members of the *ton*—acquaintances of Lady Russell or Sir Walter—they made their way to the Musgroves, who were congregated at several adjoining tables.

"Captain." Mr. Musgrove stood to greet him as they approached. "My family wishes you and Mrs. Wentworth the best that marriage can bring. Who in September would have thought we would be celebrating three marriages among those who spent many happy hours in our company throughout October and November?" The other men at the table rose to their feet as the family patriarch spoke.

"Gentlemen, please be seated." Anne gestured to the party. Frederick tightened his grip on her hand when they came to Louisa Musgrove and Captain Benwick. "Miss Musgrove," Anne gestured to Frederick, "my husband and I are pleased to wish you and Captain Benwick happiness on the announcement of your engagement."

"Mrs. Wentworth, you are most gracious," Benwick spoke up first. "You have won the love of a fine man in Captain Wentworth. I am blessed to count him among my friends."

"Thank you, Captain." Anne looked lovingly at Frederick.

Louisa leaned forward to add her own observation. "We were *surprised* to learn of your speedy engagement, Mrs. Wentworth. Little did any of us—including your sister Mary!—realize your *high regard* for Captain Wentworth. In fact, I believe some thought before I found my James, that the good Captain might be my choice. How could we know when dear Frederick upon first seeing you again, said you were so altered he should not have known you?" Her immaturity showed clearly. Benwick gave his betrothed a reprimanding look.

Frederick flinched—just a bit—and he felt Anne stiffen. "Miss Musgrove," he said, "it is delightful to see you and your intended here today." He smiled at Captain Benwick and then addressed the two of them: "My new wife and I realize our marriage is indeed unexpected. But Anne and I have known each other for many years; our regard for one another has never wavered, no matter the circumstances. When we *discovered* we both felt the same way after so many years, why, a wedding was the only logical next step." Frederick was not about to let Louisa expunge Anne in any way. He retorted, "Miss Musgrove, I apologize if you misinterpreted my friendship; I simply wished to become familiar with the family of a man, who once served under my command and to try to make myself amiable to my sister's nearest neighbors. Mrs. Charles was away at school when I first declared my love for Anne in '06. Do you not remember my stressing those years in my dinner conversation? I hoped Anne might remember what we once were to each other. Do you recall how I placed Anne in my sister's carriage when we all walked out together? I could never see her suffer and not respond. She has always owned my heart. I returned to Somerset with the pure purpose of seeing Anne again. I did not know whether she would renew her regard, but I could never move on until I knew for sure. My comment about my dear Anne was nothing more than my conceit and pride speaking for I feared she chose not to see me with her excuses for tending Little Charles. I did not give Anne credit for being the kindest woman God ever created." He smiled at the *other* happy couple, pulled Anne closer to him, and slipped his arm around her waist. "Please excuse us. We have other guests to whom to attend." Anne smiled, he bowed, and they strolled away together.

"Another thing for which I will spend my life in apology," he said close to her ear as they walked towards some of his naval buddies.

"You were perfect," Anne offered her praise. "You made Louisa question what she thought she knew about you." She glanced back over her shoulder to see a look of puzzlement plastered on Louisa's face. "I almost believed it myself."

"It is your fault, Sweetling." His voice sounded seductive again. "When I am near you, I do the most uncharacteristic things to get your attention."

Anne openly laughed at his out and out lie, knowing what, in reality, happened with Louisa. "I think from now on your version of our resurging connection will be what I repeat on every occasion where confabulation is necessary."

"You may embellish it as you see fit, Sweetling. I give it to you to do with as you please." He wrapped his arms around her, moving the two of them together in an embrace, and then kissing her in front of everyone gathered there. Instead of being embarrassed by his actions, she reciprocated by encircling his waist with her arms and laying her head briefly on his chest. Laughing at their open display of affection, they caught hands and moved among his comrades.

"Captain, none of us at this table ever thought we would live to see the day!" Dr. Laraby said as they approached. All three men stood as Wentworth stepped in front of them.

"Anne, may I present three of my fellow officers? These are Lieutenants Michael Avendale and Matthew Harwood." He gestured to each man as they bowed to her. "And this rascal is our ship's doctor Peter Laraby—one of the finest physicians found aboard a vessel. They will join me when I return to Plymouth." As the Admiral had predicted, Frederick received his orders. He was to command a new ship—*The Resolve*. "Gentlemen, this is my wife, Anne Elliot Wentworth."

Peter Laraby continued to speak for the group. "Mrs. Wentworth, we are pleased to meet you. Our good captain kept his regard for you a secret. We will hope to wield the details from you; the man is a virtual steel trap when it comes to sharing his personal life. No doubt he did not wish to divulge information about you until you were safely married to him."

"You should be aware, Mr. Laraby, my husband taught me subterfuge before he would agree to marry me." Frederick laughed as Anne's face straightened in all sincerity, and as her words amazed his three shipmates. "Yet, you will be happy to know he just bequeathed me a story which I may repeat to my heart's desire."

"Do not forget, my Love, you have my permission to *embellish* said story, especially where these three are concerned." Frederick rested his hands on her shoulders.

"Did you hear that, Gentlemen?" Anne's voice took on an idolized, coquettish tone. "My *esteemed* husband gave me his *permission*. Am I not blessed among women?"

The three took up her tone, heartily enjoying her flaunting of her and Wentworth's courtship. "We look forward to it, Ma'am," Laraby acknowledged. "Do you intend to travel with the Captain,

Mrs. Wentworth?"

Frederick looked down at her; the question brought back the reality of their rushed marriage. "It is my wish never to part with Mrs. Wentworth." Frederick's eyes delve deep into the chocolate-gray ones looking back at him.

Anne returned her attention to the three men. "I will see you aboard ship, Gentlemen. It has been my pleasure to make the acquaintance of men with whom my husband serves his country." With that, she curtsied before stepping away to the next group. Frederick bowed, too, and then followed her.

"Thank you," he said softly, "for agreeing to come with me."

Anne gripped his arm. "I can be nowhere else," she said with determination. "I did not incur my father's wrath to be left behind."

Frederick melted with her sentiments. How often he misjudged her! Even though it hurt her to do so, Anne set him free because she thought she would hold him back in his career. Who was to say whether she might have? Some of his captures required risks he wondered if he would have taken if Anne traveled with him. He assumed for years her persuadable temper to be a weakness, but he learned at Uppercross and Lyme a resolute character possessed weakness in its absolute determination when reason should prevail.

"Let us make our final farewells," he said. They came to Lady Russell. "How may we ever thank you for what you did for us?" Frederick said as he bowed.

Lady Russell took Anne's hand in hers. "Elizabeth Stevenson was my best friend, and I grieved greatly at her passing; but she left me you—my sweet Anne, the perfect image of your mother. I loved you, Child, as my own, and when I offered my advice I did so as I thought Elizabeth might. I do not regret what I did, but I see now that I denied you time with this man because I misjudged your resiliency. That is my real regret; I never saw your full worth until you withstood both your father's and my censure. I forgot that Elizabeth, despite being both sensible and amiable, possessed a streak of stubbornness also. She became infatuated with your father, and she would brook no one denying her the man she loved. I should have remembered that about her. When you demanded our help, I suddenly pictured my dear Elizabeth standing there, saying she would have no one but Sir Walter Elliot as her husband. It was at that moment that I knew I must be Elizabeth Stevenson's true friend and help her daughter be with the man she loved. I said as much to your father. While she lived, Elizabeth humored Sir Walter and softened him and promoted his real respectability. He could deny her little."

Anne fell into the woman's arms, crying tears of happiness. "You have served me well," she assured Lady Russell. "I have loved and respected you, and that will not change. I only ask you to allow Frederick into our circle."

Lady Russell patted Anne on the back. "Captain Wentworth will have my devotion as your husband. I assure you, Anne, this will be so."

"Thank you—thank you for everything." Anne clutched Frederick's hand, and he led her away to their individual families.

"Father, we will be leaving soon," Anne said softly to Sir Walter.

"Then we will part, not knowing when we might meet again." He stood to address his middle daughter. "You will, of course, maintain your family's good name in all your dealings. First and foremost, remember you are an Elliot."

"Yes, Father, I will remember." Frederick moved behind her, lending her silent support, and Anne raised her chin and straightened her shoulders. "You and Elizabeth will be careful. Do not allow those with false faces to seek you out for your generous natures." The warning pleased Frederick. Possibly, Sir Walter would not succumb to flattery so quickly in the future. "Father, you are still a relatively young man, and no one maintains his appearance as you do." Her father smiled a little. "I would like to see you find someone to bring joy to your life. Start a new family; foil Mr. Elliot's plans for the baronetcy. I, for one, would welcome a younger brother and a new Lady Elliot. Think of it, Father: Kellynch would remain in our line of the family."

Frederick added his own insights. "I agree with my wife. The

Admiral is likely to be needed in a supporting role for our services. If so, he and my sister would have to quit Kellynch. I would not wish to see your ancestral home, Sir Walter, fall into the hands of someone who does not love it as much as you do. A man should grieve for his late wife, but twelve years is sufficient."

"Thank you, Captain. I will consider your words—and Anne's words. Perhaps I will spend some time in London when the Season begins anew. Possibly a young widow—a war widow, even, or a woman of independent means. The lady would just need to be young enough to give me a male heir. It is a thought." Sir Walter's gaze came back to Anne. "Take good care of Anne, Captain; she is her mother's daughter in every way. You will therefore be a fortunate man; my Elizabeth was a remarkable woman, one whom I did not appreciate enough until she was gone."

Frederick was touched by the words. "I will, Sir Walter."

Next came Sophia and Edward. "Anne, you will do well aboard ship," Sophia said stoutly.

"I will learn from all you told me; it will be a great adventure—my *first* adventure," Anne affirmed.

"You sail with the best," the Admiral confirmed what Anne gleamed from the various conversations she overheard today. "Your Frederick is highly esteemed by those with whom he sails and by the British Navy's high command. You will be safe with him. I am proud to be called his brother."

Frederick looked away, a bit embarrassed by such high praise from the Admiral. "My wife will probably be more in control than I." He teased to break the tension. "I have seen the ocean play lovingly at her feet as she stood on an outcropping at Lyme. While the others ran from the tide, Anne stood and welcomed it, and the sea responded by kissing her with a delicate spray. I saw that reaction only a few times; Anne is meant to be near the ocean; she loves it so, and it responds in kind."

"Your sister is the same. I first saw her when she stood along the shore at North Yarmouth, admiring the splendor of the water. I knew she had to be mine." Admiral Croft draped his arm around

Sophia's shoulder.

Sophia patted his hand. "I knew you by character long before."

"Well, and I heard of you as a very pretty girl. And what were we to wait for besides? I do not like having such things so long in hand." Benjamin Croft kissed the tip of his wife's upturned nose. "Now, Frederick has brought us a gem, Sophie."

"I have, Admiral," Frederick interrupted, trying to get a moment with Edward. "And you, my Brother," he continued, "how do I give you my gratitude?"

"You do so, Frederick, by returning to us safely. My child needs his uncle and his new aunt. Our prayers will daily be with you and your men on *The Resolve*." Edward embraced him before saying, "Now, the two of you get out of here. You waited long enough to start your life together."

"On that we agree." Frederick's smile grew by the second. "Are you ready, Mrs. Wentworth?" He turned to take Anne's hand in his.

She nodded her agreement. However, before they could escape the room, women, wishing to bid Anne farewell, beset them. Mary Musgrove and Elizabeth Elliot led the crowd.

Frederick stood patiently to the side and let the women kiss and hug Anne, but when it appeared their exit might *never* occur, he gallantly stepped into the milieu. "Excuse me, Ladies," he said, "but I seemed to have misplaced my wife. Ah, there she is!" With those words, he scooped Anne into his arms and, holding her close to his chest, strode from the room. The group of women followed the two of them, giggling and weeping. Frederick placed Anne—who herself was giggling and weeping—into the front seat of their carriage. "Wave goodbye to our families, my Love," he told her as he sprang to the seat to take up the reins.

Frederick glanced back to see women waving handkerchiefs and men holding their glasses high in a salute as he maneuvered his team into the coach traffic of Bath Street. Anne swiveled around to look at him after offering their party her own farewells. "Frederick Wentworth, you are incorrigible," she reprimanded him.

"That is what you used to say of me years ago, Sweetling. Why would you think I might change?" he teased. "I am of the persuasion that our marriage should not wait any longer for its beginning. Even *you* could not fault me for that, I think."

Anne tried to look stern, but the effort was useless. "It was quite romantic," she admitted, "to be carried off by the man I love."

Frederick lowered his head to kiss her lips. They would travel to an inn outside Bath to spend their wedding night. Frederick had secured the best rooms and ordered a private meal for them. Footmen had delivered their bags that morning to the inn. Anne sat as close to him as propriety allowed, and Frederick dropped one of his hands into her lap. Turning his palm up, he waited for her to place her hand in his. "I love you," he murmured, "more than life itself."

"And I love you," Anne responded. "I always have—I always will."

CHAPTER 20

Light, so low upon earth,
You send a flash to the sun.
Here is the golden close of love,
All my wooing is done.
—Alfred Lord Tennyson, "Marriage Morning"

By the time they reached the inn, it was late afternoon. The sunny day had become overcast and threatened rain. Frederick put up the roof of the landaulette, but a chill set in by the time they reached their destination. Frederick loosened his coat and wrapped Anne in it as well. "I will not have you catch your death of cold on our wedding day," he insisted. Both lap blankets became tucked around her also.

"What of you, my Love?" she asked as she snuggled into his chest.

"First, I am more used to the elements, having spent years in all sorts of weather aboard ship. Second, my coats are much heavier than your muslin and cloak. But, most important, to be able to hold you in my arms and feel you pressed to me, I would suffer the worst winter has to offer. A temperamental spring day means nothing. If you will just kiss me occasionally, I will stay as warm as on a summer day."

"You are not what you appear to be," she noted as she wrapped her arms around his waist. "I would venture to say most people see you as the disciplined sea captain, ever observant—brave to the end."

"And you do not see me that way, Sweetling?" He kissed the tip of her upturned nose.

Her voice was thoughtful. "I see that man; but there is so much more to you. I see a man who loves to tease—who is thoughtful and considerate—who is sensitive—and who is passionate."

"I am passionate about you, Sweetling." They rode in silence for a few minutes. "Anne?"

"Yes, Love."

"I will be tender this evening."

She paused before answering. "I know.—I am not afraid."

"Promise me," he began again. "Promise me if you are uncomfortable in any way you will tell me. I will not have you lie there and be only a vessel for my pleasure. That is not what love is." He kissed the top of her head. "I assume you had no one with whom to speak about physical love?"

"I did—I did speak to your sister. Truthfully, much of what she said was shocking, but I am glad Sophia was so *direct*." She blushed at speaking so openly with him.

Frederick pulled the carriage to a halt, and he and Anne looked down on a small town. "I suppose we should move farther apart before we enter the village. We would not wish to scandalize the residents with our behavior." Anne began to shift away from him, but he pulled her to him one more time, kissing her properly. Lips posed above each other, he nearly growled, "Of course, I promise scandalous behavior in the privacy of our own room."

She laughed and leaned in for another intimate kiss, taking Frederick by surprise.

When they separated, he was breathing hard. "You, Anne Wentworth, are a dangerous woman." Then he laughed. "Let us go, Love. I need to get to know my wife a bit better." He flicked the reins across the horses' backs, and the carriage sprang forward.

They took a light meal as soon as they arrived. Having eaten little at the wedding breakfast, they were both famished; then they took a walk about the village. Anne bought some ribbon to trim one of her day dresses and a couple of men's handkerchiefs that she planned to monogram with his initials as a present for him. He bought a couple of bars of lavender-scented soap so Anne might have them aboard ship. Having asked Sophia's opinion, Frederick had already packed a bag of essentials—luxuries on a ship—so Anne would not have to do without her favorite toiletries. He had sent them ahead to Plymouth in preparation for their departure.

"When do we need to be in Plymouth?" she asked as they strolled along the wooden walkway.

"Benjamin will send one of the coaches for us on Monday. A groomsman will drive our carriage back to Kellynch for safekeeping while we are away." Frederick steered her around a sizable mud hole before continuing. "I need to be at the ship by Thursday, but I would prefer to actually take possession of it and walk its decks on Wednesday. By leaving early Monday morning, we should arrive by late afternoon, soon enough for me to inform the Central Office of my change in marital status. I thought on Tuesday we might attend the performance at the Theatre Royal II before we set sail. Would you like that?"

"It would be pleasant to spend an evening on your arm."

Frederick spoke with regret. "I am sorry, Anne. You deserve a wedding trip to the Continent, instead of a few nights at a country inn before I drag you off to a crowded ship—and a war."

"Oh, Frederick, do you really think I care about those things? I will spend three glorious days and nights in your arms! Then I will visit a bustling seaport for the first time—shipyards and battleships everywhere. I am most *eager* to see it."

After several moments, he said, "I am a lucky man."

"And you adore me?" she asked.

"That I do," he whispered. "I love you more than you will ever know."

After supper, Frederick took her in his arms. "I will join the men downstairs for a drink, but I shall have the maid bring you up a bath first. I return in an hour. That should give you plenty of time to prepare."

"I will be ready." Anne went up on her tiptoes to kiss his mouth again. Knowing what the night would bring, Frederick closed his eyes to push desire away for just a little longer.

Reluctantly, he let her go. "I will be back soon." He squeezed her hand and then quickly strode from the room.

Frederick sipped on a tankard of ale and pretended to listen to the men talk of crops and the weather—but his mind was elsewhere.

Heart pounding, an hour later, he slipped back into the room, securing the lock behind him. Taking a deep breath, he flexed and relaxed his hands several times to relieve the tension building quickly in his limbs. The room was warm, thanks to the fire burning in the hearth, and he needed a few seconds for his vision to adjust to the dim light.

"Frederick?" Anne's soft voice brought his eyes to her. She stood in the middle of the room, hair draped over her shoulders and hanging loosely down her back. The glow from the fire picked up the auburn highlights, giving her curls an inner shine. Barefoot, she stood innocently staring at him; her white dressing gown clung to her delicate, shapely body.

Frederick struggled to say the words he wanted her to know. "You are exquisite," he muttered hoarsely. Then he crossed the room in a couple of strides and took her in his arms.

The feel of her body without corsets or chemise or layers of dress nearly did him in. He forced himself to go slowly, although his body demanded immediate action. He stroked her hair, allowing his fingers to trail down to the ends and then rested them on her slim waist. Beginning with slightly parted lips and then using his tongue to coax her mouth to respond to his, he bent to kiss her. Anne pressed closer to him, twining her hands around his neck. "Ah, Anne, I thought this night would never come."

"I am ready, my Darling," she whispered near his ear.

It took no other enticement to convince him. Frederick scooped her into his arms and headed toward the bed, already turned down for the night. Carrying her close to him, he asked, "Can you hear my heart? It stopped beating years ago; now it can take up again." Frederick laid her gently across the bed, and her hair spread out across the pillow completing the picture from his dream.

Looking down at her, he began to unbutton his jacket. "Your beauty stuns me," he spoke reverently, enthralled by her appearance.

Anne stretched her arms out to him, and Frederick leaned over and blew out the single candle—only the glow of the fire showed in the room. Then he slid into bed with her. "I love you, Anne Elliot Wentworth. I have loved no one but you. You are my life."

"This is our first night together," she whispered in his ear. "The first night of thousands to come." She kissed him then—and after that, no more words were needed. They knew from the first day they met—from the first time they danced—from the first time they kissed. This was where they were meant to be.

★ ★ ★

On Saturday, they took the landaulette out for a ride about the countryside, taking in the beautiful vistas. Frederick ordered a picnic lunch packed by the innkeeper's wife and laid claim to extra blankets for the drive. The sun shone brightly, although the air still held a brisk coolness.

Choosing a rocky outcropping overlooking a panoramic glade and orchard, he spread the blanket on the flat ledge and then he helped Anne settle there. She sat with her knees pulled up and her arms wrapped about them. Watching her intently, he relished the image of Anne tilting her face up to the sun. "It is such a beautiful day," she said.

Frederick leaned over to kiss her upturned lips as he placed the picnic basket beside her. "*Perfectly* beautiful," he murmured. He laid the extra blanket to her left in case she needed the additional warmth, and then he stretched out his full length, lying on his back and covering his face with his hat.

After ten minutes of silence, Anne's voice broke through. "Did you bring me all the way out here so you might catch up on your sleep?"

He removed the hat and rolled to his side, propping himself up on one elbow. "I enjoyed the warmth of the sun, and I admit it could easily lull me to sleep. I got little rest last night."

"Neither did I," she asserted.

Frederick laughed before taking her hand in his. "I recall," he murmured and flashed a wicked smile. "Would you like a repeat performance?" He moved up to kiss her earlobe. "I would be willing to service your needs, Sweetling."

"Why do you not serve the food instead?" Anne suggested, a little scandalized.

"Ah, Sweetheart, you wound me greatly, but I am here to please you." Frederick sat up to open the basket. "Now, let us see what Mrs. Francis has created for us." He removed the contents of the basket and then piled roasted chicken, dark bread, cheese, and fresh fruit on the plates. "What do you think, Love? Is this not a grand meal?" He poured them each a large glass of wine.

"It is, Frederick." Anne leaned in to kiss his wine-touched lips. "It is the best meal ever served to me."

He wrapped his arms around her. "Do you love being married as much as I do?"

Anne turned to sit back against him after feeding Frederick a mouthful of cheese and bread. "Married life is very satisfying, Mr. Wentworth." She wiggled up next to him, and he automatically began to kiss the nape of her neck. The freedom to touch each other became more intoxicating with each new exploration. "Will it always be this way?" she asked.

"I would hope so," he spoke next to her ear. "Twenty years from now, it will not be so adventurous, but I guarantee the passion and the desire will still be there."

"Can you imagine us twenty years from now?"

Frederick traced his fingers up and down her arm. "I see us in an estate—near the sea, of course—where we will entertain our neighbors. Our children will be strong as their father and as beautiful as their mother, and they will accept only love matches—the same as their parents." This was a defining moment; he and Anne actually had a future. Speaking of children and of a home out loud seemed very prophetic—almost mystical.

"How many children?" she asked.

He encircled her in his embrace. "Two—maybe three."

"Two," she decided.

"Two it is, Mrs. Wentworth."

The afternoon passed too quickly, but they spent their time together speaking of commitment—to something greater—something beyond them. They planned their life—talked of where to live, how to arrange the house, what qualities to instill in their children, and what role each would play. They learned about each other intimately the night before; they learned how to make the marriage work during that impromptu Saturday afternoon picnic.

On Sunday, they joined the villagers at the local church to give thanks for their love and to pray for the safety of all the men with whom Frederick would sail.

When the Admiral's coach rolled into the inn yard early Monday morning, the reality of what would change when they reached Plymouth gripped them. "Frederick, I am frightened," she whispered once they were on their way.

He took her hand in his. "I would be telling a lie if I told you there is no danger. Of course, in war there is always danger." Frederick lifted her chin to force Anne to look at him. "There are dangers even when there is not a war. Women die regularly in childbirth. Poverty claims hundreds daily. Men lose their homes and property to gambling and overspending, sending their families into bankruptcy. A gentleman can easily greet death simply by stepping into a busy street and meeting a runaway carriage. We cannot control our fate, Anne; all we can do is exercise caution and reason. I am known for those qualities. I will never put you or the men on my ship at risk simply to win a government prize. I value human life too much."

"I know," she spoke the words softly but with a degree of determination. "Change is frightening, though."

"I understand, my Love. It is more of a change for you than it is for me. You are giving up your way of life, all you knew. You must promise, just as you did on our first night together, you will tell me when things are too much—too much change at once. There is *nothing* you can say to me that will lessen my love for you."

"I promise." Anne brought his hand to her mouth. She kissed his palm and then followed his lifeline with her index finger. "You will have a long life," she predicted in a voice that was husky with emotion.

Frederick took the glove from her hand and examined her palm. "And you, too." Then he aligned their palms, so their lifelines touched each other. "We will have a long life *together*." His fingers interlaced with hers. "As our hands are linked together, so is our fate. We belong to each other—you and I."

"You and I." She smiled, more serenely now. "Our fates predetermined."

"Yes, our fates have brought us full circle, back to each other." He wrapped his other hand around their two and squeezed them together. "We are bound together, and nothing will pull us apart. I need you near me, Anne, and then I can do anything."

★ ★ ★

"Captain, we are coming into the Sound," Harwood reported.

His assistant helped Frederick to finish dressing. "Thank you, Lieutenant; I will be ready."

"The crew are pleased to have you up and about, Sir." Harwood began to straighten the quarters.

"My recovery was difficult for a while, and I do thank you and the other officers for the part you played; I am doing well. Yet, four and a half months at sea are long enough. I do not know about you, Harwood, but I am ready for some dry land." Frederick straightened the cuff of his uniform's sleeve as his assistant brushed down the back of the coat. "Are the prisoners ready for the transfer?"

"They are, Sir. Our men will sail the French sloop into the bay behind us. That one, plus the frigate we captured earlier, should serve us well."

"I admit to looking forward to this payout. I promised Mrs. Wentworth a place of her own when this action is over." Frederick wrapped the belt from his saber around his waist.

"How much longer do you think we will be, Captain?"

"The war, you mean?—It cannot last much longer. When we took on supplies at Gibraltar, Wellington had Napoleon on the run. That was nearly a month ago: I cannot imagine Bonaparte can hold out much longer. That is one of my first tasks when we are in port—we need an update as to if we go back out again." Frederick slid on his gloves.

"What will we do with the American—the one who shot you?" Harwood opened the door for Frederick.

"I will turn him over to the Central Office as soon as we dock: I am sure they will be most eager to question him." Frederick nodded to both men. "Let us greet England." They followed him to the main deck.

Anne stayed in the background, allowing Frederick to lead his men home to England. His was the most serious injury of their journey, but they made it home safely because he had trained them to operate efficiently without him. A month into their orders, they had captured a French frigate, which was already disassembled, and the prisoners were on one of the many ships anchored off Plymouth's coast. Today, they brought in the sloop as a second prize.

Frederick led Anne to one of the railings so he could speak with her privately. "You will wait on board with the men until I return for you. It may take several hours to turn over all the records to the Central Office."

"I understand. It will give me time to finish packing."

"Shall I send one of the men to help you?"

"No, my Love, I can handle it. I would be mortified if one of the crew saw my private papers or, even worse, my undergarments." She flushed with embarrassment at the thought.

He smiled at her. "Only I am allowed to make you blush."

"That is your prerogative," she taunted. "Now, go about your duties; I will be fine," she assured him.

"We will dine at the Royal Hotel tonight. You enjoyed staying there when we first came to Plymouth."

"That sounds delightful. Now, off with you." With that, Anne walked briskly toward her quarters. Frederick's eyes followed her—if she only knew how essential she was to him!

Returning to his officers, who were gathered on deck, Frederick addressed them: "Gentlemen, without your devotion to duty, we might be coming home to England with news of our losses; instead, we enter this port with everyone safe and sound. I salute your efforts. I will note them in my official report. I take Avendale and Harwood with me. The rest of you see to securing *The Resolve*. I will return with our new orders and leave for everyone."

"Yes, Captain." The men dispersed to do his bidding, knowing in a few hours, they would see loved ones again.

Strolling down the gangplank, seeing Benjamin waiting surprised him. "Frederick, my Boy, Sophie will be so happy to know you are safe! She worried so. As soon as I heard it was *The Resolve* coming in, I hurried down to see for myself." He started to give Frederick a warm hug, but Frederick backed away.

"Forgive me, Admiral. I suffered an injury in our most recent encounter. I am well now, but still a bit sore. Is Sophia in Plymouth, too? Anne will be happy to see her."

"Your sister is still at Kellynch. I am traveling back and forth, mostly between Bath and here, but occasionally to Bristol in support of the Central Office. I am only at Kellynch a few days a week, but I cannot leave Sophie there alone for very long. I *should* wait for your sister to tell you, but I will not. Sophie, after all these years, is with child. Once I found out, I could not subject her to a return to the sea; that is why I am acting as an adviser to these various groups."

"Sophia? You are to be a father, Benjamin? How magnificent! And how are Edward and Christine?" Frederick's mind rushed through the many things he wanted to ask his sister's husband as they walked briskly toward the Central Office for Naval Affairs.

"Christine is in her confinement. Our brother is distraught if his letters are any indication. Of course, in six months Edward will be able to return my ridicule. Let us get you clearance, and then I want to see that wife of yours. We have not laid eyes on either of you since you rode away from your wedding breakfast. How did Mrs. Wentworth take to the sea?"

"As if she was born aboard a warship," Frederick asserted. "Truthfully, Benjamin, if Anne had not been with me, I am not sure I would have survived. Dr. Laraby says she tended me for almost five days straight while my fever raged on. Benjamin, Anne was of all I thought. Only when I opened my eyes and found her there, did I have a will to go on. If this happened years ago . . . ." They stopped walking when Frederick touched the Admiral's arm.

"Then I am pleased you and Miss Anne found your way back to each other. I would not want to have to tell Sophie or Edward of your demise. Did you lose any men?" They began to walk again, and Frederick's two lieutenants followed closely behind them.

"Not a one, Admiral."

"Excellent! The high command will be pleased to hear it." Benjamin patted him on the back. "Here we are." The Admiral indicated the door to a small storefront office. Frederick and his men followed Benjamin into the darkened room.

"Wentworth!" Pennington, a Vice Admiral of the Red, came forward to meet them. "You have returned! That means we have all our ships back but two. We are certainly glad you made it in safely. Have a seat, Gentlemen." He gestured to two chairs at the end of the table. "Sit there, Wentworth. I want to hear all the news before you write up your report."

Benjamin took the seat next to Frederick's. "I am not sure, Sir, where you want me to begin; I assume you read the report of our earlier capture—the frigate."

"Certainly, Captain, but what of this latest prize? My spies on the dock tell me you brought in a French sloop."

"My men, Sir, did the *bringing*; I am afraid I was severely injured when we made our assault. As we prepared to board the sloop, an American took me into his sights and unloaded into me. If it were not for the men of my crew and the ship's doctor, I would not have survived. Fortunately, we had no other serious injuries—and no casualties."

"An American, you say?" Admiral Pennington questioned.

"Yes, Sir; the last I remember, the man shouted out some insult directed at the King." Frederick turned to his two lieutenants. "Might either one of you give the Vice-Admiral more facts on the American prisoner?"

Lieutenant Harwood spoke up first. "The prisoner surely was

not happy with our takeover of the French ship; he put up quite a fight. Needless to say, many of our men were upset with his attack on the Captain; he suffered the wrath of several of them before we could secure his safety. He shouted his curses for several days, but as we came closer to English soil, he became more docile—accepting his fate. It appears that the ship, as noted in our log, was a private one, sailing under the French flag—mostly mercenaries onboard."

Benjamin turned to Avendale. "Did the American give any indication as to why he was on this ship?"

Avendale shared what he knew. "In the past few days, the American has been more open with information. One of our men speaks French, and he managed to hold several conversations with him. The prisoner's father, evidently, was of French extraction, having settled in a predominantly French community of New Orleans in the Americas. He said he was sent by a group of French sympathizers to help Bonaparte. We thought that to be ridiculous. I mean, what would Bony do with an American? Why would America want to fight this crazy French war? They surely cannot still be fighting the War of 1812? It was three years ago, after all."

"Some do not end their fighting with the cessation of the war," Pennington remarked. "And what the American said may not be so bizarre."

"What do you mean, Sir?" Frederick stopped filling the water glass before him and turned his attention fully on Admiral Pennington.

Instead of answering, Pennington instructed Frederick, "Tell us what you know of Bonaparte."

Frederick told Pennington what he had said to Harwood earlier. "We found out at Gibraltar that Wellington defeated Bonaparte at Waterloo. That was in the middle of June. We know little else of the scope of the war since that time. We have not been in port for almost a month. The men on *The Resolve* carried on after my injury, but towing the French sloop slowed down our return."

"Then you do not know that Napoleon surrendered to the *Bellerophon's* captain two days ago? Bony tried to make his escape: He planned to take refuge in the United States. Two French ships anchored off the Atlantic coast prepared to receive Napoleon, but the *Bellerophon* blocked the port and his escape. It is rumored that there was to be a third—maybe even a fourth— ship, each with American sympathizers to aid in the Emperor's escape."

"Are—are you suggesting—?" Frederick stammered.

Pennington interrupted him. "It is possible, Captain. It would explain why the American chose to make *you* his target. If you remove the head, the body dies."

"Not with Captain Wentworth," Harwood interjected. "He taught us that our duty comes before everything."

"Yes, yes," said Pennington. "That is the British way; laudable as it is, we would expect nothing less from the commander of one of our ships." Yet, even Pennington knew how unusual it was for a crew to be so well trained and so devoted to their commander. It spoke volumes of the type of man Frederick Wentworth was.

"Let me see if I understand, Sir." Frederick tried to clear his thinking. "First, the war is essentially over, and very soon my men and I will be returning to civilian life." Pennington nodded his head in agreement. "*And* my crew quite possibly captured a French ship transporting an American sent to relay Bonaparte to safety in the United States."

"That is what it sounds like, Captain Wentworth," Pennington confirmed.

Benjamin began to laugh. "If this plays out, Frederick, you and your men will be national heroes. You will have foiled part of Bony's plan to leave France behind. It is said he missed his first means of escape, and the *LaSalle* was Bonaparte's last hope." Frederick sat silent in disbelief. "You have to admire the man," Benjamin continued. "Bonaparte's rise to power came as a result of his ability and his ambition, not as a man of rank or privilege. He had no noble title—he is actually from a poor family of Corsica. He was trained as an artillery officer and now is a symbol—a product of the new France."

"Bony's story is like yours, Captain," Avendale said. "Unlike many of our officers, you have no title, but I would rather follow you into battle than any other officer under which I ever served. You were trained as a naval officer. Your lives have parallels; do you not see it?"

"It will make a great story for the War Office." Pennington knew how it would play out in the newspapers.

Frederick protested, "I want no parallels with Bonaparte!"

"Let us get all the particulars on paper," Pennington encouraged.

Frederick turned to his brother by marriage. "Admiral, might I impose on you to return to *The Resolve* and retrieve Anne? Please take her to the Royal Hotel. I promised her we would stay there for a few days—at least, until this is complete."

"It would be my pleasure. Mrs. Wentworth is an exceptional woman. Wait until you meet her, Pennington." Benjamin Croft stood to take his leave.

Pennington called to the Admiral's retreating form, "Croft, see if Mrs. Wentworth will join us for dinner? I will bring my Miranda along; she will enjoy the company of another lady."

"Admiral," Frederick interceded, "after you have Anne settled in one of the hotel rooms, be sure to advise the hotel dining room of our party."

Benjamin waved his hand in recognition of what the men said. He knew exactly how to arrange the evening; the Admiral would make sure Anne understood that her husband, under subtly worded orders, would dine this evening with one of his commanding officers. Frederick needed her support tonight; a naval wife could make or break her husband's career. Frederick had probably planned an intimate meal for his bride, but that would have to wait. Her husband's career came first this evening. Besides, if Anne Wentworth could entertain the supercilious creatures who populated her father's drawing room, Frederick had no cause for alarm; but to err on the side of caution, Benjamin Croft would guarantee Frederick's success with gentle hints to Sir Walter's second daughter.

CHAPTER 21

O, my Luve's like a red, red rose,
That's newly sprung in June.
O, my Luve's like the melodie,
That's sweetly play'd in tune.
—Robert Burns, "O, My Luve's Like a Red, Red Rose"

They spent six weeks in Plymouth waiting for something to change. Although pressed repeatedly by the allied armies, the French continued to hold out, not accepting their defeat. The Wentworths let a small cottage on the outskirts of the town for privacy and to economize. Frederick and Anne had decided to save his prize money to purchase their own home. Despite never having once prepared her own meal, Anne became quite adept at improvisation. Used to fending for himself, Frederick assisted her. Some of their fondest moments resulted from disastrous attempts in the kitchen. They would laugh hysterically in each other's arms, settle for bread and tea, and spend the night in passionate lovemaking.

At the beginning of August, he received word from Edward that he and Christine had welcomed a son, Edward James. Frederick promised in his return letter that he and Anne would visit as soon as the Navy released him from his duties.

In September, the story of the action taken by *The Resolve* and of Wentworth's injury became well known in Plymouth, and he and Anne retreated to Kellynch to stay with the Admiral and Sophia. Frederick worried how the move would affect Anne—returning to her childhood home, but as a guest. Yet, Anne reasoned she should be there for Sophia, before his sister's lying-in. "We can revisit the lake," she whispered in his ear as Frederick took Anne into his arms.

"Have you ever made love in the open?" he teased, as he trailed a line of kisses down Anne's neck.

"Frederick!" she protested, trying to shove away from him by placing her hands firmly against his chest.

He raised his eyebrows, feigning innocence.

Finally, she burst out laughing. "You know full well I have never made love anywhere but in our bed!"

"Then perhaps we should make love in *your* bed," he suggested.

"*My* bed?" Anne looked confused.

He offered in explanation, "Your bedchamber—the one in the east wing."

"My old room?" she whispered. "You would want to make love there? Why, Frederick?"

He was quiet for a moment and then responded, "When I returned to Lyme—the time I left you the note regarding Louisa's progress . . ." Anne looked at him intently, trying to understand the emotions behind his words. "I went to your room and spent time there—alone. I imagined you there—touching your favorite things. My heart felt heavy—I accepted the fact you would never be mine; I would never know happiness. I laid across your bed, trying to recall the smell of lavender on your pillow—hugging it to me, imagining you in my arms—staring up at the canopy, and feeling a pain in my heart—the loneliness consuming my soul."

Anne understood; she knew how she would feel if she found herself in the house where Frederick grew into manhood. "Ah," she said quietly. Then she said, "We would have the wing all to ourselves."

"As if we were alone in our own house," he murmured.

"Kellynch would feel like home again to me." Her eyes lit with excitement. "Would you enjoy staying in the east wing?" she asked.

Frederick pulled her closer. "Would I enjoy making my wife happy? Would I enjoy having you entirely to myself—hearing you cry out my name in ecstasy? I assume your question is rhetorical, my Dear." He kissed her passionately. "I will have Ned move us into your room this afternoon," he said huskily when he came up for air.

"Thank you, Frederick." She kissed his ear as she inched closer to him. "You the kindest, most considerate man . . . ."

"Do not tell anyone else." He turned her chin so she faced him. "Kind and considerate are not qualities for which the Navy looks in their captains." By then, they were lost to their combined desire. Frederick pulled her down with him as he leaned back on the chaise. "I love you," he gasped as Anne moved across him. "I love you—forever."

★ ★ ★

The news of his commendation shocked their little household and gave them a reason for celebration. "A Rear Admiral of the White!" Anne danced around the room, waving the letter through the air as if it were a butterfly's wings. "How many bars and medals is that on your dress uniform?" she inquired sweetly. She laughed as she spun around him one more time.

"Enough to impress even your father, I suppose." Frederick smiled to see her so happy. "Of course, it is not as many as Benjamin."

"You, my Husband, will be the best-looking Rear Admiral in the whole British Navy," Anne declared as she went up on her tip-toes to nibble on his bottom lip.

"Now, you sound like your father," he teased.

She chuckled. "Well, my father cannot be wrong *all* the time."

Frederick snorted, choking back the laughter bubbling in his throat. "Sir Walter Elliot speaks the truth. What a novel idea that is!"

Anne cried, "Let us take the landaulette and visit Mary and Charles. I will take pleasure in sharing your advancement with my sister." Anne wrapped her arms around his neck. "My sister always appreciated the fact you were richer than either Captain Benwick or Charles Hayter."

"And that is important because?" Frederick took an interest in this new side of his wife.

"Because Mary is an Elliot, and she will rush from what she considers her sickbed to share her news with Charles's family—to let Charles's family know I am now married to a Rear Admiral of the White and . . ."

"And Louisa is married to retired Captain Benwick." Frederick finished her sentence. "I am surprised, my Love; I never knew you to be so concerned about *status*."

Anne dropped her eyes. "I suppose, like Mary, I, too, am an Elliot; I should be ashamed for having such thoughts."

"But you are not?" Frederick mocked.

"No," she sighed. "No, not yet, at any rate. Since our wedding breakfast, I keep hearing Louisa's voice saying, '*I believe some thought before I found my James, that the good Captain might be my choice.*' If I am taking Louisa Musgrove's leftovers, I perversely want her to realize she threw away the wrong man."

Frederick kissed her forehead. "I will ask Ned to call for the carriage. Wear your heavy cloak, my Love." He laughed as he headed toward the hallway. "If you wish to turn green with jealousy, I do not want you to turn blue from the cold as well. The colors are complementary, after all."

"Thank you, Frederick," she said to his retreating form.

He spun around to face her. Giving Anne a very exaggerated bow, he declared in his most military-sounding voice, "That is Rear Admiral Wentworth to you, Ma'am." Then he disappeared through the open door.

Laughing loudly, Anne called to his departing footsteps. "Yes, Sir!"

★ ★ ★

In late November, after a night of difficult labor, Sophia delivered a beautiful baby girl, whom she immediately named Cassandra Rose, after her late mother. Benjamin Croft paced the floors for hours, waiting impatiently for his child, but no baby would have a more doting father.

"She is quite the most adorable child God ever created," the Admiral said softly as he held the sleeping baby to him. "Is she not beautiful, Frederick?" He gently pushed the swaddling blankets away from the child's face to give his brother a look at his daughter.

"Cassandra Rose will break many hearts, Benjamin." Frederick gazed down at the child. "You will need a military escort wherever she goes."

"I never knew—I mean, Sophia and I never thought this could happen. Maybe all those years at sea kept Sophie from..." Benjamin lightly touched his daughter's face.

Frederick placed his arm around the Admiral's shoulder. Still looking down at the sleeping child, he barely whispered, "Your and Sophia's time at sea had nothing to do with my sister waiting until she was six and thirty to deliver her first child. It is just simply God's plan. The same as it was God's plan that I return to the service alone all those years ago—because I needed to be there for my men when we were at war—the same as Anne needed to be with me on my most recent voyage or else I would have died. God decided that you and Sophia needed a child, and I will bet a year's wages He thinks you need more than one. Sophia will look grand with a crew of little Crofts trailing along behind her, and you, my Admiral—my brother in marriage—will have your proverbial hands full."

★ ★ ★

"We will take a house together close to Mayfair," Benjamin Croft said as they all sat relaxing in his study at Kellynch. "Edward and Christine will join us there."

Frederick sat back in his chair. He turned the invitation, which had come that morning, over again and again in his hand. With France's signing of the Treaty of Paris in late November, about the same time Sophia had given birth to Cassandra Rose, the country went wild for anything military. The war, now at an end, demanded a celebration, and the Prince of Wales knew exactly what to do. He and his inner circle would recognize the most prestigious of the British war heroes at Carlton House, while all those who had served their country would receive military honors with parades and such. Those invited to Carlton House would spend the evening, along with Prinny, with leaders of the allied countries and other dignitaries: Field Marshal Gebhard Blucher; Prussian General Gneiseneau; the Grand Duchess Catherine and her brother, the Czar of Russia; Prince Frederick of the Netherlands; Francis I of Austria; Levin August, better known as Count von Bennigsen, the

King of Prussia; and William II of the Netherlands, who reportedly would marry Princess Charlotte of Wales.

Sophia took the card from Frederick's hand and read it aloud: "The Prince of Wales requests the pleasure of the company of Rear Admiral of the White Frederick Wentworth and Mrs. Anne Wentworth at an evening of celebration."

"It reads the same as the one Benjamin received," Frederick assured her as he took back the card.

Anne sat quietly, spellbound with the news. "We are invited to Carlton House." She exhaled slowly. "The Prince of Wales and the Queen will both likely be there."

"Yes, Love," Frederick reiterated. Although the news stunned him also, Anne's reaction amused him more. "You and my sister both read the card."

"Frederick, we cannot—" she started her protest, but realized the effort was fruitless.

Frederick crossed to where she sat, joining her on the settee. "Of course, Mrs. Wentworth, I will send our regrets to the Queen of England," he chastised sarcastically.

"But–But, Frederick," she stammered, "I never had a Season or was presented at court."

"Anne, you are a married woman; you need neither of those in this case. We will not even be speaking to any of the royals; there will be hundreds of people there. It is a State dinner; Benjamin and I will be part of the pomp and circumstance of the evening—that is all. We are likely to be seated at one of the back tables; yet, we will be able to tell our children we were part of history. Besides," he whispered in a conspiratorial tone, "think how jealous Mary and Elizabeth will be."

Anne's countenance turned to one of wicked delight. "They *will*, will they not?"

He whispered even lower. "Mrs. Benwick will not be invited."

"I love you," she giggled as the words burst from her mouth.

He laughed as he took her hand in his and settled back into the furniture. He stretched out his legs to their full length. "How could you not? I am, after all, a Rear Admiral of the White."

"*Now* who sounds like my father?"

Frederick looked sharply at Anne and pretended to be offended. "I take your words to heart, Mrs. Wentworth. You are right; I will not speak thusly again."

Immediately, tears formed in Anne's eyes. "Oh, my Love, I apologize. I never meant to criticize you." Tears flowed freely down her face. "I would never censure you so; it was a joke. You must believe me."

Frederick swept her into his arms, ignoring the fact they sat in a room with Sophia and Benjamin. "Sweetheart, I teased you as I always do; I never thought your words to be criticism."

Although she fought to control them, still the tears streamed out of her eyes, leaving trails of wet powder on her face. "I do not know why I am crying; I feel like such a fool. Sophia—Benjamin, I never meant to make you uncomfortable," she called out to them.

"You are just nervous, Anne," the Admiral assured her. "You are to be in the same room as the reigning monarchs. Who would not be nervous? I am nervous. Are you not, Sophia?"

"But none of *you* cry, even *Sophia!* What is wrong with *me?*" Sobs began all over again. This time they came because she knew she was the only one who had cried over the news.

"Come, Love." Frederick coaxed her onto his lap. "You are one of the strongest women I know. I recall you were not afraid of armed French ships. You will easily win the approval of any dignitary we might see—or meet." He wiped away her tears with a handkerchief. "You are incomparable."

Anne snuggled into his chest as she encircled his neck with her arms. "Thank you for loving me even with all my insecurities," she whispered in his ear.

Frederick would have loved to kiss her—to make love to her. Instead, he simply pulled her closer and stroked her hair. Out of the corner of his eye, he noted Sophia and the Admiral slipping from the room.

"You are tired," he said softly. "Let me take you to our room;

you need to rest." He lifted Anne to carry her to their quarters.

"Will we sleep?" she said dreamily.

Frederick chuckled. "You are a tempting one, Sweetling, but I will insist you sleep. At least, initially," he added as an afterthought.

"Initially," she murmured, nearly asleep already. "I love you, Frederick. You are too good to me."

"Nothing is ever good enough for you, Anne—nothing could match your love." Frederick kissed the top of her head as he carried her down the long deserted corridor to their room.

★ ★ ★

"You are not eating this morning?" Sophia asked as Anne pushed her plate away. They would leave for London that day, nearly a month before the celebration at Carlton House. The four of them would take a house together on the edge of Mayfair.

Married nearly a year, Anne looked forward to seeing her father and her sister Elizabeth again. Sir Walter had taken her and Frederick's advice. He had given up the house in Bath and took one in a reasonably fashionable area of London. According to Lady Russell's most recent letter, Sir Walter actively wooed a war widow—a Mrs. Bradley. Elizabeth—who had not written to Anne since Anne and Frederick's wedding—had tried to sabotage the relationship, but Sir Walter denied his eldest daughter's wishes. The eldest Elliot had suddenly found herself supplanted by a woman two years her junior. Anne would see the situation for herself at the end of the week, when she and Frederick dined with her family.

"I did eat a little." Anne nodded her thanks to the footman who removed the plate. "I will take something at the posting inn; I am sure we will stop several times today." She took a sip of her tea. "Besides, I am so nervous that my stomach is in knots."

"Have you had to use your chamber pot, I mean for your *stomach* condition?" Sophia held her teacup to her mouth, but she did not drink. Instead, she watched Anne carefully over the rim of the cup.

"Yes—but only yesterday and today. You do not suppose I am coming down with something? That would be *disastrous*; this is Frederick's big moment."

Sophia put the cup down, fully interested. "How long has your stomach been bothering you?"

Anne thought back—trying to give an accurate answer. "About a week, I suppose. It is worse in the morning—dry toast usually does the trick, though."

"Anne, when were your last courses?"

Anne's head snapped around. "What do you mean, Sophia? I *cannot* be!"

"Morning nausea—emotionally crying for no real reason— exhausted all the time. Think about it, Anne; it says 'with child' to me. Why can you not be carrying Frederick's baby? Do not tell me it is your age; I am nearly seven years older than you, and Cassandra Rose says it is possible." Sophia coolly summarized what Anne already suspected—but did not allow herself to truly consider.

Panicking, she begged Frederick's sister. "I will not tell Frederick until I am sure. Please, Sophia, you must say nothing. I cannot raise Frederick's hopes, only to have them dashed. These next few weeks are too important to let my nerves be mistaken for the possibility—the reality of—a child."

"I will say nothing," Sophia assured her. "But you must watch carefully. The next few weeks will be filled with ceremony after ceremony. Do not let the demands of Frederick's obligations risk your health or that of a child. My brother would *never* allow harm to come to you. His career—everything—is secondary to the love Frederick feels for you."

"I will exercise caution until I know for sure," Anne promised.

★ ★ ★

"Anne!" Sir Walter scrambled to his feet as a footman announced her and Frederick. "My, do you not look well! Your complexion glows, and you look less thin in your person and in your cheeks. Have you been using Gowland's lotion as I suggested?"

"No, Father—nothing at all," she replied as she offered him a kiss on the cheek.

"Certainly you cannot do better than continue as you are; you cannot be better than well." Her father moved past her to greet

Frederick, who stood to the side, amused by what Sir Walter chose as the first thing to say to his daughter after they had been apart for nearly a year. "Captain," the man offered his hand, "it has been a long time, Sir."

"Father, remember I wrote—Frederick is now a Rear Admiral of the White?"

"Of course, you did," Sir Walter looked at Frederick with a new respect. "How could I commit such a faux pas?"

"It is perfectly understandable, Sir. I am afraid I, too, am unaccustomed to the title." Frederick took Sir Walter's hand, vowing to be civil to the man.

"Come, I have someone I wish you to meet." Sir Walter gestured to a woman of approximately Anne's age. Raven-haired with astonishing blue eyes, the lady was taller than Anne by at least three inches. She had a small waist and a well-developed bust line, which her gown of lavender, a color often worn by a widow after her mourning period, prominently displayed. "This is Mrs. Amelia Bradley. Mrs. Bradley, this is my second daughter, Anne Wentworth, and her husband, Rear Admiral Frederick Wentworth."

Frederick bowed and Anne curtsied; Mrs. Bradley responded in kind. "Mrs. Bradley," Anne took the lead, "it is pleasant to meet you, at last. We have heard much of you from Lady Russell."

"I hope Lady Russell spoke of my *finer* qualities," the woman answered charmingly.

"I assure you, Ma'am," Frederick led Anne to a nearby chair, "that we heard a glowing account."

Mrs. Bradley nodded to a wing chair for Frederick's use. "I am pleased to hear it," she murmured. "Your father speaks often of your union, Admiral Wentworth. Sir Walter became quite enthralled by stories of your recent captures; I cannot *imagine* the dangers, Sir! And you, Mrs. Wentworth," she continued, "traveled with your husband?"

"I did, Mrs. Bradley," Anne spoke softly. "A woman should follow her husband."

Frederick interrupted, "My wife is adamant about our not

being separated, as am I. We waited many years to share a life together." He cleared his throat. "You may be unaware, Mrs. Bradley, of how close I came to death's door in this most recent journey; if Anne had not traveled with me—to tend me—I likely would have succumbed to my wounds."

"Really, Wentworth?" Sir Walter questioned him. "I never supposed *Anne* to be capable of handling such a crisis!"

"Then you, Sir, misjudge your daughter. Anne is sensible, compassionate, and intelligent. She can be stubborn, but sometimes that trait is the one that the situation demands. I have heard Anne compared to the late Lady Elliot. No one is more capable than Anne."

"We-Well," Sir Walter stammered, "I expect that I still see Anne as the little girl always with a book in her hand—lost in her world of make believe."

Anne, ever the diplomat in the family, added quickly, "I suspect I am a combination of both the fanciful girl and the sagacious woman—both the little girl and the grown-up Anne."

Mrs. Bradley joined in again. "I imagine you would be, Mrs. Wentworth. Most women are, although the men in our lives sometimes see us as one dimensional."

Frederick took the woman's words to heart; he imagined she spoke from first hand experience when dealing with Sir Walter. "I understood, Mrs. Bradley," he returned his attention to the woman seated before him, "that your late husband served in the Iberian campaign?"

"He did, Sir." Amelia Bradley paused. "Stephen lost his life trying to break Napoleon's military hold on the rest of Europe."

"Did you follow the drum, Ma'am?" Anne asked.

"No—No, Mrs. Wentworth, I do not possess your determination. I wish I had been there when Stephen…" Her words trailed off. "But I suppose that there would have been nothing I could do."

"The men who served in both Andalusia and in Portugal dealt Napoleon a major blow—but they suffered unbelievable losses. Your husband, Ma'am, was very brave."

"Thank you—you are most kind, Sir."

An awkward pause ensued. Anne knew talk of Mrs. Bradley's late husband probably wounded Sir Walter's ego, so she changed the subject. "Father, where is Elizabeth this evening? I had hoped to see her."

"Elizabeth is out with Mr. Stitt and his family at the theater."

"Mr. Stitt?" Frederick asked in an amused tone.

"A nobody," Sir Walter noted. "Mr. Stitt has made his own way—he has wealth, although he has no title. Owns a silver mine or some sort of hole in the ground—near Cornwall, I believe. Of course, I dare not object; the man is your sister's first serious suitor in several years. At least, he can afford her tastes; if he presents himself, I will agree most readily."

"Father!" Anne protested.

Just then, a footman announced dinner, and they moved to the dining room. Anne took her father's arm, and Frederick escorted Mrs. Bradley. Mrs. Bradley and Sir Walter sat at opposite ends of the table. Anne and Frederick occupied the middle. The dinner was in four courses, and the conversation remained cordial throughout.

"And you will be in town through the end of the month?" Sir Walter asked after motioning for the last course to be removed from the table.

"We will, Sir." Frederick placed his cutlery to the side of his setting. "We took a house with the Admiral and Sophia; my brother will join us after a fortnight."

Mrs. Bradley noted, "That is quite a household."

"You and I, my Dear," Sir Walter directed his attention to his lady friend, "will need to call on the Admiral and Mrs. Croft. They are my tenants at Kellynch Hall."

"As are Frederick and I, Father. We have been in Somersetshire since last September."

"Oh yes, of course," Sir Walter placated.

Mrs. Bradley stood, acting as the lady of the house, obviously, with Sir Walter's consent. "Mrs. Wentworth, why do we not retire to the drawing room and leave the men to their cigars and port?"

"Thank you, Mrs. Bradley." Anne followed the woman to her

feet, as did Frederick and Sir Walter. "Frederick—Father, we will see you in a few minutes." And with curtsies, the ladies left the room.

"Well, Wentworth, what will it be?" Sir Walter led Frederick into his study.

Frederick settled in a chair opposite Sir Walter's desk. "A brandy or a glass of port will be fine, Sir."

The older man handed him a brandy, and Frederick took a sip. "I am glad we have this time alone, Wentworth. I have something I need to discuss with you."

"Certainly, Sir Walter. What might that be?" Frederick asked cautiously.

Sir Walter came around the desk to sit next to Frederick. "As you and my daughter might surmise, I plan to offer for Mrs. Bradley soon. She is an attractive woman and young enough to bear me additional heirs. I find her company most pleasant, and, I believe, we will get along well together. She has her widow's pension and an unentailed piece of property left to her by her father, as well as a good living from her husband's investments."

"I see," Frederick mused. "Of course, Anne and I wish you much happiness. But how does your offer to Mrs. Bradley affect us? What do you need of me, Sir Walter?"

Elliot swished the brandy around in his glass. "I wish to take Mrs. Bradley to Kellynch as my wife. I will be terminating the Admiral's lease on the estate when the terms are up in September."

"And you expect me to deliver that message to my family?" Frederick hated being put in the middle—in such a position.

Sir Walter shook his head, a bit offended. "I would not ask it of my daughter's husband; I will speak for myself, Wentworth." Elliot took a large gulp of his drink before going on. "However, you must understand that I have done nothing to date because you and Anne are also at Kellynch. I cannot turn my daughter out, but I also cannot take my bride into a household predisposed to taking orders from both your sister and your wife."

Frederick paused—extending his thinking time before responding. "Then you would like to know when I will become the type of husband I always claimed I would be to Anne and when I plan to give my wife a proper place of her own?"

"That is not the way I would have phrased it, but it is the crux of the matter."

Frederick stared at his wife's father, disbelief playing through his body. *Calm down, Wentworth*, he told himself. *This foolish man's self-centered view of the world is not news to you.* "We have two prospective homes in mind, both appropriate for Anne's station in life." Frederick began to check off the details in his head. "I assure you, Sir Walter, once this month of celebration is complete, your daughter and I will make a choice. We are most eager to have a place of our own. With the war finally over, my services will no longer be needed; I will remain in an advisory position only. I will take a half pension, if necessary, but Anne and I will soon vacate Kellynch, and you and Mrs. Bradley can live there in wedded bliss." Frederick could not resist saying this last in a slightly sarcastic tone.

Evidently Sir Walter heard the sarcasm in Frederick's voice. "I did not mean to offend you, Wentworth." Yet, his tone said otherwise.

At that, Frederick lost his tenuous hold on his temper. Even with his promotion and his recognition from the Crown, Sir Walter still judged him poorly. The man's interest in Frederick's career came only as a reflection of what glory he might bring to the Elliot name. He would never be good enough for Anne in Sir Walter's opinion. "Sir Walter, you have done nothing but insult me every chance you had for the past ten years. Until I came to you a year ago to ask for permission a second time to marry Anne, I was nothing more than a bowing acquaintance. I know I am a disappointment, in your estimation, but I tolerate your censure for Anne's sake. Here, however, are the facts. As a Rear Admiral of the White, I possess nearly as much social clout as do you. You have the inherited position, which I will never have, but it is I, at this time, who has the fortune. You foolishly ran through yours and now must marry a woman of independent wealth in order to save your name and your estate. I, on the other hand, married the woman I love. I supported Anne's idea of your reclaiming your home. I would think that counted for something, but now you take this opportunity—the first time we have seen each other in over a year—the first time you have seen your own child—to promote your own interests. Go ahead and marry for convenience; marry for money. That is the way of the aristocracy! Do not have second thoughts about Anne's future. I will provide for my wife!"

Sir Walter flinched at the tone of authority in Frederick's voice. Only this man—Anne's husband—ever spoke to him as such. He countered, "And what of your sister and the Admiral?"

"You pompous prat!" Frederick cursed under his breath. "I knew you lacked the courage to deal honorably with my family! However, do not concern yourself with principles. I feel confident in safely saying that as Sophia and the Admiral are new parents, I doubt they will wish to remain long at Kellynch. When she starts walking, Cassandra Rose will want to actually touch things—not live in a museum! I will tell my sister of your intentions. If you are finished, Sir Walter, I would prefer to return to my wife's company." He set the glass down hard on the table, sloshing some of the brandy onto his hand.

★ ★ ★

"How long have you known my father, Mrs. Bradley?" Anne helped herself to a cup of tea before taking a seat on one of the settees in the drawing room.

The other woman took a seat in one of the overstuffed wing chairs, and set her cup and saucer on an end table. "A little more than three months."

"Do you have an understanding?" Anne asked. She sipped slowly, letting the the brew fill her senses.

"I should not speak for Sir Walter, but I am confident we are moving in that direction." She straightened the seams of her dress as it draped over her lap. "Do you object to our possible union, Mrs. Wentworth?"

Anne took her time before answering. "If my father is satisfied, then I have no objections."

"Your sister Elizabeth is not so accepting of our relationship,"

Mrs. Bradley confided.

"When our mother passed, my father foolishly gave all his attention to my eldest sister. Since she was seventeen, Elizabeth has acted as the mistress of Kellynch. She would not be happy to be supplanted by anyone; it is her identity, after all. Mary is Mrs. Musgrove, and Elizabeth was the mistress of Kellynch. Until Frederick came along, I had no identity; my perspective is different from theirs."

"Hmm," Mrs. Bradley said.

Anne took another sip of her tea. "Tell me more about yourself, Mrs. Bradley."

The other woman smiled charmingly. "May I call you Anne?"

Anne half smiled. "As long as I may call you Amelia."

Mrs. Bradley nodded. "You know of my previous marriage. I married Stephen at nineteen and was a widow by two and twenty. I am a year older than you and two years Elizabeth's junior. I am independently wealthy—a gentleman's daughter, but I would like a title to go along with my wealth. Many men find me too old; it is not as if I could have a Season at my age and with my marital status. I want a family, Anne. Your father wants a second family, possibly an heir to save his estate. Sir Walter says that, at your suggestion, he is in London with just that purpose. I am not a foolish woman, Anne. Neither am I overly emotional. Your father and I get along well together. Ours will not be a love match, but I hope it will be more than one of convenience; yet, if it is not, both of us will understand. Your father and I both married for love the first time. At least, I assume Sir Walter married the late Lady Elliot out of love; he speaks of her fondly."

"Amelia, you should know that my father can be difficult. He is not known for his business sense; you will need to practice economy in the home. Like my mother, you will need to find a way to humor him and even to soften bits of his personality. You will have to work to conceal his failings and promote his respectability."

"I see," Amelia said, as if Anne had shared the secrets of the universe.

"Will you wish to move into Kellynch upon your marriage?"

Anne inquired. "I ask because Frederick's sister, her husband, and their child have lived there some eighteen months. Frederick and I will move out soon—after these celebratory events, but Sophia and the Admiral remain. They should be given proper notice."

Amelia put down her cup. "As you indicated moments ago, Sir Walter could economize in almost any place other than London; it is expensive to live here—to maintain a lifestyle here. The purpose of marrying your father is to assume the position of his wife—his title and his estate. Otherwise, the relationship might not seem so promising. I have a small estate—one not entailed—given to me by my father, but I cannot imagine Sir Walter would wish to live there. As I want a title, your father, likewise, wishes to save his estate and family line. I will sell my property and use the money to make Kellynch Hall solvent."

Curious, Anne asked, "Where is your property?"

Amelia picked up her teacup again. "Oxfordshire—it is in Oxfordshire. It is a small affair with a decent house—repaired recently, as I anticipated selling it—around fifty tenants—about three thousand per year annual clearance, if my man of business keeps accurate books. I have a reliable steward who maintains it while I am away."

"It sounds very pleasant," Anne said wistfully.

Amelia turned her head to look at Anne sharply. "Would you and Admiral Wentworth be interested in it? I would not mind keeping it in the family."

"Frederick and I seek something close to the sea. I do not think my husband could tolerate being landlocked."

"That is too bad; it seemed like a perfect solution for all of us." Amelia looked toward the open door. "I believe I hear the gentlemen coming this way."

"Amelia," Anne lowered her voice, trying to make sure Frederick did not hear. "Would you consider the Admiral and Sophia to be family? Might I discreetly mention your estate to Frederick's sister? Since the birth of their child in November, they both seem more intent on putting down roots. Kellynch thrives under their care, but I believe they would like a place of their own."

"I would gladly entertain their inquiries. It will be our secret until your husband's family chooses to make it public."

Nothing more could be said as the men reentered the room. Anne could tell immediately that Frederick and her father had argued; both men looked unhappily tense. After thirty minutes of strained conversation, she feigned a headache to curtail the evening.

As Frederick led her to a waiting coach, he guided her along in a preoccupied way with his hand on her elbow. When Anne nearly stumbled getting into the coach, he came to his senses.

"I am sorry, Anne. My mind is elsewhere."

"I suspect that you are still brooding about something stupid my father said." She settled herself into the warmth of the coach.

Frederick climbed in after her, shaking his head. "The man certainly knows how to make me lose reason!" He took her hand as he settled himself next to her. "But you do not deserve my wrath; I beg your forgiveness."

"What is there to forgive? Did you not defend my honor this evening?" She kissed his cheek as the coach lurched forward, ending up in his responsive arms as they swayed into the night carriage traffic. Despite his recent annoyance, her presence lightened his mood. "Now, this is the perfect way for you to beg my forgiveness," she joked.

Frederick wrapped her in his embrace, tightening his hold. He began to drape kisses along her face. "Forgive me," he murmured with each kiss.

"Say it again," Anne teased as he hit one of her sensitive spots. "Again, please," she gasped when Frederick kept up his assault. Her moan announced his total forgiveness—no further talk needed.

CHAPTER 22

So, we'll go no more a-roving
So late into the night,
Though the heart be still as loving,
And the moon be still as bright.
—Lord Byron, "We'll Go No More A-Roving"

"Where are we going this evening?" Frederick's secret had piqued her interest. They had spent every evening over the past fortnight at one event or another—one evening, a ball; another, a soiree; still another, a concert—but tonight would be different. They were on their own; Sophia and Benjamin had begged off to spend the evening with Cassandra Rose.

"You will see."

Frustrated, Anne sat back in the carriage; Frederick sat across from her, staring out the coach's window, pretending to be interested in the increasing darkness. "How long will you make me wait before you share our destination?"

Anne's pleading pleased him; he loved to surprise her—to see the pure joy in her eyes when she experienced something new. "It is something special—just for you," was all he divulged.

Finally, the coach halted in front of a concert house—actually, the best concert house in London. For a moment, she sat mesmerized by the impressive facade of the building. Then she asked, "A concert?" As he helped her from the carriage, Frederick remained silent; instead, he took Anne's arm on his and led her into the crowded, brightly lit hall.

In a private box overlooking the stage, he seated her and then secured champagne from a server before closing the curtain, sealing them away from the throng. "May I say you look very beautiful tonight, Mrs. Wentworth," he whispered close to her ear. Even in the dimly lit theater, he could see her blush.

"Frederick, what is the program?"

"Why not read the playbill, my Love?" Smiling, he sat back in the cushioned chair.

Anne began to thumb through the pages. "Madame Tresurré!" she whispered loudly.

"I have heard that the lady is exceptional." His smile grew with the look of bewilderment on Anne's face.

"I have heard, Sir, from one who experienced Italian arias in their natural setting, that her performance is a disappointment."

"What a foolish person to think so," Frederick mocked himself. "I would imagine whoever told you such lies must have been pre-occupied with something else rather than truly listening to the performance."

"Then we will enjoy the music together." She moved closer to him—as close as propriety would allow. "Do you suppose love songs are on the program?"

"I am sure they are, Sweetling." He took her hand and returned it to his arm. "Will you translate the Italian for me?"

Anne tightened her grasp. "What makes you think I speak Italian well enough to translate for a man as well traveled as you, my Husband?"

Frederick grew serious for a moment. "I want what Mr. Elliot and my conceit robbed me of that evening a year ago. I want to experience the music the way it should be—with a person so in tune with herself that she becomes part of the music. That concert in Bath was nearly the end of our relationship; I came close to giving up. I walked away from the most important person in my life. In retrospect, it was a low moment—a memory I would just as soon forget. Therefore, I propose we replace the anxiety and the depression we felt that evening in Bath with a new memory, one where no one else exists but you and me—nothing but us and the music."

"It amazes me that a man who has known the savagery of war can be such a romantic." Anne slid her gloved hand into his, allowing Frederick to pull her hand into his lap.

"Because I faced death and came away only scathed, I seek out the joys that life brings. For me, the most joyful moments are those I share with you; only with you do I feel whole again." The lights began to dim throughout the theater, but their eyes remained on each other. Only when the acclaimed soprano took the stage did they turn their attention to the performance. Then Frederick and Anne traveled together to magical musical realms, their personal connection unbroken.

★ ★ ★

They would leave London at the end of the week after experiencing a whirlwind of celebratory rituals. Edward and Christine had joined them ten days prior, bringing young Edward with them. The couples set up a nursery, and Sophia noted how often Anne went there to hold the babies.

"You should be getting dressed." Speaking softly, Sophia stood in the doorway.

Anne shifted young Edward in her arms. "Is he not beautiful?" Anne's light touch traced the outline of the child's face. "I could look at him for hours."

Sophia stepped into the room, peeking in the crib at her own Cassandra Rose. "Everything else fades into insignificance when one looks into the face of a child." She walked to where Anne sat. "Here, let me take him. You cannot be late tonight; the Prince Regent and the Queen await."

"I suppose I should be about it." Anne stood, but she did not make a move to leave the comfort of the room. Sophia handed the sleeping Edward to the nursery maid, and then rejoined her brother's wife. She wrapped her arm around Anne's waist to urge her to move. They were nearly to the door when Anne acknowledged, "I have not had my courses for three months now."

"I know." Sophia turned Anne toward her. "I can tell by the shine of your hair and the glow of your complexion. Women know these things without being told. Are you not happy?"

"Yes—oh yes. I have always longed for children."

Sophia looked concerned. "Then what, pray tell, is the matter?"

"Have you noticed that Frederick never comes in here unless someone insists? What if he does not want children—I mean, we spoke of it before we married, but it has been a year, and my husband seems oblivious to the fact that he has no child."

"Oh, Anne." Sophia pulled her along into the hallway. "You really do not think Frederick might not want children? Do you believe he will not be happy with the news?"

"I do not want to lose him, Sophia. What if he turns from me—from our child? I could not bear it! When you and I first suspected my condition, I was sure he would be happy with the prospect; yet, now I am not so confident. Frederick has all these plans for a house and an estate and—"

"Anne," Sophia interrupted her, "for a woman of such great intelligence, you know so little of life. If Frederick feigned disinterest in children, it was for *your* sake. As small children, the three of us used to play at knights and Celtic warriors and everything imaginable for a child, and in each play, we always imagined these heroes with their families. We feared a separation when our parents passed, and the three of us swore that staying together as a family would be the most important ideal in our lives. Frederick would be content with a household of children, one child, or no children if he had your love; but I guarantee you my brother will be ecstatic with your news. Has he not the most loving heart?"

"Yes—yes, he is the most *romantic* man under that stiff exterior," Anne said shyly.

Sophia smiled with the knowledge that her brother had finally found happiness. "Do you not think he possesses the capacity to love his own child? His heart is large enough to love all those in his life. The man is built to love and protect. How can you doubt it?"

"I never doubt my husband," Anne spoke with determination. "I doubt myself often, but never Frederick. I simply fear disappointing him; I did so all those years ago."

"Trust me," Sophia said as she walked Anne toward her chambers. "Frederick would rather have your news than all the recognitions he will receive tonight."

Anne smiled that Madonna-like smile commonplace among mothers and mothers-to-be. "Thank you, Sophia. You have put my mind at ease. I will tell him this evening when we return."

★ ★ ★

Being announced, the Wentworths and the Crofts walked proudly into the dining hall at Carlton House. A naval attaché to the court had called upon them two days earlier to review the protocol at a dinner with royalty present. They were as prepared as one can be— but then again, one can never be fully prepared for the grace, the splendor, and the dignity of such an occasion.

The light of hundreds of candles flickered off the gold trim of the ceiling. Chandeliers hung low, their light shimmering over the gold-edged place settings and goblets upon the cream-colored linen of the tables. Wall sconces every few feet added to the brightness; it was as if one stepped into the brightness of day. Bouquets of fresh flowers perfumed the air, while guests crushed dried rose petals and lavender under their feet as they walked about.

Women wearing gowns of various shades of the rainbow—and some wearing plumes that arched high out of their hair—moved about the room on the arms of handsomely dressed gentlemen. The shimmer of the material and the sparkle of their jewels added to the glow of the evening.

Anne wore a custard-tinted empire-waist gown of satin, and Frederick thought her the most arrestingly beautiful woman he ever saw. A pearl necklace adorned her throat, and beaded pearl pins held the complicated upsweep of her hair in a sleek design. Frederick, who wore his full dress uniform, looked large and powerful and perfectly in control. Together, they were a striking pair, and more than one head turned upon their entrance.

The Crofts sat at one of the many tables dedicated to the Navy, while Frederick and Anne found themselves at a table headed by Vice Admiral Pennington. Lieutenants Harwood and Avendale, along with Dr. Laraby, represented *The Resolve*, while like officers from the *Bellerophon* also occupied the table.

"So, Wentworth, did you share your news with your wife?" Pennington called from his end of the table.

Frederick looked up suddenly, discomfited by the question. "Unfortunately, I arrived home too late to fully give it my attention, Admiral." He took a sip of a very fine white wine.

"*One* of you must tell me the news!" cried Anne.

Frederick cleared his throat and put down his wineglass. "I am sure, Mrs. Wentworth, you will find this news amusing. The Navy Board has chosen to release five sets of captain's logs as books to the public. My log from the last months of my service—the capture of the two French ships and the American traitor will be the first one released. The book publisher asked that I review the entries and add any pertinent details—embellish so to speak."

Anne offered one of her beguiling smiles, and he knew immediately where her mind would go. "Embellish?" she laughed. "They will allow you, my Husband, to embellish your log? The publisher must have heard of your storytelling prowess."

Avendale's new wife, Margaret exclaimed, "So, you will be an author!"

"Of sorts. But I do not expect, Mrs. Avendale, to compete with Mrs. Ratcliffe, if that is what you mean."

Anne laughed, although she tried to stifle it. "No, Mrs. Avendale, I cannot see Admiral Wentworth competing with the new Gothic writers—no castles or strange prophecies or damsels in distress aboard a ship."

Frederick loved her taunt; her quick wit never ceased to amaze him. "Maybe I will be able to compete with your favorite writer, my Love. What is her name?"

"We readers are unsure. Her first book *Sense and Sensibility* simply reads 'by a Lady.' The second reads 'by the author of *Sense and Sensibility*.' Hers are novels of our time, speaking of the social classes and the economic structure, which paralyzed our efforts for independent thinking. But they are books of hope because one can see the changes coming whether those in charge choose to recognize it or not."

Mrs. Avendale took on a quizzical look. "I thought they were simply love stories."

Frederick smiled at the woman. "My wife is a great believer in crossing cultural lines, but I am sure she enjoyed the romance part of the book, as well, for she has a very tender heart."

"If it is the captain's log, then we shall all receive a mention," Dr. Laraby observed.

Admiral Pennington confirmed, "I expect you will. When Admiral Wentworth was disabled, others filled in the report—the log. It will reflect the two captures and the Admiral's struggle to survive. The publisher anticipates that the British public will be enthralled by the drama. We jumped the gun, so to speak; the Army has not deployed its high rollers, as of yet. The Battle of Copen-hagen—and probably that of San Domingo—as well as the Battle of the Nile will also be released. Did you not see action in some of those, Wentworth?"

"I did, Admiral, at both San Domingo and Copenhagen."

"Then maybe we can tie the logs together that way. Your story in one log will lead to another log, in which you play a different role. Excellent idea, if I do say so myself! I will run it by the higher-ups tomorrow." He returned his attention to Anne. "Mrs. Went-worth, your husband's log will be the first one released; you must be very pleased."

"Admiral Pennington, I assure you that I am extraordinarily proud of my husband."

"I thought," Frederick whispered privately, "I might persuade you to help me review the logs; you have a gift for words."

Anne smiled mischievously. "Sir, I am not so *persuadable* as I once was."

"I did not think you were, Madam," he retorted slyly. "But I believe my charm might overcome your reservations."

She giggled. "It is possible that it might, Admiral Wentworth." She took a leisurely sip of her excellent red wine.

The attaché, who had attended them previously, appeared at the table, interrupting their conversation. "Admiral Wentworth, His

Majesty George IV wishes to speak to you and Mrs. Wentworth."

"Sp–Speak to us? Now?" Frederick stammered. He touched his napkin to his lips.

The man nodded, and Frederick stood quickly, reaching for Anne's hand, which had begun to tremble. As they walked the long aisle between the tables toward the head table, the man instructed him, "You are quite tall, Admiral. His Majesty is not, so sit when you speak with him."

Frederick nodded and then steadied Anne as she rushed along beside him. Touching her elbow, he balanced her as they wove their way between tables and among the serving staff. "Are you all right, Sweetling?" he asked as they followed the attaché, who was hurriedly leading the way.

"We have been summoned to meet the heir to our country's throne. How should I be?" Anne responded, sounding frightened. Frederick was not sure that her teeth were not chattering, although to him, the room suddenly felt very stuffy and warm. Unconsciously, he ran a finger around his collar, feeling it tightening on him.

Anne nearly swooned as they came within sight of the Prince Regent. "My legs!" she hissed to Frederick. "They are rubber!"

"I am here," he murmured.

Despite what she knew he must be feeling, he looked self-assured; for that, Anne was suddenly grateful. They were together—she and Frederick could do *anything* together. She took a deep breath and then straightened her shoulders. "I am ready," she told him as he directed her the last few feet before being presented to George IV and his special guests.

"I never thought otherwise, my Love." He placed her hand on his arm as they stepped in front of their future king.

"Your Majesty," the attaché spoke once the Prince Regent turned his head to look in their direction. "May I present Rear Admiral Frederick Wentworth and his wife Mrs. Anne Wentworth?" Both men made a proper bow as Anne dipped into a deep curtsy.

No one raised his eyes or spoke until the Prince spoke. "Admiral Wentworth, would you and your wife care to join us for a few minutes?"

"We would be honored, Your Majesty." Frederick's voice changed in timbre. He handed Anne into the nearest chair and took the one set at an angle from the Prince, making the disparity in their heights less obvious.

"Are you enjoying yourself, Mrs. Wentworth?" the Prince asked nonchalantly.

Anne swallowed hard before answering. "It is a magnificent gathering, Your Highness."

"Then you approve, Madam?" He seemed amused by her innocence, and his tone spoke volumes. "Have you not been to Carlton House previously?"

"No, Your Highness. I mean, I have not been to your home previously." A tone of disapproval crept into her voice; she did not like being the object of his entertainment. "As far as approving of the supper," she blurted out, "one would be foolish to disapprove of what one's monarch offered." Suddenly, she wished that she had not opened her mouth.

A long pause added to the tension before the Prince laughed. "A woman with spunk, Admiral Wentworth! You may have your hands full." He motioned to the man on Anne's left. "This is Prince Metternich of Austria, Madam."

Anne dropped her eyes, but did not stand to curtsy. "It is with pleasure that I greet you, Prince Metternich."

"Mrs. Wentworth," the Austrian spoke in heavily accented English, "we understand that we owe your husband a great debt."

"I am sure my husband does not feel he alone is worthy of such accolades, Prince Metternich."

The Prince Regent interrupted, "Is that true, Admiral Wentworth? Does your wife speak your thoughts on the matter?"

Frederick spoke with as much dignity as he could muster under the circumstances: "My wife is extremely loyal and honest. My men—my crew—were as much a part of the success of our campaign as I was. In fact, they carried on most efficiently once I became injured."

"Then you give them the credit for the captures?" the Austrian prince questioned.

"We are a crew, Prince Metternich; each of us relies on all the others to survive. Like a chain, we are only as strong as our weakest link." Anne stared at him in disbelief; her softhearted husband appeared a rock of granite.

George IV laughed heartily, as did the minions seated at his table. "A lesson we are pleased Bonaparte never learned. Tell me, Wentworth, from where you hail," Prinny demanded.

"From Herefordshire, Your Highness."

"And your parents?"

"Edward and Cassandra, Your Majesty, of simple birth if that is your question, my Prince."

"Was I misinformed?" Prinny looked almost embarrassed. "I thought you were from Somerset, Admiral."

"My wife and I currently reside in Somerset with my sister and her husband, Admiral Croft. We are at Kellynch Hall, Your Highness."

"At Kellynch?" the Prince Regent now seemed completely interested. "Sir Walter Elliot's seat?"

"The very one, Your Highness. My wife is Sir Walter's daughter."

Prinny directed his comment to Anne. "Your father, Mrs. Wentworth, is well known as a pompous ass!"

"I am aware of his reputation." Anne, thankfully, did not crack a smile. The rest of the Prince's table, however, burst into laughter again, as if on cue.

The woman to the Prince's right inquired, "Then are you not Lady Wentworth?"

Anne allowed a smile to turn up the corners of her mouth. "My husband has no title, Madam."

The Prince Regent leaned forward and flirtatiously took Anne's hand in his while Frederick fought the urge to snatch it out of his grasp. Prinny knew exactly what he was doing—a test, so to speak, of the Wentworths' reported devotion to each other. He brushed his lips across Anne's knuckles. "Tell me, Mrs. Wentworth, when did you meet the Admiral?"

Anne flushed a little but spoke forthrightly, "Your Highness, my husband and I fell in love when I was but nineteen, and he had just received his first command. We never loved another or even considered another worthy of our attention, although we spent many years apart."

"Not even a prince, Mrs. Wentworth?" Prinny prodded her. Frederick bit back the anger swelling in his chest.

Anne gazed at the heir to the throne. "Your Majesty, although you have the world to offer, I never wanted the world; I turned down riches and a title, preferring to marry the Admiral. I do not regret my decision."

"Mrs. Wentworth, you are incomparable!" the Prince exclaimed. "I do not know when I last so enjoyed a conversation." He purposefully placed Anne's hand in Frederick's. "You are a lucky man, Wentworth."

"Thank you, Your Highness; it is a fact of which I am well aware," Frederick forced pleasantry into his tone, although inside, he seethed.

Anne had recognized the Duke of Mayfield earlier, so when he asked about her father, she was not surprised. "Mrs. Wentworth, is Sir Walter not set to marry Mrs. Amelia Bradley?"

"He is, Your Grace." Anne squeezed Frederick's hand, glad to have him so close.

The Duke continued, "And will he not return to Kellynch when he marries?"

"My father—Sir Walter," Frederick began, "will return to Kellynch Hall soon—at the end of the Season. Having recently begun their family, my sister and her husband are considering a place of their own in Oxfordshire. My wife and I seek a like estate of our own, now that the war with France is at an end."

"So, Sir Walter marries Mrs. Stephen Bradley, a war widow," the tipsy Duke said sarcastically. "He marries *her* for her money, and she marries *him* for his title. Then *he* displaces his own daughter, as well as two men who, between them, have served this country for nearly three decades." The alcohol gave the Duke courage he might not possess otherwise. "It seems a shame, Your Highness; that we have this evening to celebrate war heroes like Wentworth here, only to find out that we *displace* them."

"My wife and I appreciate your concern, Your Grace," Frederick added with a nod to those at the Prince's table, "but we encouraged my wife's father to remarry. He has only daughters and his immediate family would otherwise lose the estate to a cousin, a man who may own the title but not care for the position it gives him. I have earned enough from my service to provide for Mrs. Wentworth."

The Prince rejoined the conversation. "Your consideration and foresight speak well of you, Admiral Wentworth. You reflect estimably on our country's Navy, as a gentleman of reason and of vision. Your country and your future King thank you for your service."

Realizing their time with Prinny and his inner circle had come to an end, Frederick rose to his feet and helped Anne to hers. "Your Majesty," Frederick said as he lowered his body in a bow, "Mrs. Wentworth and I thank you most sincerely for the honor." Anne curtsied elaborately.

Then—as coached by the attaché—Frederick and Anne took several steps backward. Frederick bowed and Anne curtsied again, and they turned quickly to leave.

"Nothing like an inquisition!" Frederick chuckled as they approached their own table once more.

Anne swayed against him, feeling all the adrenaline drain from her. "I never realized the royal court cared so much for gossip. Perhaps I should have provided a copy of my family tree as a parting gift."

Frederick took hold of her arm. "I would prefer not to have to relate even half of that conversation with our tablemates. May we simply tell them that Prince George wanted me to describe the boarding of the French sloop and you to describe my recovery?"

Anne glanced quickly at his fellow crew members, who were waiting for the retelling. "I agree; telling your men the Prince wanted to gossip about my father and wanted to make you jealous is not my idea of pleasant dinner conversation."

"Our Monarch succeeded in one way; I seriously considered planting him a facer if he held your hand much longer," he whispered close to her ear.

"Thank you, my Husband, for showing restraint. Finding you in a cell at the Old Bailey tomorrow morning is not how I wish to end my time in London." Anne took his arm to return to the table.

They told their diplomatic version of the conversation to anyone who would listen. During the main course, the captain of the *Bellerophon* told a similar tale. Anne and Frederick wondered if he "lied" also or whether the Prince's party had actually spoken of Bonaparte's capture with him.

As the party's entertainment began to wind down. Frederick and Anne prepared to take their leave and rejoin Sophia and Benjamin for the ride home. However, before they could make their goodbyes, the attaché reappeared at the table. "Admiral Wentworth," the man spoke softly, "his Majesty requests to speak to you again." Frederick laid his napkin on the table, preparing to stand when the man spoke in more confidence, "Come alone, Sir."

Anne's eyebrows shot up and she smiled at her husband, silently sending him courage. "Frederick?" Anne reached for him instinctively.

He helped her to her feet. "Go wait with Benjamin and Sophia, my Love. Whatever it is Prince George wants, I will handle it." Uncharacteristically, he kissed her cheek before turning to follow the court's messenger. Frederick had no idea what to expect. Prince George had earned a reputation for his magnanimous character, as well as his frivolous one. With the turn of the earlier conversation, Frederick had no idea what to expect when he approached the table again. For all he knew, the Prince might demand the pleasure of Anne's company in private; it was not beyond him. *That will not happen.* Frederick certainly would not look the other way, no matter what it cost him.

He waited with the court's emissary for nearly ten minutes before the Prince chose to recognize his presence. "Admiral Wentworth," Prinny called out, "you returned!" Frederick could hear the slur of his speech and knew that he dealt with a powerful man in his cups. As a ship's captain, he had handled many an insensible man, but Prince George was his country's future leader.

Frederick bowed low. "As you requested, Your Majesty."

"Come closer, Wentworth." He gestured to the same chair, which Frederick occupied earlier.

Frederick sat down and asked guardedly, "May I be of service, Your Highness?"

"Actually, Admiral, I have decided to be of service to *you*," he said loudly.

"I beg your pardon, Your Majesty, but I do not understand."

The Prince gestured to the other side of the table, and the Duke of Mayfield took over the explanation. Frederick noted how the other guests at the table all stared at him—silly, drunken smiles plastered on many of their faces, as if they all shared some delicious secret. "According to our sources—Sir William Dunlap, to be precise," the Duke's speech was even more slurred than the Prince's, "your wife's father's family was granted its title by Charles II."

Frederick said cautiously, "I believe Your Grace is correct in this matter."

"Of *course*, I am correct," Mayfield asserted.

"Charles," Prince George laughed at what he would say before he said it, "was a two. Charles Two. I am a four; that makes me twice as powerful. Is that not right, Admiral?"

Frederick wanted to smile; Prince George was a lousy drunk. "Four is twice as strong as two, Your Highness," he said, as seriously as he could.

"Charles Two gave the Elliots a baronetcy. I am a four; I will give you more. That rhymes," he cackled, as did the rest of his table. The Prince snapped his fingers, and one of the footmen placed a folded document shield in his hand. "Admiral Wentworth, I need you to stand, but I think *I* will not stand. *We* will do this seated. Sir Walter Elliot is a nincompoop, but you are a sensible man. England needs sensible men, Wentworth. Your wife's father is a mere baronet, but from this day forward, you and your children will have a title greater than that man's. I give you this!" He held out the document, and Frederick tentatively took it.

Gingerly, he unfolded the paper and began to read.

"What do you think, Wentworth?" the Prince asked; he was puffed up like a bantam rooster.

"It is phenomenal, Your Majesty; I do not know what to say except to offer my devotion and my appreciation." Frederick began to read the paper again—a royal proclamation—including the King's seal and the Queen's signature under that of George IV.

"My man will call on you tomorrow morning with all the details. He will tell you of the property and of your duties to the Crown. I expect that you should return to Mrs. Wentworth, Admiral. She is likely to be missing you."

"Yes, Your Highness." Frederick got to his feet and began his obligatory bow out of the group's sight. "Your kindness will never be forgotten." He nodded to the Duke, who seemed to have engineered the honor.

As he backed away, Frederick wondered what had just occurred. No one would believe it; he was not sure even he did, although he clutched the proof of it tightly in his hand.

When he reached Anne, she was extremely curious, but he told her nothing. "In the carriage," was all Frederick said as he hustled her from the room; Benjamin and Sophia closely followed.

Finally settled in their coach, Anne could contain herself no longer. "Tell me!" she demanded.

"I considered it, and I may wait until tomorrow. Our Prince George may change his mind, after all." He leaned back into the cushioned upholstery and pretended to close his eyes for sleep.

Anne noted the smile, however, and she allowed herself the liberty of reclining against his shoulder. "Then I suppose I will wait to tell you what *I* know." Anne snuggled into his arm, relaxing her weight against him.

"You have no secrets from me," Frederick mumbled, trying to sound sleepy.

Anne yawned before saying, "If you say so, my Dear." She shut her eyes and sighed heavily.

"Will either of you tell Sophia or me?" Benjamin asked, too curious to wait.

Anne chuckled, but she did not open her eyes. "Sophia already knows my secret," she mumbled dreamily.

Frederick sat up now, suddenly aware that Anne might not be mocking him. "What is your secret, Anne?"

"You first," she stated firmly.

Frederick turned to his sister. "Sophia?"

"Leave me out of your domestic squabbles." Sophia draped a leg over Benjamin's knee. He removed her slipper and began to massage her foot.

"Anne?" Frederick's attention reverted to his wife.

She looked away—out the coach's window. The coach lantern illuminated her profile. "It is nothing, Frederick; I only wanted you to share what Prince George said."

Frederick turned her chin to face him. "You are a terrible liar, Sweetling, but I will share with you my news; then you must share as well." He took a deep breath. "Prince George or the Duke of Mayfield or someone else at that table dislikes your father intensely. The more they drank, evidently, the more they mulled over our answers to what the group had asked about our life together. In short, Prince George has bestowed a title on me, on you, and on any children."

Silence.

Undaunted, he continued, "I am now Frederick James Wentworth, Viscount Orland of Hanson Hall in Dorset."

Frederick waited, but still no one spoke; suspended in disbelief, they stared at him, waiting for the punch line. "Viscount?" Sophia asked. She laughed, but with a suspicious overtone. "My brother is a viscount?"

"Yes." Frederick never took his eyes off Anne. "I am Viscount Orland. Anne is Viscountess Orland." She still did not move, barely blinking—barely breathing. "Anne?" He patted her hand and smiled. "Say something, Anne."

She swallowed down her incredulity; her lips moved, but no sound came out. Finally, after several failed attempts, she stammered, "Frederick, this is not amusing."

He put one arm around her and placed the proclamation in her hands. "It is so dark in here you probably cannot read the paper you hold, but it says you are married to a viscount. Prince George's man will call on us tomorrow with specific details."

Benjamin began to laugh heartily, and Sophia soon joined in. Anne, understanding that Frederick spoke the truth, exploded with laughter.

Benjamin chortled, "Rear Admiral *and* a title before you are forty. You are one lucky salt, Frederick!"

Frederick burst into laughter and attempted to summarize his conversation with the inebriated prince. "Prince George…said he was…was a four…made him…made him stronger…stronger than Charles…Charles Two…Charles II." The laughter came easily now to all four of them as they each succumbed to his obvious joy. "Charles gave…gave your father…a baronetcy…George gave me twice…twice a baronet…a *viscount!*"

Anne collapsed into his arms, howling with unladylike laughter, burying her head against his chest. "My *father*"—she got the words out—"My *father* will have to bow to you."

Her words brought a loud burst of laughter from Sophia, who buried her fist in her mouth to smother what now was uncontrollable happiness emanating from the coach's passengers. "Both your sisters will have to bow to you, Anne. Will not Elizabeth love that?"

"Elizabeth!" Anne shrieked. "Poor Mary!"

"Mrs. Charles will be green with envy, Anne," Benjamin added. "She will probably take to her bed for a month."

Frederick became more serious. "I could give Edward a better living if he wants it—on our estate."

"Let us wait for that," Anne, ever the reasonable one, said. "We do not know the condition of the estate. It could be run down—near ruin." She wiped the happy tears from her cheeks.

"Even if it is, we will make it work—you and I, Anne; it will be ours. I promised you years ago I would give you all you deserved. We will have a house in London; I will sit in Parliament; I will be the voice of those veterans coming home to England and encourage England to protect *them*, now that they have protected *us*."

"I knew you would find an altruistic reason for our good luck. You will continue to protect your men." Anne stroked his cheek with the back of her hand. Without thinking, she added, "Our baby will have the best of fathers."

"Baby?" Frederick latched onto the word.

Again, everything in the carriage grew stone quiet. Sophia whimpered with expectation.

The light from the lantern suddenly seemed very strong. "Yes," Anne managed to say. Looking into Frederick's eyes, she repeated, "Yes. I am with child."

"When?" he demanded.

"Late summer," she murmured. "I felt the quickening begin earlier in the week."

"You felt our child move?" Frederick's large palm moved to cover her stomach. "Will you tell me when it happens next?"

"Yes."

But he did not hear; he was taking her into her arms and embracing her. "I love you," he murmured in her ear. "I have *always* loved you."

"Forgive us," Anne apologized to the other occupants of the carriage. "We should not share such intimate moments in front of you."

"What is there to forgive?" Benjamin started. "You just learned the most perfect news—you are to be parents."

"Say it again—make it so," Frederick demanded of no one in particular.

Anne clutched at his hand. "We are to have a child, my Love."

Sophia chided in, "A baby of your own, Frederick."

"Maybe a son to inherit your new title," Benjamin teased.

Anne joined in the taunt. "Or a daughter who will wrap you around her finger."

"I do not care which," Frederick declared. "A child! What was it you said, Benjamin? The future is a place for dreams, and those dreams lie in our children." He turned to his wife. "Thank you, Anne. Despite what we earned from the Prince this evening, your gift is greater than any wealth or title. Even if we were in a simple cottage, I would be a rich man at this moment." He pulled her into his embrace, holding Anne's head to his chest where she might hear his heartbeat. He kissed the top of her head.

Sophia resisted the urge to tell Anne "I told you so." Instead, she switched her position and swiveled into Benjamin's arms. "We *are* a happy foursome tonight. The Admiral and I learned today that Mrs. Bradley has accepted our offer for the Oxfordshire property."

Benjamin pulled her closer. "Our man of business saw the property last week and assures us that it meets all our needs. It is about half the size of Kellynch, but it will be roots for Sophie and me and for our daughter."

"And maybe someday for your son," Anne whispered.

Benjamin chuckled. "The Wentworths have settled down, Miss Anne, and we are reaping the benefits."

Anne sleepily laid her head against Frederick's shoulder. "Admiral, we married into the best."

"We did, Miss Anne; we certainly did."

CHAPTER 23

It is not while beauty and youth are thine own,
And thy cheeks unprofaned by a tear,
That the fervor and faith of a soul can be known,
To which time will but make thee more dear.
—Thomas Moore, "Believe Me,
If All Those Endearing Young Charms"

When the footman announced Lord Wallingford, Frederick greeted him in the rented study. The rest of the household prepared for their departure on Saturday. Benjamin and Edward supervised the packing, making sure the belongings, recently merged, were separated along property lines. Anne, Sophie, and Christine paid a final call on Bond Street, securing London's latest fashions.

"Viscount Orland." Wallingford bowed to Frederick upon his entrance.

Frederick laughed lightly. "You are the first to call me such, Lord Wallingford. I am afraid the name still sounds foreign to me. I am barely adjusting to my new rank—a new title may come more slowly." Frederick led the man to matching wing chairs in front of the hearth. "May I offer you refreshments, Sir?"

Wallingford declined with thanks. Then he settled into the chair, laying his papers across his lap. Once settled comfortably, he addressed Frederick again. "As you know, I am here to discuss the property bestowed upon you by our Prince."

"Mrs. Wentworth—the voice of reason in this household—has convinced herself and me, to a certain extent, that this gift from our Prince Regent has some sort of catch. The estate, for example, she believes to be in ruins. Will I need to spend all my prize money bringing it back to life?"

"Your wife is obviously astute, but she is mistaken about the estate. I assure you the property is in repair and productive; it will bring you a comfortable living. The house is immaculate. And the title is sound. You will be the third-highest-ranking family in the area. His Majesty would not put you in the position of having to pull rank on some of the older members of the aristocracy by placing you above them. You would never be accepted in the community in such a case."

After years of reading between the line of military orders, Frederick recognized a stall. "And it is important to his His Majesty that I be accepted in the community?"

"Yes, Admiral, it is," Wallingford acknowledged.

Frederick smiled slightly. "Then I was *chosen* for something? This is not simply a gift from my future king?"

Wallingford gave him a brief nod. "You wish me to be honest?"

"Preferably."

Wallingford nodded and rifled through his stack of papers. "The gift of which you speak is as I described—the house, the land, and the title. And they are all yours. They will remain in your family, but for such an honor, the Crown expects reimbursement."

Frederick's eyebrows shot up, but he forced himself to remain calm. "Please continue."

Wallingford cleared his throat. "You and a few select others were *chosen*, as you say, based on your military careers—on the report of your loyalty to England—but, more importantly, on the report of your leadership—your men's training—the way they respect you and respond to your expertise. His Majesty was not drunk yesterday evening; that was a ruse. Many of the honorees who spoke to the Prince and his guests simply talked of their military experiences."

"He spoke to us of my wife's father," Frederick mused. "In most unflattering terms, I might add."

"Part of the ruse," Wallingford assured him. "The Central Office for Naval Affairs has a plan, approved by the Crown Prince. During this war, a system of smugglers, as well as traitors—many of them

French sympathizers—increased in numbers. Unfortunately, without a war on, the public will look the other way; the conspirators will thrive without censure. We cannot allow that to happen. That is where you and those others *chosen* come in. We need our own system of people in place throughout England to combat whatever is thrown at us.

"Each of those the Central Office identifies will become part of communities where we need them to be our eyes and ears. Some chosen are already established in their home counties. Each recruit to our cause receives *payment* catered to his needs. One, for example, needs money to make his business solvent; another needs a brother saved from transport to Australia. We needed a point man, a person to coordinate our efforts along the Channel. What better way than to reward a war hero with a title and an estate for his wife."

Frederick could not resist asking, "How much does the Central Office know of my personal life?"

Wallingford laughed, recognizing Frederick's solitary temperament. "Probably more than you care for them to, Admiral. They have monitored your career since before you took command of the *Laconia*—probably as far back as your first meeting with Anne Elliot."

Frederick sat forward suddenly. "I will not endanger my wife and our child—not even for a title and an estate," he asserted vehemently.

"Then you are to be a father?" Wallingford noted.

"I am, Sir; please understand Anne is the only person—the most important person in my life." Frederick's voice was firm. "Loyalty to her and our child comes before even loyalty to my country."

"We never doubted that, Lord Orland. In fact, we are banking on your desire to give Mrs. Wentworth what you openly expressed on more than one occasion—to give her what she deserved—a title and an estate."

Frederick asked suddenly, "How does this work?"

"It is uncomplicated, Sir. You and Mrs. Wentworth take possession of Hanson Hall and make it your home. You insert yourself into the local society and become the person everyone trusts—to whom everyone talks freely. We will help you to establish connections with our trusted assistants. We chose Dorset specifically for its location—*close* to Cornwall and its strong smuggling business, but *not* Cornwall, where no one accepts strangers at face value. Lord Orland's demise without an heir left us the perfect opening to establish a presence in the area. Your capture of the American gives the Crown a logical excuse—one that people will easily accept—to reward your efforts with a property and a title."

Frederick had to know. "How dangerous is this?"

Wallingford smiled again. "Not dangerous at all in comparison with the work you have been doing for the Crown until quite recently."

"Honesty, please, Lord Wallington!" Frederick demanded.

Wallingford's genial nature allowed him to easily gain a person's trust; secretly, he admired Frederick for not capitulating to his charm. "Anytime, Admiral, a man faces those who wish to overthrow our government or who wish to defraud businesses, there is danger. But you will not be fighting in hand-to-hand combat; you will be facing down some of the most manipulative people in our realm. You need to depend heavily on your intuition to recognize those who are scheming. We have others in place to capture those involved or to help a person escape. What we do *not* have is a manager—a captain. We strongly believe you are the man for that job."

"What if I refuse?" Frederick asked.

Wallingford picked up his papers. "Then you go on with your life; you draw your half pay until the country calls you to service again. You tell Mrs. Wentworth the Prince took back what he gave you in a drunken stupor."

Frederick retorted, "So if I want the title and the estate for Anne, then I do what is asked of me."

"That pretty much sums up the situation. So, what will it be, Admiral Wentworth?" Wallingford gave him another charming smile.

Frederick sat back, contemplating the situation. He was silent for nearly five minutes—so long Wallingford's practiced confidence took a hit. "May I see the papers you brought?" Frederick finally said.

"Let us move to the desk, Admiral. We may spread out the map of your new property. It has renovated stables and barns and even a system in place for indoor running water. It is very close to the shoreline. Have I mentioned that before?"

"No, Lord Wallingford, you did not." Frederick had made his decision. He would do what he had to do for Anne to have what she deserved.

As Wallingford spread out the map on the desk, he added, "You may not, Wentworth, tell anyone of your arrangement. Not Admiral Croft—and, especially, not Mrs. Wentworth. I will serve as your contact. You will report to me in most of your endeavors; I will apprise you of what you will need to know."

"I am at your service, Lord Wallingford."

"Wentworth, we will get along splendidly." He spread out the rolled paper and began to point to the topographical elements of interest on the map. "The parkland drops down to the sea at this point."

After being sequestered for nearly an hour, reviewing the legal papers involving the Prince's gift and Frederick's service to the Crown, he straightened upon hearing Anne return to the house. "I believe I hear Mrs. Wentworth; my sister, Mrs. Croft; and my brother's wife, Christine Wentworth. I will introduce you to my wife. If we are to be acquaintances, Mrs. Wentworth should become familiar to you."

Wallingford began gathering his papers. "That will not be necessary, Lord Orland."

Before Frederick could respond with the obvious question of "Why not?" Anne lightly tapped on the door and entered without waiting for her husband's bidding. "Frederick," she began, but then froze. She had not expected him to be with someone else. "I apologize; I did not realize you entertained company."

Frederick crossed the room as she spoke and took up a position in front of her. "No, my Dear, I am happy you came in when you did; I would like for you to meet someone." He placed her hand on his arm to walk her toward the desk. Wallingford still had his back to them, gathering the last of the papers dealing with Frederick's service to the government. "This, Anne, is Lord Wallingford; he brought the papers from the Prince regarding the estate. We were just going over them."

Wallingford straightened and slowly turned, the usual charming smile plastered on his face. "Hello, Anne," he said casually.

She gasped. "Marcus? "It *is* you! Marcus Lansing! You assumed your father's title?" She left Frederick looking shocked and offered Wallingford a quick embrace.

Annoyance laced Frederick's next words. "I was unaware, Wallingford, that you were familiar with Mrs. Wentworth."

Anne explained, "Marcus attended a boys' boarding school outside Bath before going off to the university. The girls' school I attended often joined Marcus's school at dances. Plus, our fathers were classmates at Cambridge, we would occasionally visit his family."

"I see," said Frederick. *Why did I trust Wallingford to tell me the whole truth?* It was a lesson he would not forget.

"I was a gangly boy with two left feet. Your wife, Lord Orland, took pity on me and my inability to keep time to the music." Wallingford smiled pleasantly at Anne. "She has always had a kind heart."

As if he needed to stake his claim to her, Frederick took Anne's hand and brought the back of it to his lips. "My wife's heart is the kindest of them all; I am blessed to have her regard."

"Oh, Frederick," she protested half-heartedly. Then Anne focused on something else her former friend said. "Did Marcus say Lord Orland?"

"I did, Mrs. Wentworth." Wallingford gestured to the open map. "I was showing your husband the property. Would you like to see for yourself?"

"Certainly, if you would not mind." She made her way to the desk. "Is our new estate close to yours, Marcus?" Anne asked as she leaned over the paper to analyze it.

"Your estate, Wallingford?" Frederick tried to sound casual, but he seethed with anger at how much the man had withheld.

Marcus Lansing pointed to the shoreline so Anne might see for herself where the property lay before he answered. "You recall, Wentworth, that I mentioned two others in Dorset would outrank you in title and size of their estates."

Frederick responded warily, "Yes."

"I would be one of those two." Wallingford said softly as he pointed out the location of the house in relationship to the parkland for Anne's inspection. "My estate borders Somerset on the other side of the county. As you are now both Wentworth and Orland, I am both Marcus Lansing and Wallingford."

"And would you be number one or number two on the list?"

"Marcus is an earl," Anne interrupted. "As was his father before him."

"An earl?" Frederick said. "Is there a *Countess* Wallingford?"

Marcus laughed. "Sadly, no. I was in service to our Prince until recently. Dorset has an extensive coastline, and the government needed me to help in Lyme and Bath and Swanage. So unfortunately, I neglected my private life. Maybe Mrs. Wentworth will have a soft heart and introduce me to someone as kind as she."

Anne's eyes sparkled. She patted Wallingford's hand as she said, "I will keep an eye out for someone special." Then she turned to Frederick. "You will assume the title you are being offered?"

"I told Lord Wallingford I would." Frederick looked at the man sharply while he continued to address Anne. "Unless you have an objection, my Dear?"

"Oh, no, Frederick; it looks wonderful. May we visit the property one day next week?" Anne rushed to his side again; she looked up at him with those doe-like eyes, which mesmerized him years ago.

Frederick turned to his wife. "Of course, my Love," he agreed. Then he turned to the Prince's representative. "Welcome your newest neighbors, Wallingford." Frederick shook the man's hand, and Anne hugged Wallingford again and kissed him on the cheek.

Wallingford looked very pleased with Frederick's decision. "Your Prince will be most gratified by the news."

★ ★ ★

Although Wallingford offered to escort them on their visit to their new property, Frederick and Anne wanted to see the area for themselves first. Lyme and Bath and even Plymouth outlined the county, but he was as unfamiliar with this part of England as she was.

"It is beautiful, Frederick." Anne clutched his hand as they stood looking out over the bay from one of the highest vantage points above Swanage. They had traveled through hay meadows and wooded areas and the countryside; now, they stood braced against the wind, looking out over a coastal cliff and limestone outcroppings.

Frederick had rented a coach, and they spent the past few days visiting the sights about the county. They had spent much of this day exploring the ruins of Corfe Castle, a medieval castle, which, according to their tour guide, had come to prominence during the time of William the Conqueror. The tour guide had been a font of information, informing them that the castle had been a royal residence during the medieval period; King Edward II had been imprisoned there; and King John had kept his crown jewels there. Henry VII had given the castle to his mother, but Henry VIII reclaimed it when he came to the throne. His daughter, Queen Elizabeth I, had sold the castle to one of her favorite courtiers, Sir Christopher Hatton, who fortified it during England's defense against the Spanish Armada, a fact which had greatly impressed Frederick. The tour guide had gone on to say that Sir John Bankes, the Lord Chief Justice to Charles I, had owned it during the Civil War in the mid-1600s, but the Parliamentary forces had left it in ruins. Now it stood in mute testament to the violence of English history. At the bottom of the hill leading to the shell, picturesque stone houses peppered the village, where Anne had purchased gifts in the local shops for the Admiral and Sophia.

Swanage Bay, four and half miles southeast of the remains, offered their current view. "King Alfred fought a fierce naval battle against the Danes in this very bay in 877," Frederick shared as he laid his arm lightly about her shoulder. "They say Ballard Cliff is very dangerous—the sea quite treacherous in those parts, although I do not know that firsthand, for I never dropped anchor in these waters."

"You know so much of the world," she whispered near his ear as she willingly turned in his arms. "I feel so protected when I am with you."

"Do you, my Love?" he asked as he used his finger to tilt her chin upward where he might kiss her.

Anne knew, instinctively, he still brooded over her recent meeting with Marcus Lansing; she would give him what he needed in terms of reassurance. She snaked her arms around his neck. "I never felt safe any place else; I never felt love any place else. Frederick, you are the only man I could ever love; you must know that."

"I do know, Anne, but I am conceited enough to want to hear it from your mouth." He kissed her again. "What a deliciously beautiful mouth it is." Frederick's lips lingered over hers, running his tongue teasingly along her bottom lip and teeth. "I love drinking from your lips."

When he released her, she turned back to the view. "Fascinating!" Anne reveled in the feel of the wind on her face and in her hair while the sun warmed her. Suddenly, she stiffened in his arms. "Frederick, give me your hand." Curious, he complied. She took his palm and placed it on her abdomen. "Feel."

A tiny foot kicked him. Or was it a miniature hand that punched him? He laughed with delight. The sensation spread through him. "Our child is strong!" he asserted. She laughed and nodded her agreement. "Our love grows within you; it is God's work," he whispered.

"Indeed, my Husband. This baby will know a man of strength, but also a man of love." She kissed his palm.

"Come, Sweetling," he said at last. "Tomorrow we see our new home. I sent word to the staff to expect us in the afternoon."

Frederick scooped Anne into his arms and carried her back to the carriage. "I do believe you have put on weight," he said, pretending to stagger.

She giggled. "You are carrying *two* people, my Husband." Then Anne rested her head on his shoulder and lay comfortably in his arms as he approached the waiting coach. "Our child and our home—I was not certain this day would ever come."

"The day is here, sweet Anne; you will have everything you desire."

★ ★ ★

The parkland surrounding the house stretched out for a half mile before the road beside it dipped down to a wooden bridge crossing one of the many creeks leading to the River Stour. Then the road climbed once more toward the red brick house with elaborate gingerbread trim and rows and rows of windows facing the noonday sun. The sunlight danced on the window panes and turned the streaming rays to fractured colors of the rainbow. The house looked as though it belonged in a fairy tale.

"Welcome to your home, my Love," Frederick announced as the coach crossed the wide cobblestone path leading to the house's entrance. Purple-clad servants hurried down the steps of the entrance to greet them. The coach's steps were lowered, and Frederick climbed out to stand on his own property. He reached in and took Anne's hand, guiding her to his side. "Viscountess Orland," he spoke softly "your new house awaits."

"Marcus was right," she whispered, "it looks sound."

"Hopefully," he murmured close to her ear, "the rooms are not gutted."

A stately butler in black came forward. "Viscount Orland. Viscountess Orland." He bowed and then gestured toward the house. "My name is Mr. Smythe; I am in charge of the household staff. If you will follow me, I will show you about the house."

"Thank you, Mr. Smythe." Frederick acknowledged several of the other waiting staff with a nod of his head. "Lady Orland and I appreciate your attention to detail." As they followed the man through the entrance, Frederick informed the man, "Today, we want simply to become familiar with the house and the immediate grounds. Tomorrow, I would like to speak with the steward. Is he available?"

"I will send word, Lord Orland." The butler paused before speaking, "May I say, Sir, we are happy to have a new viscount in residence; it has been nearly a year; Lord Orland, we understand you are a decorated military man."

"My husband is a Rear Admiral of the White," Anne blurted out. "You may tell the staff their new master is a national hero—a man who served England for more than a decade. They have much of which to be proud."

"My wife," he half laughed as he handed his outer coat to one of the waiting footmen, "is my staunchest admirer."

Mr. Smythe smiled, nodded his head, and indicated the foyer. "As one can see, the house is in good repair. Madam, would you like me to show you and Lord Orland the rooms?"

"I hope it will not offend you, Mr. Smythe, but we would prefer to explore the house on our own. Please instruct the household staff to go about their regular duties. We are not here to censure—only to learn what our new home has to offer."

"Very well, Madam; I will have the luggage brought in and placed in the master chambers. If you or Lord Orland need anything, simply pull the cord." With that, the butler disappeared, and several other servants scrambled to their stations.

Frederick offered Anne his arm. "Are you ready, Mrs. Wentworth?"

Anne gave him her most beguiling smile. "I prefer the name Wentworth to all the other names to which I have been addressed in my life." She took his arm as they strolled into the room on their right, and they took their first look at what would be their abode for the rest of their lives.

"It is the name you were born to share." His breath caressed her cheek. "And this, Sweetling is the home we were born to share."

"Our child will inherit this estate, Frederick. It is our future; the Wentworth name will be a part of England's history. Your dedication—your determination—created the opportunity for us to shape our identity. Let us make the Wentworth name stand for all that is best in English society."

He gently guided her into his embrace. "We will act with decorum, with compassion, with empathy, and with kindness. You, my Love, will be a model of English grace and womanhood. I will try to live up to your image of the man to whom you gave your heart."

"There is no one above you, my Husband; you are already the best man I have ever known. You deal with people honestly and honorably; that is a very rare quality." She stroked the underside of his jawline with her fingertips. "Now, your child and I," she teased him, "wish to see our new home. I need to set up a proper nursery. This is a very active child." Anne gently touched her stomach. "I have the feeling he will be a handful, and I will not have a chance to catch up if I procrastinate now."

"He?" Frederick asked with amusement.

Anne turned to take his hand. "Or she." Dropping his hand and taking a few steps away from him, she looked back over her shoulder and added, "Or they."

"No *theys*, Anne Wentworth," he warned as he caught up with her. "One crew member at a time, do you hear me?" But he beamed with happiness. "I love you, Mrs. Wentworth," he said as he bent to kiss her lips.

When they separated, Anne whispered, "Let us find the master bedroom."

He murmured huskily, "It probably would not be a good first impression if the servants found us sharing an intimate moment, would it?"

"Probably not." Anne took his hand. "Let us go and claim this house as our own."

CHAPTER 24

And in Life's noisiest hour,
There whispers still the ceaseless Love of Thee,
The heart's Self-solace and soliloquy.
—Samuel Taylor Coleridge, "The Presence of Love"

Over the next two months, they established themselves in the community. Having been raised in Kellynch Hall, Anne understood the running of a household. And so she ran Hanson Hall with sensibleness, authority, and compassion. Frederick reflected that if Anne had been the oldest sister, instead of Elizabeth, Sir Walter might never have had to leave Kellynch Hall. Of course, that would have meant that Sophia and Benjamin would never have come to Somerset, and he would never have returned and found Anne. On that count, Frederick thanked his lucky stars to have a father as inept as Sir Walter.

For his part, Frederick managed quite well on the land. Although he had spent most of his adult life on the sea, he understood hard work and how to command men without domination. He learned quickly in whom he could place his confidence in dealing with supplies—with materials—with construction. And Frederick judiciously placed men whom he knew he could trust in positions on the estate. He learned much from them. When Edward and Christine decided they would remain in Shropshire, he offered the living to Lieutenant Avendale, who jumped at the chance to be closer to his wife's home of Bristol. Lieutenant Harwood joined his staff as an apprentice to the estate's steward, Mr. Lawrence. The steward had informed Frederick the first day they met that he wished to pension out soon, and as Harwood's father had held a similar position in West Sussex, his former lieutenant had some knowledge of the responsibilities involved.

Two of his former able seamen became cottagers on his estate, and he found a like situation for another on a neighboring property. As news got out of how he had helped those who had served with him previously, Frederick regularly received pleas from men who had returned from military service but found no employment. As often as he could, he located places for shopkeepers, farmers, or tradesmen, especially if they had served valiantly. Dr. Laraby, for example, opened an office in Hurn with Frederick's financial assistance. Occasionally, a shirker would beseech him for help; in those cases, he politely replied that he knew of nothing available for the man at the time. He would not help those who had shunned their duties aboard ship. He now had more than a dozen men strategically positioned throughout the county whom he implicitly trusted.

With each placement, when his former crewmember professed gratitude and offered Frederick his allegiance, he gave him a speech: "I may be Viscount Orland to everyone else, but to you, I am still *Captain Wentworth*. All I ask is for you to help me become a part of this community. As a titled gentleman, I am responsible for the lives of many people in the area. If you hear of anything out of the ordinary, I ask you to let me know, no matter how insignificant it may seem. If you learn of a tradesman who cheats his customers, I want to know. If you find a group of men up to no good, please send me word. If you do this, you repay me for my kindness. You will make my life on the land as productive as you did with my tenure on the sea." Each man implicitly trusted his captain and readily agreed—his was a small price to pay for the respectability and the manhood he gave them.

Wallingford called upon them several times and gave Frederick tours of the area, introducing him to people in place to aid the British government's cause. Frederick listened carefully and made his own evaluations. Since the day Wallingford revealed having known Anne previously, Frederick had held back in believing Marcus Lansing completely, possibly out of jealousy or possibly out of something else he could not explain. Wallingford appeared to have Frederick's best interests at heart, but he knew that appearances could be deceiving.

★ ★ ★

Frederick and Anne volunteered to host the community picnic for the village of Hurn's annual Midsummer's Day celebration. At the picnic, they would meet many whom they did not know. People would judge them by how the Wentworths performed on this particular occasion. Frederick held no doubts Anne would excel in every manner—the woman possessed a way about her. Anyone who had ever met *his Anne* fell in love with her gentle nature. He worried more about his own acceptance. At sea, Frederick had understood the natural practice of taking orders from those above and giving orders to those of lower ranks. In local issues, he found those in power were more ruthless than any pirate or mercenary he had ever met. The business of politics required him to be genial and pleasant to people for whom he cared little. Idle banter was dull to him; Frederick considered himself a man of action, not social tedium; the game played by those in power certainly tried his patience.

Since he had agreed to Wallingford's proposition, Frederick had spent many hours analyzing his own disposition. Essentially, he was a loner; perhaps that was why he had been so successful as a naval officer. He had learned the proper way—the naval way—to handle most situations. But with strangers, he generally held back. It was only with Anne that he had never known a facade—only with Anne had he felt comfortable from the beginning. Self-sufficiency highlighted his life—his haven of strength. When he looked at Edward and Sophia, he saw the same stubbornness of spirit, which made him determined to mold Fate—to cheat it, actually. Making small talk with total strangers was, for Frederick, exquisite torture. He did not look forward to the hours of playing the perfect host.

Anne suddenly appeared before him, clasping the bodice of her dress to her bosom. "Would you lace me?" she asked charmingly.

"Madam, where is your maid?" As he questioned her, he took up the ribbons and began to slip the ends through the eyelets.

"I married you. Why do I need a maid?" She glanced over her

shoulder at him.

He continued to crisscross the laces, and then he tied the ends of the ribbons. "You are looking well, my Love."

"I am looking pleasingly plump is what you mean," Anne corrected.

Frederick smiled wickedly before asserting, "Pregnancy becomes you, Lady Orland." He pulled her into his embrace. "Your curves have become more—*curvaceous.*"

"You like resting your head on my very ample bosom," she teased.

Never tiring of her closeness, Frederick bent to kiss her. Holding only inches from her mouth, he continued to nibble on her bottom lip. "I never previously complained about the size of your breasts, my Love. I found them quite enticing, in fact."

"You are such a cad, Frederick Wentworth!" Anne turned around to kiss him before drawing away from him. "You look very handsome today, my Love."

Frederick pulled at his shirt's neckline. "And I thought that full dress uniforms were uncomfortable!"

Anne chuckled. "You look quite dashing in your waistcoat and white cravat."

"Are you flirting with me, Mrs. Wentworth?" he asked as he reached for his handkerchief and watch fob.

Anne twirled once to let the movement of her dress catch his attention. "I might be, my Lord. Is it working?"

Frederick's eyes followed her as she made her way to the door. "If you, my Viscountess, wish to know whether your feminine charms still have power over me, let me show you up close and personal." He strode towards her before coming up short, posing over her, forcing Anne to look up in his eyes. "You, Anne Elliot Wentworth, have only to smile at me or raise your eyes to mine or even walk into a room, and I am yours completely. I lost my heart to you long ago." His finger traced a line from her temple to her lips. "I will come to you more often than you may want—yet, I can do nothing less for you possess me body and soul."

"I choose to take my comfort in your arms, my Husband; I never suspected love required such complete surrender, but I gladly run the white banner up the flag pole of life and turn over my whole self to you. This child and I are blessed to find the love in your heart. My present and future are forever bound to you."

Frederick forced himself to breathe. It struck him once again how lonely he had been all those years without her. He turned to offer her his elbow. "Let us go meet our neighbors, Lady Orland."

She lightly placed her hand on his forearm. "Of course, Lord Orland."

The earlier overcast skies had cleared by noon. People from all walks of life peppered the lawn with their blankets and their games, content to enjoy the lovely weather and to see the new viscount and viscountess. All sorts of foodstuffs covered the linen-lined tables. Although each family had contributed at least one dish to the assortment, the bulk of the offerings came from Hanson Hall: roast beef, cheese, fresh fruit, roasted rabbit and pheasant, dark bread, boiled carrots and potatoes, seed-cakes, berry tarts, and lemonade. Anne had even hired a quartet of fiddlers to provide music throughout the day.

"Lady Orland." One of the cottagers approached her as Anne made her way down one of the slopes. The woman curtsied, a feat hard to accomplish on an incline. "Me name be Mrs. Miller. Me family it lives past the second hedgerow."

Anne reached out and touched the woman's arm. "Mrs. Miller, the Viscount and I are pleased that you are here. I hope you find everything satisfactory. As this is our first Midsummer's Day celebration, we were unsure as to the traditions."

Mrs. Miller flushed. "Ma'am, it be one of the best we seen. Me family just wishes to say we be happy you and Lord Orland come to stay. Me be a midwifin' if you need me for the babe."

"Thank you, Mrs. Miller. Thank you so much." Anne started on her way, but the woman had one more thing to say.

"We be hearin' the new Master, he be a hero. That be true?"

"Lord Orland is a Rear Admiral in the British Navy. George IV awarded him a title because of his actions in the war." As she spoke, Anne's eyes automatically searched the crowd for Frederick. "My husband is an honorable and brave man." Her gaze found Frederick's back.

"The Master also be a hero by makin' a difference to some," Mrs. Miller continued. "We be judgin' how he treat us—those who work for him. He deal honestly with me man—first time in many years. We be glad you and he and this babe come so we have a place. None of us be wantin' to leave the land. We be workin' hard for him; you tell your man—the Master—that."

The woman's words humbled Anne. "I assure you, Mrs. Miller, Lord Orland will be moved by your sentiments; he is a man who accepts responsibility seriously. You tell Mr. Miller and the others that if we make mistakes or if there are things we need to address, they need to speak to Lord Orland or to Mr. Lawrence. He will listen; he may not be able to solve every issue, but my husband will deal with them fairly."

"Yes, Mistress Orland." The woman made another awkward curtsy and then moved back to her family.

Frederick walked the grounds for the third time, stopping to speak to as many people as he could: cottagers, shopkeepers, tradesmen, and landed gentry. With each, he tried to learn something about the person—the name, especially; he had learned long ago that being able to call a sailor by his name was the start of establishing a relationship of mutual respect. He watched his wife orchestrate the food and the games. It was time, he decided, to insist that Anne find her own patch of shade. Going on six months of pregnancy, she had no business overtaxing her energies. On his most recent pass through the crowd, he had recruited Mr. Harwood and Mrs. Avendale to take over some of the responsibilities.

"Captain," Mr. Avendale said to Frederick as his former commanding officer circumnavigated the terrace, "may I speak to you?"

"Certainly." Frederick walked Mr. Avendale back into the house, where they might talk privately. Once alone, he asked, "What may I do for you, Lieutenant?"

"When you gave me this position, Sir, you asked me to keep my ears open and to let you know if I heard anything unusual."

Frederick stiffened. "Do you have something for me?" He motioned Avendale to a nearby chair and took a seat himself.

"Day before yesterday, Mrs. Thomason came to see me. Her brother, Jatson Laurie, has fallen in with some men whom Mrs. Thomason believes are unsavory characters. Anyway, she wanted me to intervene with Mr. Laurie. From what I understand, Laurie is involved in some kind of smuggling ring. Many small-time smugglers sold brandy and cigars and such taken from French ships during the war. The local law officials have looked the other way for much of this trade, but Laurie appears to be involved in something bigger. If my limited sources are correct, something big is going down in a warehouse outside Studland this evening. Most people in this part of the county travel from here to Wimborne Minster for the celebratory Midsummer's Day fireworks. The ports and the warehouses are likely to be deserted."

"Do we know in what these men are involved?" Frederick steepled his fingers as he tried to come up with a plan.

Avendale hesitated. "Mrs. Thomason seems to think her brother might be involved in something dangerous. He was told to bring a gun. No one would shoot someone over some cigars, no matter how fine they might be. It has to be something more lucrative than that, Captain."

Frederick paused for several moments, considering whom he should trust. Finally, he spoke. "Avendale, I need for you to do something for me. I cannot be seen contacting our men, so I want you to find Mr. Harwood and tell him what you just told me. I want all our former crew members to meet me at eleven tonight on the north side of the Studland Bay warehouse district. If they need horses, have Harwood make arrangements to use horses from my stable; tell each of them to come prepared to fight."

"Yes, Sir." Avendale moved to follow Frederick's orders.

"Michael," Frederick called after him, "you are not to come with us. I need someone whom the locals will trust, and I will not ask a curate to pick up a gun."

★ ★ ★

Luckily for Frederick, the picnic exhausted Anne, so she retired early. She fell asleep quickly—but Frederick lay beside her, wide awake, brooding about what was to come, what could happen that evening.

He had made a commitment in exchange for an estate and a title for Anne's sake; but—insofar as it was possible—he would fulfill his commitment on *his* terms. Tonight, he would lead his men into the unknown. He had never felt so uncertain—not since his first naval command mission. *Am I asking my men to do the impossible? What if someone dies?*

He slipped out of bed sometime later. Now, he stood looking down at the sleeping figure of the woman who owned his heart. "I love you, my Anne," he whispered, before quietly leaving her chamber for his dressing room. He dressed in casual attire—breeches, boots, a cambric shirt open at the neck, and a greatcoat.

Frederick and Matthew Harwood left the estate via horseback in time to reach their meeting point long before his men. After serving under him for several years, Harwood knew Frederick *needed* to assess the scene prior to the others' arrival. After riding in silence for nearly a half hour, Harwood finally asked, "Do we have any idea what we face tonight?"

"If you ask whether I have thought this through, I assure you I have, Lieutenant." That was all he said, because his plan was woefully lacking in specifics. Tonight he would learn firsthand how to be an agent for the government. He wondered—too late—whether he should have contacted Marcus Lansing, after all. "Will the others join us?"

"The men will be there, Captain—I guess I should say Admiral—or Lord Orland?" Harwood's voice betrayed his nervousness.

Wentworth mentally cringed with the knowledge that his men would put their lives on the line simply because he asked them to. "I prefer Captain to the other titles; it seems a more comfortable fit."

Finally arriving in Studland, Frederick and Harwood made their way through the deserted streets and alleys surrounding the warehouses. They left their horses tied up in the wooded area outside the village and moved through the shadows. As predicted, villagers throughout the county had celebrated during the day, so anyone who might have legitmate business in the warehouse district at this hour was home sleeping it off. However, when they spotted the warehouse in question, several men buzzed about it. Two stood guard at the entrance while the others unloaded barrels from wagons, evidently cargo from the ship sitting in Studland Bay.

"Are they armed?" Harwood whispered from their vantage point between two buildings facing the warehouse.

Frederick nodded slightly and put away his spyglass. "The two out front are. We should assume the others are as well." He paused for a moment before continuing. "I need for you to sneak back to the horses and meet the men. I am going around to the back to see if I can get a better look. If I am caught, you are not to stage a rescue; I will not have men's lives put in danger to save me. You will ride hard to find Lord Wallingford and tell him what I did, and he will know what to do. Do you understand me on this, Harwood?"

"Yes, Sir—I understand." Frederick heard the man's breath catch in his words.

"If I think we have a chance to stop this, I will follow you to meet the men. Now, move out, Harwood."

Hesitating briefly, Harwood turned to leave. "Be careful, Captain. Your missus needs you."

"I am fully aware of that, Lieutenant. Now, hurry."

★ ★ ★

The ease with which he managed to find his way to the back of the warehouse surprised Frederick. He had expected it to be better protected, especially considering the cargo was probably illegal, *but the gang foresaw no trouble*. The men separated the items into four distinct areas—just as someone might divide furniture for the rooms of a house.

He worked his way through the shadows. His height made it difficult to secure places to hide, as the cargo was not stacked. He hunched over to hurry from one area to another, trying to get close enough to survey the unloading. He wanted to know what the thieves moved and how much resistance his men might face. Yet, afraid to get any closer, Frederick hid behind some barrels near the steps, slipping back into the orifice beneath the stairs.

Hearing the planks above his head creak, Frederick moved so that he was flush against the back wall, pulling his dark coat about him to make himself less visible in the dim shadows. Then people—three, from what he could tell—began to descend the steps slowly—first one and then another and then another.

Not even breathing, he demanded silence, although his pulse thrummed in his ears, and Frederick wondered how the men could not hear it. He wanted desperately to know who these men were, but he forced himself to remain patient and just watch and listen.

"The pictures go to my special client," a man in a dark gray coat spoke as he stepped to a lower level. "He pays well, and we can use the money to buy additional hulls."

"What of the brandy?" Another man posed on the upper steps. All Frederick could see of him was his boots. Frederick sank even farther back against the wall, trying to make himself as small as possible. He could not confront these men alone; he must learn as much as he could before going for help.

A local, speaking in a Dorsetshire accent, descended next. "The brandy be for sale to pay me men."

"Is everything else in place?" The first man now stood so close to him that Frederick feared he would turn to see him hiding in the shadows.

"Lord Cochrane understands we do this for him. He sent specific instructions." With that, the men began to walk toward the warehouse's main opening, and Frederick slowly peeled himself off the wall, preparing to move out the way he had come in. He wished he knew more, but he could not risk staying any longer. He rushed from one cluster of barrels to another, pausing only long enough to allow guards or workers to pass. Finally reaching the door, he edged it open, barely wide enough to slip his body through. He did not relax until he was well away from the building.

Frederick circled the area, coming out on a different pathway, before setting out for the meeting place on foot. Proceeding through the wooded farmland surrounding the village, he followed the hedgerows rather than cutting directly across the fields. It was a clear night; even without a full moon, he could see quite easily. Arriving near the copse of trees hiding his men, he let out the pre-arranged whistle before entering the wooded circle and heard Harwood whistle in return. All the men—his men—waited for him. Harwood rushed forward to meet him. "What did you find, Captain?" The other men closed ranks to hear his story.

"First," Frederick began, "I want each of you to know what I am asking you to do is dangerous. Also, this is not like when we took ships and shared prize money. With this mission, you simply get what little I can give you; so if you want out, no one will consider it a shame, for you have already served your country and me most faithfully."

"We follow you, Captain." Harwood spoke first, but the others echoed his sentiments.

"Then this is what I know. A group of smugglers are, as I speak, moving cargo into a warehouse, evidently to separate it before distributing it to different interested parties. There must be four distinct types of commodities—for they divide the containers as such. I overheard some men speaking of pictures, and I observed large wooden crates, which must contain framed artwork, probably smuggled out of France to satisfy a member of the aristocracy. They also spoke of brandy, and I noted appropriate-sized casks in which, I suspect, the brandy can be found."

"What of the other items, Captain?" John Langley, his former quartermaster and one of the men he placed in a shopkeeper's position, asked the question all of them were thinking.

"Truthfully, Langley, I do not know. Barrels of some sort were being unloaded, but no markings showed. And something smelled like rotten fish or rotten eggs, but I do not know what it was."

Harwood asked, "How many men?"

Frederick mentally counted the men he had seen. "A half

dozen moved the supplies in and out; I counted four guards—two front and two on the sides; and there were three others—those are the ones I overheard speaking about the brandy and the crates."

"Thirteen men then!" George Shipley, a lately minted midshipman, replied, his tone more forceful than his words.

Frederick looked around the group to assure that they each understood what he said. "Again, what I ask of each of you is not a requirement to maintain the position in which I placed you. I will *not* force anyone to become a part of this. These men we seek betray our government, making a quick profit at the expense of hard-working people like yourselves. They set themselves above the law. My interference will make some enemies—those who wish to forge an alliance with France being among them. If you come with me tonight, you will be a part of something great. We have left our ship, but the battle for a free England still remains. Yet, each of you must decide whether you wish to fight. As for myself, I fight for my wife and my unborn child; I want them to live in a country where such crimes are not tolerated by a titled man or a tradesman or a farmer." Frederick's expression became grim.

There was silence, and then John Langley asked, "How do we proceed, Captain?"

"First, we need a distraction to divert the attention of the guards in front while the majority of us slip into the back of the warehouse."

"Drunks are common along the docks and in the warehouse district," a mast captain added. "One of us could be obnoxiously drunk."

Langley thought out loud, "We need to recruit some women to help us next time. A woman could pretend to be a lady of the evening and distract the guards."

Frederick raised an eyebrow. "Next time," he said. "But what about tonight, gentlemen? Who among you can be the most obnoxious?"

All eyes immediately fell on Christian Hollmes, a tall, broad-shouldered, lean, but muscular, man, with calloused hands and tanned skin. "I guess I am your man, Captain," he said jovially as the others slapped him on the back.

"Good," Wentworth commented. "You are large enough to handle any trouble once we are discovered. We are counting on you, Hollmes."

"Do not worry, Captain," he assured.

"Gentlemen, we set sail in unknown waters—very dangerous waters. Think of your first boarding of an enemy ship. None of us knew what to do the first time. It will be the same tonight. Be safe—take no undue chances. Capture whom you can, but do not follow a man into the night—into the unknown. I want no casualties. None of us has spent much time battling the enemy on land. Let us learn from tonight's encounter."

As he led the men back along the hedgerows toward the warehouse, Frederick thought about why he was undertaking this perilous mission. He desired a proper home for *his Anne* and their child. Also, he had made a promise to the British government, and he was a man of his word. Further, he *hated* being under Wallingford's watchful eye; if he must act in the name of the government, he would do it on his terms. Finally, he took responsibility as Viscount Orland. All seemed logical reasons—rationales for his actions—but were they the whole truth? In reality, he did not know.

CHAPTER 25

Now thou hast loved me one whole day,
Tomorrow when thou leav'st, what wilt thou say?
Wilt thou then antedate some new-made vow?
Or say that now
We are not just those persons which we were?
—John Donne, "Woman's Constancy"

When the men signaled to one another that they were in position to enter the back of the warehouse, Hollmes—shirttail out of his breeches, face smudged with soot, and ale obtained from a flask Shipley carried, splashed on his person—staggered forward out of the shadows. He greeted the two men standing guard. Everyone else seemed to be inside. "Hey, Boys, what be here?" Hollmes called out as he lunged against the wagon, pretending to be barely able to stand.

The two guards searched the darkness to see if he came alone. "Nothin' for your concern. Be gone with ya'," the larger one warned while they both brought up their guns, prepared to deal with a drunken intrusion.

"Ya' got drink in there, Boys?" Hollmes staggered closer.

"We be tellin' ya' no more. Ya' need to be leavin'," the man's tone became more demanding.

Hollmes plastered on his silliest smile as he stepped forward one more time. "Share ye drink with ole Toby. I be needin' a drink bad."

The smaller guard reached out to steady Hollmes's movements. Chuckling lightly, he spoke a little less intimidatingly, "Ye be drunk enough, ole Toby."

Realizing he would never have a better opportunity, Hollmes moved quickly. Grabbing both men by their necks, with one swift, powerful thrust, he clanged their heads together, dazing them both.

He let the smaller man slide to his knees while he turned and delivered a well-placed upper cut to the larger of the two. A sharp crack of the guard's jaw told Hollmes he would have no more worries from him for a while. The smaller man then staggered to his feet, preparing to shoot Hollmes in the back. Used to hand-to-hand combat during boardings, in which the enemy came from all directions at once, Hollmes spun, leg extended, and took out the second guard's footing. Then he hauled the man back up against the warehouse wall and applied a profound pressure to the man's neck. In a few seconds, the guard's limp body slumped against him. Quickly, he moved to drag the bodies out of the light in case someone else came along.

In the back of the warehouse, as Christian Hollmes stepped from the shadows, Frederick, Harwood, Langley, Shipley, and three others slipped through the rear door. Frederick placed a man at each entrance to prevent anyone escaping, and then he sent Timothy Smallridge and Lucas Kendrick to the building's roof to work their way down from the upper floor. They were his best climbers on board *The Resolve*—no rope or ladder ever stopped either of them.

Hearing the commotion in the front, several men rushed for the main entrance, but Hollmes managed to swing the door shut just as they reached it. In the confusion of their attempted escape, they did not check to see if the door was bolted closed; instead, en masse, they immediately turned toward the other exit, running to find safe refuge.

From his vantage point behind a cluster of barrels, Frederick waited until the group was center court in the warehouse before signaling his men, and then they all stood, guns pointed at the retreating thieves. "Stand and deliver," Shipley demanded, as the robbers skidded to a halt and prepared to defend themselves.

A few of them foolishly reached for their weapons before realizing men with guns, loaded and cocked, surrounded them. A man near the front slowly put his hands in the air. "Who be you?" he demanded, although he evidently planned to surrender without a fight. Frederick recognized the voice as being that of the local he had heard on the steps.

"Interested citizens," Shipley responded as they edged from behind the barrels to take the guns held by those they surrounded.

The man leading the group pointed at the cargo. "Interested in what?" He grinned; a flash of movement in his eyes told Frederick that he planned something.

Without speaking, Frederick motioned ever so slightly with his head, and Harwood nodded in response. They both stepped to the back of the group and took up positions holding hostages to persuade those in the front to abandon any thoughts of a fight. When the group leader noted their changed circumstances, he shoved his hands a bit higher. "How 'bout some Frenchie brandy, Boys?"

Shipley, by silent consent, still spoke for Frederick's men. Wentworth did not wish to appear to be in charge. "We will help ourselves, But first, where are the rest of your men?"

The same man spoke for the smugglers. "What other men?' He kept his eyes noncommittal.

Shipley knew now the man spoke half-truths. They stood facing each other—sizing each other up. Shipley shot a glance toward Frederick; he caught it and raised an eyebrow. Then Frederick took the gun he held next to the temple of his hostage and pushed it hard against his head, as if he planned to pull the trigger. The hostage gulped out the word, "Upstairs."

"Shut up!" the gang's leader ordered.

"Ye shut up!" the scruffy-faced thief shot back.

Frederick motioned with his gun for Harwood to follow him, and they both began to edge their way up the stairs. Meanwhile, Shipley motioned to the others to tie up the ones they had caught. Moving cautiously forward and letting his gun hand lead, Frederick's mind remained alert although his chest felt tight with dread—one small step at a time, ever closer to the upper levels. He knew by now Kendrick and Smallridge had to be in place and were probably herding those remaining in the warehouse toward him.

But when the attack came, it still took him by surprise. A club came down hard on his forearm, and the gun skittered across the floor. With his other arm, Frederick reached up to grasp his opponent's jacket to try to pull the man off balance. In doing so, they became entangled, and they began to wrestle, tumbling down the short flight of stairs. Frederick sensed, rather than felt, Harwood jump clear of this struggle, as well as a perfectly tossed cask of brandy smashed and dripping onto the packed-dirt floor. Banging first against the wall and then against the railing, Frederick held on until they came crashing down in a heap of bone and muscle, slamming into the hardened ground, which served as the floor of the building. Somehow, he ended up on top of his attacker, and he heard the air rush from the man's lungs as Frederick's weight hit him full force. Jostling to gain the advantage, Frederick pulled his knee up to first strike the man between his outstretched thighs and then to kneel on the man's chest, the packed weight of his body pushing down as his knee came under the man's chin and cut off his air supply. "Move, bastard, and I will kill you," he growled close to the man's face.

Sounds of gunfire from above sent Harwood scrambling up the steps, but moments later he reappeared, leading at gunpoint another of the gang of smugglers ahead of him. Kendrick and Smallridge followed, and Frederick gave a silent prayer that all of his men were well. The rest of his men appeared; Hollmes shoved his two captors toward the others. "Are you all right, Sir?" Harwood asked, close to him.

"Yes," he whispered, aware of his racing pulse. "Let us lock these men up until we see what we have." Frederick rolled off the man and landed in the puddle of brandy.

They pushed all twelve into a small toolshed inside the warehouse. "Barely enough room to stand!" the men complained, but Frederick's crew turned a deaf ear. Prisoners secured at last, his men began to survey the accumulated goods. Breaking open one of the casks of brandy, they found cups enough for all of them to share before taking an inventory of what they had recovered.

Frederick and Harwood moved to a table to find any paperwork associated with the haul. Frederick's arm throbbed from the pain of the blow, but he simply gritted his teeth. He buttoned his greatcoat to chest level and slid his arm through the opening, bracing the arm to his body, like a sling.

Harwood teased, "You remind me of Napoleon."

"No Bonaparte jokes, if you please, Mr. Harwood," Frederick warned. "I keep telling you I am too tall."

Frederick poured himself one drink; tossed it back, and then poured another to steady his nerves before returning to the task at hand. After a celebratory toast, his men went to work examining what they had found. A smooth brandy was a hot commodity in those parts. The men reported the number of casks at fifty, counting the one from which they already drunk and the one with its contents sloshed on the floor. Opening the crates, Frederick recognized the works of Jacques-Louis David, the dazzling costumes and jewelry fashionable at the court of Napoleon Bonaparte clearly evident in each portrait. Another crate held work from François Gérard, known for his portrait of Madame de Talleyrand. "I prefer landscapes," Harwood commented when the man held up the painting for Frederick to see. "What will we do with those?" he asked as Frederick indicated for the men to replace the piece in the crate.

"Maybe I should make a contribution to my Prince—repayment for the gift of my title."

Finally, the men came to the barrels at the far end of the warehouse. "Whew! These surely stink, Captain, even before we have taken the lids off," Shipley sang out.

"What is in them is all I want to know," Frederick responded. "Leave them capped after that."

They found metal bars to break the seals. Frederick and Harwood ambled over to take a look at the first one, opened by John Langley. "What the hell is that?" Harwood mumbled as he dipped his finger into a black liquid with the consistency of a thick pudding.

"Coal tar," Cavton Harris asserted as he touched the liquid.

Frederick turned on the man. "Are you sure, Cav?"

"Positive, Captain."

Langley wiped his hand on his pants. "Why would someone

smuggle in coal tar?"

"It has lots of uses," Harris assured them, "but why steal it, and why in such huge quantities?"

Frederick waved them on. "Let us see what stinks so badly."

They had barely cracked the lid on one of the other barrels before they all reached for handkerchiefs to cover their noses and mouths. "I—I am afraid to ask," Frederick stammered as he backed away from the cylinder.

Tears coming to his eyes, Shipley quickly returned the lid to its place. "Pray tell, *what* is that?" He gasped and coughed to clear his throat.

"Fire and brimstone," Tweed Swift, a former gunnery mate, stated flatly.

"Explain," Frederick demanded.

"Sulfur, Sir. I know the smell well. The Bible calls it brimstone; therefore, the phrase 'fire and brimstone.' It was a favorite saying when we loaded the guns on *The Resolve*. Sulfur is an ingredient in gunpowder."

Harwood moved up beside him. "Again, why would anyone smuggle sulfur? It makes no sense."

"Harwood, did you ever hear of Captain Sir Thomas, Lord Cochrane?" Frederick's mind raced through the possibilites.

Harwood laughed good-naturedly. "Who has not heard of *Le Loup des Mers*, the Sea Wolf? With the frigate *Pallas*, he alone earned seventy-five thousand pounds sterling in prize money. But Lord Cochrane is in gaol, Sir—part of the London Stock Exchange scandal, a little over a year ago—lost his knighthood—dismissed from the Royal Navy—everything."

"Then tell me why I overheard those men tonight talking of corresponding with Lord Cochrane?" Frederick muttered, exceedingly unsettled.

"A different Lord Cochrane—I do not know, Captain." Harwood looked concerned. "If the thieves know Cochrane, it has something to do with the sulfur and the coal tar. It is not likely a man in gaol has use for fancy portraits or French brandy."

Swift added grimly, "A man could use the sulfur and coal tar if he wanted a big fire or a big explosion."

"Big . . . like a wall . . . or building . . . or a ship?" Frederick tried to understand the scope of what his man proposed.

"Certainly like a ship. There is enough coal tar and sulfur here to bring down Whitehall or, at least do heavy damage to the War Offices. Saint James even if one wanted to hurt the king. Maybe they planned on breaking Lord Cochrane out of gaol." Swift thought the idea absurd but a possibility.

Harwood's tone grew much harder—more distant. "What do you want to do about all this, Captain?"

Frederick had formulated a plan while hiding in the warehouse. "I do not want anyone to get his hands on what we have here, especially considering the dire consequences of mixing these two elements together. Could we load the sulfur and coal tar back onto the wagons and store them in the barn in the north pasture? No one goes up there this time of year. We will find a way of disposing of the barrels—a few at a time. Harville could use some of each in his furniture business. Molten sulfur makes decorative inlays."

Swift suggested, "We could spread some of the sulfur on the land. It is a slow-release fertilizer—best when it is wet, though."

"What else?" Frederick wondered.

"Me Ma uses pure powdered sulfur as a medicinal tonic and as a way to clean out the bowels," Kendrick thought out loud.

"Good," Frederick noted. "We will figure out ways to get rid of it, little by little—make sure, however, it is not used for gunpowder. What about the coal tar?"

"Besides being used in dye treatments for fabrics, a person can use it to seal roofs—makes a watertight seal."

The ideas came fast. "My grandmother used it for any skin irritation. The woman swore by it."

"Put some in paint. It helps to make the wall warmer. The cottagers could use it before the winter comes to keep out the cold."

"All right," Frederick interrupted. "We have ideas; we do not need to settle it all tonight, but we do need to move these barrels before we turn those men over to the authorities. We will leave two of the paintings and some casks of the brandy as evidence. If the gang planned a jailbreak, they will not divulge the presence of the sulfur or the coal tar. Each of you take three casks of brandy. Sell it about the country or drink it. I will not ask what you do with it. However, you should be able to get a pretty penny for them at some of the inns, if that is what you choose."

"Thank you, Captain," Shipley spoke for all of them.

Frederick's unnerving smile reappeared. "You might as well be paid for your work somehow. Now let us hurry; we should all be home in bed before dawn."

Two hours later, Harwood took the reins of one wagon and Shipley took the reins of the other. "We will all meet you at the north barn tomorrow before dusk to unload. Simply park the wagon out of sight," Frederick ordered. "Take five casks of brandy back to Hanson Hall for me, will you, Harwood?"

"Certainly, Captain." He and Harwood exchanged a glance. "Will you be all right, Sir? I mean getting home."

"I can still ride a horse, Harwood, but how I will explain my arm to Mrs. Wentworth is not something about which I care to think."

Harwood grinned. "You could claim she had a nightmare and kicked you out of bed, Sir."

"Mrs. Wentworth is not that gullible!" Frederick snorted.

"Good luck, Captain," Shipley called as they moved out.

Although the middle of the night, Frederick first made a call on the Harbor Master's office, leaving a note giving specific directions to the warehouse and the men locked in the shed. In the note, he told the Harbor Master that Jatson Laurie was the informant and to go easy on him, but make it look as if Laurie was guilty also. That was the most he could do for Mrs. Thomason. He hoped for some sort of mercy for the woman's sake. However, Laurie had participated in the smuggling gang of his own free will.

Having set the door unlatched when he left, at a quarter after four in the morning, he sneaked back into his house. Frederick knew within an hour the servants would be up and preparing for the day. Exhausted, and more than a bit sore, he wove his way through the corridors to his chambers. Passing Anne's door, he hesitated, considering going in to face her. But reflecting that discretion was the better part of valor, Frederick simply touched the door lightly before moving on. He turned the knob to his own door quietly. In the early light of dawn, he could just make out the shapes of the furniture.

Carefully, he unbuttoned his coat with his free hand and tried to shrug out of it without moving his arm. Halfway in and halfway out, he realized he would need to use his forearm and hand or forever be stuck partially clothed. Taking his left hand to move his right, he concentrated completely, so as not to make any sound. So focused on the task at hand, Frederick did not realize Anne had stepped from his dressing room and stood behind him. When her hand touched his shoulder to ease the coat away, he gasped—both out of pain and out of surprise.

"I will not ask why you were out all night, Frederick." She lowered the coat from his left arm before coming to face him. She walked to the nightstand and lit a candle and then finished removing the coat. "But you will allow me to tend my husband without complaint." Her voice sounded cold, and tears streamed down her face.

"Anne," he started, but she shushed him and began to cut the shirt away.

"The shirt is ruined; we should not try to take it over your head. I have my scissors here." Her voice was barely audible, but Frederick stood and let her minister to him. "I will send to the village for Dr. Laraby."

Frederick nodded, but he said no more. She filled a basin with water and forced him to sit while she bathed his arms and then his face—his chest and his back. "You have bruises," she whispered as she sent the soapy rag across his shoulder blades. "Some scratches, too, although they do not look deep. I will wash you; you are dirty and smell of brandy and sweat."

Frederick simply leaned back against the chair and watched her carefully. The tears still cascaded down her cheeks, and he took his thumb to wipe them away.

Still not speaking, she brought him a glass of wine. He took a sip before setting it on the table. She stood by the fire, warming her hands. "Thank you, Anne," he whispered softly.

"Do *not*..." she hissed, and then her voice trailed off.

"Do not *what*?" he demanded. "Do not thank my wife for tending my wounds?" Despite the pain in his arm, he found himself beside her. "Do not tell her she is my world?" With his left hand, he turned her chin, forcing Anne to look at him. He pulled her to him, allowing her to sob into his shoulder. Her tears ran down his arm and chest. "Ask me, Anne—ask me where I was tonight," he pleaded into her hair.

"It is *none* of my *affair*. I am simply the mistress of your house; I know where a man goes when he no longer desires his pregnant wife."

Her words stunned him; Frederick expected her to be confused concerning his whereabouts—to be angry, even, because he had not told her—but, stupidly, he never thought she would think him untrue. "Anne, there is no one for me but you, pregnant or not. This was no night of debauchery."

"Then *what*?" she asked, her eyes blazing. "How did you come by your injury?"

"That is better," he said softly. "I will tell you everything. Send someone for Laraby, and then come join me in our sitting room." He kissed her forehead and walked through the door to the room they shared.

A few minutes later, she stood in the doorway. "I brought a blanket for your shoulders," she said as she entered the room. Her eyes and nose were red from weeping.

Frederick leaned forward to allow her to drape the coverlet around his bare back. "Come sit with me," he demanded.

Anne seated herself beside him, but she made a point of not touching him.

"Do you wish to talk?" he asked as he pulled the blanket closer.

"I suppose we should; I do not like for us to be at odds." Anne slid her hand to his knee, bending to her need to touch him. "If you are willing to explain, I will listen."

"Will you look at me, Anne?" he asked as he took her hand and raised it to his lips. He pressed her hand to his cheek, trying to think of a way to make her understand. In some ways, he almost wished he could keep the lie of a mistress, but he saw the hurt in her eyes and knew she became the Anne created by Sir Walter and her sisters—the one who lacked confidence; Frederick would face her anger from the truth rather than have her become that wall-flower again. "I will tell you the whole story," he declared, "but you must promise not to interrupt until I finish. Then I will answer your questions."

"Very well."

Frederick took a deep breath. He was about to reveal to Anne secrets that Marcus Lansing—Lord Wallingford—had explicitly warned him not to tell her. "You were right when you thought Hanson Hall held a catch. Marcus Lansing, as you know, brought me the details of the Prince's offer, but he also brought me the terms of my accession to the title. The Central Office recruited me to spearhead the search for smugglers and traitors working out of Cornwall and through the Channel." He saw her eyes grow wide with dismay, but as promised, she held her tongue.

"However, once I accepted the position, I began to wonder about Wallingford, who is my governmental contact in Dorset. At first, I admit to being a bit jealous of the fact that you two were old friends." Anne looked stunned, but she remained silent. Embarrassed, Frederick continued, "But now, it is more than that, Anne. I cannot feel good about what he offers.

"So, I set up my own network. I have Avendale and Harwood and Shipley and several others. I asked them to keep their eyes and ears open and to tell me if they took note of anything unusual. Today, during the picnic, Avendale brought me news I could not ignore.

"Harwood and I, along with ten others I trust, stopped a smuggling group at Studland Harbor. Unfortunately, I fought with one of the men after he struck my arm with a club. That is what you see on my body."

"Frederick!" she gasped. "Oh, God, was anyone else hurt?"

Anne had forgotten her promise to keep silent, but he would not remind her of it. "No one."

"Tell me the rest," she insisted. "I need to know in what you were involved."

"Wallingford warned me not to speak of our deal with anyone, especially you. I never wanted you to know of the danger, but, Anne, I can make a difference here. My men have a new life where they can keep their honor while providing for their families. You should have seen them this evening. I told each of them he did not need to prove himself, but they stayed, despite the danger. They want to rid England of its traitors. How could they not? We fought for years— only to come home to enemies within our own borders."

"I see." Head down, she pondered what he had said for several minutes. Frederick silently watched her. Then she raised her head and said, "Of course, they would. It takes a special type of man to place his life on the line for his country." She stroked his bare arm as she spoke. "How could I be so stupid to think otherwise? I am mortified by my ignorance. Can you ever forgive me?"

"For being jealous?" he taunted.

Anne blushed and looked away quickly. "Yes—I was jealous— green with envy. I tried to make myself into the kind of woman who accepts her husband's appetites, but I could not. I was devastated to think you might choose someone else; I just could not fathom why you would leave our bed."

"You should know I would never leave you unless another person was in danger."

She suddenly understood what he was saying. He loved her— only her, but sometimes he must answer the call to help others. It was his nature. "God has a new path for you."

"For us," he corrected. "I need your support. God returned me to the sea when my men needed me, and then he brought me home to you. Now, he presents me with a whole new challenge.

With this title, I can give honorable men a new start, and I can affect England's future. Yet, none of it means anything without you. I need for you to continue to do what you did today—develop relationships—reach those whom I cannot reach. I do not possess your natural ease with people."

"What did you find tonight?"

Anne had not agreed to help—but she had not refused either; she simply accepted what he told her, and for that, Frederick was more than thankful. "Mrs. Thomason told Mr. Avendale that her brother was involved in something dangerous. She was right, but it was not what I expected. We found French brandy, which made sense. We also found some paintings—portraits by François Gérard and Jacques-Louis David."

"Gérard and David! You trifle with me!"

"No, it is as I speak. Yet, we found something even more bizarre in that Studland warehouse—barrels of coal tar and of sulfur."

His disclosure baffled her. "Coal tar?" Anne questioned. "Why would anyone want coal tar, or sulfur, for that matter?"

"It is not even that we found such an unusual haul; it is the large quantity of barrels which surprised us. According to Tweed Swift, we could blow up all of Whitehall and maybe even part of St. James with it."

"Why?" she demanded. "Why would anyone smuggle raw materials when they could simply use an explosive?"

"When I reconnoitered the warehouse before we went in as a group, I overheard some men talking of Sir Thomas, Lord Cochrane. Maybe you remember reading of him in the Navy Lists. However, Harwood says Lord Thomas is in prison. We thought maybe they wanted to blow up his gaol—to release him." Frederick needed to make some sense of a senseless night; he hoped Anne might see something he did not.

"But I still wonder why they had so much. I cannot imagine they would need more than a small portion to even bring down a wall. You said there were barrels."

"That there were."

"Did the captured men confess anything?"

Feeling a prickly uneasiness, Frederick tried to come to some conclusions. "We did not question the men; I left them locked up in the warehouse and sent word to the Harbor Master. He will question them. I left two of the portraits and some of the brandy as evidence, but we moved everything else to the barns in the north pasture. We will find ways to use the sulfur and coal tar. Harwood says we can use the coal tar for roofs and sealing and the sulfur for fertilizer. I gave each man three casks of brandy to sell or drink as he sees fit. I thought it best not to be directly attached to the investigation."

"Will the thieves not recognize you? Will they not accuse you of having the barrels?" Anne asked worriedly.

"I thought of that. If they would say I have it, I would get Wallingford involved—turn over what we found, if necessary; but I do not believe that will happen. *Someone* planned something large, and these men probably knew little of the complete plan. I just wish I could find out more without involving Marcus Lansing." Frederick caught her hand and squeezed it gently.

A light tap on the door ended their conversation. Dr. Laraby swept into the room. "Wentworth," he stated as he rushed through the door. "I hear you had an accident."

"His horse was temperamental," Anne insisted for the benefit of the servants standing in the background.

Laraby understood without being told something was amiss. "Let me take a look."

"Thank you, doctor; my husband tolerates my need to feel he is well." Anne appeared flustered, even though a moment ago she was perfectly calm. Frederick realized she performed for the staff; that is what she wanted them to think. Why else would she send for the doctor at such an hour?

Laraby moved the arm tentatively. "Rotate your wrist as much as you can."

Frederick did so through gritted teeth.

"You have a broken wrist and what appears to be a fractured bone in your arm. You must have tried to catch yourself with that arm." Laraby knew his captain had not fallen from a horse, but he did not feel a need to inquire further. "I will set it for you; you will heal nicely."

"Thank you for coming so quickly, Doctor. I wish I could have convinced my husband to see you before such an ungodly hour, but he did not want to disturb everyone's holiday. Then the pain worsened." She continued to fuss over Frederick as servants brought in the supplies the doctor needed. "Next time, my Dear, please listen to me."

"I will, Sweetling." Frederick smiled at her. "I am still learning to be a proper husband." Anne instructed a servant to bring Frederick more wine to ease his discomfort.

Laraby went to work immediately, and in a short time Frederick's hand was in a cast and his arm in a sling. "That should do it for you, Wentworth. I will check on you late tomorrow. I am sure you and Lady Orland would both like some rest now."

"Come by around three," Frederick stated, but Laraby knew it to be an order.

"Yes, Admiral. Until tomorrow." The doctor left, followed closely by the servants.

"Do you think you can sleep? The doctor left some laudanum if you need it."

Frederick rose and took her hand. "Will you lie with me? I need you close."

She slid into his one-armed embrace. "Come, let us make you more physically comfortable. We will use your bed; it is larger, and I am less likely to hit your hand. I will fix you a dose of the medicine Laraby prescribed."

Once they were contentedly settled, Anne snuggled into his back as best she could, given her bulk. "Thank you, Anne, for understanding my need to do this my way." His words began to slur. "I know...Lansing is an old friend...but I must make this mine." He began to drift off to sleep.

"Frederick, there is something you should know."

He caught her hand to his chest. "What is that, Sweetling?"

"Marcus used to brag of Sir Thomas's conquests when we were in school, and then again when I saw him a couple of times at parties and such; it must have been in '09 or so, and he could speak of nothing else. Marcus Lansing—Lord Wallingford—is Lord Cochrane's cousin. You were right to not fully trust Marcus."

"Neither should you, Anne," he warned.

She slid her arm up and down his chest. "I needed to know all this; do not shut me out of your life again."

"Never, my Love," he mumbled. "You and I will see things through together."

EPILOGUE

And looking to the Heaven, that bends above you,
How oft! I bless the Lot, that made me love you.
—Samuel Taylor Coleridge, "The Presence of Love"

Frederick rode hard, trying to reach Hanson Hall before dark. He had taken the last of the sulfur and coal tar to Harville and Rushick in Brighton. A week after the midnight raid on the warehouse, Wallingford had showed up, unannounced, at the estate. He wanted to know about Frederick's involvement in the matter. By that time, he and Anne had discussed the best way to handle the situation. Frederick told Lansing he and Harwood had stumbled on the ring when he was trying to find the brother of one of his cottagers. When Lansing asked if he had led the raid, he assured the man that he had participated, but was not the spokesman for the group. His only interest lay in securing Laurie's release. Later, when it became known in aristocratic circles that he possessed several of the portraits, Frederick claimed he had purchased them from an unknown seller in order to save them from being destroyed. To prove his point, he donated one of the paintings to the Royal Academy and sent another as a gift to George IV. Of course, Anne insisted on keeping the smallest one to display in Hanson Hall. Frederick still wondered about Lansing's connection to the event. Had the man been involved somehow? Did he have prior knowledge of the thievery? In questioning Admiral Pennington and Benjamin, he learned that Lord Cochrane had some revolutionary ideas on how to win the war, but no one knew exactly what those ideas were. In addition, Frederick realized something else after the fact: The man in the gray coat was not among their captures. It took two months to dispose of all the barrels, but now each of his cottagers had a sealed roof and walls. The fallow fields lay thick with sulfur; in addition, Dr. Laraby had claimed some of it.

Today, he rode for another reason. He had spent the night with Thomas and Milly, but one of his footmen had awoken the household before dawn with the news that Anne was to deliver their child. She was a few weeks early, and Frederick worried for her health. He wished now he had never left her. He had changed horses several times on his trip, and he was not sure he should not do so again. He was finally in Dorset, but he doubted the one he rode would make it all the way to Hanson Hall.

"Wentworth!" Lucas Kendrick suddenly appeared on the road. Frederick pulled up the reins on his horse.

"I am hurrying, Kendrick!" he called. "Mrs. Wentworth delivers our child."

"I was sent to meet you. Take this horse; it is fresh, and you will get there faster. Shipley waits about twenty miles down the road with another."

Frederick slid from the saddle and hurried to his friend's horse. "Thank you, Kendrick, for thinking of this."

"I cannot take the credit. It was your wife; she says she needs you home!" Kendrick called as Frederick rode away at a full gallop.

He traded horses with Shipley with seven miles to go. Horses from his own stable held up better than the nags he had secured at the posting inns across Hampshire. He rode across the wooden bridge leading to the cobbled curve in front of the house. Then Frederick slid from the horse as a footman reached for the reins. He nearly bolted through the door just as Mr. Smythe opened it. Throwing his coat at one of the men, he demanded, "Where is she?"

"Lady Orland is in her room. Mrs. Miller is with her, and Dr. Laraby is standing by if he is needed." Smythe led the way as Frederick scrambled up the stairs.

"Then I am in time?" he begged.

Smythe could not keep up with him, and so he called after Frederick's retreating form, "I believe you are, Sir."

Skidding to a stop in front of Anne's door, he hesitated, wondering whether he should knock before entering. But he heard the unmistakable wail of a baby, and he burst through the door, completely out of breath. Mrs. Miller and Harriet, Anne's maid, bustled about the room in a flurry of activity, but his eyes fell on the body reclining against the bed. Her hair plastered her head, and her pale face looked exhausted—the veins in her neck and across her temple were blue lines on white. His heart leapt at the sight of her—*his Anne*—so fragile—so vulnerable! She looked broken and twisted, and he moved to straighten her in the bed; then he saw the blood covering her legs and the linens. "Dear God, Anne!" he cried out in fright, as he dropped to his knees beside her.

Her eyes fluttered open and then closed again, but a smile took hold of the corners of her mouth. "You made it." Her lips barely moved, but he heard her.

Frederick gently kissed her forehead as he brushed the hair from her face. "I am here, my Love." He clutched at her hand, praying she was all right, but he never saw so much blood.

"Mrs. Wentworth," Mrs. Miller came forward carrying a bundle, "would ye be likin' to see ye boy?"

Frederick's head snapped around; he heard the child's cry, but he forgot it all when he saw Anne. "A boy?" he whispered loudly, his voice raspy.

"Let my husband see his heir," she wearily told the older woman.

Looking at nothing but the bundle of swaddling clothes in Mrs. Miller's hands, Frederick reached out to carefully take the child into his arms. "Be holdin' his head just so," Mrs. Miller instructed him.

Frederick nestled the child in the crook of his arm, and he turned back the blanket to gaze at the elfin face. In that moment, everything changed. "In all my life," he murmured as he slid back the blanket and touched the soft silkiness of his child's hair.

"Let me see," Anne's voice came from behind him.

Frederick bent low to lay the baby in her arms. "He is beautiful, Anne." His words rang in the silent room. "My, God, how perfect you both are!" He leaned forward and kissed the end of her nose. "I am sorry I could not get here any faster." He traced the outline of his son's face with the tip of one finger.

"And I—I am sorry," she said haltingly, "that your daughter could wait no longer."

Frederick looked confused. "Daughter?" His eyes fell on the black curls of his child's hair. "Mrs. Miller, is this not my boy?" he asked, wondering why everyone now stared at him.

"Aye, Admiral, he be ye boy." Mrs. Miller went to the far corner of the room and picked up what he suddenly realized was another child. "This here be ye gal, tho'." She placed a second child in his arms. "She be little like her Mam, but ye should hear the gal cry."

Frederick rolled back the covering blanket. In his arms lay a miniature Anne—no doubt about it—the baby would be the spitting image of *his Anne*. "Perfection again!" He laughed as he returned his attention to his wife. "You did it all without me!" he teased.

"Next time." Her eyes began to drift closed.

"We be needin' to get ye and the boy cleaned up, Lady Orland. We let His Lordship take the gal to his room." Mrs. Miller began to shoo him away as she took his son and returned him to the makeshift nursery on the far side of the room. Frederick watched it all very carefully before bending to kiss Anne once more.

Standing slowly, he noted Anne's exhaustion taking over. "I will be back shortly, my Love," he whispered to her. "Take good care of Her Ladyship," he ordered both of the women, even though he knew they would. "Come, Sweetling," he spoke softly to the child he carried. "Let me show you your new home." He left, humming a sailor's song to the child.

Strolling casually through the house, he took the newborn from room to room—cooing words of love as he went. "Would you like to see your nursery?" he asked as he walked into the room. "Is it not a fine room? Your mother prepared it well, and you, my darling daughter, will thrive in this room. It is made especially for you." He touched his daughter's hand, and the little fingers curled around his. "Your mother claims you will wrap me around these baby fingers." He touched the child's hand with his lips. "Your mother is a very smart person, and like me, my child, you are blessed to be loved by her." Frederick rubbed his cheek against the baby's hand. "I am sure they are finished; let us go find your brother."

By the time he had returned with his daughter to Anne's room, Harriet and Mrs. Miller had cleaned up the bed and Anne. With a fresh gown and her hair combed, Anne's pale skin, less pallid, showed some returning color in her cheeks, bringing him some relief. "Your daughter returns," he said jovially, coming to sit by Anne's bed. Then he handed his new daughter to Mrs. Miller.

"*My* daughter?" Anne accused. "I suppose our boy is *your* son? *My* daughter and *your* son? Is that how it will be?"

"No." He laughed lightly at her renewed playfulness. "They will be *my* daughter and *my* son when they are on their best behavior. They will be *your* children at all other times."

"That hardly seems fair," she countered. "*I* did all the hard work; *I* should reap the rewards."

Frederick touched her bottom lip with his fingertip. "Is not the fact that your husband loves you more than life itself reward enough?"

"It has its benefits," she retorted sleepily. "Are you happy, my Husband? After all, you warned me about having more than one crew member at a time."

"Ours will be a houseful, but as long as you and the children are well, I will be content. I have a daughter to protect and a son to be my heir; plus, I have their mother to love. God gave me much in one fell swoop today."

Anne slid her hand into his. "Have you considered names for our children?"

"Not at all. I assumed we still had weeks to discuss it, as you were not to deliver so soon." He brought her hand to his lips, rubbing them back and forth against her knuckles. "Do you have preferences?"

The corners of Anne's mouth turned up in delight. "I do have a thought for our daughter."

"Pray tell."

"You will think this insignificant, but it crossed my mind several times of late." She hesitated, not sure how to explain what she wanted to say. "Traditionally, I should name her after my mother Lady Elizabeth, but my sister dampens the 'enchantment' of that practice. Some would suggest we name our daughter after me, but that is not my wish. I always hated my name because it allowed my family to treat me as 'plain Anne.' I felt the name fit me quite well until you saw me—until I was no longer invisible. I do not want my daughter to be 'plain Anne.' I want my baby to have a name others will remember—a distinctive name. When we met again at the concert, you spoke of once being in Romola, Italy. I thought the city's name the most beautiful sound—the way the word rolls off the tongue. Could we name our daughter Romola? If we wish to follow the traditional route, we can use *Anne* as her middle name. Romola Anne Wentworth. What do you think?"

"Just like the child, I believe the name is perfect." Frederick would never disagree with Anne's decision. It was the ideal name for their beautiful daughter, and some day he would tell the girl of how her mother reasoned out the choice.

Anne smiled, happy that he had agreed with her suggestion. "What of our son? Do you want him to be named *Frederick*?"

"Like you, I would prefer something else. The name fits me, but as you once told me, it is a *mouthful*—Frederick James Wentworth. My grandfather was a *Robert*. What do you think? Robert James Wentworth, the Honorable Lord Orland?"

"It is an excellent choice; your family will be pleased that you honored your patriarch."

"Romola and Robert—our children, Mrs. Wentworth." He laughed as he bent to kiss the top of her head. "Can you believe all this? How we arrived at this point? In '06, would you have believed we would be married and live in this house and have these children?"

"We are living our dreams," she whispered. "Your father and mother would be so proud of the man you have become. This land will belong to Robert some day. And both he and Romola will marry for love, as their parents did."

Frederick bent to kiss her cheek. Anne closed her eyes and

relaxed. "You are exhausted, and rightly so, my Love. I will have the wet nurse take the children to the nursery for the night. You may see them in a few hours." He adjusted the bed linens about her as she settled back against the pillows.

"We will need to employ another wet nurse," she mumbled.

Frederick smiled down at her. "I will do so with tomorrow's light." He kissed her forehead. Frederick caught his breath on a sob of relief. "You and the children complete my life," he whispered. "Rest now; we will talk in the morning."

"Come lie with me," she muttered.

"I will bathe and join you," he assured her.

Sometime later, Frederick slid his long frame under the blanket. Anne slept, so he simply warmed her backside by cuddling next to her. The fragrance of her hair wafted over him as he relaxed into the familiarity of her body. He removed the strands of hair from about her face; seeing the thick lashes resting on the rise of her cheeks, Frederick realized the impact of the moment: In an instant, he had fallen in love with Anne Elliot, and, decisively, he won her. "The children are a testament to our love," he whispered to her sleeping form.

She rolled over into his embrace, snuggling into his chest. "Umm," she moaned.

"I look into your face," he murmured as his lips brushed against her cheek, "and I see God's plan at work. In His infinite wisdom, He brought me to your doorstep twice."

She snaked her arm up over his shoulder. "Do you plan to talk all evening?" her lips barely moved. "I am sleepy, and I hoped you would skip the adorations and go straight to the kissing part."

"I can be as silent as the lambs."

"Prove it," she challenged. "Just prove it."

AFTERWORD

When the Treaty of Paris was signed on November 20, 1815, Napoleon was already in exile on the tiny South Atlantic island of Saint Helena. Forced to accept the defeat of his Imperial Guard at Waterloo, Napoleon fled first to France, leaving behind coaches loaded with gold and jewelry and his private papers—his personal fortune. Reaching Paris on June 21, 1815, he still refused to admit his failure; on June 22, the Chamber of Representatives demanded that Bonaparte abdicate.

Even with his renunciation, Napoleon did not give up hopes of escaping the British and Prussian armies. On July 8, he tried to escape to the United States by boarding the French frigate *La Salle*; however, the English warship *Bellerophon* blocked the French emperor's escape. But Napoleon had contacted more than one ship and asked it to prepare to receive him. Still smarting from the War of 1812, where British embargos nearly destroyed American naval commerce, some French-born Americans reportedly sympathized with Bonaparte and tried to help him escape from the Duke of Wellesley's justice.

★ ★ ★

Captain Sir Thomas, Lord Cochrane, held radical ideas, in the form of saturation bombing and chemical warfare, on how the British should conduct naval warfare. A decorated hero, Lord Cochrane advanced quickly through naval ranks. Napoleon himself dubbed Cochrane "The Sea Wolf."

However, Cochrane fell out of favor when he first became consumed by the 1809 court-martial of Admiral James Gambier. Cochrane's inability to properly express himself in a public debate forum played out during the trial, allowing the general public to see his "imperfections." To complicate matters, he earned political enemies with his election to Parliament. A "tarnished star," Cochrane eventually went to jail, charged with illegally manipulating the London Stock Exchange in 1814.

An interesting fact about Cochrane's career was his plan to conduct chemical warfare. Even the Prince Regent approved of Cochrane's plan, and Whitehall considered the merits of it—turning it down only when British military leaders considered that the enemy might reciprocate with a like technology.

In Cochrane's plan, a hollowed-out ship's hulk would be layered with clay, scrap metal, a thick layer of powder, rows of shells, and animal carcasses. This "loaded" ship would be sent among the enemy vessels and then exploded—sending deadly mortar in a circular path. Other seemingly empty ships would be layered with clay—and then charcoal—and then sulfur, creating a floating stink bomb. The "noxious effluvia," or toxic, clouds would quickly subdue the opposition.

In 1818, released from jail, Cochrane left England and became a mercenary, not returning home until King William IV pardoned him in 1829. He continued to purport his ideas, even to Queen Victoria during the Crimean War. The details of Cochrane's plans never became public, and, with the end of the Crimean War, all thoughts of radical warfare were sealed away in the record rooms of Whitehall. Ironically, ten years after the files were unsealed, soldiers faced yellow sulfuric clouds of mustard gas during World War I.

RESOURCES

"Almack's Assembly Rooms." *Britain Express.*Violet Ashford. 2000.
    {http://www.britainexpress.com/History/almacks.htm}.

"A–Z Contents." *The Encyclopaedia of Plymouth History.* Plymouth Data
    Web Site. Sponsored by Plymouth Local Studies Library and the
    Plymouth and West Devon Record Office.
    {http://plymouthdata.info/index.htm}.

"Battle of Aix Roads." *Everything2.*The Everything Development Com-
    pany. 2002.
    {http://everything2.com/title/battle%2520of%2520Aix%2520
    Roads}.

"Battle of Copenhagen (1807)." *Nation Master.* 2003–2008.
    {http:www.nationmaster.com/encyclopedia/Battle-of-Copen-
    hagen-(1807)}.

"The Battle of Rasheed 'Roseta' March 31, 1807." *Arabic News*, 31 Mar.
    2001.
    {www.Arabicnews.com/ansub/Daily/Day/010331/2001033134
    .html}.

"The Battle of San Domingo." *National Maritime Museum.* 2008.
    {http://www.nmm.ac.uk/collections/prints/listPrints.cfm?filt
    er=maker&node=185}.

"British Royal Navy Crews." *Napoleonic Guide.* 2006.
    {http://www.napoleonguide.com/navy_crews.htm}.

"A Calendar for *Persuasion.*" *The Republic of Pemberley.*
    {http://www.jimandellen.org/austen/persuasion.calendar.
    html}.

"The Cancelled Chapters of *Persuasion.*" *The Republic of Pemberley.*
    Posted by Edith Lank, 3 Mar. 1997.
    {http://www.pemberley.com/janeinfo/pcanchap.html}.

"Children's Amusements in the Early Nineteenth Century." *Memorial
    Hall Museum.* Pocumtuck Valley Memorial Association, Deerfield,
    Massachusetts. 2008.
    {http://Memorialhall.mass.edu/classroom/curriculum_6th/

lesson13/bkgdessay1.html}.

"Cleric." *New Advent*, from *The Catholic Encyclopedia*.
{http://newadvent.org/cathen/04049b.htm}.

"Copenhagen." *Napoleonic Guide*. 2006.
{http://www.napoleonguide.com/battle_cope1801.htm}.

"Eighteenth Century Naval Ranks." *N. Cargill-Kipar*. 1999–2008.
{http://www.kipar.org/piratical-resources/british-navy-ranks.html}.

"English Report of Trafalgar." *Napoleonic Guide*. From *The Hampshire Chronicle*. 2006.
{http://www.napoleonguide.com/sailors_uktraf.htm}.

"George Gordon Byron, Lord Byron (1788–1824)." *Poem Hunter*. "Bride of Abydos, The." 2000–2008.
{http://www.poemhunter.com/poem/bride-of-abydos-the/}.

"The Lady of the Lake." *The Literature Network*. Jalic. 2000–2008.
{http://www.online-literature.com/walter_scott/2561}.

Malcomson, Robert. "During the Napoleonic Wars a British Naval Officer Proposed the Use of Saturation Bombing and Chemical Warfare." *Tripod*. Lycos. 2009.
{http://members.tripod.com/EsotericTexts07/Brit.NapChemWar.xx.htm}.

"Napoleonic Naval Balance." *Napoleonic Guide*. 2006.
{http://www.napoleonguide.com/navy_balance.htm}.

"Officer Ranks in the Royal Navy: The Naval Hierarchy Explained." *The Royal Naval Museum*. 2000.
{http://www.royalnavalmuseum.org/info_sheets_nav_rankings.htm}.

"Pictures of Corfe Castle." *Pictures of England*. 2001–2009.
{http://www.picturesofengland.com/England/Dorset/Corfe_Castle/Corfe_Castle

"Pictures of Swanage." *Pictures of England*. 2001–2009.
{http://www.picturesofengland.com/England/Dorset/Swanage}.

"Pictures of Wimborne Minster." *Pictures of England*. 2001–2009.
{http://www.picturesofengland.com/England/Dorset/Wimborne_Minster}.

"Ship of War, 1650–1815: An Age of Conflicts." *National Maritime Museum*. 2008. {http://nmm.ac.uk/visit/exhibitions/on-display/ship-of-war-1650-1815/}.

Streissguth, Thomas. *History's Greatest Defeats: The Napoleonic Wars: Defeat of the Grand Army*. San Diego: Lucent Books, 2003.

"Toys and Games." *History Lives*, a division of the Cooperman Fife and Drum Company. 2005.
{http://www.historylives.com/toysandgames.htm}.

"What Is Coal Tar?" *wiseGeek*. Conjecture Corporation. 2007.
{http://www.Wisegeek.com/what-is-coal-tar.htm}.

OTHER ULYSSES PRESS BOOKS

DARCY'S PASSIONS: *PRIDE AND PREJUDICE*
RETOLD THROUGH HIS EYES
Regina Jeffers, $14.95

Profound and amusing, this novel captures the style and humor of Jane Austen's novel while turning the entire story on its head. It presents Darcy as a man in turmoil. His duty to his family and estate demand he choose a woman of high social standing. But what his mind tells him to do and what his heart knows to be true are two different things. After rejecting Elizabeth as being unworthy, he soon discovers he's in love with her. But the independent Elizabeth rejects his marriage proposal. Devastated, he must search his soul and transform himself into the man she can love and respect.

DARCY'S TEMPTATION: A SEQUEL TO JANE
AUSTEN'S *PRIDE AND PREJUDICE*
Regina Jeffers, $14.95

By changing the narrator to Mr. Darcy, *Darcy's Temptation* turns one of the most beloved literary love affairs of all time on its head, even as it presents new plot twists and fresh insights into the characters' personalities and motivations. Four months into the new marriage, all seems well when Elizabeth discovers she is pregnant. However, a family conflict that requires Darcy's personal attention arises because of Georgiana's involvement with an activist abolitionist. On his return journey from a meeting to address this issue, a much greater danger arises. Darcy is attacked on the road and, when left helpless from his injuries, he finds himself in the care of another woman.

VAMPIRE DARCY'S DESIRE: A *PRIDE AND PREJUDICE* ADAPTATION
Regina Jeffers, $14.95

This inventive novel tells of a tormented Darcy who comes to "Netherfield" to escape the pressure on him to marry. Dispirited by his family's 200-year curse and his fate as a half-human/half-vampire damphir, Darcy would rather live forever alone than inflict the horrors of a vampire life on a beautiful wife. Destiny has other plans. Darcy meets Elizabeth and finds himself yearning for her as a man and driven to possess her as a vampire.

MR. DARCY PRESENTS HIS BRIDE: A SEQUEL TO JANE AUSTEN'S *PRIDE & PREJUDICE*
Helen Halstead, $14.95

When Elizabeth Bennet marries the brooding, passionate Mr. Darcy, she is thrown into the exciting world of London society. Elizabeth is drawn into a powerful clique for which intrigue is the stuff of life and rivalry the motive. Her success, it seems, can only come at the expense of good relations with her husband.

THE LOST YEARS OF JANE AUSTEN: A NOVEL
Barbara Ker Wilson, $14.95

There was an interval in Jane Austen's life, before any of her novels were published, when she disappeared from sight. This book seeks to fill those missing months with a visit from England to the colony of New South Wales, where the dashing Mr. D'Arcy Wentworth has settled at Homebush, a convict revolt is brewing at Castle Hill, and no one is quite certain whether the Napoleonic War has ended or not.

To order these books call 800-377-2542 or 510-601-8301, fax 510-601-8307, e-mail ulysses@ ulyssespress.com, or write to Ulysses Press, P.O. Box 3440, Berkeley, CA 94703. All retail orders are shipped free of charge. California residents must include sales tax. Allow two to three weeks for delivery.

ABOUT THE AUTHOR

Regina Jeffers, an English teacher for thirty-eight years, considers herself a Jane Austen enthusiast. She is the author of several novels, including *Darcy's Passions*, *Darcy's Temptation* and *Vampire Darcy's Desire*. A Time Warner Star Teacher and Martha Holden Jennings Scholar, Jeffers often serves as a consultant in language arts and media literacy. Currently living outside Charlotte, North Carolina, she spends her time in the classroom and with her writing.